The Modern Novel Series

A FAREWELL TO ARMS

THE MODERN NOVEL SERIES

ERNEST HEMINGWAY

A Farewell to Arms

WITH A COMMENTARY
BY
TONY TANNER

HEINEMANN EDUCATIONAL BOOKS
LONDON

Heinemann Educational Books Ltd
LONDON EDINBURGH MELBOURNE AUCKLAND TORONTO
HONG KONG SINGAPORE KUALA LUMPUR NEW DELHI
NAIROBI JOHANNESBURG LUSAKA IBADAN
KINGSTON

ISBN 0 435 17940 3

First published 1929
Commentary © Heinemann Educational Books Ltd 1971
First published in the Modern Novel Series
by permission of Jonathan Cape Ltd 1971
Reprinted 1975, 1978

Published by
Heinemann Educational Books Ltd
48 Charles Street, London W1X 8AH
Printed Offset Litho and bound in Great Britain by
Cox & Wyman Ltd, London, Fakenham and Reading

TO

G. A. P.

CONTENTS

BOOK I

CHAPTER 1

In the late summer of that year we lived in a house in a village that looked across the river and the plain to the mountains. In the bed of the river there were pebbles and boulders, dry and white in the sun, and the water was clear and swiftly moving and blue in the channels. Troops went by the house and down the road and the dust they raised powdered the leaves of the trees. The trunks of the trees too were dusty and the leaves fell early that year and we saw the troops marching along the road and the dust rising and leaves, stirred by the breeze, falling and the soldiers marching and afterwards the road bare and white except for the leaves.

The plain was rich with crops; there were many orchards of fruit trees and beyond the plain the mountains were brown and bare. There was fighting in the mountains and at night we could see the flashes from the artillery. In the dark it was like summer lightning, but the nights were cool and there was not the feeling of a storm coming.

Sometimes in the dark we heard the troops marching under the window and guns going past pulled by motor-tractors. There was much traffic at night and many mules on the roads with boxes of ammunition on each side of their pack-saddles and grey motor-trucks that carried men, and other trucks with loads covered with canvas that moved slower in the traffic. There were big guns too that passed in the day drawn by tractors, the long barrels of the guns covered with green branches and green leafy branches and vines laid over the tractors. To the north we could look across a valley and see a forest of chestnut trees and behind it another mountain on this side of the river. There was fighting for that mountain too, but it was not successful, and in the fall when the rains came the leaves all fell from the chestnut trees and the branches were bare and the trunks black with rain. The vineyards were thin and bare-branched too and all the country wet and brown and dead with the autumn. There were mists over the river and clouds on the mountain and the trucks splashed mud on the roads and the troops were muddy and wet in their capes; their rifles were wet and under their capes the two leather cartridge-boxes on the front of the belts, grey leather boxes heavy with the packs of clips of thin, long 6.5 mm. cartridges, bulged forward under the capes so that the men, passing on the road, marched as though they were six months gone with child.

There were small grey motor-cars that passed going very fast; usually there was an officer on the seat with the driver and more officers in the back seat. They splashed more mud than the camions even and if one of the officers in the back was very small and sitting between two generals, he himself so small that you could not see his face but only the top of his cap and his narrow back, and if the car went especially fast it was probably the King. He lived in Udine and came out in this way nearly every day to see how things were going, and things went very badly.

At the start of the winter came the permanent rain and with the rain came the cholera. But it was checked and in the end only seven thousand died of it in the army.

CHAPTER 2

THE next year there were many victories. The mountain that was beyond the valley and the hillside where the chestnut forest grew was captured and there were victories beyond the plain on the plateau to the south and we crossed the river in August and lived in a house in Gorizia that had a fountain and many thick shady trees in a walled garden and a wistaria vine purple on the side of the house. Now the fighting was in the next mountains beyond and was not a mile away. The town was very nice and our house was very fine. The river ran behind us and the town had been captured very handsomely but the mountains beyond it could not be taken and I was very glad the Austrians seemed to want to come back to the town some time, if the war should end, because they did not bombard it to destroy it but only a little in a military way. People lived on in it and there were hospitals and cafés and artillery up side streets and two bawdy-houses, one for troops and one for officers, and with the end of the summer, the cool nights, the fighting in the mountains beyond the town, the shell-marked iron of the railway bridge, the smashed tunnel by the river where the fighting had been, the trees around the square and the long avenue of trees that led to the square; these with there being girls in the town, the King passing in his motor-car, sometimes now seeing his face and little long-necked body and grey beard like a goat's chin-tuft; all these with the sudden interiors of houses that had lost a wall through shelling, with plaster and rubble in their gardens and sometimes in the street, and the whole thing going well on the Carso made the fall very different from the last fall when we had been in the country. The war was changed too.

The forest of oak trees on the mountain beyond the town was gone. The forest had been green in the summer when we had come into the town but now there were the stumps and the broken trunks and the ground torn up, and one day at the end of the fall when I was out where the oak forest had been I saw a cloud coming over the mountain. It came very fast and the sun went a dull yellow and then everything was grey and the sky was covered and the cloud came on down the mountain and suddenly we were in it and it was snow. The snow slanted across the wind, the bare ground was covered, the stumps of trees projected, there was snow on the guns and there were paths in the snow going back to the latrines behind trenches.

Later, below in the town, I watched the snow falling, looking out of the window of the bawdy-house, the house for officers, where I sat with a friend and two glasses drinking a bottle of Asti, and, looking out at the snow falling slowly and heavily, we knew it was all over for that year. Up the river the mountains had not been taken; none of the mountains beyond the river had been taken. That was all left for next year. My friend saw the priest from our mess going by in the street, walking carefully in the slush, and pounded on the window to attract his attention. The priest looked up. He saw us and smiled. My friend motioned for him to come in. The priest shook his head and went on. That night in the mess after the spaghetti course, which everyone ate very quickly and seriously, lifting the spaghetti on the fork until the loose strands hung clear then lowering it into the mouth, or else using a continuous lift and sucking into the mouth, helping ourselves to wine from the grass-covered gallon flask; it swung in a metal cradle and you pulled the neck of the flask down with the forefinger and the wine, clear red, tannic and lovely, poured out into the glass held with the same hand; after this course, the captain commenced picking on the priest.

The priest was young and blushed easily and wore a uniform like the rest of us but with a cross in dark red velvet above the left breast-pocket of his grey tunic. The captain spoke pidgin Italian for my doubtful benefit, in order that I might understand perfectly, that nothing should be lost.

'Priest today with girls,' the captain said looking at the priest and at me. The priest smiled and blushed and shook his head. This captain baited him often.

'Not true?' asked the captain. 'Today I see priest with girls.'

'No,' said the priest. The other officers were amused at the baiting.

'Priest not with girls,' went on the captain. 'Priest never with girls,' he explained to me. He took my glass and filled it, looking at my eyes all the time, but not losing sight of the priest.

'Priest every night five against one.' Every one at the table laughed. 'You understand? Priest every night five against one.'

He made a gesture and laughed loudly. The priest accepted it as a joke.

'The Pope wants the Austrians to win the war,' the major said. 'He loves Franz Joseph. That's where the money comes from. I am an atheist.'

'Did you ever read the *Black Pig?*' asked the lieutenant. 'I will get you a copy. It was that which shook my faith.'

'It is a filthy and vile book,' said the priest. 'You do not really like it.'

'It is very valuable,' said the lieutenant. 'It tells you about those priests. You will like it,' he said to me. I smiled at the priest and he smiled back across the candle-light. 'Don't you read it,' he said.

'I will get it for you,' said the lieutenant.

'All thinking men are atheists,' the major said. 'I do not believe in the Freemasons however.'

'I believe in the Freemasons,' the lieutenant said. 'It is a noble organization.' Someone came in and as the door opened I could see the snow falling.

'There will be no more offensive now that the snow has come,' I said.

'Certainly not,' said the major. 'You should go on leave. You should go to Rome, Naples, Sicily —'

'He should visit Amalfi,' said the lieutenant. 'I will write you cards to my family in Amalfi. They will love you like a son.'

'He should go to Palermo.'

'He ought to go to Capri.'

'I would like you to see Abruzzi and visit my family at Capracotta,' said the priest.

'Listen to him talk about the Abruzzi. There's more snow there than here. He doesn't want to see peasants. Let him go to centres of culture and civilization.'

'He should have fine girls. I will give you the addresses of places in Naples. Beautiful young girls — accompanied by their mothers. Ha! Ha! Ha!'

13

He looked at the priest and shouted, 'Every night priest five against one!' They all laughed again.

'You must go on leave at once,' the major said.

'I would like to go with you and show you things,' the lieutenant said.

'When you come back bring a phonograph.'

'Bring good opera disks.'

'Bring Caruso.'

'Don't bring Caruso. He bellows.'

'Don't you wish you could bellow like him?'

'He bellows. I say he bellows!'

'I would like you to go to Abruzzi,' the priest said. The others were shouting. 'There is good hunting. You would like the people and though it is cold it is clear and dry. You could stay with my family. My father is a famous hunter.'

'Come on,' said the captain. 'We go whore-house before it shuts.'

'Good night,' I said to the priest.

'Good night,' he said.

CHAPTER 3

When I came back to the front we still lived in that town. There were many more guns in the country around and the spring had come. The fields were green and there were small green shoots on the vines, the trees along the road had small leaves and a breeze came from the sea. I saw the town with the hill and the old castle above it in a cup in the hills with the mountains beyond, brown mountains with a little green on their slopes. In the town there were more guns, there were some new hospitals, you met British men and sometimes women, on the street, and a few more houses had been hit by shell-fire. It was warm and like the spring and I walked down the alleyway of

14

trees, warmed from the sun on the wall, and found we still lived in the same house and that it all looked the same as when I had left it. The door was open, there was a soldier sitting on a bench outside in the sun, an ambulance was waiting by the side door and inside the door, as I went in, there was the smell of marble floors and hospital. It was all as I had left it except that now it was spring. I looked in the door of the big room and saw the major sitting at his desk, the window open and the sunlight coming into the room. He did not see me and I did not know whether to go in and report or go upstairs first and clean up. I decided to go on upstairs.

The room I shared with the lieutenant Rinaldi looked out on the courtyard. The window was open, my bed was made up with blankets and my things hung on the wall, the gas-mask in an oblong tin can, the steel helmet on the same peg. At the foot of the bed was my flat trunk, and my winter boots, the leather shiny with oil, were on the trunk. My Austrian sniper's rifle with its blued octagon barrel and the lovely dark walnut, cheek-fitted, *schutzen* stock, hung over the two beds. The telescope that fitted it was, I remembered, locked in the trunk. The lieutenant, Rinaldi, lay asleep on the other bed. He woke when he heard me in the room and sat up.

'Ciaou!' he said. 'What kind of time did you have?'

'Magnificent.'

We shook hands and he put his arm around my neck and kissed me.

'Oughf,' I said.

'You're dirty,' he said. 'You ought to wash. Where did you go and what did you do? Tell me everything at once.'

'I went everywhere. Milan, Florence, Rome, Naples, Villa San Giovanni, Messina, Taormina —'

'You talk like a time-table. Did you have any beautiful adventures?'

'Yes.'

'Where?'

'Milano, Firenze, Roma, Napoli —'

'That's enough. Tell me really what was the best.'

'In Milano.'

'That was because it was first. Where did you meet her? In the Cova? Where did you go? How did you feel? Tell me everything at once. Did you stay all night?'

'Yes.'

'That's nothing. Here now we have beautiful girls. New girls never been to the front before.'

'Wonderful.'

'You don't believe me? We will go now this afternoon and see. And in the town we have beautiful English girls. I am now in love with Miss Barkley. I will take you to call. I will probably marry Miss Barkley.'

'I have to get washed and report. Doesn't anybody work now?'

'Since you are gone we have nothing but frostbites, chilblains, jaundice, gonorrhoea, self-inflicted wounds, pneumonia and hard and soft chancres. Every week someone gets wounded by rock fragments. There are a few real wounded. Next week the war starts again. Perhaps it starts again. They say so. Do you think I would do right to marry Miss Barkley — after the war of course?'

'Absolutely,' I said and poured the basin full of water.

'Tonight you will tell me everything,' said Rinaldi. 'Now I must go back to sleep to be fresh and beautiful for Miss Barkley.'

I took off my tunic and shirt and washed in the cold water in the basin. While I rubbed myself with a towel I looked around the room and out the window and at Rinaldi lying with his eyes closed on the bed. He was good-looking, was my age, and he came from Amalfi. He loved being a surgeon and we were great friends. While I was looking at him he opened his eyes.

'Have you any money?'

'Yes.'

'Loan me fifty lire.'

I dried my hands and took out my pocket-book from the inside of my tunic hanging on the wall. Rinaldi took the note, folded it without rising from the bed and slid it in his breeches pocket. He smiled, 'I must make on Miss Barkley the impression of a man of sufficient wealth. You are my great and good friend and financial protector.'

'Go to hell,' I said.

That night at the mess I sat next to the priest and he was disappointed and suddenly hurt that I had not gone to the Abruzzi. He had written to his father that I was coming and they had made preparations. I myself felt as badly as he did and could not understand why I had not gone. It was what I had wanted to do and I tried to explain how one thing had led to another and finally he saw it and understood that I had really wanted to go and it was almost all right. I had drunk much wine and afterwards coffee and Strega and I explained, winefully, how we did not do the things we wanted to do; we never did such things.

We two were talking while the others argued. I had wanted to go to Abruzzi. I had gone to no place where the roads were frozen and hard as iron, where it was clear cold and dry and the snow was dry and powdery and hare-tracks in the snow and the peasants took off their hats and called you Lord and there was good hunting. I had gone to no such place but to the smoke of cafés and nights when the room whirled and you needed to look at the wall to make it stop, nights in bed, drunk, when you knew that that was all there was, and the strange excitement of waking and not knowing who it was with you, and the world all unreal in the dark and so exciting that you must resume again unknowing and not caring in the night, sure that this was all and all and all and not caring. Suddenly to care very much and to sleep, to wake with it sometimes morning and all that had been there gone and everything sharp and hard and clear and sometimes a dispute about the cost. Sometimes still pleasant and fond and warm and breakfast and lunch. Sometimes all niceness gone and glad to get out on the street but always another day starting and then another night. I tried to tell about the night and the difference between the night and the day and how the night was better unless the day was very clean and cold and I could not tell it; as I cannot tell it now. But if you have had it you know. He had not had it but he understood that I had really wanted to go to the Abruzzi but had not gone and we were still friends, with many tastes alike, but with the difference between us. He had always known what I did not know and what, when I learned it, I was always able to forget. But I did not know that then, although I learned it later. In the meantime we were all at the mess, the meal was finished, and the argument went on. We two stopped talking and the captain shouted, 'Priest not happy. Priest not happy without girls.'

'I am happy,' said the priest.

'Priest not happy. Priest wants Austrians to win the war,' the captain said. The others listened. The priest shook his head.

'No,' he said.

'Priest wants us never to attack. Don't you want us never to attack?'

'No. If there is a war I suppose we must attack.'

'Must attack. Shall attack!'

The priest nodded.

'Leave him alone,' the major said. 'He's all right.'

'He can't do anything about it anyway,' the captain said. We all got up and left the table.

CHAPTER 4

THE battery in the next garden woke me in the morning and I saw the sun coming through the window and got out of the bed. I went to the window and looked out. The gravel paths were moist and the grass was wet with dew. The battery fired twice and the air came each time like a blow and shook the window and made the front of my pyjamas flap. I could not see the guns but they were evidently firing directly over us. It was a nuisance to have them there but it was a comfort that they were no bigger. As I looked out at the garden I heard a motor-truck starting on the road. I dressed, went downstairs, had some coffee in the kitchen and went out to the garage.

Ten cars were lined up side by side under the long shed. They were top-heavy, blunt-nosed ambulances, painted grey and built like moving-vans. The mechanics were working on one out in the yard. Three others were up in the mountains at dressing-stations.

'Do they ever shell that battery?' I asked one of the mechanics.

'No, Signor Tenente. It is protected by the little hill.'

'How's everything?'

'Not so bad. This machine is no good but the others march.' He stopped working and smiled. 'Were you on permission?'

'Yes.'

He wiped his hands on his jumper and grinned. 'You have a good time?' The others all grinned too.

'Fine,' I said. 'What's the matter with this machine?'

'It's no good. One thing after another.'

'What's the matter now?'

'New rings.'

I left them working, the car looking disgraced and empty with the engine open and parts spread on the work-bench, and went in under the shed and looked at each of the cars. They were moderately clean, a few freshly washed, the others dusty. I looked at the tyres carefully, looking for cuts or stone bruises. Everything seemed in good condition. It evidently made no difference whether I was there to look after things or not. I had imagined that the condition of the cars, whether or not things were obtainable, the smooth functioning of the business of removing wounded and sick from the dressing-stations, hauling them back from the mountains to the clearing-station and then distributing them to the hospitals named on their papers, depended to a considerable extent on myself. Evidently it did not matter whether I was there or not.

'Has there been any trouble getting parts?' I asked the sergeant mechanic.

'No, Signor Tenente.'

'Where is the gasolene park now?'

'At the same place.'

'Good,' I said and went back to the house and drank another bowl of coffee at the mess table. The coffee was a pale grey and sweet with condensed milk. Outside the window it was a lovely spring morning. There was that beginning of a feeling of dryness in the nose that meant the day would be hot later on. That day I visited the posts in the mountains and was back in town late in the afternoon.

The whole thing seemed to run better while I was away. The offensive was going to start again I heard. The division for which we worked were to attack at a place up the river and the major told me that I would see about the posts for during the attack. The attack would cross the river up above the narrow gorge and spread up the hillside. The posts for the cars would have to be as near the river as they could get and keep covered. They would, of course, be selected by the infantry but we were supposed to work it out. It was one of those things that gave you a false feeling of soldiering.

I was very dusty and dirty and went up to my room to wash. Rinaldi was sitting on the bed with a copy of Hugo's English grammar. He was dressed, wore his black boots, and his hair shone.

'Splendid,' he said when he saw me. 'You will come with me to see Miss Barkley.'

'No.'

'Yes. You will please come and make me a good impression on her.'

'All right. Wait till I get cleaned up.'

'Wash up and come as you are.'

I washed, brushed my hair and we started.

'Wait a minute,' Rinaldi said. 'Perhaps we should have a drink.' He opened his trunk and took out a bottle.

'Not Strega,' I said.

'No. Grappa.'

'All right.'

He poured two glasses and we touched them, first fingers extended. The grappa was very strong.

'Another?'

'All right,' I said. We drank the second grappa, Rinaldi put away the bottle and we went down the stairs. It was hot walking through the town but the sun was starting to go down and it was very pleasant. The British hospital was a big villa built by Germans before the war. Miss Barkley was in the garden. Another nurse was with her. We saw their white uniforms through the trees and walked towards them. Rinaldi saluted. I saluted too but more moderately.

'How do you do?' Miss Barkley said. 'You're not an Italian, are you?'

'Oh, no.'

Rinaldi was talking with the other nurse. They were laughing.

'What an odd thing — to be in the Italian army.'

'It's not really the army. It's only the ambulance.'

'It's very odd though. Why did you do it?'

'I don't know,' I said. 'There isn't always an explanation for everything.'

'Oh, isn't there? I was brought up to think there was.'

'That's awfully nice.'

'*Do* we have to go on and talk this way?'

'No,' I said.

'That's a relief. Isn't it?'

'What is the stick?' I asked. Miss Barkley was quite tall. She wore what seemed to me to be a nurse's uniform, was blonde and had a tawny skin and grey eyes. I thought she was very beautiful.

She was carrying a thin rattan stick like a toy riding-crop, bound in leather.

'It belonged to a boy who was killed last year.'

'I'm awfully sorry.'

'He was a very nice boy. He was going to marry me and he was killed on the Somme.'

'It was a ghastly show.'

'Were you there?'

'No.'

'I've heard about it,' she said. 'There's not really any war of that sort down here. They sent me the little stick. His mother sent it to me. They returned it with his things.'

'Had you been engaged long?'

'Eight years. We grew up together.'

'And why didn't you marry?'

'I don't know,' she said. 'I was a fool not to. I could have given him that anyway. But I thought it would be bad for him.'

'I see.'

'Have you ever loved anyone?'

'No,' I said.

We sat down on a bench and I looked at her.

'You have beautiful hair,' I said.

'Do you like it?'

'Very much.'

'I was going to cut it all off when he died.'

'No.'

'I wanted to do something for him. You see I didn't care about the other thing and he could have had it all. He could have had anything he wanted if I had known. I would have married him or anything. I know all about it now. But then he wanted to go to war and I didn't know.'

I did not say anything.

'I didn't know about anything then. I thought it would be worse for him. I thought perhaps he couldn't stand it and then of course he was killed and that was the end of it.'

'I don't know.'

'Oh, yes,' she said. 'That's the end of it.'

We looked at Rinaldi talking with the other nurse.

'What was her name?'

'Ferguson. Helen Ferguson. Your friend is a doctor, isn't he?'

'Yes. He's very good.'

'That's splendid. You rarely find anyone any good this close to the front. This is close to the front, isn't it?'

'Quite.'

'It's a silly front,' she said. 'But it's very beautiful. Are they going to have an offensive?'

'Yes.'

'Then we'll have to work. There's no work now.'

'Have you done nursing long?'

'Since the end of 'fifteen. I started when he did. I remember having a silly idea he might come to the hospital where I was. With a sabre cut, I suppose, and a bandage around his head. Or shot through the shoulder. Something picturesque.'

'This is the picturesque front,' I said.

'Yes,' she said. 'People can't realize what France is like. If they did it couldn't all go on. He didn't have a sabre cut. They blew him all to bits.'

I didn't say anything.

'Do you suppose it will always go on?'

'No.'

'What's to stop it?'

'It will crack somewhere.'

'We'll crack. We'll crack in France. They can't go on doing things like the Somme and not crack.'

'They won't crack here,' I said.

'You think not?'

'No. They did very well last summer.'

'They may crack,' she said. 'Anybody may crack.'

'The Germans too.'

'No,' she said. 'I think not.'

23

We went over towards Rinaldi and Miss Ferguson.

'You love Italy?' Rinaldi asked Miss Ferguson in English.

'Quite well.'

'No understand,' Rinaldi shook his head.

'Bastante bene,' I translated. He shook his head.

'That is not good. You love England?'

'Not too well. I'm Scottish, you see.'

Rinaldi looked at me blankly.

'She's Scottish, so she loves Scotland better than England,' I said in Italian.

'But Scotland is England.'

I translated this for Miss Ferguson.

'Pas encore,' said Miss Ferguson.

'Not really?'

'Never. We do not like the English.'

'Not like the English? Not like Miss Barkley?'

'Oh, that's different. She's partly Scottish too. You mustn't take everything so literally.'

After a while we said good night and left. Walking home Rinaldi said, 'Miss Barkley prefers you to me. That is very clear. But the little Scottish one is very nice.'

'Very,' I said. I had not noticed her. 'You like her?'

'No,' said Rinaldi.

CHAPTER 5

THE next afternoon I went to call on Miss Barkley again. She was not in the garden and I went to the side door of the villa where the ambulances drove up. Inside I saw the head nurse, who said Miss Barkley was on duty — 'there's a war on, you know.'

I said I knew.

'You're the American in the Italian army?' she asked.

'Yes, ma'am.'

'How did you happen to do that? Why didn't you join up with us?'

'I don't know,' I said. 'Could I join now?'

'I'm afraid not now. Tell me. Why did you join up with the Italians?'

'I was in Italy,' I said, 'and I spoke Italian.'

'Oh,' she said. 'I'm learning it. It's a beautiful language.'

'Somebody said you should be able to learn it in two weeks.'

'Oh, I'll not learn it in two weeks. I've studied it for months now. You may come and see her after seven o'clock if you wish. She'll be off then. But don't bring a lot of Italians.'

'Not even for the beautiful language?'

'No. Nor for the beautiful uniforms.'

'Good evening,' I said.

'A rivederci, Tenente.'

'A rivederla.' I saluted and went out. It was impossible to salute foreigners as an Italian, without embarrassment. The Italian salute never seemed made for export.

The day had been hot. I had been up the river to the bridgehead at Plava. It was there that the offensive was to begin. It had been impossible to advance on the far side the year before because there was only one road leading down from the pass to the pontoon bridge and it was under machine-gun and shell fire for nearly a mile. It was not wide enough either to carry all the transport for an offensive and the Austrians could make a shambles out of it. But the Italians had crossed and spread out a little way on the far side to hold about a mile and a half on the Austrian side of the river. It was a nasty place and the Austrians should not have let them hold it. I suppose it was mutual tolerance because the Austrians still kept a bridgehead further down the river. The Austrian trenches were above on the hill-side only a few yards from the Italian lines. There had been a little town but it was all rubble. There was what was left of a railway station and a smashed permanent bridge that could not be repaired and used because it was in plain sight.

I went along the narrow road down towards the river, left the car at the dressing-station under the hill, crossed the pontoon bridge, which was protected by a shoulder of the mountain, and went through the trenches in the smashed-down town and along the edge of the slope. Everybody was in the dugouts. There were racks of rockets standing to be touched off to call for help from the artillery or to signal with if the telephone wires were cut. It was quiet, hot and dirty. I looked across the wire at the Austrian lines. Nobody was in sight. I had a drink with a captain that I knew in one of the dugouts and went back across the bridge.

A new wide road was being finished that would go over the mountain and zig-zag down to the bridge. When this road was finished the offensive would start. It came down through the forest in sharp turns. The system was to bring everything down the new road and take the empty trucks, carts and loaded ambulances and all returning traffic up the old narrow road. The dressing-station was on the Austrian side of the river under the edge of the hill and stretcher-bearers would bring the wounded back across the pontoon bridge. It would be the same when the offensive started. As far as I could make out the last mile or so of the new road where it started to level out would be able to be shelled steadily by the Austrians. It looked as though it might be a mess. But I found a place where the cars would be sheltered after they had passed that last bad-looking bit and could wait for the wounded to be brought across the pontoon bridge. I would have liked to drive over the new road but it was not yet finished. It looked wide and well made with a good grade and the turns looked very impressive where you could see them through openings in the forest on the mountain side. The cars would be all right with their good metal-to-metal brakes and anyway, coming down, they would not be loaded. I drove back up the narrow road.

Two carabinieri held the car up. A shell had fallen and while we waited three others fell up the road. They were seventy-sevens and came with a whishing rush of air, a hard bright burst and flash and then grey smoke that blew across the road. The carabinieri waved us to go on. Passing where the shells had landed I avoided the small broken places and smelled the high explosive and the smell of blasted clay and stone and freshly-shattered flint. I drove back to Gorizia and our villa and, as I said, went to call on Miss Barkley, who was on duty.

At dinner I ate very quickly and left for the villa where the British had their hospital. It was really very large and beautiful and there were fine trees in the grounds. Miss Barkley was sitting on a bench in the garden. Miss Ferguson was with her. They seemed glad to see me and in a little while Miss Ferguson excused herself and went away.

'I'll leave you two,' she said. 'You get along very well without me.'

'Don't go, Helen,' Miss Barkley said.

'I'd really rather. I must write some letters.'

'Good night,' I said.

'Good night, Mr. Henry.'

'Don't write anything that will bother the censor.'

'Don't worry. I only write about what a beautiful place we live in and how brave the Italians are.'

'That way you'll be decorated.'

'That will be nice. Good night, Catherine.'

'I'll see you in a little while,' Miss Barkley said. Miss Ferguson walked away in the dark.

'She's nice,' I said.

'Oh, yes, she's very nice. She's a nurse.'

'Aren't you a nurse?'

'Oh, no. I'm something called a V.A.D. We work very hard but no one trusts us.'

'Why not?'

'They don't trust us when there's nothing going on. When there is really work they trust us.'

'What is the difference?'

27

'A nurse is like a doctor. It takes a long time to be. A V.A.D. is a short cut.'

'I see.'

'The Italians didn't want women so near the front. So we're all on very special behaviour. We don't go out.'

'I can come here though.'

'Oh, yes. We're not cloistered.'

'Let's drop the war.'

'It's very hard. There's no place to drop it.'

'Let's drop it anyway.'

'All right.'

We looked at each other in the dark. I thought she was very beautiful and I took her hand. She let me take it and I held it and put my arm around under her arm.

'No,' she said. I kept my arm where it was.

'Why not?'

'No.'

'Yes,' I said. 'Please.' I leaned forward in the dark to kiss her and there was a sharp stinging flash. She had slapped my face hard. Her hand had hit my nose and eyes, and tears came in my eyes from the reflex.

'I'm so sorry,' she said. I felt I had a certain advantage.

'You were quite right.'

'I'm dreadfully sorry,' she said. 'I just couldn't stand the nurse's-evening-off aspect of it. I didn't mean to hurt you. I did hurt you, didn't I?'

She was looking at me in the dark. I was angry and yet certain, seeing it all ahead like the moves in a chess game.

'You did exactly right,' I said. 'I don't mind at all.'

'Poor man.'

'You see I've been leading a sort of a funny life. And I never even talk English. And then you are so very beautiful.' I looked at her.

'You don't need to say a lot of nonsense. I said I was sorry. We do get along.'

28

'Yes,' I said. 'And we have gotten away from the war.'

She laughed. It was the first time I had ever heard her laugh. I watched her face.

'You are sweet,' she said.

'No, I'm not.'

'Yes. You are a dear. I'd be glad to kiss you if you don't mind.'

I looked in her eyes and put my arm around her as I had before and kissed her. I kissed her hard and held her tight and tried to open her lips; they were closed tight. I was still angry and as I held her suddenly she shivered. I held her close against me and could feel her heart beating and her lips opened and her head went back against my hand and then she was crying on my shoulder.

'Oh, darling,' she said. 'You will be good to me, won't you?'

What the hell, I thought. I stroked her hair and patted her shoulder. She was crying.

'You will, won't you?' She looked up at me. 'Because we're going to have a strange life.'

After a while I walked with her to the door of the villa and she went in and I walked home. Back at the villa I went upstairs to the room. Rinaldi was lying on his bed. He looked at me.

'So you make progress with Miss Barkley?'

'We are friends.'

'You have that pleasant air of a dog in heat.'

I did not understand the word.

'Of a what?'

He explained.

'You,' I said, 'have that pleasant air of a dog who —'

'Stop it,' he said. 'In a little while we would say insulting things.' He laughed.

'Good night,' I said.

'Good night, little puppy.'

I knocked over his candle with the pillow and got into bed in the dark.

Rinaldi picked up the candle, lit it and went on reading.

CHAPTER 6

I WAS away for two days at the posts. When I got home it was too late and I did not see Miss Barkley until the next evening. She was not in the garden and I had to wait in the office of the hospital until she came down. There were many marble busts on painted wooden pillars along the walls of the room they used for an office. The hall, too, that the office opened on, was lined with them. They had the complete marble quality of all looking alike. Sculpture had always seemed a dull business — still bronzes looked like something. But marble busts all looked like a cemetery. There was one fine cemetery though — the one at Pisa. Genoa was the place to see the bad marbles. This had been the villa of a very wealthy German and the busts must have cost him plenty. I wondered who had done them and how much he got. I tried to make out whether they were members of the family or what; but they were all uniformly classical. You could not tell anything about them.

I sat on a chair and held my cap. We were supposed to wear steel helmets even in Gorizia but they were uncomfortable and too theatrical in a town where the civilian inhabitants had not been evacuated. I wore one when we went up to the posts, and carried an English gas-mask. We were just beginning to get some of them. They were a real mask. Also we were required to wear an automatic pistol; even doctors and sanitary officers. I felt it against the back of the chair. You were liable to arrest if you did not have one worn in plain sight. Rinaldi carried a holster stuffed with toilet paper. I wore a real one and felt like a gunman until I practised firing it. It was an Astra 7.65 calibre with a short barrel and it jumped so sharply when you let it off that there was no question of hitting anything. I practised with it, holding below the target and trying to master the jerk of the ridiculous short barrel until I could hit within a yard of where I aimed at twenty paces and then the ridiculousness of carrying a pistol at all came over me and I soon forgot it and carried it flopping against the small of my back with no feeling at all except a vague sort of shame when I met English-speaking people. I sat now in the chair and an orderly of some sort looked at me disapprovingly from behind a desk while I looked at the marble floor, the pillars with the marble busts, and the frescoes on the wall and waited for Miss Barkley. The frescoes were not bad. Any frescoes were good when they started to peel and flake off.

I saw Catherine Barkley coming down the hall, and stood up. She did not seem tall walking towards me but she looked very lovely.

'Good evening, Mr. Henry,' she said.

'How do you do?' I said. The orderly was listening behind the desk.

'Shall we sit here or go out in the garden?'

'Let's go out. It's much cooler.'

I walked behind her out into the garden, the orderly looking after us. When we were out on the gravel drive she said, 'Where have you been?'

'I've been out on post.'

'You couldn't have sent me a note?'

'No,' I said. 'Not very well. I thought I was coming back.'

'You ought to have let me know, darling.'

We were off the driveway, walking under the trees. I took her hands, then stopped and kissed her.

'Isn't there anywhere we can go?'

'No,' she said. 'We have to just walk here. You've been away a long time.'

'This is the third day. But I'm back now.'

She looked at me. 'And you do love me?'

'Yes.'

'You did say you loved me, didn't you?'

'Yes,' I lied. 'I love you.' I had not said it before.

'And you call me Catherine?'

'Catherine.' We walked on a way and were stopped under a tree.

'Say, "I've come back to Catherine in the night." '

'I've come back to Catherine in the night.'

'Oh, darling, you have come back, haven't you?'

'Yes.'

'I love you so and it's been awful. You won't go away?'

'No. I'll always come back.'

'Oh, I love you so. Please put your hand there again.'

'It's not been away.' I turned her so I could see her face when I kissed her and I saw that her eyes were shut. I kissed both her shut eyes. I thought she was probably a little crazy. It was all right if she was. I did not care what I was getting into. This was better than going every evening to the house for officers where the girls climbed all over you and put your cap on backward as a sign of affection between their trips upstairs with brother officers. I knew I did not love Catherine Barkley nor had any idea of loving her. This was a game, like bridge, in which you said things instead of playing cards. Like bridge you had to pretend you were playing for money or playing for some stakes. Nobody mentioned what the stakes were. It was all right with me.

'I wish there was some place we could go,' I said. I was experiencing the masculine difficulty of making love very long standing up.

'There isn't any place,' she said. She came back from wherever she had been.

'We might sit there just for a little while.'

We sat on the flat stone bench and I held Catherine Barkley's hand. She would not let me put my arm around her.

'Are you very tired?' she asked.

'No.'

She looked down at the grass.

'This is a rotten game we play, isn't it?'

'What game?'

'Don't be dull.'

'I'm not, on purpose.'

'You're a nice boy,' she said. 'And you play it as well as you know how. But it's a rotten game.'

'Do you always know what people think?'

'Not always. But I do with you. You don't have to pretend you love me. That's over for the evening. Is there anything you'd like to talk about?'

'But I do love you.'

'Please let's not lie when we don't have to. I had a very fine little show and I'm all right now. You see I'm not mad and I'm not gone off. It's only a little sometimes.'

I pressed her hand, 'Dear Catherine.'

'It sounds very funny now — Catherine. You don't pronounce it very much alike. But you're very nice. You're a very good boy.'

'That's what the priest said.'

'Yes, you're very good. And you will come and see me?'

'Of course.'

'And you don't have to say you love me. That's all over for a while.' She stood up and put out her hand. 'Good night.'

I wanted to kiss her.

'No,' she said. 'I'm awfully tired.'

'Kiss me, though,' I said.

'I'm awfully tired, darling.'

'Kiss me.'

'Do you want to very much?'

'Yes.'

We kissed and she broke away suddenly. 'No. Good night, please, darling.' We walked to the door and I saw her go in and down the hall. I liked to watch her move. She went on down the hall. I went on home. It was a hot night and there was a good deal going on up in the mountains. I watched the flashes on San Gabriele.

I stopped in front of the Villa Rossa. The shutters were up but it was still going on inside. Somebody was singing. I went on home. Rinaldi came in while I was undressing.

'Ah, ha!' he said. 'It does not go so well. Baby is puzzled.'

'Where have you been?'

'At the Villa Rossa. It was very edifying, baby. We all sang. Where have you been?'

'Calling on the British.'

'Thank God I did not become involved with the British.'

CHAPTER 7

I CAME back the next afternoon from our first mountain post and stopped the car at the *smistâmento* where the wounded and sick were sorted by their papers and the papers marked for the different hospitals. I had been driving and I sat in the car and the driver took the papers in. It was a hot day and the sky was very bright and blue and the road was white and dusty. I sat in the high seat on the Fiat and thought about nothing. A regiment went by in the road and I watched them pass. The men were hot and sweating. Some wore their steel helmets but most of them carried them slung from their packs. Most of the helmets were too big and came down almost over the ears of the men who wore them. The officers all wore helmets; better-fitting helmets. It was half of the Brigata Basilicata. I identified them by their red and white striped collar mark. There were stragglers going by long after the regiment had passed — men who could not keep up with their platoons. They were sweaty, dusty and tired. Some looked pretty bad. A soldier came along after the last of the stragglers. He was walking with a limp. He stopped and sat down beside the road. I got down and went over.

'What's the matter?'

He looked at me, then stood up.

'I'm going on.'

'What's the trouble?'

'— the war.'

34

'What's wrong with your leg?'

'It's not my leg. I got a rupture.'

'Why don't you ride with the transport?' I asked. 'Why don't you go to the hospital?'

'They won't let me. The lieutenant said I slipped the truss on purpose.'

'Let me feel it.'

'It's way out.'

'Which side is it on?'

'Here.'

I felt it.

'Cough,' I said.

'I'm afraid it will make it bigger. It's twice as big as it was this morning.'

'Sit down,' I said. 'As soon as I get the papers on these wounded I'll take you along the road and drop you with your medical officers.'

'He'll say I did it on purpose.'

'They can't do anything,' I said. 'It's not a wound. You've had it before, haven't you?'

'But I lost the truss.'

'They'll send you to a hospital.'

'Can't I stay here, Tenente?'

'No. I haven't any papers for you.'

The driver came out of the door with the papers for the wounded in the car.

'Four for 105. Two for 132,' he said. They were hospitals beyond the river.

'You drive,' I said. I helped the soldier with the rupture up on the seat with us.

'You speak English?' he asked.

'Sure.'

'How you like this goddam war?'

'Rotten.'

'I say it's rotten. Jesus Christ, I say it's rotten.'

'Were you in the States?'

'Sure. In Pittsburg. I knew you was an American.'

'Don't I talk Italian good enough?'

'I knew you was an American all right.'

'Another American,' said the driver in Italian looking at the hernia man.

'Listen, lootenant. Do you have to take me to that regiment?'

'Yes.'

'Because the captain doctor knew I had this rupture. I threw away the goddam truss so it would get bad and I wouldn't have to go to the line again.'

'I see.'

'Couldn't you take me no place else?'

'If it was closer to the front I could take you to a first medical post. But back here you've got to have papers.'

'If I go back they'll make me get operated on and then they'll put me in the line all the time.'

I thought it over.

'You wouldn't want to go in the line all the time, would you?' he asked.

'No.'

'Jesus Christ, ain't this a goddam war?'

'Listen,' I said. 'You get out and fall down by the road and get a bump on your head and I'll pick you up on our way back and take you to a hospital. We'll stop by the road here, Aldo.' We stopped at the side of the road. I helped him down.

'I'll be right here, lieutenant,' he said.

'So long,' I said. We went on and passed the regiment about a mile ahead, then crossed the river, cloudy with snow water and running fast through the spiles of the bridge, to ride along the road across the plain and deliver the wounded at the two hospitals. I drove coming back and went fast with the empty car to find the man from Pittsburg. First we passed the regiment, hotter and slower than ever: then the stragglers. Then we saw a horse ambulance stopped by the road. Two men were lifting the hernia man to put him in. They had come back for him. He shook his head at me. His helmet was off and his forehead was bleeding below the hair line. His nose was skinned and there was dust on the bloody patch and dust in his hair.

'Look at the bump, lieutenant!' he shouted. 'Nothing to do. They come back for me.'

When I got back to the villa it was five o'clock and I went out where we washed the cars, to take a shower. Then I made out my report in my room, sitting in my trousers and an undershirt in front of the open window. In two days the offensive was to start and I would go with the cars to Plava. It was a long time since I had written to the States and I knew I should write but I had let it go so long that it was almost impossible to write now. There was nothing to write about. I sent a couple of army Zona di Guerra post-cards, crossing out everything except I am well. That should handle them. Those post-cards would be very fine in America; strange and mysterious. This was a strange and mysterious war zone but I supposed it was quite well run and grim compared to other wars with the Austrians. The Austrian army was created to give Napoleon victories; any Napoleon. I wished we had a Napoleon, but instead we had Il Generale Cadorna, fat and prosperous, and Vittorio Emmanuele, the tiny man with the long thin neck and the goat beard. Over on the right they had the Duke of Aosta. Maybe he was too good-looking to be a great general but he looked like a man. Lots of them would have liked him to be king. He looked like a king. He was the King's uncle and commanded the third army. We were in the second army. There were some British batteries up with the third army. I had met two gunners from that lot, in Milan. They were very nice and we had a big evening. They were big and shy and embarrassed and very appreciative together of anything that happened. I wished that I was with the British. It would have been much simpler. Still I would probably have been killed. Not in this ambulance business. Yes, even in the ambulance business. British ambulance drivers were killed sometimes. Well, I knew I would not be killed. Not in this war. It did not have anything to do with me. It seemed no more dangerous to me myself than war in the movies. I wished to God it was over though. Maybe it would finish this summer. Maybe the Austrians would crack. They had always cracked in other wars. What was the matter with this war? Everybody said the French were through. Rinaldi said that the French had mutinied and troops marched on Paris. I asked him what happened and he said, 'Oh, they stopped them.' I wanted to go to Austria without war. I wanted to go to the Black Forest. I wanted to go to the Hartz Mountains. Where were the Hartz Mountains anyway? They were fighting in the Carpathians. I did not want to go there anyway. It might be good though. I could go to Spain if there was no war. The sun was going down and the day was cooling off. After supper I would go and see Catherine Barkley. I wished she were here now. I wished I were in Milan with her. I would like to eat at the Cova and then walk down the Via Manzoni in the hot evening and cross over and turn off along the canal and go to the hotel with Catherine Barkley. Maybe she would. Maybe she would pretend that I was her boy that was killed and we would go in the front door and the porter would take off his cap and I would stop at the concierge's desk and ask for the key and she would stand by the elevator and then we would get in the elevator and it would go up very slowly clicking at all the floors and then our floor and the boy would open the door and stand there and she would step out and I would step out and we would walk down the hall and I would put the key in the door and open it and go in and then take down the telephone and ask them to send a bottle of capri bianco in a silver bucket full of ice and you would hear the ice against the pail coming down the corridor and the boy would knock and I would say leave it outside the door please. Because we would not wear any clothes because it was so hot and the window open and the swallows flying over the roofs of the houses and when it was dark afterwards and you went to the window very small bats hunting over the houses and close down over the trees and we would drink the capri and the door locked and it hot and only a sheet and the whole night and we would both love each other all night in the hot night in Milan. That was how it ought to be. I would eat quickly and go and see Catherine Barkley.

They talked too much at the mess and I drank wine because tonight we were not all brothers unless I drank a little and talked with the priest about Archbishop Ireland who was, it seemed, a noble man and with whose injustice, the injustices he had received and in which I participated as an American, and of which I had never heard, I feigned acquaintance. It would have been impolite not to have known something of them when I had listened to such a splendid explanation of their causes which were, after all, it seemed, misunderstandings. I thought he had a fine name and he came from Minnesota which made a lovely name: Ireland of Minnesota, Ireland of Wisconsin, Ireland of Michigan. What made it pretty was that it sounded like Island. No that wasn't it. There was more to it than that. Yes, father. That is true, father. Perhaps, father. No, father. Well, maybe yes, father. You know more about it than I do, father. The priest was good but dull. The officers were not good but dull. The King was good but dull. The wine was bad but not dull. It took the enamel off your teeth and left it on the roof of your mouth.

'And the priest was locked up,' Rocca said, 'because they found the three per cent bonds on his person. It was in France of course. Here they would never have arrested him. He denied all knowledge of the five per cent bonds. This took place at Béziers. I was there and reading of it in the paper, went to the jail and asked to see the priest. It was quite evident he had stolen the bonds.'

'I don't believe a word of this,' Rinaldi said.

'Just as you like,' Rocca said. 'But I am telling it for our priest here. It is very informative. He is a priest; he will appreciate it.'

The priest smiled. 'Go on,' he said. 'I am listening.'

'Of course some of the bonds were not accounted for but the priest had all of the three per cent bonds and several local obligations, I forget exactly what they were. So I went to the jail, now this is the point of the story, and I stood outside his cell and I said as though I were going to confession, "Bless me, father, for you have sinned." '

There was great laughter from everybody.

'And what did he say?' asked the priest. Rocca ignored this and went on to explain the joke to me. 'You see the point, don't you?' It seemed it was a very funny joke if you understood it properly.)They poured me more wine and I told the story about the English private soldier who was placed under the shower-bath. Then the major told the story of the eleven Czechoslovaks and the Hungarian corporal. After some more wine I told the story of the jockey who found the penny. The major said there was an Italian story something like that about the duchess who could not sleep at night. At this point the priest left and I told the story about the travelling salesman who arrived at five o'clock in the morning at Marseilles when the mistral was blowing. The major said he had heard a report that I could drink. I denied this. He said it was true and by the corpse of Bacchus we would test whether it was true or not. Not Bacchus, I said. Not Bacchus. Yes, Bacchus, he said. I should drink cup for cup and glass for glass with Bassi Fillipo Vicenza. Bassi said no that was no test because he had already drunk twice as much as I. I said that was a foul lie and, Bacchus or no Bacchus, Fillipo Vicenza Bassi or Bassi Fillippo Vicenza had never touched a drop all evening and what was his name anyway? He said was my name Frederico Enrico or Enrico Federico? I said let the best man win, Bacchus barred, and the major started us with red wine in mugs. Half-way through the wine I did not want any more. I remembered where I was going.

'Bassi wins,' I said. 'He's a better man than I am. I have to go.'

'He does really,' said Rinaldi. 'He has a rendezvous. I know all about it.'

'I have to go.'

'Another night,' said Bassi. 'Another night when you feel stronger.' He slapped me on the shoulder. There were lighted candles on the table. All the officers were very happy. 'Good night, gentlemen,' I said.

Rinaldi went out with me. We stood outside the door on the path and he said, 'You'd better not go up there drunk.'

'I'm not drunk, Rinin. Really.'

'You'd better chew some coffee.'

'Nonsense.'

'I'll get some, baby. You walk up and down.' He came back with a handful of roasted coffee beans.

'Chew those, baby, and God be with you.'

'Bacchus,' I said.

'I'll walk down with you.'

'I'm perfectly all right.'

We walked along together through the town and I chewed the coffee. At the gate of the driveway that led up to the British villa, Rinaldi said good night.

'Good night,' I said. 'Why don't you come in?'

He shook his head. 'No,' he said. 'I like the simpler pleasures.'

'Thank you for the coffee beans.'

'Nothing, baby. Nothing.'

I started down the driveway. The outlines of the cypresses that lined it were sharp and clear. I looked back and saw Rinaldi standing watching me and waved to him.

I sat in the reception hall of the villa waiting for Catherine Barkley to come down. Someone was coming down the hallway. I stood up, but it was not Catherine. It was Miss Ferguson.

'Hello,' she said. 'Catherine asked me to tell you she was sorry she couldn't see you this evening.'

'I'm so sorry. I hope she's not ill.'

'She's not awfully well.'

'Will you tell her how sorry I am?'

'Yes, I will.'

'Do you think it would be any good to try and see her to-morrow?'

'Yes, I do.'

'Thank you very much,' I said. 'Good night.'

I went out the door and suddenly I felt lonely and empty. I had treated seeing Catherine very lightly, I had gotten somewhat drunk and had nearly forgotten to come but when I could not see her there I was feeling lonely and hollow.

CHAPTER 8

THE next afternoon we heard there was to be an attack up the river that night and that we were to take four cars there. Nobody knew anything about it although they all spoke with great positiveness and strategical knowledge. I was riding in the first car and as we passed the entry to the British hospital I told the driver to stop. The other cars pulled up. I got out and told the drivers to go on and that if we had not caught up to them at the junction of the road to Cormons to wait there. I hurried up the driveway and inside the reception hall I asked for Miss Barkley.

'She's on duty.'

'Could I see her just for a moment?'

They sent an orderly to see and she came back with him.

'I stopped to ask if you were better. They told me you were on duty, so I asked to see you.'

'I'm quite well,' she said, 'I think the heat knocked me over yesterday.'

'I have to go.'

'I'll just step outside the door a minute.'

'And you're all right?' I asked outside.

'Yes, darling. Are you coming tonight?'

'No. I'm leaving now for a show up above Plava.'

'A show?'

'I don't think it's anything.'

'And you'll be back?'

'Tomorrow.'

She was unclasping something from her neck. She put it in my hand. 'It's a Saint Anthony,' she said. 'And come to-morrow night.'

'You're not a Catholic, are you?'

'No. But they say a Saint Anthony's very useful.'

'I'll take care of him for you. Goodbye.'

'No,' she said, 'not goodbye.'

'All right.'

'Be a good boy and be careful. No, you can't kiss me here. You can't.'

'All right.'

I looked back and saw her standing on the steps. She waved and I kissed my hand and held it out. She waved again and then I was out of the driveway and climbing up into the seat of the ambulance and we started. The Saint Anthony was in a little white metal capsule. I opened the capsule and spilled him out into my hand.

'Saint Anthony?' asked the driver.

'Yes.'

'I have one.' His right hand left the wheel and opened a button on his tunic and pulled it out from under his shirt.

'See?'

I put my Saint Anthony back in the capsule, spilled the thin gold chain together and put it all in my breast pocket.

'You don't wear him?'

'No.'

'It's better to wear him. That's what it's for.'

'All right,' I said. I undid the clasp of the gold chain and put it around my neck and clasped it. The saint hung down on the outside of my uniform and I undid the throat of my tunic, un-buttoned the shirt collar and dropped him in under the shirt. I felt him in his metal box against my chest while we drove. Then I forgot about him. After I was wounded I never found him. Someone probably got it at one of the dressing-stations.

We drove fast when we were over the bridge and soon we saw the dust of the other cars ahead down the road. The road curved and we saw the three cars looking quite small, the dust rising from the wheels and going off through the trees. We caught them and passed them and turned off on a road that climbed up into the hills. Driving in convoy is not unpleasant if you are the first car and I settled back in the seat and watched the country. We were in the foot-hills on the near side of the river and as the road mounted there were the high mountains off to the north with snow still on the tops. I looked back and saw the three cars all climbing, spaced by the interval of their dust. We passed a long column of loaded mules, the drivers walking along beside the mules wearing red fezes. They were bersaglieri.

Beyond the mule train the road was empty and we climbed through the hills and then went down over the shoulder of a long hill into a river-valley. There were trees along both sides of the road and through the right line of trees I saw the river, the water clear, fast and shallow. The river was low and there were stretches of sand and pebbles with a narrow channel of water and sometimes the water spread like a sheen over the pebbly bed. Close to the bank I saw deep pools, the water blue like the sky. I saw arched stone bridges over the river where tracks turned off from the road and we passed stone farmhouses with pear trees candelabraed against their south walls and low stone walls in the fields. The road went up the valley a long way and then we turned off and commenced to climb into the hills again. The road climbed steeply going up and back and forth through chestnut woods to level finally along a ridge. I could look down through the woods and see, far below, with the sun on it, the line of river that separated the two armies. We went along the rough new military road that followed the crest of the ridge and I looked to the north at the two ranges of mountains, green and dark to the snow-line and then white and lovely in the sun. Then, as the road mounted along the ridge, I saw a third range of mountains, higher snow mountains, that looked chalky white and furrowed, with strange planes, and then there were mountains far off beyond all these, that you could hardly tell if you really saw. Those were all the Austrians' mountains and we had nothing like them. Ahead there was a rounded turn-off in the road to the right and looking down I could see the road dropping through the trees. There were troops on this road and motor trucks and mules with mountain-guns and as we went down, keeping to the side, I could see the river far down below, the line of ties and rails running along it, the old bridge where the railway crossed to the other side and across, under a hill beyond the river, the broken houses of the little town that was to be taken.

It was nearly dark when we came down and turned on to the main road that ran beside the river.

CHAPTER 9

THE road was crowded and there were screens of corn stalk and straw matting on both sides and matting over the top so that it was like the entrance at a circus or a native village. We drove slowly in this matting-covered tunnel and came out on to a bare cleared space where the railway station had been. The road here was below the level of the river bank and all along the side of the sunken road there were holes dug in the bank with infantry in them. The sun was going down and looking up along the bank as we drove I saw the Austrian observation balloons above the hills on the other side dark against the sunset. We parked the cars beyond a brickyard. The ovens and some deep holes had been equipped as dressing-stations. There were three doctors that I knew. I talked with the major and learned that when it should start and our cars should be loaded we would drive them back along the screened road and up to the main road along the ridge where there would be a post and other cars to clear them. He hoped the road would not jam. It was a one-road show. The road was screened because it was in sight of the Austrians across the river. Here at the brickyard we were sheltered from rifle or machine-gun fire by the river bank. There was one smashed bridge across the river. They were going to put over another bridge when the bombardment started and some troops were to cross at the shallows up above at the bend of the river. The major was a little man with upturned moustaches. He had been in the war in Libya and wore two wound-stripes. He said that if the thing went well he would see that I was decorated. I said I hoped it would go well but that he was too kind. I asked him if there was a big dugout where the drivers could stay and he sent a soldier to show me. I went with him and found the dugout, which was very good. The drivers were pleased with it and I left them there. The major asked me to have a drink with him and two other officers. We drank rum and it was very friendly. Outside it was getting dark. I asked what time the attack was to be and they said as soon as it was dark. I went back to the drivers. They were sitting in the dugout talking and when I came in they stopped. I gave them each a package of cigarettes, Macedonias, loosely packed cigarettes that spilled tobacco and needed to have the ends twisted before you smoked them. Manera lit his lighter and passed it around. The lighter was shaped like a Fiat radiator. I told them what I had heard.

'Why didn't we see the post when we came down?' Passini asked.

'It was just beyond where we turned off.'

'That road will be a dirty mess,' Manera said.

'They'll shell hell out of us.'

46

'Probably.'

'What about eating, lieutenant? We won't get a chance to eat after this thing starts.'

'I'll go and see now,' I said.

'You want us to stay here or can we look around?'

'Better stay here.'

I went back to the major's dugout and he said the field kitchen would be along and the drivers could come and get their stew. He would loan them mess tins if they did not have them. I said I thought they had them. I went back and told the drivers I would get them as soon as the food came. Manera said he hoped it would come before the bombardment started. They were silent until I went out. They were all mechanics and hated the war.

I went out to look at the cars and see what was going on and then came back and sat down in the dugout with the four drivers. We sat on the ground with our backs against the wall and smoked. Outside it was nearly dark. The earth of the dugout was warm and dry and I let my shoulders back against the wall, sitting on the small of my back, and relaxed.

'Who goes to the attack?' asked Gavuzzi.

'Bersaglieri.'

'All bersaglieri?'

'I think so.'

'There aren't enough troops here for a real attack.'

'It is probably to draw attention from where the real attack will be.'

'Do the men know that who attack?'

'I don't think so.'

'Of course they don't,' Manera said. 'They wouldn't attack if they did.'

'Yes they would,' Passini said. 'Bersaglieri are fools.'

'They are brave and have good discipline,' I said.

'They are big through the chest by measurement, and healthy. But they are still fools.'

'The granatieri are tall,' Manera said. This was a joke. They all laughed.

'Were you there, Tenente, when they wouldn't attack and they shot every tenth man?'

'No.'

'It is true. They lined them up afterward and took every tenth man. Carabinieri shot them.'

'Carabinieri,' said Passini and spat on the floor. 'But those grenadiers; all over six feet. They wouldn't attack.'

'If everybody would not attack the war would be over,' Manera said.

'It wasn't that way with the granatieri. They were afraid. The officers all came from such good families.'

'Some of the officers went alone.'

'A sergeant shot two officers who would not get out.'

'Some troops went out.'

'Those that went out were not lined up when they took the tenth men.'

'One of those shot by the carabinieri is from my town,' Passini said. 'He was a big smart tall boy to be in the granatieri. Always in Rome. Always with the girls. Always with the carabinieri.' He laughed. 'Now they have a guard outside his house with a bayonet and nobody can come to see his mother and father and sisters and his father loses his civil rights and cannot even vote. They are all without law to protect them. Anybody can take their property.'

'If it wasn't that that happens to their families nobody would go to the attack.'

'Yes. Alpini would. These V.E. soldiers would. Some bersaglieri.'

'Bersaglieri have run too. Now they try to forget it.'

'You should not let us talk this way, Tenente. Evviva l'esercito!' Passini said sarcastically.

'I know how you talk,' I said. 'But as long as you drive the cars and behave — '

'— and don't talk so other officers can hear,' Manera finished.

'I believe we should get the war over,' I said. 'It would not finish it if one side stopped fighting. It would only be worse if we stopped fighting.'

'It could not be worse,' Passini said respectfully. 'There is nothing worse than war.'

'Defeat is worse.'

'I do not believe it,' Passini said still respectfully. 'What is defeat? You go home.'

'They come after you. They take your home. They take your sisters.'

'I don't believe it,' Passini said. 'They can't do that to everybody. Let everybody defend his home. Let them keep their sisters in the house.'

'They hang you. They come and make you be a soldier again. Not in the auto-ambulance, in the infantry.'

'They can't hang everyone.'

'An outside nation can't make you be a soldier,' Manera said. 'At the first battle you all run.'

'Like the Tchecos.'

'I think you do not know anything about being conquered and so you think it is not bad.'

'Tenente,' Passini said. 'We understand you let us talk. Listen. There is nothing as bad as war. We in the auto-ambulance cannot even realize at all how bad it is. When people realize how bad it is they cannot do anything to stop it because they go crazy. There are some people who never realize. There are people who are afraid of their officers. It is with them that war is made.'

'I know it is bad but we must finish it.'

'It doesn't finish. There is no finish to a war.'

'Yes there is.'

Passini shook his head.

'War is not won by victory. What if we take San Gabriele? What if we take the Carso and Monfalcone and Trieste? Where are we then? Did you see all the far mountains today? Do you think we could take all them too? Only if the Austrians stop fighting. One side must stop fighting. Why don't we stop fighting? If they come down into Italy they will get tired and go away. They have their own country. But no, instead there is a war.'

'You're an orator.'

'We think. We read. We are not peasants. We are mechanics. But even the peasants know better than to believe in a war. Everybody hates this war.'

'There is a class that controls a country that is stupid and does not realize anything and never can. That is why we have this war.'

'Also they make money out of it.'

'Most of them don't,' said Passini. 'They are too stupid. They do it for nothing. For stupidity.'

'We must shut up,' said Manera. 'We talk too much even for the Tenente.'

'He likes it,' said Passini. 'We will convert him.'

'But now we will shut up,' Manera said.

'Do we eat yet, Tenente?' Gavuzzi asked.

'I will go and see,' I said. Gordini stood up and went outside with me.

'Is there anything I can do, Tenente? Can I help in any way?' He was the quietest one of the four.

'Come with me if you want,' I said, 'and we'll see.'

It was dark outside and the long light from the searchlights was moving over the mountains. There were big searchlights on that front mounted on camions that you passed sometimes on the roads at night, close behind the lines, the camion stopped a little off the road, an officer directing the light and the crew scared. We crossed the brickyard, and stopped at the main dressing-station. There was a little shelter of green branches outside over the entrance and in the dark the night wind rustled the leaves dried by the sun. Inside there was a light. The major was at the telephone sitting on a box. One of the medical captains said the attack had been put forward an hour. He offered me a glass of cognac. I looked at the board tables, the instruments shining in the light, the basins and the stoppered bottles. Gordini stood behind me. The major got up from the telephone.

'It starts now,' he said. 'It has been put back again.'

I looked outside, it was dark and the Austrian searchlights were moving on the mountains behind us. It was quiet for a moment still, then from all the guns behind us the bombardment started.

'Savoia,' said the major.

'About the soup, major,' I said. He did not hear me. I repeated it.

'It hasn't come up.'

A big shell came in and burst outside in the brickyard. Another burst and in the noise you could hear the smaller noise of the brick and dirt raining down.

'What is there to eat?'

'We have a little pasta asciutta,' the major said.

'I'll take what you can give me.'

The major spoke to an orderly who went out of sight in the back and came back with a metal basin of cold cooked macaroni. I handed it to Gordini.

'Have you any cheese?'

The major spoke grudgingly to the orderly who ducked back into the hole again and came out with a quarter of a white cheese.

'Thank you very much,' I said.

'You'd better not go out.'

Outside something was set down beside the entrance. One of the two men who had carried it looked in.

'Bring him in,' said the major. 'What's the matter with you? Do you want us to come outside and get him?'

The two stretcher-bearers picked up the man under the arms and by the legs and brought him in.

'Slit the tunic,' the major said.

He held a forceps with some gauze in the end. The two captains took off their coats. 'Get out of here,' the major said to the two stretcher-bearers.

'Come on,' I said to Gordini.

'You better wait until the shelling is over,' the major said over his shoulder.

'They want to eat,' I said.

'As you wish.'

Outside we ran across the brickyard. A shell burst short near the river bank. Then there was one that we did not hear coming until the sudden rush. We both went flat and with the flash and bump of the burst and the smell heard the singing off of the fragments and the rattle of falling brick. Gordini got up and ran for the dugout. I was after him, holding the cheese, its smooth surface covered with brick dust. Inside the dugout were the three drivers sitting against the wall, smoking.

'Here, you patriots,' I said.

'How are the cars?' Manera asked.

'All right.'

'Did they scare you, Tenente?'

'You're damned right,' I said.

I took out my knife, opened it, wiped off the blade and pared off the dirty outside surface of the cheese. Gavuzzi handed me the basin of macaroni.

'Start in to eat, Tenente.'

'No,' I said. 'Put it on the floor. We'll all eat.'

'There are no forks.'

'What the hell,' I said in English.

I cut the cheese into pieces and laid them on the macaroni.

'Sit down to it,' I said. They sat down and waited. I put thumb and fingers into the macaroni and lifted. A mass loosened.

'Lift it high, Tenente.'

I lifted it to arm's length and the strands cleared. I lowered it into the mouth, sucked and snapped in the ends, and chewed, then took a bite of cheese, chewed, and then a drink of the wine.

It tasted of rusty metal. I handed the canteen back to Passini.

'It's rotten,' he said. 'It's been in there too long. I had it in the car.'

They were all eating, holding their chins close over the basin, tipping their heads back, sucking in the ends. I took another mouthful and some cheese and a rinse of wine. Something landed outside that shook the earth.

'Four hundred twenty or minnenwerfer,' Gavuzzi said.

'There aren't any four hundred twenties in the mountains,' I said.

'They have big Skoda guns. I've seen the holes.'

'Three hundred fives.'

We went on eating. There was a cough, a noise like a railway engine starting and then an explosion that shook the earth again.

'This isn't a deep dugout,' Passini said.

'That was a big trench-mortar.'

'Yes, sir.'

I ate the end of my piece of cheese and took a swallow of wine. Through the other noise I heard a cough, then came the chuh-chuh-chuh-chuh—then there was a flash, as a blast-furnace door is swung open, and a roar that started white and went red and on and on in a rushing wind. I tried to breathe but my breath would not come and I felt myself rush bodily out of myself and out and out and out and all the time bodily in the wind. I went out swiftly, all of myself and I knew I was dead and that it had all been a mistake to think you just died. Then I floated, and instead of going on I felt myself slide back. I breathed and I was back. The ground was torn up and in front of my head there was a splintered beam of wood. In the jolt of my head I heard somebody crying. I thought somebody was screaming. I tried to move but I could not move. I heard the machine-guns and rifles firing across the river and all along the river. There was a great splashing and I saw the star-shells go up and burst and float whitely and rockets going up and heard the bombs, all this in a moment, and then I heard close to me someone saying, 'Mamma mia! Oh, mamma mia!' I pulled and twisted and got my legs loose finally and turned around and touched him. It was Passini and when I touched him he screamed. His legs were towards me and I saw in the dark and the light that they were both smashed above the knee. One leg was gone and the other was held by tendons and part of the trouser and the stump twitched and jerked as though it were not connected. He bit his arm and moaned, 'Oh, Mamma mia, mamma mia,' then, 'Dio ti salvi, Maria. Dio ti salvi, Maria. Oh Jesus shoot me Christ shoot me, Mamma mia, mamma mia, oh purest lovely Mary shoot me. Stop it. Stop it. Stop it. Oh Jesus lovely Mary stop it. Oh oh oh oh,' then choking, 'Mamma, mamma mia.' Then he was quiet, biting his arm, the stump of his leg twitching.

'Portaferiti!' I shouted holding my hands cupped. 'Portaferiti!' I tried to get closer to Passini to try to put a tourniquet on the legs but I could not move. I tried again and my legs moved a little. I could pull backwards along with my arms and elbows. Passini was quiet now. I sat beside him, undid my tunic and tried to rip the tail of my shirt. It would not rip and I bit the edge of the cloth to start it. Then I thought of his puttees. I had on wool stockings but Passini wore puttees. All the drivers wore puttees. But Passini had only one leg. I unwound the puttee and while I was doing it I saw there was no need to try and make a tourniquet because he was dead already. I made sure he was dead. There were three others to locate. I sat up straight and as I did so something inside my head moved like the weights on a doll's eyes and it hit me inside behind my eyeballs. My legs felt warm and wet and my shoes were wet and warm inside. I knew that I was hit and leaned over and put my hand on my knee. My knee wasn't there. My hand went in and my knee was down on my shin. I wiped my hand on my shirt and another floating light came very slowly down and I looked at my leg and was very afraid. 'Oh, God,' I said, 'get me out of here.' I knew, however, that there had been three others. There were four drivers. Passini was dead. That left three. Someone took hold of me under the arms and somebody else lifted my legs.

'There are three others,' I said. 'One is dead.'

'It's Manera. We went for a stretcher but there wasn't any. How are you, Tenente?'

'Where are Gordini and Gavuzzi?'

'Gordini's at the post getting bandaged. Gavuzzi has your legs. Hold on to my neck, Tenente. Are you badly hit?'

'In the leg. How is Gordini?'

'He's all right. It was a big trench-mortar shell.'

'Passini's dead.'

'Yes. He's dead.'

A shell fell close and they both dropped to the ground and dropped me. 'I'm sorry, Tenente,' said Manera. 'Hang on to my neck.'

'If you drop me again.'

'It was because we were scared.'

'Are you unwounded?'

'We are both wounded a little.'

'Can Gordini drive?'

'I don't think so.'

They dropped me once more before we reached the post.

'You sons of bitches,' I said.

'I am sorry, Tenente,' Manera said. 'We won't drop you again.'

Outside the post a great many of us lay on the ground in the dark. They carried wounded in and brought them out. I could see the light come out from the dressing-station when the curtain opened and they brought someone in or out. The dead were off to one side. The doctors were working with their sleeves up to their shoulders and were red as butchers. There were not enough stretchers. Some of the wounded were noisy but most were quiet. The wind blew the leaves in the bower over the door of the dressing-station and the night was getting cold. Stretcher-bearers came in all the time, put their stretchers down, unloaded them and went away. As soon as I got to the dressing-station Manera brought a medical sergeant out and he put bandages on both my legs. He said there was so much dirt blown into the wound that there had not been much haemorrhage. They would take me as soon as possible. He went back inside. Gordini could not drive, Manera said. His shoulder was smashed and his head was hurt. He had not felt bad but now the shoulder had stiffened. He was sitting up beside one of the brick walls. Manera and Gavuzzi each went off with a load of wounded. They could drive all right. The British had come with three ambulances and they had two men on each ambulance. One of their drivers came over to me, brought by Gordini who looked very white and sick. The Britisher leaned over.

'Are you badly hit?' he asked. He was a tall man and wore steel-rimmed spectacles.

'In the legs.'

'It's not serious, I hope. Will you have a cigarette?'

'Thanks.'

'They tell me you've lost two drivers.'

'Yes. One killed and the fellow that brought you.'

'What rotten luck. Would you like us to take the cars?'

'That's what I wanted to ask you.'

'We'd take quite good care of them and return them to the Villa. 206, aren't you?'

'Yes.'

'It's a charming place. I've seen you about. They tell me you're an American.'

'Yes.'

'I'm English.'

'No!'

'Yes, English. Did you think I was Italian? There were some Italians with one of our units.'

'It would be fine if you would take the cars,' I said.

'We'll be most careful of them,' he straightened up. 'This chap of yours was very anxious for me to see you.' He patted

Gordini on the shoulder. Gordini winced and smiled. The Englishman broke into voluble and perfect Italian. 'Now everything is arranged. I've seen your Tenente. We will take over the two cars. You won't worry now.' He broke off, 'I must do something about getting you out of here. I'll see the medical wallahs. We'll take you back with us.'

He walked across to the dressing-station, stepping carefully among the wounded. I saw the blanket open, the light came out and he went in.

'He will look after you, Tenente,' Gordini said.

'How are you, Franco?'

'I am all right.' He sat down beside me. In a moment the blanket in front of the dressing-station opened and two stretcher-bearers came out followed by the tall Englishman. He brought them over to me.

'Here is the American Tenente,' he said in Italian.

'I'd rather wait,' I said. 'There are much worse wounded than me. I'm all right.'

'Come, come,' he said. 'Don't be a bloody hero.' Then in Italian: 'Lift him very carefully about the legs. His legs are very painful. He is the legitimate son of President Wilson.' They picked me up and took me into the dressing-room. Inside they were operating on all the tables. The little major looked at us furious. He recognized me and waved a forceps.

'Ça va bien?'

'Ça va.'

'I have brought him in,' the tall Englishman said in Italian. 'The only son of the American Ambassador. He will be here until you are ready to take him. Then I shall take him with my first load.' He bent over me. 'I'll look up their adjutant to do your papers and it will all go much faster.' He stooped to go under the doorway and went out. The major was unhooking the forceps now, dropping them in a basin. I followed his hands with my eyes. Now he was bandaging. Then the stretcher-bearers took the man off the table.

'I'll take the American Tenente,' one of the captains said. They lifted me on to the table. It was hard and slippery. There were many strong smells, chemical smells and the sweet smell of blood. They took off my trousers and the medical captain commenced dictating to the sergeant-adjutant while he worked, 'Multiple superficial wounds of the left and right thigh and left and right knee and right foot. Profound wounds of right knee and foot. Lacerations of the scalp' — he probed — (Does that hurt?) (Christ, yes!) 'with possible fracture of the skull. Incurred in the line of duty. That's what keeps you from being court-martialled for self-inflicted wounds,' he said. 'Would you like a drink of brandy? How did you run into this thing anyway? What were you trying to do? Commit suicide? Antitetanus please, and mark a cross on both legs. Thank you. I'll clean this up a little, wash it out, and put on a dressing. Your blood coagulates beautifully.'

The adjutant, looking up from the paper, 'What inflicted the wounds?'

The medical captain, 'What hit you?'

Me, with the eyes shut, 'A trench-mortar shell.'

The captain, doing things that hurt sharply and severing tissue — 'Are you sure?'

Me — trying to lie still and feeling my stomach flutter when the flesh was cut, 'I think so.'

Captain doctor — (interested in something he was finding), 'Fragments of enemy trench-mortar shell. Now I'll probe for some of this if you like but it's not necessary. I'll paint all this and — Does that sting? Good, that's nothing to how it will feel later. The pain hasn't started yet. Bring him a glass of brandy. The shock dulls the pain; but this is all right, you have nothing to worry about if it doesn't infect and it rarely does now. How is your head?'

'It's very bad,' I said.

'Better not drink too much brandy then. If you've got a fracture you don't want inflammation. How does that feel?'

Sweat ran all over me.

'Good Christ!' I said.

'I guess you've got a fracture all right. I'll wrap you up and don't bounce your head around.' He bandaged, his hands moving very fast and the bandage coming taut and sure. 'All right, good luck and Vive la France.'

'He's an American,' one of the other captains said.

'I thought you said he was a Frenchman. He talks French,' the captain said. 'I've known him before. I always thought he was French.' He drank a half tumbler of cognac. 'Bring on something serious. Get some more of that anti-tetanus.' The captain waved to me. They lifted me and the blanket-flap went across my face as we went out. Outside the sergeant-adjutant knelt down beside me where I lay, 'Name?' he asked softly. 'Middle name? First name? Rank? Where born? What class? What corps?' and so on. 'I'm sorry for your head, Tenente. I hope you feel better. I'm sending you now with the English ambulance.'

'I'm all right,' I said. 'Thank you very much.' The pain that the major had spoken about had started and all that was happening was without interest or relation. After a while the English ambulance came up and they put me on to a stretcher and lifted the stretcher up to the ambulance level and shoved it in. There was another stretcher by the side with a man on it whose nose I could see, waxy-looking, out of the bandages. He breathed very heavily. There were stretchers lifted and slid into the slings above. The tall English driver came around and looked in. 'I'll take it very easily,' he said. 'I hope you'll be comfy.' I felt the engine start, felt him climb up into the front seat, felt the brake come off and the clutch go in, then we started. I lay still and let the pain ride.

As the ambulance climbed along the road, it was slow in the traffic, sometimes it stopped, sometimes it backed on a turn, then finally it climbed quite fast. I felt something dripping. At first it dropped slowly and regularly, then it pattered into a stream. I shouted to the driver. He stopped the car and looked in through the hole behind his seat.

'What is it?'

'The man on the stretcher over me has a haemorrhage.'

'We're not far from the top. I wouldn't be able to get the stretcher out alone.' He started the car. The stream kept on. In the dark I could not see where it came from the canvas overhead. I tried to move sideways so that it did not fall on me. Where it had run down under my shirt it was warm and sticky. I was cold and my leg hurt so that it made me sick. After a while the stream from the stretcher above lessened and started to drip again and I heard and felt the canvas above move as the man on the stretcher settled more comfortably.

'How is he?' the Englishman called back. 'We're almost up.'

'He's dead I think,' I said.

The drops fell very slowly, as they fall from an icicle after the sun has gone. It was cold in the car in the night as the road climbed. At the post on the top they took the stretcher out and put another in and we went on.

CHAPTER 10

In the ward at the field hospital they told me a visitor was coming to see me in the afternoon. It was a hot day and there were many flies in the room. My orderly had cut paper into strips and tied the strips to a stick to make a brush that swished the flies away. I watched them settle on the ceiling. When he stopped swishing and fell asleep they came down and I blew them away and finally covered my face with my hands and slept too. It was very hot and when I woke my legs itched. I waked the orderly and he poured mineral water on the dressings. That made the bed damp and cool. Those of us that were awake talked across the ward. The afternoon was a quiet time. In the morning they came to each bed in turn, three men nurses and a doctor and picked you up out of bed and carried you into the dressing-room so that the beds could be made while we were having our wounds dressed. It was not a pleasant trip to the dressing-room and I did not know until later that beds could be made with men in them. My orderly had finished pouring water and the bed felt cool and lovely and I was telling him where to scratch on the soles of my feet against the itching when one of the doctors brought in Rinaldi. He came in very fast and bent down over the bed and kissed me. I saw he wore gloves.

'How are you, baby? How do you feel? I bring you this — ' It was a bottle of cognac. The orderly brought a chair and he sat down, 'and good news. You will be decorated. They want to get you the medaglia d'argento but perhaps they can get only the bronze.'

'What for?'

'Because you are gravely wounded. They say if you can prove you did any heroic act you can get the silver. Otherwise it will be the bronze. Tell me exactly what happened. Did you do any heroic act?'

'No,' I said. 'I was blown up while we were eating cheese.'

'Be serious. You must have done something heroic either before or after. Remember carefully.'

'I did not.'

'Didn't you carry anybody on your back? Gordini says you carried several people on your back but the medical major at the first post declares it is impossible. He has to sign the proposition for the citation.'

'I didn't carry anybody. I couldn't move.'

'That doesn't matter,' said Rinaldi.

He took off his gloves.

'I think we can get you the silver. Didn't you refuse to be medically aided before the others?'

'Not very firmly.'

'That doesn't matter. Look how you are wounded. Look at

your valorous conduct in asking to go always to the first line. Besides, the operation was successful.'

'Did they cross the river all right?'

'Enormously. They take nearly a thousand prisoners. It's in the bulletin. Didn't you see it?'

'No.'

'I'll bring it to you. It is a successful *coup de main*.'

'How is everything?'

'Splendid. We are all splendid. Everybody is proud of you. Tell me just exactly how it happened. I am positive you will get the silver. Go on tell me. Tell me all about it.' He paused and thought. 'Maybe you will get an English medal too. There was an English there. I'll go and see him and ask if he will recommend you. He ought to be able to do something. Do you suffer much? Have a drink. Orderly, go get a corkscrew. Oh you should see what I did in the removal of three metres of small intestine and better now than ever. It is one for *The Lancet*. You do me a translation and I will send it to *The Lancet*. Every day I am better. Poor dear baby, how do you feel? Where is that damn corkscrew? You are so brave and quiet I forget you are suffering.' He slapped his gloves on the edge of the bed.

'Here is the corkscrew, Signor Tenente,' the orderly said.

'Open the bottle. Bring a glass. Drink that, baby. How is your poor head? I looked at your papers. You haven't any fracture. That major at the first post was a hog-butcher. I would take you and never hurt you. I never hurt anybody. I learn how to do it. Every day I learn to do things smoother and better. You must forgive me for talking so much, baby. I am very moved to see you badly wounded. There, drink that. It's good. It cost fifteen lire. It ought to be good. Five stars. After I leave here I'll go see that English and he'll get you an English medal.'

'They don't give them like that.'

'You are so modest. I will send the liaison officer. He can handle the English.'

'Have you seen Miss Barkley?'

'I will bring her here. I will go now and bring her here.'

'Don't go,' I said. 'Tell me about Gorizia. How are the girls?'

'There are no girls. For two weeks now they haven't changed them. I don't go there any more. It is disgraceful. They aren't girls; they are old war comrades.'

'You don't go at all?'

'I just go to see if there is anything new. I stop by. They all ask for you. It is a disgrace that they should stay so long that they become friends.'

'Maybe girls don't want to go to the front any more.'

'Of course they do. They have plenty of girls. It is just bad administration. They are keeping them for the pleasure of dug-out hiders in the rear.'

'Poor Rinaldi,' I said. 'All alone at the war with no new girls.'

Rinaldi poured himself another glass of the cognac.

'I don't think it will hurt you, baby. You take it.'

I drank the cognac and felt it warm all the way down. Rinaldi poured another glass. He was quieter now. He held up the glass. 'To your valorous wounds. To the silver medal. Tell me, baby, when you lie here all the time in the hot weather don't you get excited?'

'Sometimes.'

'I can't imagine lying like that. I would go crazy.'

'You are crazy.'

'I wish you were back. No one to come in at night from adventures. No one to make fun of. No one to lend me money. No blood brother and room mate. Why do you get yourself wounded?'

'You can make fun of the priest.'

'That priest. It isn't me that makes fun of him. It is the captain. I like him. If you must have a priest have that priest. He's coming to see you. He makes big preparations.'

'I like him.'

'Oh, I knew it. Sometimes I think you and he are a little that way. You know.'

'No, you don't.'

'Yes, I do sometimes. A little that way like the number of the first regiment of the Brigata Ancona.'

'Oh, go to hell.'

He stood up and put on his gloves.

'Oh, I love to tease you, baby. With your priest and your English girl, and really you are just like me underneath.'

'No, I'm not.'

'Yes, we are. You are really an Italian. All fire and smoke and nothing inside. You only pretend to be American. We are brothers and we love each other.'

'Be good while I'm gone,' I said.

'I will send Miss Barkley. You are better with her without me. You are purer and sweeter.'

'Oh, go to hell.'

'I will send her. Your lovely cool goddess. English goddess. My God, what would a man do with a woman like that except worship her? What else is an Englishwoman good for?'

'You are an ignorant foul-mouthed dago.'

'A what?'

'An ignorant wop.'

'Wop. You are a frozen-faced . . . wop.'

'You are ignorant. Stupid.' I saw that word pricked him and kept on. 'Uninformed. Inexperienced, stupid from inexperience.'

'Truly? I tell you something about your good women. Your goddesses. There is only one difference between taking a girl who has always been good and a woman. With a girl it is painful. That's all I know.' He slapped the bed with his glove. 'And you never know if the girl will really like it.'

'Don't get angry.'

'I'm not angry. I just tell you, baby, for your own good. To save you trouble.'

'That's the only difference?'

'Yes. But millions of fools like you don't know it.'

'You were sweet to tell me.'

'We won't quarrel, baby. I love you too much. But don't be a fool.'

'No. I'll be wise like you.'

'Don't be angry, baby. Laugh. Take a drink. I must go, really.'

'You're a good old boy.'

'Now you see. Underneath we are the same. We are war brothers. Kiss me goodbye.'

'You're sloppy.'

'No. I am just more affectionate.'

I felt his breath come towards me. 'Goodbye. I come to see you again soon.' His breath went away. 'I won't kiss you if you don't want. I'll send your English girl. Goodbye, baby. The cognac is under the bed. Get well soon.'

He was gone.

CHAPTER 11

IT was dusk when the priest came. They had brought the soup and afterwards taken away the bowls and I was lying looking at the rows of beds and out the window at the tree-top that moved a little in the evening breeze. The breeze came in through the window and it was cooler with the evening. The flies were on the ceiling now and on the electric light bulbs that hung on wires. The lights were only turned on when someone was brought in at night or when something was being done. It made me feel very young to have the dark come after the dusk and then remain. It was like being put to bed after early supper. The orderly came down between the beds and stopped. Someone was with him. It was the priest. He stood there small, brown-faced, and embarrassed.

'How do you do?' he asked. He put some packages down by the bed, on the floor.

'All right, father.'

He sat down in the chair that had been brought for Rinaldi and looked out of the window embarrassedly. I noticed his face looked very tired.

'I can only stay a minute,' he said. 'It is late.'

'It's not late. How is the mess?'

He smiled. 'I am still a great joke.' He sounded tired too. 'Thank God they are all well.'

'I am so glad you are all right,' he said. 'I hope you don't suffer.' He seemed very tired and I was not used to see him tired.

'Not any more.'

'I miss you at the mess.'

'I wish I were there. I always enjoyed our talking.'

'I brought you a few little things,' he said. He picked up the packages. 'This is mosquito netting. This is a bottle of vermouth. You like vermouth? These are English papers.'

'Please open them.'

He was pleased and undid them. I held the mosquito netting in my hands. The vermouth he held up for me to see and then put it on the floor beside the bed. I held up one of the sheaf of English papers. I could read the headlines by turning it so the half-light from the window was on it. It was the *News of the World*.

'The others are illustrated,' he said.

'It will be a great happiness to read them. Where did you get them?'

'I sent for them to Mestre. I will have more.'

'You were very good to come, father. Will you drink a glass of vermouth?'

'Thank you. You keep it. It's for you.'

'No, drink a glass.'

'All right. I will bring you more then.'

The orderly brought the glasses and opened the bottle. He broke off the cork and the end had to be shoved down into the bottle. I could see the priest was disappointed but he said, 'That's all right. It's no matter.'

'Here's to your health, father.'

'To your better health.'

Afterwards he held the glass in his hand and we looked at one another. Sometimes we talked and were good friends but to-night it was difficult.

'What's the matter, father? You seem very tired.'

'I am tired but I have no right to be.'

'It's the heat.'

'No. This is only the spring. I feel very low.'

'You have the war disgust?'

'No. But I hate the war.'

'I don't enjoy it,' I said. He shook his head and looked out of the window.

'You do not mind it. You do not see it. You must forgive me. I know you are wounded.'

'That is an accident.'

'Still even wounded you do not see it. I can tell. I do not see it myself, but I feel it a little.'

'When I was wounded we were talking about it. Passini was talking.'

The priest put down the glass. He was thinking about something else.

'I know them because I am like they are,' he said.

'You are different, though.'

'But really I am like they are.'

'The officers don't see anything.'

'Some of them do. Some are very delicate and feel worse than any of us.'

'They are mostly different.'

'It is not education or money. It is something else. Even if they had education or money men like Passini would not wish to be officers. I would not be an officer.'

'You rank as an officer. I am an officer.'

67

'I am not really. You are not even an Italian. You are a foreigner. But you are nearer the officers than you are to the men.'

'What is the difference?'

'I cannot say it easily. There are people who would make war. In this country there are many like that. There are other people who would not make war.'

'But the first ones make them do it.'

'Yes.'

'And I help them.'

'You are a foreigner. You are a patriot.'

'And the ones who would not make war? Can they stop it?'

'I do not know.'

He looked out of the window again. I watched his face.

'Have they ever been able to stop it?'

'They are not organized to stop things and when they get organized their leaders sell them out.'

'Then it's hopeless?'

'It is never hopeless. But sometimes I cannot hope. I try always to hope, but sometimes I cannot.'

'Maybe the war will be over.'

'I hope so.'

'What will you do then?'

'If it is possible I will return to the Abruzzi.'

His brown face was suddenly very happy.

'You love the Abruzzi!'

'Yes, I love it very much.'

'You ought to go there then.'

'I would be too happy. If I could live there and love God and serve Him.'

'And be respected?' I said.

'Yes and be respected. Why not?'

'No reason not. You should be respected.'

'It does not matter. But there in my country it is understood that a man may love God. It is not a dirty joke.'

'I understand.'

He looked at me and smiled.

'You understand, but you do not love God.'

'No.'

'You do not love Him at all?' he asked.

'I am afraid of Him in the night sometimes.'

'You should love Him.'

'I don't love much.'

'Yes,' he said. 'You do. What you tell me about in the nights. That is not love. That is only passion and lust. When you love you wish to do things for. You wish to sacrifice for. You wish to serve.'

'I don't love.'

'You will. I know you will. Then you will be happy.'

'I'm happy. I've always been happy.'

'It is another thing. You cannot know about it unless you have it.'

'Well,' I said. 'If I ever get it I will tell you.'

'I stay too long and talk too much.' He was worried that he really did.

'No. Don't go. How about loving women? If I really loved some woman, would it be like that?'

'I don't know about that. I never loved any woman.'

'What about your mother?'

'Yes, I must have loved my mother.'

'Did you always love God?'

'Ever since I was a little boy.'

'Well,' I said. I did not know what to say. 'You are a fine boy,' I said.

'I am a boy,' he said. 'But you call me father.'

'That's politeness.'

He smiled.

'I must go, really,' he said. 'You do not want me for anything?' he asked hopefully.

'No. Just to talk.'

'I will take your greetings to the mess.'

'Thank you for the many fine presents.'

'Nothing.'

'Come and see me again.'

'Yes. Goodbye,' he patted my hand.

'So long,' I said in dialect.

'Ciaou,' he repeated.

It was dark in the room and the orderly, who had sat by the foot of the bed, got up and went out with him. I liked him very much and I hoped he would get back to the Abruzzi some time. He had a rotten life in the mess and he was fine about it, but I thought how he would be in his own country. At Capracotta, he had told me, there were trout in the stream below the town. It was forbidden to play the flute at night. When the young men serenaded only the flute was forbidden. Why, I had asked. Because it was bad for the girls to hear the flute at night. The peasants all called you 'Don' and when you met them they took off their hats. His father hunted every day and stopped to eat at the houses of peasants. They were always honoured. For a foreigner to hunt he must present a certificate that he had never been arrested. There were bears on the Gran Sasso D'Italia, but it was a long way. Aquila was a fine town. It was cool in the summer at night and the spring in Abruzzi was the most beautiful in Italy. But what was lovely was the fall to go hunting through the chestnut woods. The birds were all good because they fed on grapes and you never took a lunch because the peasants were always honoured if you would eat with them at their houses. After a while I went to sleep.

CHAPTER 12

THE room was long with windows on the right-hand side and a door at the far end that went into the dressing-room. The row of beds that mine was in faced the windows and another row, under the windows, faced the wall. If you lay on your left side you could see the dressing-room door. There was another door at the far end that people sometimes came in by. If anyone were going to die they put a screen around the bed so you could not see them die, but only the shoes and puttees of doctors and men nurses showed under the bottom of the screen and sometimes at the end there would be whispering. Then the priest would come out from behind the screen and afterwards the men nurses would go back behind the screen to come out again carrying the one who was dead with a blanket over him down the corridor between the beds and someone folded the screen and took it away.

That morning the major in charge of the ward asked me if I felt that I could travel the next day. I said I could. He said then they would ship me out early in the morning. He said I would be better off making the trip now before it got too hot.

When they lifted you up out of bed to carry you into the dressing-room you could look out of the window and see the new graves in the garden. A soldier sat outside the door that opened on to the garden, making crosses and painting on them the names, rank, and regiment of the men who were buried in the garden. He also ran errands for the ward, and in his spare time made me a cigarette-lighter out of an empty Austrian rifle-cartridge. The doctors were very nice and seemed very capable. They were anxious to ship me to Milan, where there were better X-ray facilities and where, after the operation, I could take mechanico-therapy. I wanted to go to Milan too. They wanted to get us all out and back as far as possible because all the beds were needed for the offensive, when it should start.

The night before I left the field hospital Rinaldi came in to see me with the major from our mess. They said that I would go to an American hospital in Milan that had just been installed. Some American ambulance units were to be sent down, and this hospital would look after them and any other Americans on service in Italy. There were many in the Red Cross. The States had declared war on Germany, but not on Austria.

The Italians were sure America would declare war on Austria, too, and they were very exicted about any Americans coming down, even the Red Cross. They asked me if I thought President Wilson would declare war on Austria and I said it was only a matter of days. I did not know what we had against Austria, but it seemed logical that they should declare war on her if they did on Germany. They asked me if we would declare war on Turkey. I said that was doubtful. Turkey, I said, was our national bird, but the joke translated so badly and they were so puzzled and suspicious that I said yes, we would probably declare war on Turkey. And on Bulgaria? We had drunk several glasses of brandy and I said yes by God on Bulgaria too and on Japan. But, they said, Japan is an ally of England. You can't trust the bloody English. The Japanese want Hawaii, I said. Where is Hawaii? It is in the Pacific Ocean. Why do the Japanese want it? They don't really want it, I said. That is all talk. The Japanese are a wonderful little people, fond of dancing and light wines. Like the French, said the major. We will get Nice and Savoia from the French. We will get Corsica and all the Adriatic coast-line, Rinaldi said. Italy will return to the splendours of Rome, said the major. I don't like Rome, I said. It is hot and full of fleas. You don't like Rome? Yes, I love Rome. Rome is the mother of nations. I will never forget Romulus suckling the Tiber. What? Nothing. Let's all go to Rome. Let's go to Rome tonight and never come back. Rome is a beautiful city, said the major. The mother and father of nations, I said. Roma is feminine, said Rinaldi. It cannot be the father. Who is the father, then, the Holy Ghost? Don't blaspheme. I wasn't blaspheming, I was asking for information. You are drunk, baby. Who made me drunk? I made you drunk, said the major. I made you drunk because I love you and because America is in the war. Up to the hilt, I said. You go away in the morning, baby, Rinaldi said. To Rome, I said. No, to Milan. To Milan, said the major, to the Crystal Palace, to the Cova, to Campari's, to Biffi's, to the galleria. You lucky boy. To the Gran Italia, I said, where I will borrow money from George. To the Scala, said Rinaldi. You will go to the Scala. Every night, I said. You won't be able to afford it every night, said the major.

The tickets are very expensive. I will draw a sight draft on my grandfather, I said. A what? A sight draft. He has to pay or I go to jail. Mr. Cunningham at the bank does it. I live by sight drafts. Can a grandfather jail a patriotic grandson who is dying that Italy may live? Live the American Garibaldi, said Rinaldi. Evviva the sight drafts, I said. We must be quiet, said the major. Already we have been asked many times to be quiet. Do you go tomorrow really, Federico? He goes to the American hospital, I tell you, Rinaldi said. To the beautiful nurses. Not the nurses with beards of the field hospital. Yes, yes, said the major, I know he goes to the American hospital. I don't mind their beards, I said. If any man wants to raise a beard, let him. Why don't you raise a beard, Signor Maggiore? It could not go in a gas-mask. Yes, it could. Anything can go in a gas-mask. I've vomited into a gas-mask. Don't be so loud, Baby, Rinaldi said. We all know you have been at the front. Oh, you fine baby, what will I do while you are gone? We must go, said the major. This becomes sentimental. Listen, I have a surprise for you. Your English. You know? The English you go to see every night at their hospital? She is going to Milan too. She goes with another to be at the American hospital. They had not got nurses yet from America. I talked today with the head of their riparto. They have too many women here at the front. They send some back. How do you like that, baby? All right. Yes? You go to live in a big city and have your English there to cuddle you. Why don't I get wounded? Maybe you will, I said. We must go, said the major. We drink and make noise and disturb Federico. Don't go. Yes, we must go. Goodbye. Good luck. Many things. Ciaou. Ciaou. Ciaou. Come back quickly, baby. Rinaldi kissed me. You smell of lysol. Goodbye, baby. Goodbye, Many things. The major patted my shoulder. They tiptoed out. I found I was quite drunk, but went to sleep.

The next day in the morning we left for Milan and arrived forty-eight hours later. It was a bad trip. We were side-tracked for a long time this side of Mestre and children came and peeked in. I got a little boy to go for a bottle of cognac, but he came back and said he could only get grappa. I told him to get it, and when it came I gave him the change, and the man beside me and I got drunk and slept until past Vicenza, where I woke up and was very sick on the floor. It did not matter, because the man on that side had been very sick on the floor several times before. Afterwards I thought I could not stand the thirst and in the yards outside of Verona I called to a soldier who was walking up and down beside the train and he got me a drink of water. I woke Georgetti, the other boy who was drunk, and offered him some water. He said to pour it on his shoulder and went back to sleep. The soldier would not take the penny I offered him and brought me a pulpy orange. I sucked on that and spat out the pith and watched the soldier pass up and down past a freight-car outside and after a while the train gave a jerk and started.

BOOK II

CHAPTER 13

WE got into Milan early in the morning and they unloaded us in the freight-yard. An ambulance took me to the American hospital. Riding in the ambulance on a stretcher I could not tell what part of the town we were passing through, but when they unloaded the stretcher I saw a market-place and an open wine shop with a girl sweeping out. They were watering the street and it smelled of the early morning. They put the stretcher down and went in. The porter came out with them. He had grey moustaches, wore a doorman's cap and was in his shirt-sleeves. The stretcher would not go into the elevator and they discussed whether it was better to lift me off the stretcher and go up in the elevator or carry the stretcher up the stairs. I listened to them discussing it. They decided on the elevator. They lifted me from the stretcher. 'Go easy,' I said. 'Take it softly.'

In the elevator we were crowded and as my legs bent the pain was very bad. 'Straighten out the legs,' I said.

'We can't, Signor Tenente. There isn't room.' The man who said this had his arm around me and my arm was around his neck. His breath came in my face metallic with garlic and red wine.

'Be gentle,' the other man said.

'Son of a bitch who isn't gentle.'

'Be gentle, I say,' the man with my feet repeated.

I saw the doors of the elevator closed, and the grille shut and the fourth-floor button pushed by the porter. The porter looked worried. The elevator rose slowly.

'Heavy?' I asked the man with the garlic.

'Nothing,' he said. His face was sweating and he grunted. The elevator rose steadily and stopped. The man holding the

75

feet opened the door and stepped out. We were on a balcony. There were several doors with brass knobs. The man carrying the feet pushed a button that rang a bell. We heard it inside the doors. No one came. Then the porter came up the stairs.

'Where are they?' the stretcher-bearers asked.

'I don't know,' said the porter. 'They sleep downstairs.'

'Get somebody.'

The porter rang the bell, then knocked on the door, then he opened the door and went in. When he came back there was an elderly woman wearing glasses with him. Her hair was loose and half-falling, and she wore a nurse's dress.

'I can't understand,' she said. 'I can't understand Italian.'

'I can speak English,' I said. 'They want to put me somewhere.'

'None of the rooms are ready. There isn't any patient expected.' She tucked at her hair and looked at me near-sightedly.

'Show them any room where they can put me.'

'I don't know,' she said. 'There's no patient expected. I couldn't put you in just any room.'

'Any room will do,' I said. Then to the porter in Italian, 'Find an empty room.'

'They are all empty,' said the porter. 'You are the first patient.' He held his cap in his hand and looked at the elderly nurse.

'For Christ's sweet sake take me to some room.' The pain had gone on and on with the legs bent, and I could feel it going in and out of the bone. The porter went in the door, followed by the grey-haired woman, then came hurrying back. 'Follow me,' he said. They carried me down a long hallway and into a room with drawn blinds. It smelled of new furniture. There was a bed and a big wardrobe with a mirror. They laid me down on the bed.

'I can't put on sheets,' the woman said. 'The sheets are locked up.'

I did not speak to her. 'There is money in my pocket,' I said to the porter. 'In the buttoned-down pocket.' The porter took out the money. The two stretcher-bearers stood beside the bed holding their caps. 'Give them five lire apiece and five lire for yourself. My papers are in the other pocket. You may give them to the nurse.'

The stretcher-bearers saluted and said thank you. 'Goodbye,' I said. 'And many thanks.' They saluted again and went out.

'Those papers,' I said to the nurse, 'describe my case and the treatment already given.'

The woman picked them up and looked at them through her glasses. There were three papers and they were folded. 'I don't know what to do,' she said. 'I can't read Italian. I can't do anything without the doctor's orders.' She commenced to cry and put the papers in her apron pocket. 'Are you an American?' she asked crying.

'Yes. Please put the papers on the table by the bed.'

It was dim and cool in the room. As I lay on the bed I could see the big mirror on the other side of the room, but could not see what it reflected. The porter stood by the bed. He had a nice face and was very kind.

'You can go,' I said to him. 'You can go too,' I said to the nurse. 'What is your name?'

'Mrs. Walker.'

'You can go, Mrs. Walker. I think I will go to sleep.'

I was alone in the room. It was cool and did not smell like a hospital. The mattress was firm and comfortable, and I lay without moving, hardly breathing, happy in feeling the pain lessen. After a while I wanted a drink of water and found the bell on a cord by the bed and rang it, but nobody came. I went to sleep.

When I woke I looked around. There was sunlight coming in through the shutters. I saw the big armoire, the bare walls, and two chairs. My legs in the dirty bandages stuck straight out in the bed. I was careful not to move them. I was thirsty and I reached for the bell and pushed the button. I heard the door open and looked and it was a nurse. She looked young and pretty.

'Good morning,' I said.

'Good morning,' she said and came over to the bed. 'We haven't been able to get the doctor. He's gone to Lake Como. No one knew there was a patient coming. What's wrong with you, anyway?'

'I'm wounded. In the legs and feet and my head is hurt.'

'What's your name?'

'Henry. Frederic Henry.'

'I'll wash you up. But we can't do anything to the dressings until the doctor comes.'

'Is Miss Barkley here?'

'No. There's no one by that name here.'

'Who was the woman who cried when I came in?'

The nurse laughed. 'That's Mrs. Walker. She was on night-duty and she'd been asleep. She wasn't expecting anyone.'

While we were talking she was undressing me, and when I was undressed, except for the bandages, she washed me, very gently and smoothly. The washing felt very good. There was a bandage on my head, but she washed all around the edge.

'Where were you wounded?'

'On the Isonzo, north of Plava.'

'Where is that?'

'North of Gorizia.'

I could see that none of the places meant anything to her.

'Do you have a lot of pain?'

'No. Not much now.'

She put a thermometer in my mouth.

'The Italians put it under the arm,' I said.

'Don't talk.'

When she took the thermometer out she read it and then shook it.

'What's the temperature?'

'You're not supposed to know that.'

'Tell me what it is.'

'It's almost normal.'

'I never have any fever. My legs are full of old iron too.'

'What do you mean?'

'They're full of trench-mortar fragments, old screws and bed-springs and things.'

She shook her head and smiled.

'If you had any foreign bodies in your legs they would set up an inflammation and you'd have fever.'

'All right,' I said. 'We'll see what comes out.'

She went out of the room and came back with the old nurse of the early morning. Together they made the bed with me in it. That was new to me and an admirable proceeding.

'Who is in charge here?'

'Miss Van Campen.'

'How many nurses are there?'

'Just us two.'

'Won't there be more?'

'Some more are coming.'

'When will they get here?'

'I don't know. You ask a great many questions for a sick boy.'

'I'm not sick,' I said, 'I'm wounded.'

They had finished making the bed and I lay with a clean smooth sheet under me and another sheet over me. Mrs. Walker went out and came back with a pyjama jacket. They put that on me and I felt very clean and dressed.

'You're awfully nice to me,' I said. The nurse called Miss Gage giggled. 'Could I have a drink of water?' I asked.

'Certainly. Then you can have breakfast.'

'I don't want breakfast. Can I have the shutters opened, please?'

The light had been dim in the room and when the shutters were opened it was bright sunlight and I looked out on a balcony and beyond were the tiled roofs of houses and chimneys. I looked out over the tiled roofs and saw white clouds and the sky very blue.

'Don't you know when the other nurses are coming?'

'Why? Don't we take good care of you?'

'You're very nice.'

'Would you like to use the bedpan?'

'I might try.'

They helped me and held me up, but it was not any use. Afterwards I lay and looked out the open doors on to the balcony.

'When does the doctor come?'

'When he gets back. We've tried to telephone to Lake Como for him.'

'Aren't there any other doctors?'

'He's the doctor for the hospital.'

Miss Gage brought a pitcher of water and a glass. I drank three glasses and then they left me and I looked out the window a while and went back to sleep. I ate some lunch and in the afternoon Miss Van Campen, the superintendent, came up to see me. She did not like me and I did not like her. She was small and neatly suspicious and too good for her position. She asked many questions and seemed to think it was somewhat disgraceful that I was with the Italians.

'Can I have wine with the meals?' I asked her.

'Only if the doctor prescribes it.'

'I can't have it until he comes?'

'Absolutely not.'

'You plan on having him come eventually?'

'We've telephoned him at Lake Como.'

She went out and Miss Gage came back.

'Why were you rude to Miss Van Campen?' she asked after she had done something for me very skilfully.

'I didn't mean to be. But she was snooty.'

'She said you were domineering and rude.'

'I wasn't. But what's the idea of a hospital without a doctor?'

'He's coming. They've telephoned for him to Lake Como.'

'What does he do there? Swim?'

'No. He has a clinic there.'

'Why don't they get another doctor?'

'Hush! Hush! Be a good boy and he'll come.'

I sent for the porter and when he came I told him in Italian to get me a bottle of Cinzano at the wine shop, a fiasco of chianti and the evening papers. He went away and brought them wrapped in newspaper, unwrapped them, and then I asked him to draw the corks and put the wine and vermouth under the bed. They left me alone and I lay in bed and read the papers a while, the news from the front, and the list of dead officers with their decorations and then reached down and brought up the bottle of Cinzano and held it straight up on my stomach, the cool glass against my stomach, and took little drinks, making rings on my stomach from holding the bottle there between drinks, and watched it get dark outside over the roofs of the town. The swallows circled around and I watched them and the night hawks flying above the roofs and drank the Cinzano. Miss Gage brought up a glass with some egg-nog in it. I lowered the vermouth bottle to the other side of the bed when she came in.

'Miss Van Campen had some sherry put in this,' she said. 'You shouldn't be rude to her. She's not young and this hospital is a big responsibility for her. Mrs. Walker's too old and she's no use to her.'

'She's a splendid woman,' I said. 'Thank her very much.'

'I'm going to bring your supper right away.'

'That's all right,' I said. 'I'm not hungry.'

When she brought the tray and put it on the bed-table I thanked her and ate a little of the supper. Afterwards it was dark outside and I could see the beams of the searchlights moving in the sky. I watched for a while and then went to sleep. I slept heavily, except once I woke sweating and scared and then went back to sleep, trying to stay outside of my dream. I woke for good long before it was light and heard roosters crowing, and stayed on awake until it began to be light. I was tired and once it was really light I went back to sleep again.

CHAPTER 14

It was bright sunlight in the room when I woke. I thought I was back at the front and stretched out in bed. My legs hurt me and I looked down at them, still in the dirty bandages, and seeing them knew where I was. I reached up for the bell-cord and pushed the button. I heard it buzz down the hall and then someone coming on rubber soles along the hall. It was Miss Gage and she looked a little older in the bright sunlight and not so pretty.

'Good morning,' she said. 'Did you have a good night?'

'Yes, thanks, very much,' I said. 'Can I have a barber?'

'I came in to see you and you were asleep with this in the bed with you.'

She opened the armoire door and held up the vermouth bottle. It was nearly empty. 'I put the other bottle from under the bed in there too,' she said. 'Why didn't you ask me for a glass?'

'I thought maybe you wouldn't let me have it.'

'I'd have had some with you.'

'You're a fine girl.'

'It isn't good for you to drink alone,' she said. 'You mustn't do it.'

'All right.'

'Your friend Miss Barkley's come,' she said.

'Really?'

'Yes. I don't like her.'

'You will like her. She's awfully nice.'

She shook her head. 'I'm sure she's fine. Can you move just a little to this side? That's fine. I'll clean you up for breakfast.' She washed me with a cloth and soap and warm water. 'Hold your shoulder up,' she said. 'That's fine.'

'Can I have the barber before breakfast?'

'I'll send the porter for him.' She went out and came back. 'He's gone for him,' she said and dipped the cloth she held in the basin of water.

The barber came with the porter. He was a man of about

fifty, with an upturned moustache. Miss Gage was finished with me and went out, and the barber lathered my face and shaved. He was very solemn and refrained from talking.

'What's the matter? Don't you know any news?' I asked.

'What news?'

'Any news. What's happened in the town?'

'It is time of war,' he said. 'The enemy's ears are everywhere.'

I looked up at him. 'Please hold your face still,' he said and went on shaving. 'I will tell nothing.'

'What's the matter with you?' I asked.

'I am an Italian. I will not communicate with the enemy.'

I let it go at that. If he was crazy, the sooner I could get out from under the razor the better. Once I tried to get a good look at him. 'Beware,' he said. 'The razor is sharp.'

I paid him when it was over and tipped him half a lira. He returned the coins.

'I will not. I am not at the front. But I am an Italian.'

'Get to hell out of here.'

'With your permission,' he said and wrapped his razors in newspaper. He went out, leaving the five copper coins on the table beside the bed. I rang the bell. Miss Gage came in. 'Would you ask the porter to come, please?'

'All right.'

The porter came in. He was trying to keep from laughing.

'Is that barber crazy?'

'No, signorino. He made a mistake. He doesn't understand very well and he thought I said you were an Austrian officer.'

'Oh,' I said.

'Ho, ho, ho!' the porter laughed. 'He was funny. One move from you, he said, and he would have — ' He drew his forefinger across his throat.

'Ho, ho, ho!' He tried to keep from laughing. 'When I tell him you were not an Austrian. Ho, ho, ho!'

'Ho, ho, ho!' I said bitterly. 'How funny if he would cut my throat. Ho, ho, ho!'

'No, signorino. No, no. He was so frightened of an Austrian. Ho, ho, ho.'

'Ho, ho, ho!' I said. 'Get out of here!'

He went out and I heard him laughing in the hall. I heard someone coming down the hallway. I looked towards the door. It was Catherine Barkley.

She came in the room and over to the bed.

'Hello, darling,' she said. She looked fresh and young and very beautiful. I thought I had never seen anyone so beautiful.

'Hello,' I said. When I saw her I was in love with her. Everything turned over inside of me. She looked towards the door, saw there was no one, then she sat on the side of the bed and leaned over and kissed me. I pulled her down and kissed her and felt her heart beating.

'You sweet,' I said. 'Weren't you wonderful to come here?'

'It wasn't very hard. It may be hard to stay.'

'You've got to stay,' I said. 'Oh, you're wonderful.' I was crazy about her. I could not believe she was really there and held her tight to me.

'You mustn't,' she said. 'You're not well enough.'

'Yes. I am. Come on.'

'No. You're not strong enough.'

'Yes. I am. Yes. Please.'

'You do love me?'

'I really love you. I'm crazy about you. Come on, please.'

'Feel our hearts beating?'

'I don't care about our hearts. I want you. I'm just mad about you.'

'You really love me?'

'Don't keep on saying that. Come on. Please, please, Catherine.'

'All right, but only for a minute.'

'All right,' I said. 'Shut the door.'

'You can't. You shouldn't — '

'Come on. Don't talk. Please come on.'

Catherine sat in a chair by the bed. The door was open into the hall. The wildness was gone and I felt finer than I had ever felt.

She asked, 'Now do you believe I love you?'

'Oh, you're lovely,' I said. 'You've got to stay. They can't send you away. I'm crazy in love with you.'

'We'll have to be awfully careful. That was just madness. We can't do that.'

'We can at night.'

'We'll have to be awfully careful. You'll have to be careful in front of other people.'

'I will.'

'You'll have to be. You're sweet. You do love me, don't you?'

'Don't say that again. You don't know what that does to me.'

'I'll be careful then. I don't want to do anything more to you. I have to go now, darling, really.'

'Come back right away.'

'I'll come when I can.'

'Goodbye.'

'Goodbye, sweet.'

She went out. God knows I had not wanted to fall in love with her. I had not wanted to fall in love with anyone. But God knows I had and I lay on the bed in the room of the hospital in Milan and all sorts of things went through my head and finally Miss Gage came in.

'The doctor's coming,' she said. 'He telephoned from Lake Como.'

'When does he get here?'

'He'll be here this afternoon.'

CHAPTER 15

NOTHING happened until afternoon. The doctor was a thin quiet little man who seemed disturbed by the war. He took out a number of small steel splinters from my thighs with delicate and refined distaste. He used a local anæsthetic called something or other 'snow', which froze the tissue and avoided pain until the probe, the scalpel or the forceps got below the frozen portion. The anæsthetized area was clearly defined by the patient, and after a time the doctor's fragile delicacy was exhausted and he said it would be better to have an X-ray. Probing was unsatisfactory, he said.

The X-ray was taken at the Ospedale Maggiore, and the doctor who did it was excitable, efficient and cheerful. It was arranged by holding up the shoulders, that the patient should see personally some of the larger foreign bodies through the machine. The plates were to be sent over. The doctor requested me to write in his pocket notebook, my name, and regiment and some sentiment. He declared that the foreign bodies were ugly, nasty, brutal. The Austrians were sons of bitches. How many had I killed? I had not killed any, but I was anxious to please—and I said I had killed plenty. Miss Gage was with me and the doctor put his arm around her and said she was more beautiful than Cleopatra. Did she understand that? Cleopatra the former queen of Egypt. Yes, by God she was. We returned to the little hospital in the ambulance, and after a while and much lifting I was upstairs and in bed again. The plates came that afternoon, the doctor had said by God he would have them that afternoon and he did. Catherine Barkley showed them to me. They were in red envelopes and she took them out of the envelopes and held them up to the light and we both looked.

'That's your right leg,' she said, then put the plate back in the envelope. 'This is your left.'

'Put them away,' I said, 'and come over to the bed.'

'I can't,' she said. 'I just brought them in for a second to show you.'

She went out and I lay there. It was a hot afternoon and I was sick of lying in bed. I sent the porter for the papers, all the papers he could get.

Before he came back three doctors came into the room. I have noticed that doctors who fail in the practice of medicine have a tendency to seek one another's company and aid in consultation. A doctor who cannot take out your appendix properly will recommend to you a doctor who will be unable to remove your tonsils with success. These were three such doctors.

'This is the young man,' said the house doctor with the delicate hands.

'How do you do?' said the tall gaunt doctor with the beard. The third doctor, who carried the X-ray plates in their red envelopes, said nothing.

'Remove the dressings?' questioned the bearded doctor.

'Certainly. Remove the dressings, please, nurse,' the house doctor said to Miss Gage. Miss Gage removed the dressings. I looked down at the legs. At the field hospital they had the look of not too freshly ground hamburger steak. Now they were crusted and the knee was swollen and discoloured, and the calf sunken, but there was no pus.

'Very clean,' said the house doctor. 'Very clean and nice.'

'Um,' said the doctor with the beard. The third doctor looked over the house doctor's shoulder.

'Please move the knee,' said the bearded doctor.

'I can't.'

'Test the articulation?' the bearded doctor questioned. He had a stripe beside the three stars on his sleeve. That meant he was a first captain.

'Certainly,' the house doctor said. Two of them took hold of my right leg very gingerly and bent it.

'That hurts,' I said.

87

'Yes, yes. A little further, doctor.'

'That's enough. That's as far as it goes,' I said.

'Partial articulation,' said the first captain. He straightened up. 'May I see the plates again, please, doctor?' The third doctor handed him one of the plates. 'No. The left leg, please.'

'That is the left leg, doctor.'

'You are right. I was looking from a different angle.' He returned the plate. The other plate he examined for some time. 'You see, doctor?' he pointed to one of the foreign bodies which showed spherical and clear against the light. They examined the plate for some time.

'Only one thing I can say,' the first captain with the beard said. 'It is a question of time. Three months, six months probably.'

'Certainly the synovial fluid must re-form.'

'Certainly. It is a question of time. I could not conscientiously open a knee like that before the projectile was encysted.'

'I agree with you, doctor.'

'Six months for what?' I asked.

'Six months for the projectile to encyst before the knee can be opened safely.'

'I don't believe it,' I said.

'Do you want to keep your knee, young man?'

'No,' I said.

'What?'

'I want it cut off,' I said, 'so I can wear a hook on it.'

'What do you mean? A hook?'

'He is joking,' said the house doctor. He patted my shoulder very delicately. 'He wants to keep his knee. This is a very brave young man. He has been proposed for the silver medal of valour.'

'All my felicitations,' said the first captain. He shook my hand. 'I can only say that to be on the safe side you should wait at least six months before opening such a knee. You are welcome of course to another opinion.'

'Thank you very much,' I said. 'I value your opinion.'

The first captain looked at his watch.

'We must go,' he said. 'All my best wishes.'

'All my best wishes and many thanks,' I said. I shook hands with the third doctor, Capitan Varini-Tenente Enry, and they all three went out of the room.

'Miss Gage,' I called. She came in. 'Please ask the house doctor to come back a minute.'

He came in holding his cap and stood by the bed. 'Did you wish to see me?'

'Yes. I can't wait six months to be operated on. My God, doctor, did you ever stay in bed six months?'

'You won't be in bed all the time. You must first have the wounds exposed to the sun. Then afterwards you can be on crutches.'

'For six months and then have an operation?'

'That is the safe way. The foreign bodies must be allowed to encyst and the synovial fluid will re-form. Then it will be safe to open up the knee.'

'Do you really think yourself I will have to wait that long?'

'That is the safe way.'

'Who is that first captain?'

'He is a very excellent surgeon of Milan.'

'He's a first captain, isn't he?'

'Yes, but he is an excellent surgeon.'

'I don't want my leg fooled with by a first captain. If he was any good he would be made a major. I know what a first captain is, doctor.'

'He is an excellent surgeon and I would rather have his judgment than any surgeon I know.'

'Could another surgeon see it?'

'Certainly, if you wish. But I would take Dr. Barella's opinion myself.'

'Could you ask another surgeon to come and see it?'

'I will ask Valentini to come.'

'Who is he?'

'He is a surgeon of the Ospedale Maggiore.'

'Good. I appreciate it very much. You understand, doctor, I couldn't stay in bed six months.'

'You would not be in bed. You would first take a sun cure. Then you could have light exercise. Then when it was encysted we would operate.'

'But I can't wait six months.'

The doctor spread his delicate fingers on the cap he held and smiled. 'You are in such a hurry to get back to the front?'

'Why not?'

'It is very beautiful,' he said. 'You are a noble young man.' He stooped over and kissed me very delicately on the forehead. 'I will send for Valentini. Do not worry and excite yourself. Be a good boy.'

'Will you have a drink?' I asked.

'No thank you. I never drink alcohol.'

'Just have one.' I rang for the porter to bring glasses.

'No. No thank you. They are waiting for me.'

'Goodbye,' I said.

'Goodbye.'

Two hours later Dr. Valentini came into the room. He was in a great hurry and the points of his moustache stood straight up. He was a major, his face was tanned and he laughed all the time.

'How did you do it, this rotten thing?' he asked. 'Let me see the plates. Yes. Yes. That's it. You look healthy as a goat. Who's the pretty girl? Is she your girl? I thought so. Isn't this a bloody war? How does that feel? You are a fine boy. I'll make you better than new. Does that hurt? You bet it hurts. How they love to hurt you, these doctors. What have they done for you so far? Can't that girl talk Italian? She should learn. What a lovely girl. I could teach her. I will be a patient here myself. No, but I will do all your maternity work free. Does she understand that? She will make you a fine boy. A fine blonde like she is. That's fine. That's all right. What a lovely girl. Ask her if she eats supper with me. No, I don't take her away from you. Thank you. Thank you very much, miss. That's all.'

'That's all I want to know.' He patted me on the shoulder. 'Leave the dressings off.'

'Will you have a drink, Dr. Valentini?'

'A drink? Certainly. I will have ten drinks. Where are they?'

'In the armoire. Miss Barkley will get the bottle.'

'Cheery oh. Cheery oh to you, miss. What a lovely girl. I will bring you better cognac than that.' He wiped his moustache.

'When do you think it can be operated on?'

'Tomorrow morning. Not before. Your stomach must be emptied. You must be washed out. I will see the old lady downstairs and leave instructions. Goodbye. I see you tomorrow. I'll bring you better cognac than that. You are very comfortable here. Goodbye. Until tomorrow. Get a good sleep. I'll see you early.' He waved from the doorway, his moustaches went straight up, his brown face was smiling. There was a star in a box on his sleeve because he was a major.

CHAPTER 16

THAT night a bat flew into the room through the open door that led on to the balcony and through which we watched the night over the roofs of the town. It was dark in our room except for the small light of the night over the town and the bat was not frightened, but hunted in the room as though he had been outside. We lay and watched him and I do not think he saw us, because we lay so still. After he went out we saw a searchlight come on and watched the beam move across the sky and then go off and it was dark again. A breeze came in the night and we heard the men of the anti-aircraft gun on the next roof talking. It was cool and they were putting on their capes. I worried in the night about someone coming up, but Catherine said they were all asleep. Once in the night we went to sleep and when I woke she was not there, but I heard her coming along the hall and the door opened and she came back to the bed and said it was all right she had been downstairs and they were all asleep. She had been outside Miss Van Campen's door and heard her breathing in her sleep. She brought crackers and we ate them and drank some vermouth. We were very hungry, but she said that would all have to be gotten out of me in the morning. I went to sleep again in the morning when it was light and when I was awake I found she was gone again. She came in looking fresh and lovely and sat on the bed, and the sun rose while I had the thermometer in my mouth, and we smelled the dew on the roofs and then the coffee of the men at the gun on the next roof.

'I wish we could go for a walk,' Catherine said. 'I'd wheel you if we had a chair.'

'How would I get into the chair?'

'We'd do it.'

'We could go out to the park and have breakfast outdoors.' I looked out the open doorway.

'What we'll really do,' she said, 'is get you ready for your friend, Dr. Valentini.'

'I thought he was grand.'

'I didn't like him as much as you did. But I imagine he's very good.'

'Come back to bed, Catherine, please,' I said.

'I can't. Didn't we have a lovely night?'

'And can you be on night-duty tonight?'

'I probably will. But you won't want me.'

'Yes, I will.'

'No, you won't. You've never been operated on. You don't know how you'll be.'

'I'll be all right.'

'You'll be sick and I won't be anything to you.'

'Come back then now.'

'No,' she said. 'I have to do the chart, darling, and fix you up.'

'You don't really love me or you'd come back again.'

'You're such a silly boy.' She kissed me. 'That's all right for the chart. Your temperature's always normal. You've such a lovely temperature.'

'You've got a lovely everything.'

'Oh, no. You have the lovely temperature. I'm awfully proud of your temperature.'

'Maybe all our children will have fine temperatures.'

'Our children will probably have beastly temperatures.'

'What do you have to do to get me ready for Valentini?'

'Not much. But quite unpleasant.'

'I wish you didn't have to do it.'

'I don't. I don't want anyone else to touch you. I'm silly. I get furious if they touch you.'

'Even Ferguson?'

'Especially Ferguson and Gage and the other, what's her name?'

'Walker?'

'That's it. They've too many nurses here now. There must be some more patients or they'll send us away. They have four nurses now.'

'Perhaps there'll be some. They need that many nurses. It's quite a big hospital.'

'I hope some will come. What would I do if they sent me away? They will unless there are more patients.'

'I'd go too.'

'Don't be silly. You can't go yet. But get well quickly, darling, and we will go somewhere.'

'And then what?'

'Maybe the war will be over. It can't always go on.'

'I'll get well,' I said. 'Valentini will fix me.'

'He should with those moustaches. And, darling, when you're going under the ether, just think about something else — not us. Because people get very blabby under an anaesthetic.'

'What should I think about?'

'Anything. Anything but us. Think about your people. Or even any other girl.'

'No.'

'Say your prayers then. That ought to create a splendid impression.'

'Maybe I won't talk.'

'That's true. Often people don't talk.'

'I won't talk.'

'Don't brag, darling. Please don't brag. You're so sweet and you don't have to brag.'

'I won't talk a word.'

'Now you're bragging, darling. You know you don't need to brag. Just start your prayers or poetry or something when they tell you to breathe deeply. You'll be lovely that way and I'll be so proud of you. I'm very proud of you anyway. You have such a lovely temperature and you sleep like a little boy with your arm around the pillow and think it's me. Or is it some other girl? Some fine Italian girl?'

'It's you.'

'Of course it's me. Oh, I do love you, and Valentini will make you a fine leg. I'm glad I don't have to watch it.'

'And you'll be on night-duty tonight.'

'Yes. But you won't care.'

'You wait and see.'

'There, darling. Now you're all clean inside and out. Tell me. How many people have you ever loved?'

'Nobody.'

'Not even me?'

'Yes, you.'

'How many others really?'

'None.'

'How many have you — how do you say it? — stayed with?'

'None.'

'You're lying to me.'

'Yes.'

'It's all right. Keep right on lying to me. That's what I want you to do. Were they pretty?'

'I never stayed with anyone.'

'That's right. Were they very attractive?'

'I don't know anything about it.'

'You're just mine. That's true and you've never belonged to anyone else. But I don't care if you have. I'm not afraid of them. But don't tell me about them. When a man stays with a girl when does she say how much it costs?'

'I don't know.'

'Of course not. Does she say she loves him? Tell me that. I want to know that.'

'Yes. If he wants her to.'

'Does he say he loves her? Tell me, please. It's important.'

'He does if he wants to.'

'But you never did? Really?'

'No.'

'Not really. Tell me the truth?'

'No,' I lied.

'You wouldn't,' she said. 'I knew you wouldn't. Oh, I love you, darling.'

Outside the sun was up over the roofs and I could see the points of the cathedral with the sunlight on them. I was clean inside and outside and waiting for the doctor.

'And that's it?' Catherine said. 'She says just what he wants her to?'

'Not always.'

'But I will. I'll say just what you wish and I'll do what you wish and then you will never want any other girls, will you?' She looked at me very happily. 'I'll do what you want and say what you want and then I'll be a great success, won't I?'

95

'Yes.'

'What would you like me to do now that you're all ready?'

'Come to the bed again.'

'All right. I'll come.'

'Oh, darling, darling, darling,' I said.

'You see,' she said. 'I do anything you want.'

'You're so lovely.'

'I'm afraid I'm not very good at it yet.'

'You're lovely.'

'I want what you want. There isn't any me any more. Just what you want.'

'You sweet.'

'I'm good. Aren't I good? You don't want any other girls, do you?'

'No.'

'You see? I'm good. I do what you want.'

CHAPTER 17

WHEN I was awake after the operation I had not been away. You do not go away. They only choke you. It is not like dying, it is just a chemical choking, so you do not feel, and afterwards you might as well have been drunk except that when you throw up nothing comes but bile and you do not feel better afterwards. I saw sandbags at the end of the bed. They were on pipes that came out of the cast. After a while I saw Miss Gage and she said, 'How is it now?'

'Better,' I said.

'He did a wonderful job on your knee.'

'How long did it take?'

'Two hours and a half.'

'Did I say anything silly?'

'Not a thing. Don't talk. Just be quiet.'

I was sick and Catherine was right. It did not make any difference who was on night-duty.

There were three other patients in the hospital now, a thin boy in the Red Cross from Georgia with malaria, a nice boy, also thin, from New York, with malaria and jaundice, and a fine boy who had tried to unscrew the fuse-cap from a combination shrapnel and high explosive shell for a souvenir. This was a shrapnel shell used by the Austrians in the mountains with a nose-cap which went on after the burst and exploded on contact.

Catherine Barkley was greatly liked by the nurses because she would do night-duty indefinitely. She had quite a little work with the malaria people, the boy who had unscrewed the nose-cap was a friend of ours and never rang at night unless it was necessary, but between the times of working we were together. I loved her very much and she loved me. I slept in the daytime and we wrote notes during the day when we were awake and sent them by Ferguson. Ferguson was a fine girl. I never learned anything about her except that she had a brother in the Fifty-Second Division and a brother in Mesopotamia and she was very good to Catherine Barkley.

'Will you come to our wedding, Fergy?' I said to her once.

'You'll never get married.'

'We will.'

'No you won't.'

'Why not?'

'You'll fight before you'll marry.'

'We never fight.'

'You've time yet.'

'We don't fight.'

'You'll die then. Fight or die. That's what people do. They don't marry.'

I reached for her hand. 'Don't take hold of me,' she said. 'I'm not crying. Maybe you'll be all right you two. But watch out you don't get her into trouble. You get her in trouble and I'll kill you.'

'I won't get her in trouble.'

'Well watch out then. I hope you'll be all right. You have a good time.'

'We have a fine time.'

'Don't fight then and don't get her into trouble.'

'I won't.'

'Mind you watch out. I don't want her with any of these war babies.'

'You're a fine girl, Fergy.'

'I'm not. Don't try to flatter me. How does your leg feel?'

'Fine.'

'How is your head?' She touched the top of it with her fingers. It was sensitive like a foot that had gone to sleep. 'It's never bothered me.'

'A bump like that could make you crazy. It never bothers you?'

'No.'

'You're a lucky young man. Have you the letter done? I'm going down.'

'It's here,' I said.

'You ought to ask her not to do night-duty for a while. She's getting very tired.'

'All right. I will.'

'I want to do it but she won't let me. The others are glad to let her have it. You might give her just a little rest.'

'All right.'

'Miss Van Campen spoke about you sleeping all the forenoons.'

'She would.'

'It would be better if you let her stay off nights a little while.'

'I want her to.'

'You do not. But if you would make her I'd respect you for it.'

'I'll make her.'

'I don't believe it.' She took the note and went out. I rang the bell and in a little while Miss Gage came in.

'What's the matter?'

'I just wanted to talk to you. Don't you think Miss Barkley ought to go off night-duty for a while? She looks awfully tired. Why does she stay on so long?'

Miss Gage looked at me.

'I'm a friend of yours,' she said. 'You don't have to talk to me like that.'

'What do you mean?'

'Don't be silly. Was that all you wanted?'

'Do you want a vermouth?'

'All right. Then I have to go.' She got out the bottle from the armoire and brought a glass.

'You take the glass,' I said. 'I'll drink out of the bottle.'

'Here's to you,' said Miss Gage.

'What did Van Campen say about me sleeping late in the mornings?'

'She just jawed about it. She calls you our privileged patient.'

'To hell with her.'

'She isn't mean,' Miss Gage said. 'She's just old and cranky. She never liked you.'

'No.'

'Well, I do. And I'm your friend. Don't forget that.'

'You're awfully damned nice.'

'No. I know who you think is nice. But I'm your friend. How does your leg feel?'

'Fine.'

'I'll bring some cold mineral water to pour over it. It must itch under the cast. It's hot outside.'

'You're awfully nice.'

'Does it itch much?'

'No. It's fine.'

'I'll fix those sandbags better.' She leaned over. 'I'm your friend.'

'I know you are.'

'No you don't. But you will some day.'

Catherine Barkley took three nights off night-duty, and then she came back on again. It was as though we met again after each of us had been away on a long journey.

CHAPTER 18

WE had a lovely time that summer. When I could go out we rode in a carriage in the park. I remember the carriage, the horse going slowly, and up ahead the back of the driver with his varnished high hat, and Catherine Barkley sitting beside me. If we let our hands touch, just the side of my hand touching hers, we were excited. Afterwards when I could get around on crutches we went to dinner at Biffi's or the Gran Italia and sat at the tables outside on the floor of the galleria. The waiters came in and out and there were people going by and candles with shades on the tablecloths and after we decided that we liked the Gran Italia best, George, the head-waiter, saved us a table. He was a fine waiter and we let him order the meal while we looked at the people, and the great galleria in the dusk and each other. We drank dry white capri iced in a bucket; although we tried many of the other wines, fresa, barbera and the sweet white wines. They had no wine waiter because of the war and George would smile ashamedly when I asked about wines like fresa.

'If you imagine a country that makes a wine because it tastes like strawberries,' he said.

'Why shouldn't it?' Catherine asked. 'It sounds splendid.'

'You try it, lady,' said George. 'if you want to. But let me bring a little bottle of margaux for the Tenente.'

'I'll try it too, George.'

'Sir, I can't recommend you to. It doesn't even taste like strawberries.'

'It might,' said Catherine. 'It would be wonderful if it did.'

'I'll bring it,' said George, 'and when the lady is satisfied I'll take it away.'

It was not much of a wine. As he said it did not even taste like strawberries. We went back to capri. One evening I was short of money and George loaned me a hundred lire. 'That's all right, Tenente,' he said. 'I know how it is. I know how a man gets short. If you or the lady need money I've always got money.'

After dinner we walked through the galleria, past the other restaurants and the shops with their steel shutters down, and stopped at the little place where they sold sandwiches; ham and lettuce sandwiches and anchovy sandwiches made of very tiny brown glazed rolls and only about as long as your finger. They were to eat in the night when we were hungry. Then we got into an open carriage outside the galleria in front of the cathedral and rode to the hospital. At the door of the hospital the porter came out to help with the crutches. I paid the driver, and then we rode upstairs in the elevator. Catherine got off at the lower floor where the nurses lived and I went on up and went down the hall on crutches to my room; sometimes I undressed and got into bed and sometimes I sat out on the balcony with my leg up on another chair and watched the swallows over the roofs and waited for Catherine. When she came upstairs it was as though she had been away on a long trip and I went along the hall with her on the crutches and carried the basins and waited outside the doors, or went in with her; it depending on whether they were friends of ours or not, and when she had done all there was to be done we sat out on the balcony outside my room. Afterwards I went to bed and when they were all asleep and she was sure they would not call she came in. I loved to take her hair down and she sat on the bed and kept very still, except suddenly she would dip down to kiss me while I was doing it, and I would take out the pins and lay them on the sheet and it would be loose and I would watch her while she kept very still and then take out the last two pins and it would all come down and she would drop her head and we would both be inside of it, and it was the feeling of inside a tent or behind a falls.

She had wonderfully beautiful hair and I would lie sometimes and watch her twisting it up in the light that came in the open door and it shone even in the night as water shines sometimes just before it is really daylight. She had a lovely face and body and lovely smooth skin too. We would be lying together and I would touch her cheeks and her forehead and under her eyes and her chin and throat with the tips of my fingers and say, 'Smooth as piano keys', and she would stroke my chin with her finger and say, 'Smooth as emery paper and very hard on piano keys.'

'Is it rough?'

'No, darling. I was just making fun of you.'

It was lovely in the nights and if we could only touch each other we were happy. Besides all the big times we had many small ways of making love and we tried putting thoughts in the other one's head while we were in different rooms. It seemed to work sometimes but that was probably because we were thinking the same thing anyway.

We said to each other that we were married the first day she had come to the hospital and we counted months from our wedding day. I wanted to be really married but Catherine said that if we were they would send her away and if we merely started on the formalities they would watch her and would break us up. We would have to be married under Italian law and the formalities were terrific. I wanted us to be married really because I worried about having a child if I thought about it, but we pretended to ourselves we were married and did not worry much and I suppose I enjoyed not being married, really. I know one night we talked about it and Catherine said, 'But, darling, they'd send me away.'

'Maybe they wouldn't.'

'They would. They'd send me home and then we would be apart until after the war.'

'I'd come on leave.'

'You couldn't get to Scotland and back on a leave. Besides, I won't leave you. What good would it do to marry now? We're really married. I couldn't be any more married.'

'I only wanted to for you.'

'There isn't any me. I'm you. Don't make up a separate me.'

'I thought girls always wanted to be married.'

'They do. But, darling, I am married. I'm married to you. Don't I make you a good wife?'

'You're a lovely wife.'

'You see, darling, I had one experience of waiting to be married.'

'I don't want to hear about it.'

'You know I don't love anyone but you. You shouldn't mind because someone else loved me.'

'I do.'

'You shouldn't be jealous of someone who's dead when you have everything.'

'No, but I don't want to hear about it.'

'Poor darling. And I know you've been with all kinds of girls and it doesn't matter to me.'

'Couldn't we be married privately some way? Then if anything happened to me or if you had a child.'

'There's no way to be married except by church or state. We are married privately. You see, darling, it would mean everything to me if I had any religion. But I haven't any religion.'

'You gave me the Saint Anthony.'

'That was for luck. Someone gave it to me.'

'Then nothing worries you?'

'Only being sent away from you. You're my religion. You're all I've got.'

'All right. But I'll marry you the day you say.'

'Don't talk as though you had to make an honest woman of me, darling. I'm a very honest woman. You can't be ashamed of something if you're only happy and proud of it. Aren't you happy?'

'But you won't ever leave me for someone else?'

'No, darling. I won't ever leave you for someone else. I suppose all sorts of dreadful things will happen to us. But you don't have to worry about that.'

'I don't. But I love you so much and you did love someone else before.'

'And what happened to him?'

'He died.'

'Yes and if he hadn't I wouldn't have met you. I'm not unfaithful, darling. I've plenty of faults but I'm very faithful. You'll be sick of me I'll be so faithful.'

'I'll have to go back to the front pretty soon.'

'We won't think about that until you go. You see I'm happy, darling, and we have a lovely time. I haven't been happy for a long time and when I met you perhaps I was nearly crazy. Perhaps I was crazy. But now we're happy and we love each other. Do let's please just be happy. You are happy, aren't you? Is there anything I do you don't like? Can I do anything to please you? Would you like me to take down my hair? Do you want to play?'

'Yes and come to bed.'

'All right. I'll go and see the patients first.'

CHAPTER 19

THE summer went that way. I do not remember much about the days, except that they were hot and that there were many victories in the papers. I was very healthy and my legs healed quickly so that it was not very long after I was first on crutches before I was through with them and walking with a cane. Then

I started treatments at the Ospedale Maggiore for bending the knees, mechanical treatments, baking in a box of mirrors with violet rays, massage, and baths. I went over there afternoons, and afterwards stopped at the café and had a drink and read the papers. I did not roam around the town; but wanted to get home to the hospital from the café. All I wanted was to see Catherine. The rest of the time I was glad to kill. Mostly I slept in the mornings, and in the afternoons, sometimes, I went to the races, and late to the mechanical-therapy treatments. Sometimes I stopped in at the Anglo-American Club and sat in a deep leather-cushioned chair in front of the window and read the magazines. They would not let us go out together when I was off crutches because it was unseemly for a nurse to be seen unchaperoned with a patient who did not look as though he needed attendance, so we were not together much in the afternoons. Although sometimes we could go out to dinner if Ferguson went along. Miss Van Campen had accepted the status that we were great friends because she got a great amount of work out of Catherine. She thought Catherine came from very good people and that prejudiced her in her favour finally. Miss Van Campen admired family very much and came from an excellent family herself. The hospital was quite busy, too, and that kept her occupied. It was a hot summer and I knew many people in Milan but always was anxious to get back home to the hospital as soon as the afternoon was over. At the front they were advancing on the Carso, they had taken Kuk across from Plava and were taking the Bainsizza plateau. The West front did not sound so good. It looked as though the war were going on for a long time. We were in the war now but I thought it would take a year to get any great amount of troops over and train them for combat. Next year would be a bad year, or a good year maybe. The Italians were using up an awful amount of men. I did not see how it could go on. Even if they took all the Bainsizza and Monte San Gabriele there were plenty of mountains beyond for the Austrians. I had seen them. All the highest mountains were beyond. On the

Carso they were going forward but there were marshes and swamps down by the sea. Napoleon would have whipped the Austrians on the plains. He never would have fought them in the mountains. He would have let them come down and whipped them around Verona. Still nobody was whipping anyone on the Western front. Perhaps wars weren't won any more. Maybe they went on forever. Maybe it was another Hundred Years' War. I put the paper back on the rack and left the club. I went down the steps carefully and walked up the Via Manzoni. Outside the Gran Hotel I met old Meyers and his wife getting out of a carriage. They were coming back from the races. She was a big-busted woman in black satin. He was short and old, with a white moustache and walked flat-footed with a cane.

'How do you do? How do you do?' She shook hands. 'Hello,' said Meyers.

'How were the races?'

'Fine. They were just lovely. I had three winners.'

'How did you do?' I asked Meyers.

'All right. I had a winner.'

'I never know how he does,' Mrs. Meyers said. 'He never tells me.'

'I do all right,' Meyers said. He was being cordial. 'You ought to come out.' While he talked you had the impression that he was not looking at you or that he mistook you for someone else.

'I will,' I said.

'I'm coming up to the hospital to see you,' Mrs. Meyers said. 'I have some things for my boys. You're all my boys. You certainly are my dear boys.'

'They'll be glad to see you.'

'Those dear boys. You too. You're one of my boys.'

'I have to get back,' I said.

'You give my love to all those dear boys. I've got lots of things to bring. I've some fine Marsala and cakes.'

'Goodbye,' I said. 'They'll be awfully glad to see you.'

'Goodbye,' said Meyers. 'You come around to the galleria. You know where my table is. We're all there every afternoon.' I went on up the street. I wanted to buy something at the Cova to take to Catherine. Inside, at the Cova, I bought a box of chocolate and while the girl wrapped it up I walked over to the bar. There were a couple of British and some aviators. I had a martini alone, paid for it, picked up the box of chocolate at the outside counter and walked on home toward the hospital. Outside the little bar up the street from the Scala there were some people I knew, a vice-consul, two fellows who studied singing, and Ettore Moretti, an Italian from San Francisco who was in the Italian army. I had a drink with them. One of the singers was named Ralph Simmons, and he was singing under the name of Enrico Del Credo. I never knew how well he could sing but he was always on the point of something very big happening. He was fat and looked shopworn around the nose and mouth as though he had hay-fever. He had come back from singing in Piacenza. He had sung Tosca and it had been wonderful.

'Of course you've never heard me sing,' he said.

'When will you sing here?'

'I'll be at the Scala in the fall.'

'I'll bet they throw the benches at you,' Ettore said. 'Did you hear how they threw the benches at him in Modena?'

'It's a damned lie.'

'They threw the benches at him,' Ettore said. 'I was there. I threw six benches myself.'

'You're just a wop from Frisco.'

'He can't pronounce Italian,' Ettore said. 'Everywhere he goes they throw the benches at him.'

'Piacenza's the toughest house to sing in the north of Italy,' the other tenor said. 'Believe me that's a tough little house to sing.' This tenor's name was Edgar Saunders, and he sang under the name of Edouardo Giovanni.

'I'd like to be there to see them throw the benches at you.' Ettore said. 'You can't sing Italian.'

'He's a nut,' said Edgar Saunders. 'All he knows how to say is throw benches.'

'That's all they know how to do when you two sing,' Ettore said. 'Then when you go to America you'll tell about your triumphs at the Scala. They wouldn't let you get by the first note at the Scala.'

'I'll sing at the Scala, Simmons said. 'I'm going to sing Tosca in October.'

'We'll go, won't we, Mac?' Ettore said to the vice-consul. 'They'll need somebody to protect them.'

'Maybe the American army will be there to protect them,' the vice-consul said. 'Do you want another drink, Simmons? You want a drink, Saunders?'

'All right,' said Saunders.

'I hear you're going to get the silver medal,' Ettore said to me. 'What kind of citation you going to get?'

'I don't know. I don't know I'm going to get it.'

'You're going to get it. Oh boy, the girls at the Cova will think you're fine then. They'll all think you killed two hundred Austrians or captured a whole trench by yourself. Believe me, I got to work for my decorations.'

'How many have you got, Ettore?' asked the vice-consul.

'He's got everything,' Simmons said. 'He's the boy they're running the war for.'

'I've got the bronze twice and three silver medals,' said Ettore. 'But the papers on only one have come through.'

'What's the matter with the others?' asked Simmons.

'The action wasn't successful,' said Ettore. 'When the action isn't successful they hold up all the medals.'

'How many times have you been wounded, Ettore?'

'Three times bad. I got three wound-stripes. See?' He pulled his sleeve around. The stripes were parallel silver lines on a black background sewed to the cloth of the sleeve about eight inches below the shoulder.

'You got one too,' Ettore said to me. 'Believe me they're fine to have. I'd rather have them than medals. Believe me, boy, when you get three you've got something. You only get one for a wound that puts you three months in the hospital.'

'Where were you wounded, Ettore?' asked the vice-consul.

Ettore pulled up his sleeve. 'Here,' he showed the deep smooth red scar. 'Here on my leg. I can't show you that because I got puttees on; and in the foot. There's dead bone in my foot that stinks right now. Every morning I take new little pieces out and it stinks all the time.'

'What hit you?' asked Simmons.

'A hand grenade. One of those potato mashers. It just blew the whole side of my foot off. You know those potato mashers?' He turned to me.

'Sure.'

'I saw the son of a bitch throw it,' Ettore said. 'It knocked me down and I thought I was dead all right but those damn potato mashers haven't got anything in them. I shot the son of a bitch with my rifle. I always carry a rifle so they can't tell I'm an officer.'

'How did he look?' asked Simmons.

'That was the only one he had,' Ettore said. 'I don't know why he threw it. I guess he always wanted to throw one. He never saw any real fighting probably. I shot the son of a bitch all right.'

'How did he look when you shot him?' Simmons asked.

'Hell, how should I know,' said Ettore. 'I shot him in the belly. I was afraid I'd miss him if I shot him in the head.'

'How long have you been an officer, Ettore?' I asked.

'Two years. I'm going to be a captain. How long have you been a lieutenant?'

'Going on three years.'

'You can't be a captain because you don't know the Italian language well enough,' Ettore said. 'You can talk but you can't read and write well enough. You got to have an education to be a captain. Why don't you go in the American army?'

'Maybe I will.'

'I wish to God I could. Oh boy, how much does a captain get, Mac?'

'I don't know exactly. Around two hundred and fifty dollars, I think.'

'Jesus Christ, what I could do with two hundred and fifty dollars. You better get in the American army quick, Fred. See if you can't get me in.'

'All right.'

'I can command a company in Italian. I could learn it in English easy.'

'You'd be a general,' said Simmons.

'No, I don't know enough to be a general. A general's got to know a hell of a lot. You guys think there ain't anything to war. You ain't got brains enough to be a second-class corporal.'

'Thank God I don't have to be,' Simmons said.

'Maybe you will if they round up all you slackers. Oh boy, I'd like to have you two in my platoon. Mac too. I'd make you my orderly, Mac.'

'You're a great boy, Ettore,' Mac said. 'But I'm afraid you're a militarist.'

'I'll be a colonel before the war's over,' Ettore said.

'If they don't kill you.'

'They won't kill me.' He touched the stars at his collar with his thumb and forefinger. 'See me do that? We always touch our stars if anybody mentions getting killed.'

'Let's go, Sim,' said Saunders standing up.

'All right.'

'So long,' I said. 'I have to go too.' It was a quarter to six by the clock inside the bar. 'Ciaou, Ettore.'

'Ciaou, Fred,' said Ettore. 'That's pretty fine you're going to get the silver medal.'

'I don't know I'll get it.'

'You'll get it all right, Fred. I heard you were going to get it all right.'

'Well, so long,' I said. 'Keep out of trouble, Ettore.'

'Don't you worry about me. I don't drink and I don't run around. I'm no boozer and whorehound. I know what's good for me.'

'So long,' I said. 'I'm glad you're going to be promoted captain.'

'I don't have to wait to be promoted. I'm going to be a captain for merit of war. You know. Three stars with the crossed swords and crown above. That's me.'

'Good luck.'

'Good luck. When you going back to the front?'

'Pretty soon.'

'Well, I'll see you around.'

'So long.'

'So long. Don't take any bad nickels.'

I walked on down a back street that led to a cross-cut to the hospital. Ettore was twenty-three. He had been brought up by an uncle in San Francisco and was visiting his father and mother in Torino when war was declared. He had a sister, who had been sent to America with him at the same time to live with the uncle, who would graduate from normal school this year. He was a legitimate hero who bored every one he met. Catherine could not stand him.

'We have heroes too,' she said. 'But usually, darling, they're much quieter.'

'I don't mind him.'

'I wouldn't mind him if he wasn't so conceited and didn't bore me, and bore me, and bore me.'

'He bores me.'

'You're sweet to say so, darling. But you don't need to. You can picture him at the front and you know he's useful but he's so much the type of boy I don't care for.'

'I know.'

'You're awfully sweet to know, and I try and like him but he's a dreadful, dreadful boy really.'

'He said this afternoon he was going to be a captain.'

'I'm glad,' said Catherine. 'That should please him.'

'Wouldn't you like me to have some more exalted rank?'

'No, darling. I only want you to have enough rank so that we're admitted to the better restaurants.'

'That's just the rank I have.'

'You have a splendid rank. I don't want you to have any more rank. It might go to your head. Oh, darling, I'm awfully glad you're not conceited. I'd have married you even if you were conceited but it's very restful to have a husband who's not conceited.'

We were talking softly out on the balcony. The moon was supposed to rise but there was a mist over the town and it did not come up and in a little while it started to drizzle and we came in. Outside the mist turned to rain and in a little while it was raining hard and we heard it drumming on the roof. I got up and stood at the door to see if it was raining in but it wasn't so I left the door open.

'Who else did you see?' Catherine asked.

'Mr. and Mrs. Meyers.'

'They're a strange lot.'

'He's supposed to have been in the penitentiary at home. They let him out to die.'

'And he lived happily in Milan for ever after.'

'I don't know how happily.'

'Happily enough after jail I should think.'

'She's bringing some things here.'

'She brings splendid things. Were you her dear boy?'

'One of them.'

'You are all her dear boys,' Catherine said. 'She prefers the dear boys. Listen to it rain.'

'It's raining hard.'

'And you'll always love me, won't you?'

'Yes.'

'And the rain won't make any difference?'

'No.'

'That's good. Because I'm afraid of the rain.'

'Why?' I was sleepy. Outside the rain was falling steadily.

'I don't know, darling. I've always been afraid of the rain.

'I like it.'

'I like to walk in it. But it's very hard on loving.'

'I'll love you always.'

'I'll love you in the rain and in the snow and in the hail and —
what else is there?'

'I don't know. I guess I'm sleepy.'

'Go to sleep, darling, and I'll love you no matter how it is.'

'You're not really afraid of the rain are you?'

'Not when I'm with you.'

'Why are you afraid of it?'

'I don't know.'

'Tell me.'

'Don't make me.'

'Tell me.'

'No.'

'Tell me.'

'All right. I'm afraid of the rain because sometimes I see me
dead in it.'

'No.'

'And sometimes I see you dead in it.'

'That's more likely.'

'No it's not, darling. Because I can keep you safe. I know I
can. But nobody can help themselves.'

'Please stop it. I don't want you to get Scotch and crazy to
night. We won't be together much longer.'

'No, but I am Scotch and crazy. But I'll stop it. It's all
nonsense.'

'Yes it's all nonsense.'

'It's all nonsense. It's only nonsense. I'm not afraid of the
rain. I'm not afraid of the rain. Oh, oh, God, I wish I wasn't.'
She was crying. I comforted her and she stopped crying. But
outside it kept on raining.

CHAPTER 20

ONE day in the afternoon we went to the races. Ferguson went too and Crowell Rodgers, the boy who had been wounded in the eyes by the explosion of the shell nose-cap. The girls dressed to go after lunch while Crowell and I sat on the bed in his room and read the past performances of the horses and the predictions in the racing paper. Crowell's head was bandaged and he did not care much about these races but read the racing paper constantly and kept track of all the horses for something to do. He said the horses were a terrible lot but they were all the horses we had. Old Meyers liked him and gave him tips. Meyers won on nearly every race but disliked to give tips because it brought down the prices. The racing was very crooked. Men who had been ruled off the turf everywhere else were racing in Italy. Meyers' information was good but I hated to ask him because sometimes he did not answer, and always you could see it hurt him to tell you, but he felt obligated to tell us for some reason and he hated less to tell Crowell. Crowell's eyes had been hurt, one was hurt badly, and Meyers had trouble with his eyes and so he liked Crowell. Meyers never told his wife what horses he was playing and she won or lost, mostly lost, and talked all the time.

We four drove out to San Siro in an open carriage. It was a lovely day and we drove out through the park and out along the tramway and out of town where the road was dusty. There were villas with iron fences and big overgrown gardens and ditches with water flowing and green vegetable gardens with dust on the leaves. We could look across the plain and see farmhouses and the rich green farms with their irrigation ditches and the mountains to the north. There were many carriages going into the race-track and the men at the gate let us in without cards because we were in uniform. We left the carriage, bought programmes, and walked across the infield and then across the smooth thick turf of the course to the paddock. The grand stands were old and made of wood and the betting booths were under the stands and in a row out near the stables. There was a crowd of soldiers along the fence in the infield. The paddock was fairly well filled with people and they were walking the horses around in a ring under the trees behind the grand stand. We saw people we knew and got chairs for Ferguson and Catherine and watched the horses.

They went around one after the other their heads down, the grooms leading them. One horse, a purplish black, Crowell swore was dyed that colour. We watched him and it seemed possible. He had only come out just before the bell rang to saddle. We looked him up in the programme from the number on the groom's arm and it was listed a black gelding named Japalac. The race was for horses that had never won a race worth one thousand lire or more. Catherine was sure his colour had been changed. Ferguson said she could not tell. I thought he looked suspicious. We all agreed we ought to back him and pooled one hundred lire. The odds sheets showed he would pay thirty-five to one. Crowell went over and bought the tickets while we watched the jockeys ride around once more and then go out under the trees to the track and gallop slowly up to the turn where the start was to be.

We went up in the grand stand to watch the race. They had no elastic barrier at San Siro then and the starter lined up all the horses, they looked very small way up the track, and then sent them off with a crack of his long whip. They came past us with the black horse well in front and on the turn he was running away from the others. I watched them on the far side with the glasses and saw the jockey fighting to hold him in but he could not hold him and when they came around the turn and into the stretch the black horse was fifteen lengths ahead of the others. He went way on up and around the turn after the finish.

'Isn't it wonderful,' Catherine said. 'We'll have over three thousand lire. He must be a splendid horse.'

'I hope his colour doesn't run,' Crowell said, 'before they pay off.'

'He was really a lovely horse,' Catherine said. 'I wonder if Mr. Meyers backed him.'

'Did you have the winner!' I called to Meyers. He nodded.

'I didn't,' Mrs. Meyers said. 'Who did you children bet on?'

'Japalac.'

'Really? He's thirty-five to one!'

'We liked his colour.'

'I didn't. I thought he looked seedy. They told me not to back him.

'He won't pay much,' Meyers said.

'He's marked thirty-five to one in the quotes,' I said.

'He won't pay much. At the last minute,' Meyers said, 'they put a lot of money on him.'

'Who?'

'Kempton and the boys. You'll see. He won't pay two to one.'

'Then we won't get three thousand lire,' Catherine said. 'I don't like this crooked racing!'

'We'll get two hundred lire.'

'That's nothing. That doesn't do us any good. I thought we were going to get three thousand.'

'It's crooked and disgusting,' Ferguson said.

'Of course,' said Catherine, 'if it hadn't been crooked we'd never have backed him at all. But I would have liked the three thousand lire.'

'Let's go down and get a drink and see what they pay,' Crowell said. We went out to where they posted the numbers and the bell rang to pay off and they put up 18.50 after Japalac to win. That meant he paid less than even money on a ten-lire bet.

We went to the bar under the grand stand and had a whisky and soda apiece. We ran into a couple of Italians we knew and McAdams, the vice-consul, and they came up with us when we joined the girls. The Italians were full of manners and McAdams talked to Catherine while we went down to bet again. Mr. Meyers was standing near the pari mutuel.

'Ask him what he played,' I said to Crowell.

'What are you on, Mr. Meyers?' Crowell asked. Meyers took out his programme and pointed to the number five with his pencil.

'Do you mind if we play him too?' Crowell asked.

'Go ahead. Go ahead. But don't tell my wife I gave it to you.'

'Will you have a drink?' I asked.

'No thanks. I never drink.'

We put a hundred lire on number five to win and a hundred to place and then had another whisky and soda apiece. I was feeling very good and we picked up a couple more Italians, who each had a drink with us, and went back to the girls. These Italians were also very mannered and matched manners with the two we had collected before. In a little while no one could sit down. I gave the tickets to Catherine.

'What horse is it?'

'I don't know. Mr. Meyers' choice.'

'Don't you even know the name?'

'No. You can find it on the programme. Number five I think.'

'You have touching faith,' she said. The number five won but did not pay anything. Mr. Meyers was angry.

'You have to put up two hundred lire to make twenty,' he said. 'Twelve lire for ten. It's not worth it. My wife lost twenty lire.'

'I'll go down with you,' Catherine said to me. The Italians all stood up. We went downstairs and out to the paddock.

'Do you like this?' Catherine asked.

'Yes. I guess I do.'

'It's all right, I suppose,' she said. 'But, darling, I can't stand to see so many people.'

'We don't see many.'

'No. But those Meyers and the man from the bank with his wife and daughters —'

'He cashes my sight drafts,' I said.

'Yes but someone else would if he didn't. Those last four boys were awful.'

'We can stay out here and watch the race from the fence.'

'That will be lovely. And, darling, let's back a horse we've never heard of and that Mr. Meyers won't be backing.'

'All right.'

We backed a horse named Light For Me that finished fourth in a field of five. We leaned on the fence and watched the horses go by, their hoofs thudding as they went past, and saw the mountains off in the distance and Milan beyond the trees and the fields.

'I feel so much cleaner,' Catherine said. The horses were coming back, through the gate, wet and sweating, the jockeys quieting them and riding up to dismount under the trees.

'Wouldn't you like a drink? We could have one out here and see the horses.'

'I'll get them,' I said.

'The boy will bring them.' Catherine said. She put her hand up and the boy came out from the Padoga bar beside the stables. We sat down at a round iron table.

'Don't you like it better when we're alone?'

'Yes,' I said.

'I felt very lonely when they were all there.'

'It's grand here,' I said.

'Yes. It's really a pretty course.'

'It's nice.'

'Don't let me spoil your fun, darling. I'll go back whenever you want.'

'No,' I said. 'We'll stay here and have our drink. Then we'll go down and stand at the water-jump for the steeplechase.'

'You're awfully good to me,' she said.

After we had been alone awhile we were glad to see the others again. We had a good time.

CHAPTER 21

In September the first cool nights came, then the days were cool and the leaves on the trees in the park began to turn colour and we knew the summer was gone. The fighting at the front went very badly and they could not take San Gabriele. The fighting on the Bainsizza plateau was over and by the middle of the month the fighting for San Gabriele was about over too. They could not take it. Ettore was gone back to the front. The horses were gone to Rome and there was no more racing. Cowell had gone to Rome, too, to be sent back to America. There were riots twice in the town against the war and bad rioting in Turin. A British major at the club told me the Italians had lost one hundred and fifty thousand men on the Bainsizza plateau and on San Gabriele. He said they had lost forty thousand on the Carso besides. We had a drink and he talked. He said the fighting was over for the year down here and that the Italians had bitten off more than they could chew. He said the offensive in Flanders was going to the bad. If they killed men as they did this fall the Allies would be cooked in another year. He said we were all cooked but we were all right as long as we did not know it. We were all cooked. The thing was not to recognize it. The last country to realize they were cooked would win the war. We had another drink. Was I on somebody's staff? No. He was. We were alone in the club sitting back in one of the big leather sofas. His boots were smoothly polished dull leather. They were beautiful boots. He said it was all rot. They thought only in divisions and man-power. They all squabbled about divisions and only killed them when they got them. They were all cooked. The Germans won the victories. By God they were soldiers. The old Hun was a soldier. But they were cooked too. We were all cooked. I asked about Russia. He said they were cooked already. I'd soon see they were cooked. Then the Austrians were cooked too. If they got some Hun divisions they could do it. Did he think they would attack this fall? Of course they would. The

Italians were cooked. Everybody knew they were cooked. The old Hun would come down through the Trentino and cut the railway at Vicenza and then where would the Italians be? They tried that in 'sixteen, I said. Not with Germans. Yes, I said. But they probably wouldn't do that, he said. It was too simple. They'd try something complicated and get royally cooked. I had to go, I said. I had to get back to the hospital. 'Goodbye,' he said. Then cheerily, 'Every sort of luck!' There was a great contrast between his world pessimism and personal cheeriness.

I stopped at a barber shop and was shaved and went home to the hospital. My leg was as well as it would get for a long time. I had been up for examination three days before. There were still some treatments to take before my course at the Ospedale Maggiore was finished and I walked along the side street practising not limping. An old man was cutting silhouettes under an arcade. I stopped to watch him. Two girls were posing and he cut their silhouettes together, snipping very fast and looking at them, his head on one side. The girls were giggling. He showed me the silhouettes before he pasted them on white paper and handed them to the girls.

'They're beautiful,' he said. 'How about you, Tenente?'

The girls went away looking at their silhouettes and laughing. They were nice-looking girls. One of them worked in the wine shop across from the hospital.

'All right,' I said.

'Take your cap off.'

'No. With it on.'

'It will not be so beautiful,' the old man said. 'But,' he brightened, 'it will be more military.'

He snipped away at the black paper, then separated the two thicknesses and pasted the profiles on a card and handed them to me.

'How much?'

'That's all right.' He waved his hand. 'I just made them for you.'

'Please.' I brought out some coppers. 'For pleasure.'

'No. I did them for a pleasure. Give them to your girl.'

'Many thanks until we meet.'

'Until I see thee.'

I went on to the hospital. There were some letters, an official one, and some others. I was to have three weeks' convalescent leave and then return to the front. I read it over carefully. Well, that was that. The convalescent leave started October fourth when my course was finished. Three weeks was twenty-one days. That made October twenty-fifth. I told them I would not be in and went to the restaurant a little way up the street from the hospital for supper and read my letters and the *Corriere della Sera* at the table. There was a letter from my grandfather, containing family news, patriotic encouragement, a draft for two hundred dollars, and a few clippings; a dull letter from the priest at our mess; a letter from a man I knew who was flying with the French and had gotten in with a wild gang and was telling about it, and a note from Rinaldi asking me how long I was going to skulk in Milano and what was all the news? He wanted me to bring him phonograph records and enclosed a list. I drank a small bottle of chianti with the meal, had a coffee afterwards with a glass of cognac, finished the paper, put my letters in my pocket, left the paper on the table with the tip and went out. In my room at the hospital I undressed, put on pyjamas and a dressing-gown, pulled down the curtains on the door that opened on to the balcony and sitting up in bed read Boston papers from a pile Mrs. Meyers had left for her boys at the hospital. The Chicago White Sox were winning the American League pennant and the New York Giants were leading the National League. Babe Ruth was a pitcher then playing for Boston. The papers were dull, the news was local and stale, and the war news was all old. The American news was all training camps. I was glad I wasn't in a training camp. The baseball news was all I could read and I did not have the slightest interest in it. A number of papers together made it impossible to read with interest. It was not very timely but I read at it for a while. I wondered if America really got into the war, if they would close down the major leagues. They probably wouldn't. There was still racing in Milan and the war could not be much worse. They had stopped racing in France. That was where our horse Japalac came from. Catherine was not due on duty until nine o'clock. I heard her passing along the floor when she first came on duty and once saw her pass in the hall. She went to several other rooms and finally came into mine.

'I'm late, darling,' she said. 'There was a lot to do. How are you?'

I told her about my papers and the leave.

'That's lovely,' she said. 'Where do you want to go?'

'Nowhere. I want to stay here.'

'That's silly. You pick a place to go and I'll come too.'

'How will you work it?'

'I don't know. But I will.'

'You're pretty wonderful.'

'No, I'm not. But life isn't hard to manage when you've nothing to lose.'

'How do you mean?'

'Nothing. I was only thinking how small obstacles seemed that once were so big.'

'I should think it might be hard to manage.'

'No it won't, darling. If necessary I'll simply leave. But it won't come to that.'

'Where should we go?'

'I don't care. Anywhere you want. Anywhere we don't know people.'

'Don't you care where we go?'

'No. I'll like any place.'

She seemed upset and taut.

'What's the matter, Catherine?'

'Nothing. Nothing's the matter.'

'Yes there is.'

'No, nothing. Really nothing.'

'I know there is. Tell me, darling. You can tell me.'

'It's nothing.'

'Tell me.'

'I don't want to. I'm afraid I'll make you unhappy or worry you.'

'No it won't.'

'You're sure? It doesn't worry me but I'm afraid to worry you.'

'It won't if it doesn't worry you.'

'I don't want to tell.'

'Tell it.'

'Do I have to?'

'Yes.'

'I'm going to have a baby, darling. It's almost three months along. You're not worried, are you? Please, please don't. You mustn't worry.'

'All right.'

'Is it all right?'

'Of course.'

'I did everything. I took everything but it didn't make any difference.'

'I'm not worried.'

'I couldn't help it, darling, and I haven't worried about it. You mustn't worry or feel badly.'

'I only worry about you.'

'That's it. That's what you mustn't do. People have babies all the time. Everybody has babies. It's a natural thing.'

'You're pretty wonderful.'

'No I'm not. But you mustn't mind, darling. I'll try and not make trouble for you. I know I've made trouble before. But haven't I been a good girl until now? You never knew it, did you?'

'No.'

'It will all be like that. You simply mustn't worry. I can see you're worrying. Stop it. Stop it right away. Wouldn't you like a drink, darling? I know a drink always makes you feel cheerful.'

'No. I feel cheerful. And you're pretty wonderful.'

'No I'm not. But I'll fix everything to be together if you pick out a place for us to go. It ought to be lovely in October. We'll have a lovely time, darling, and I'll write you every day while you're at the front.'

'Where will you be?'

'I don't know yet. But somewhere splendid. I'll look after all that.'

We were quiet awhile and did not talk. Catherine was sitting on the bed and I was looking at her but we did not touch each other. We were apart as when someone comes into a room and people are self-conscious. She put out her hand and took mine.

'You aren't angry are you, darling?'

'No.'

'And you don't feel trapped?'

'Maybe a little. But not by you.'

'I didn't mean by me. You mustn't be stupid. I meant trapped at all.'

'You always feel trapped biologically.'

She went away a long way without stirring or removing her hand.

'Always isn't a pretty word.'

'I'm sorry.'

'It's all right. But you see I've never had a baby and I've never even loved anyone. And I've tried to be the way you wanted and then you talk about "always".'

'I could cut off my tongue,' I offered.

'Oh, darling!' she came back from wherever she had been. 'You mustn't mind me.' We were both together again and the self-consciousness was gone. 'We really are the same one and we mustn't misunderstand on purpose.'

'We won't.'

'But people do. They love each other and they misunderstand

on purpose and they fight and then suddenly they aren't the same one.'

'We won't fight.'

'We mustn't. Because there's only us two and in the world there's all the rest of them. If anything comes between us we're gone and then they have us.'

'They won't get us,' I said. 'Because you're too brave. Nothing ever happens to the brave.'

'They die of course.'

'But only once.'

'I don't know. Who said that?'

'The coward dies a thousand deaths, the brave but one?'

'Of course. Who said it?'

'I don't know.'

'He was probably a coward,' she said. 'He knew a great deal about cowards but nothing about the brave. The brave dies perhaps two thousand deaths if he's intelligent. He simply doesn't mention them.'

'I don't know. It's hard to see inside the head of the brave.'

'Yes. That's how they keep that way.'

'You're an authority.'

'You're right, darling. That was deserved.'

'You're brave.'

'No, she said. 'But I would like to be.'

'I'm not,' I said, 'I know where I stand. I've been out long enough to know. I'm like a ball-player that bats two hundred and thirty and knows he's no better.'

'What is a ball-player that bats two hundred and thirty? It's awfully impressive.'

'It's not. It means a mediocre hitter in baseball.'

'But still a hitter,' she prodded me.

'I guess we're both conceited,' I said. 'But you are brave.'

'No. But I hope to be.'

'We're both brave,' I said. 'And I'm very brave when I've had a drink.'

'We're splendid people,' Catherine said. She went over to the armoire and brought me the cognac and a glass. 'Have a drink, darling,' she said. 'You've been awfully good.'

'I don't really want one.'

'Take one.'

'All right.' I poured the water glass a third full of cognac and drank it off.

'That was very big,' she said. 'I know brandy is for heroes. But you shouldn't exaggerate.'

'Where will we live after the war?'

'In an old people's home probably,' she said. 'For three years I looked forward very childishly to the war ending at Christmas. But now I look forward till when our son will be a lieutenant-commander.'

'Maybe he'll be a general.'

'If it's a hundred years' war he'll have time to try both of the services.'

'Don't you want a drink?'

'No. It always makes you happy, darling, and it only makes me dizzy.'

'Didn't you ever drink brandy?'

'No, darling. I'm a very old-fashioned wife.'

I reached down to the floor for the bottle and poured another drink.

'I'd better go to have a look at your compatriots,' Catherine said. 'Perhaps you'll read the papers until I come back.'

'Do you have to go?'

'Now or later.'

'All right. Now.'

'I'll come back later.'

'I'll have finished the papers,' I said.

CHAPTER 22

It turned cold that night and the next day it was raining. Coming home from the Ospedale Maggiore it rained very hard and I was wet when I came in. Up in my room the rain was coming down heavily outside on the balcony, and the wind blew it against the glass doors. I changed my clothing and drank some brandy but the brandy did not taste good. I felt sick in the night and in the morning after breakfast I was nauseated.

'There is no doubt about it,' the house surgeon said. 'Look at the whites of his eyes, Miss.'

Miss Gage looked. They had me look in a glass. The whites of the eyes were yellow and it was the jaundice. I was sick for two weeks with it. For that reason we did not spend a convalescent leave together. We had planned to go to Pallanza on Lago Maggiore. It is nice there in the fall when the leaves turn. There are walks you can take and you can troll for trout in the lake. It would have been better than Stresa because there are fewer people at Pallanza. Stresa is so easy to get to from Milan that there are always people you know. There is a nice village at Pallanza and you can row out to the islands where the fishermen live and there is a restaurant on the biggest island. But we did not go.

One day while I was in bed with jaundice Miss Van Campen came in the room, opened the door into the armoire and saw the empty bottles there. I had sent a load of them down by the porter and I believe she must have seen them going out and come up to find some more. They were mostly vermouth bottles, marsala bottles, capri bottles, empty chianti flasks and a few cognac bottles. The porter had carried out the large bottles those that had held vermouth, and the straw-covered chianti flasks, and left the brandy bottles for the last. It was the brandy bottles and a bottle shaped like a bear which had held kümmel that Miss Van Campen found. The bear-shaped bottle enraged her particularly. She held it up, the bear was sitting up on his haunches with his paws up, there was a cork in his glass head and a few sticky crystals at the bottom. I laughed.

'It was kümmel,' I said. 'The best kümmel comes in those bear-shaped bottles. It comes from Russia.'

'Those are all brandy bottles, aren't they?' Miss Van Campen asked.

'I can't see them all,' I said. 'But they probably are.'

'How long has this been going on?'

'I bought them and brought them in myself,' I said. 'I have had Italian officers visit me frequently and I have kept brandy to offer them.'

'You haven't been drinking it yourself?' she said.

'I have also drunk it myself.'

'Brandy,' she said. 'Eleven empty bottles of brandy and that bear liquid.'

'Kümmel.'

'I will send for someone to take them away. Those are all the empty bottles you have?'

'For the moment.'

'And I was pitying you having jaundice. Pity is something that is wasted on you.'

'Thank you.'

'I suppose you can't be blamed for not wanting to go back to the front. But I should think you would try something more intelligent than producing jaundice with alcoholism.'

'With what?'

'With alcoholism. You heard me say it.' I did not say anything. 'Unless you find something else I'm afraid you will have to go back to the front when you are through with your jaundice. I don't believe self-inflicted jaundice entitles you to a convalescent leave.'

'You don't?'

'I do not.'

'Have you ever had jaundice, Miss Van Campen?'

'No, but I have seen a great deal of it.'

'You noticed how the patients enjoyed it?'

'I suppose it is better than the front.'

'Miss Van Campen,' I said, 'did you ever know a man who tried to disable himself by kicking himself in the privates?'

Miss Van Campen ignored the actual question. She had to ignore it or leave the room. She was not ready to leave because she had disliked me for a long time and she was now cashing in.

'I have known many men to escape the front through self-inflicted wounds.'

'That wasn't the question. I have seen self-inflicted wounds also. I asked you if you had ever known a man who had tried to disable himself by kicking himself in the privates. Because that is the nearest sensation to jaundice and it is a sensation that I believe few women have ever experienced. That was why I asked you if you had ever had jaundice. Miss Van Campen, because' — Miss Van Campen left the room. Later Miss Gage came in.

'What did you say to Van Campen? She was furious.'

'We were comparing sensations. I was going to suggest that she had never experienced childbirth — '

'You're a fool,' Gage said. 'She's after your scalp.'

'She has my scalp,' I said. 'She's lost me my leave and she might try and get me court-martialled. She's mean enough.'

'She never liked you,' Gage said. 'What's it about?'

'She says I've drunk myself into jaundice so as not to go back to the front.'

'Pooh,' said Gage. 'I'll swear you've never taken a drink. Everybody will swear you've never taken a drink.'

'She found the bottles.'

'I've told you a hundred times to clear out those bottles. Where are they now?'

'In the armoire.'

'Have you a suitcase?'

'No. Put them in that rucksack.'

Miss Gage packed the bottles in the rucksack. 'I'll give them to the porter,' she said. She started for the door.

'Just a minute,' Miss Van Campen said. 'I'll take those bottles.' She had the porter with her. 'Carry them, please,' she said. 'I want to show them to the doctor when I make my report.'

She went down the hall. The porter carried the sack. He knew what was in it.

Nothing happened except that I lost my leave.

CHAPTER 23

THE night I was to return to the front I sent the porter down to hold a seat for me on the train when it came from Turin. The train was to leave at midnight. It was made up at Turin and reached Milan about half-past ten at night and lay in the station until time to leave. You had to be there when it came in to get a seat. The porter took a friend with him, a machine-gunner on leave who worked in a tailor shop, and was sure that between them they could hold a place. I gave them money for platform tickets and had them take my baggage. There was a big rucksack and two musettes.

I said goodbye at the hospital at about five o'clock and went out. The porter had my baggage in his lodge and I told him I would be at the station a little before midnight. His wife called me 'Signorino' and cried. She wiped her eyes and shook hands and then cried again. I patted her on the back and she cried once more. She had done my mending and was a very short dumpy happy-faced woman with white hair. When she cried her whole face went to pieces. I went down to the corner where there was a wine shop and waited inside looking out the window. It was dark outside and cold and misty. I paid for my coffee and grappa and I watched the people going by in the light from the window.

I saw Catherine and knocked on the window. She looked, saw me and smiled, and I went out to meet her. She was wearing a dark blue cape and a soft felt hat. We walked along together, along the sidewalk past the wine shops, then across the market square and up the street and through the archway to the cathedral square. There were street-car tracks and beyond them was the cathedral. It was white and wet in the mist. We crossed the tram tracks. On the left were the shops, their windows lighted, and the entrance to the galleria. There was a fog in the square and when we came close to the front of the cathedral it was very big and the stone was wet.

'Would you like to go in?'

'No,' Catherine said. We walked along. There was a soldier standing with his girl in the shadow of one of the stone buttresses ahead of us and we passed them. They were standing tight up against the stone and he had put his cape around her.

'They're like us,' I said.

'Nobody is like us,' Catherine said. She did not mean it happily.

'I wish they had some place to go.'

'It mightn't do them any good.'

'I don't know. Everybody ought to have some place to go.'

'They have the cathedral,' Catherine said. We were past it now. We crossed the far end of the square and looked back at the cathedral. It was fine in the mist. We were standing in front of the leather goods shop. There were riding boots, a rucksack and ski boots in the window. Each article was set apart as an exhibit; the rucksack in the centre, the riding boots on one side and the ski boots on the other. The leather was dark and oiled smooth as a used saddle. The electric light made high lights on the dull oiled leather.

'We'll ski some time.'

'In two months there will be ski-ing at Mürren,' Catherine said.

'Let's go there.'

'All right,' she said. We went on past other windows and turned down a side street.

'I've never been this way.'

'This is the way I go to the hospital,' I said It was a narrow street and we kept on the right-hand side. There were many people passing in the fog. There were shops and all the windows were lighted. We looked in a window at a pile of cheeses. I stopped in front of an armourer's shop.

'Come in a minute. I have to buy a gun.'

'What sort of gun?'

'A pistol.' We went in and I unbuttoned my belt and laid it with the empty holster on the counter. Two women were behind the counter. The women brought out several pistols.

'It must fit this,' I said, opening the holster. It was a grey leather holster and I had bought it second-hand to wear in the town.

'Have they good pistols?' Catherine asked.

'They're all about the same. Can I try this one?' I asked the woman.

'I have no place now to shoot,' she said. 'But it is very good. You will not make a mistake with it.'

I snapped it and pulled back the action. The spring was rather strong but it worked smoothly. I sighted it and snapped it again.

'It is used,' the woman said. 'It belonged to an officer who was an excellent shot.'

'Did you sell it to him?'

'Yes.'

'How did you get it back?'

'From his orderly.'

'Maybe you have mine,' I said. 'How much is this?'

'Fifty lire. It is very cheap.'

'All right. I want two extra clips and a box of cartridges.'

She brought them from under the counter.

'Have you any need for a sword?' she asked. 'I have some used swords very cheap.'

'I'm going to the front,' I said.

'Oh, yes, then you won't need a sword,' she said.

I paid for the cartridges and the pistol, filled the magazine and put it in place, put the pistol in my empty holster, filled the extra clips with cartridges and put them in the leather slots on the holster and then buckled on my belt. The pistol felt heavy on the belt. Still, I thought, it was better to have a regulation pistol. You could always get cartridges.

'Now we're fully armed,' I said. 'That was the one thing I had to remember to do. Someone got my other one going to the hospital.

'I hope it's a good pistol,' Catherine said.

'Was there anything else?' the woman asked.

'I don't believe so.'

'The pistol has a lanyard,' she said.

'So I noticed.' The woman wanted to sell something else. 'You don't need a whistle?'

'I don't believe so.'

The woman said goodbye and we went out on to the sidewalk. Catherine looked in the window. The woman looked out and bowed to us.

'What are those little mirrors set in wood for?'

'They're for attracting birds. They twirl them out in the field and larks see them and come out and the Italians shoot them.'

'They are an ingenious people,' Catherine said. 'You don't shoot larks do you, darling, in America?'

'Not especially.'

We crossed the street and started to walk up the other side.

'I feel better now,' Catherine said. 'I felt terrible when we started.'

'We always feel good when we're together.'

'We always will be together.'

'Yes, except that I'm going away at midnight.'

'Don't think about it, darling.'

We walked on up the street. The fog made the lights yellow.

'Aren't you tired?' Catherine asked.

'How about you?'

'I'm all right. It's fun to walk.'

'But let's not do it too long.'

'No.'

We turned down a side street where there were no lights and walked in the street. I stopped and kissed Catherine. While I kissed her I felt her hand on my shoulder. She had pulled my cape around her so it covered both of us. We were standing in the street against a high wall.

'Let's go some place,' I said.

'Good,' said Catherine. We walked on along the street until it came out on to a wider street that was beside a canal. On the other side was a brick wall and buildings. Ahead, down the street, I saw a street-car cross a bridge.

'We can get a cab up at the bridge,' I said. We stood on the bridge in the fog waiting for a carriage. Several street-cars passed, full of people going home. Then a carriage came along but there was someone in it. The fog was turning to rain.

'We could walk or take a tram,' Catherine said.

'One will be along,' I said. 'They go by here.'

'Here one comes,' she said.

The driver stopped his horse and lowered the metal sign on his meter. The top of the carriage was up and there were drops of water on the driver's coat. His varnished hat was shining in the wet. We sat back in the seat together and the top of the carriage made it dark.

'Where did you tell him to go?'

'To the station. There's a hotel across from the station where we can go.'

'We can go the way we are? Without luggage?'

'Yes,' I said.

It was a long ride to the station up side streets in the rain.

'Won't we have dinner?' Catherine asked. 'I'm afraid I'll be hungry.'

'We'll have it in our room.'

'I haven't anything to wear. I haven't even a nightgown.'

'We'll get one,' I said and called to the driver.

'Go to the Via Manzoni and up that.' He nodded and turned off to the left at the next corner. On the big street Catherine watched for a shop.

'Here's a place,' she said. I stopped the driver and Catherine got out, walked across the sidewalk and went inside. I sat back in the carriage and waited for her. It was raining and I could smell the wet street and the horse steaming in the rain. She came back with a package and got in and we drove on.

'I was very extravagant, darling,' she said, 'but it's a fine night-gown.'

At the hotel I asked Catherine to wait in the carriage while I went in and spoke to the manager. There were plenty of rooms. Then I went out to the carriage, paid the driver, and Catherine and I walked in together. The small boy in buttons carried the package. The manager bowed us towards the elevator. There was much red plush and brass. The manager went up in the elevator with us.

'Monsieur and Madame wish dinner in their room?'

'Yes. Will you have the menu brought up?' I said.

'You wish something special for dinner. Some game or a soufflé?'

The elevator passed three floors with a click each time, then clicked and stopped.

'What have you as game?'

'I could get a pheasant, or a woodcock.'

'A woodcock,' I said. We walked down the corridor. The carpet was worn. There were many doors. The manager stopped and unlocked a door and opened it.

'Here you are. A lovely room.'

The small boy in buttons put the package on the table in the centre of the room. The manager opened the curtains.

'It is foggy outside,' he said. The room was furnished in red plush. There were many mirrors, two chairs and a large bed with a satin coverlet. A door led to the bathroom.

'I will send up the menu,' the manager said. He bowed and went out.

I went to the window and looked out, then pulled a cord that shut the thick plush curtains. Catherine was sitting on the bed looking at the cut glass chandelier. She had taken her hat off and her hair shone under the light. She saw herself in one of the mirrors and put her hands to her hair. I saw her in three other mirrors. She did not look happy. She let her cape fall on the bed.

'What's the matter, darling?'

'I never felt like a whore before,' she said. I went over to the window and pulled the curtain aside and looked out. I had not thought it would be like this.

'You're not a whore.'

'I know it, darling. But it isn't nice to feel like one.' Her voice was dry and flat.

'This was the best hotel we could get in,' I said. I looked out the window. Across the square were the lights of the station. There were carriages going by on the street and I saw the trees in the park. The lights from the hotel shone on the wet pavement. Oh, hell, I thought, do we have to argue now?

'Come over here, please,' Catherine said. The flatness was all gone out of her voice. 'Come over, please. I'm a good girl again.' I looked over at the bed. She was smiling.

I went over and sat on the bed beside her and kissed her.

'You're my good girl.'

'I'm certainly yours,' she said.

After we had eaten we felt fine, and then after, we felt very happy and in a little time the room felt like our own home. My room at the hospital had been our own home and this room was our home too in the same way.

Catherine wore my tunic over her shoulders while we ate. We were very hungry and the meal was good and we drank a bottle of capri and a bottle of St. Éstèphe. I drank most of it but Catherine drank some and it made her feel splendid. For dinner we had a woodcock with soufflé potatoes and purée de marron, a salad and zabaione for dessert.

'It's a fine room,' Catherine said. 'It's a lovely room. We should have stayed here all the time we've been in Milan.'

'It's a funny room. But it's nice.'

'Vice is a wonderful thing,' Catherine said. 'The people who go in for it seem to have good taste about it. The red plush is really fine. It's just the thing. And the mirrors are very attractive.'

'You're a lovely girl.'

'I don't know how a room like this would be for waking up in the morning. But it's really a splendid room.' I poured another glass of St. Éstèphe.

'I wish we could do something really sinful,' Catherine said. 'Everything we do seems so innocent and simple. I can't believe we do anything wrong.'

'You're a grand girl.'

'I only feel hungry. I get terribly hungry.'

'You're a fine simple girl,' I said.

'I am a simple girl. No one ever understood it except you.'

'Once when I first met you I spent an afternoon thinking how we would go to the Hotel Cavour together and how it would be.'

'That was awfully cheeky of you. This isn't the Cavour is it?'

'No. They wouldn't have taken us in there.'

'They'll take us in some time. But that's how we differ, darling. I never thought about anything.'

'Didn't you ever at all?'

'A little,' she said.

'Oh you're a lovely girl.'

I poured another glass of wine.

'I'm a very simple girl,' Catherine said.

'I didn't think so at first. I thought you were a crazy girl.'

'I was a little crazy. But I wasn't crazy in any complicated manner. I didn't confuse you did I, darling?'

'Wine is a grand thing,' I said. 'It makes you forget all the bad.'

'It's lovely,' said Catherine. 'But it's given my father gout very badly.'

'Have you a father?'

'Yes,' said Catherine. 'He has gout. You won't ever have to meet him. Haven't you a father?'

'No,' I said. 'A step-father.'

'Will I like him?'

'You won't have to meet him.'

'We have such a fine time,' Catherine said. 'I don't take any interest in anything else any more. I'm so very happy married to you.'

The waiter came and took away the things. After a while we were very still and we could hear the rain. Down below on the street a motor-car honked.

> ' "And always at my back I hear
> Time's wingèd chariot hurrying near," '

I said.

'I know that poem,' Catherine said. 'It's by Marvell. But it's about a girl who wouldn't live with a man.'

My head felt very clear and cold and I wanted to talk facts.

'Where will you have the baby?'

'I don't know. The best place I can find.'

'How will you arrange it?'

'The best way I can. Don't worry, darling. We may have several babies before the war is over.'

'It's nearly time to go.'

'I know. You can make it time if you want.'

'No.'

'Then don't worry, darling. You were fine until now and now you are worrying.'

'I won't. How often will you write?'

'Every day. Do they read your letters?'

'They can't read English enough to hurt any.'

'I'll make them very confusing,' Catherine said.

'But not too confusing.'

'I'll just make them a little confusing.'

'I'm afraid we have to start to go.'

'All right, darling.'

'I hate to leave our fine house.'

'So do I.'

'But we have to go.'

'All right. But we're never settled in our home very long.'

'We will be.'

'I'll have a fine home for you when you come back.'

'Maybe I'll be back right away.'

'Perhaps you'll be hurt just a little in the foot.'

'Or the lobe of the ear.'

'No. I want your ears the way they are.'

'And not my feet?'

'Your feet have been hit already.'

'We have to go, darling. Really.'

'All right. You go first.'

CHAPTER 24

WE walked down the stairs instead of taking the elevator. The carpet on the stairs was worn. I had paid for the dinner when it came up and the waiter, who had brought it, was sitting on a chair near the door. He jumped up and bowed and I went with him into the side room and paid the bill for the room. The manager had remembered me as a friend and refused payment in advance but when he retired he had remembered to have the waiter stationed at the door so that I should not get out without paying. I suppose that had happened; even with his friends. One had so many friends in a war.

I asked the waiter to get us a carriage and he took Catherine's package that I was carrying and went out with an umbrella. Outside through the window we saw him crossing the street in the rain. We stood in the side room and looked out the window.

'How do you feel, Cat?'

'Sleepy.'

'I feel hollow and hungry.'

'Have you anything to eat?'

'Yes, in my musette.'

I saw the carriage coming. It stopped, the horse's head hanging in the rain, and the waiter stepped out, opened his umbrella, and came towards the hotel. We met him at the door and walked out under the umbrella down the wet walk to the carriage at the curb. Water was running in the gutter.

'There is your package on the seat,' the waiter said. He stood with the umbrella until we were in and I had tipped him.

'Many thanks. Pleasant journey,' he said. The coachman lifted the reins and the horse started. The waiter turned away under the umbrella and went towards the hotel. We drove down the street and turned to the left, then came around to the right in front of the station. There were two carabinieri standing under the light just out of the rain. The light shone on their hats. The rain fell clear and transparent against the light from the station. A porter came out from under the shelter of the station, his shoulders up against the rain.

'No,' I said. 'Thanks. I don't need thee.'

He went back under the shelter of the archway. I turned to Catherine. Her face was in the shadow from the hood of the carriage.

'We might as well say goodbye.'

'I can't go in?'

'No,'

'Goodbye, Cat.'

'Will you tell him the hospital?'

'Yes.'

I told the driver the address to drive to. He nodded.

'Goodbye,' I said. 'Take good care of yourself and young Catherine.'

'Goodbye, darling.'

'Goodbye,' I said. I stepped out into the rain and the carriage started. Catherine leaned out and I saw her face in the light. She smiled and waved. The carriage went up the street. Catherine pointed in toward the archway. I looked, there were only the two carabinieri and the archway. I realized she meant for me to get in out of the rain. I went in and stood and watched the carriage turn the corner. Then I started through the station and down the runway to the train.

The porter was on the platform looking for me. I followed him into the train crowding past people and along the aisle and in through a door to where the machine-gunner sat in the corner of a full compartment. My rucksack and musettes were above his head on the luggage rack. There were many men standing in the corridor and the men in the compartment all looked at us when we came in. There were not enough places in the train and everyone was hostile. The machine-gunner stood up for me to sit down. Someone tapped me on the shoulder. I looked around. It was a very tall gaunt captain of artillery with a red scar along his jaw. He had looked through the glass on the corridor and then come in.

'What do you say?' I asked. I had turned and faced him. He was taller than me and his face was very thin under the shadow of his cap-visor and the scar was new and shiny. Everyone in the compartment was looking at me.

'You can't do that,' he said. 'You can't have a soldier save you a place.'

'I have done it.'

He swallowed and I saw his Adam's apple go up and then down. The machine-gunner stood in front of the place. Other men looked in through the glass. No one in the compartment said anything.

'You have no right to do that. I was here two hours before you came.'

'What do you want?'

'The seat.'

'So do I.'

I watched his face and could feel the whole compartment against me. I did not blame them. He was in the right. But I wanted the seat. Still no one said anything.

Oh, hell, I thought.

'Sit down, Signor Capitano,' I said. The machine-gunner moved out of the way and the tall captain sat down. He looked at me. His face seemed hurt. But he had the seat. 'Get my things,' I said to the machine-gunner. We went out in the corridor. The train was full and I knew there was no chance of a place. I gave the porter and the machine-gunner ten lire apiece. They went down the corridor and outside on the platform looking in the windows but there were no places.

'Maybe some will get off at Brescia,' the porter said.

'More will get on at Brescia,' said the machine-gunner. I said goodbye to them and we shook hands and they left. They both felt badly. Inside the train we were all standing in the corridor when the train started. I watched the lights of the station and the yards as we went out. It was still raining and soon the windows were wet and you could not see out. Later I slept on the floor of the corridor; first putting my pocket-book with my money and papers in it inside my shirt and trousers so that it was inside the leg of my breeches. I slept all night, waking at Brescia and Verona when more men got on the train, but going back to sleep at once. I had my head on one of the musettes and my arms around the other and I could feel the pack and they could all walk over me if they wouldn't step on me. Men were sleeping on the floor all down the corridor. Others stood holding on to the window rods or leaning against the doors. That train was always crowded.

BOOK III

CHAPTER 25

Now in the fall the trees were all bare and the roads were muddy. I rode to Gorizia from Udine on a camion. We passed other camions on the road and I looked at the country. The mulberry trees were bare and the fields were brown. There were wet dead leaves on the road from the rows of bare trees and men were working on the road, tamping stone in the ruts from piles of crushed stone along the side of the road between the trees. We saw the town with a mist over it that cut off the mountains. We crossed the river and I saw that it was running high. It had been raining in the mountains. We came into the town past the factories and then the houses and villas and I saw that many more houses had been hit. On a narrow street we passed a British Red Cross ambulance. The driver wore a cap and his face was thin and very tanned. I did not know him. I got down from the camion in the big square in front of the Town Major's house, the driver handed down my rucksack and I put it on and swung on the two musettes and walked to our villa. It did not feel like a home-coming.

I walked down the damp gravel driveway looking at the villa through the trees. The windows were all shut but the door was open. I went in and found the major sitting at a table in the bare room with maps and typed sheets of paper on the wall.

'Hello,' he said. 'How are you?' He looked older and drier.

'I'm good,' I said. 'How is everything?'

'It's all over,' he said. 'Take off your kit and sit down.' I put my pack and the two musettes on the floor and my cap on the pack. I brought the other chair over from the wall and sat down by the desk.

'It's been a bad summer,' the major said. 'Are you strong now?'

'Yes.'

'Did you ever get the decorations?'

'Yes. I got them fine. Thank you very much.'

'Let's see them.'

I opened my cape so he could see the two ribbons.

'Did you get the boxes with the medals?'

'No. Just the papers.'

'The boxes will come later. That takes more time.'

'What do you want me to do?'

'The cars are all away. There are six up north at Caporetto. You know Caporetto?'

'Yes,' I said. I remember it as a little white town with a campanile in a valley. It was a clean little town and there was a fine fountain in the square.

'They are working from there. There are many sick now. The fighting is over.'

'Where are the others?'

'There are two up in the mountains and four still on the Bainsizza. The other two ambulance sections are in the Carso with the third army.'

'What do you wish me to do?'

'You can go and take over the four cars on the Bainsizza if you like. Gino has been up there a long time. You haven't seen it up there, have you?'

'No.'

'It was very bad. We lost three cars.'

'I heard about it.'

'Yes, Rinaldi wrote you.'

'Where is Rinaldi?'

'He is here at the hospital. He has had a summer and fall of it.'

'I believe it.'

'It has been bad,' the major said. 'You couldn't believe how bad it's been. I've often thought you were lucky to be hit when you were.'

'I know I was.'

'Next year will be worse,' the major said. 'Perhaps they will attack now. They say they are to attack but I can't believe it. It is too late. You saw the river?'

'Yes. It's high already.'

'I don't believe they will attack now that the rains have started. We will have the snow soon. What about your countrymen? Will there be other Americans besides yourself?'

'They are training an army of ten million.'

'I hope we get some of them. But the French will hog them all. We'll never get any down here. All right. You stay here tonight and go out tomorrow with the little car and send Gino back. I'll send somebody with you that knows the road. Gino will tell you everything. They are shelling quite a little still but it is all over. You will want to see the Bainsizza.'

'I'm glad to see it. I am glad to be back with you again, Signor Maggiore.'

He smiled. 'You are very good to say so. I am very tired of this war. If I was away I do not believe I would come back.'

'Is it so bad?'

'Yes. It is so bad and worse. Go get cleaned up and find your friend Rinaldi.'

I went out and carried my bags up the stairs. Rinaldi was not in the room but his things were there and I sat down on the bed and unwrapped my puttees and took the shoe off my right foot. Then I lay back on the bed. I was tired and my right foot hurt. It seemed silly to lie on the bed with one shoe off, so I sat up and unlaced the other shoe and dropped it on the floor, then lay back on the blanket again. The room was stuffy with the window closed but I was too tired to get up and open it. I saw my things were all in one corner of the room. Outside it was getting dark. I lay on the bed and thought about Catherine and waited for Rinaldi. I was going to try not to think about Catherine except at night before I went to sleep. But now I was tired and there was nothing to do, so I lay and thought about her. I was thinking about her when Rinaldi came in. He looked just the same. Perhaps he was a little thinner.

'Well, baby,' he said. I sat up on the bed. He came over, sat down and put his arm around me. 'Good old baby.' He whacked me on the back and I held both his arms.

'Old baby,' he said. 'Let me see your knee.'

'I'll have to take off my breeches.'

'Take off your breeches, baby. We're all friends here. I want to see what kind of a job they did.' I stood up, took off the breeches and pulled off the knee-brace. Rinaldi sat on the floor and bent the knee gently back and forth. He ran his finger along the scar; put his thumbs together over the kneecap and rocked the knee gently with his fingers.

'Is that all the articulation you have?'

'Yes.'

'It's a crime to send you back. They ought to get complete articulation.'

'It's a lot better than it was. It was stiff as a board.'

Rinaldi bent it more. I watched his hands. He had fine surgeon's hands. I looked at the top of his head, his hair shiny and parted smoothly. He bent the knee too far.

'Ouch!' I said.

'You ought to have more treatment on it with the machines,' Rinaldi said.

'It's better than it was.'

'I see that, baby. This is something I know more about than you.' He stood up and sat down on the bed. 'The knee itself is a good job.' He was through with the knee. 'Tell me all about everything.'

'There's nothing to tell,' I said. 'I've led a quiet life.'

'You act like a married man,' he said. 'What's the matter with you?'

'Nothing,' I said. 'What's the matter with you?'

'This war is killing me,' Rinaldi said, 'I am very depressed by it.' He folded his hands over his knee.

146

'Oh,' I said.

'What's the matter? Can't I even have human impulses?'

'No. I can see you've been having a fine time. Tell me.'

'All summer and all fall I've operated. I work all the time. I do everybody's work. All the hard ones they leave to me. By God, baby, I am becoming a lovely surgeon.'

'That sounds better.'

'I never think. No, by God, I don't think; I operate.'

'That's right.'

'But now, baby, it's all over. I don't operate now and I feel like hell. This is a terrible war, baby. You believe me when I say it. Now you cheer me up. Did you bring the phonograph records?'

'Yes.'

They were wrapped in paper in a cardboard box in my rucksack. I was too tired to get them out.

'Don't you feel good yourself, baby?'

'I feel like hell.'

'This war is terrible,' Rinaldi said. 'Come on. We'll both get drunk and be cheerful. Then we'll go get the ashes dragged. Then we'll feel fine.'

'I've had the jaundice,' I said, 'and I can't get drunk.'

'Oh, baby, how you've come back to me. You come back serious and with a liver. I tell you this war is a bad thing. Why did we make it anyway?'

'We'll have a drink. I don't want to get drunk but we'll have a drink.'

Rinaldi went across the room to the washstand and brought back two glasses and a bottle of cognac.

'It's Austrian cognac,' he said. 'Seven stars. It's all they captured on San Gabriele.'

'Were you up there?'

'No. I haven't been anywhere. I've been here all the time operating. Look, baby, that is your old toothbrushing glass. I kept it all the time to remind me of you.'

'To remind you to brush your teeth.'

'No. I have my own too. I kept this to remind me of you trying to brush away the Villa Rossa from your teeth in the morning, swearing and eating aspirin and cursing harlots. Every time I see that glass I think of you trying to clean your conscience with a toothbrush.' He came over to the bed. 'Kiss me once and tell me you're not serious.'

'I never kiss you. You're an ape.'

'I know, you are the fine good Anglo-Saxon boy. I know. You are the remorse boy, I know. I will wait till I see the Anglo-Saxon brushing away harlotry with a toothbrush.'

'Put some cognac in the glass.'

We touched glasses and drank. Rinaldi laughed at me.

'I will get you drunk and take out your liver and put you in a good Italian liver and make you a man again.'

I held the glass for some more cognac. It was dark outside now. Holding the glass of cognac, I went over and opened the window. The rain had stopped falling. It was colder outside and there was a mist in the trees.

'Don't throw the cognac out the window,' Rinaldi said. 'If you can't drink it give it to me.'

'Go and drown yourself,' I said. I was glad to see Rinaldi again. He had spent two years teasing me and I had always liked it. We understood each other very well.

'Are you married?' he asked from the bed. I was standing against the wall by the window.

'Not yet.'

'Are you in love?'

'Yes.'

'With that English girl?'

'Yes.'

'Poor baby. Is she good to you?'

'Of course.'

'I mean is she good to you practically speaking?'

'Shut up.'

'I will. You will see I am a man of extreme delicacy. Does she — ?'

'Rinin,' I said, 'please shut up. If you want to be my friend shut up.'

'I don't *want* to be your friend, baby. I *am* your friend.'

'Then shut up.'

'All right.'

I went over to the bed and sat down beside Rinaldi. He was holding his glass and looking at the floor.

'You see how it is, Rinin?'

'Oh, yes. All my life I encounter sacred subjects. But very few with you. I suppose you must have them too.' He looked at the floor.

'You haven't any?'

'No.'

'Not any?'

'No.'

'I can say this about your mother and that about your sister?'

'And that about *your* sister,' Rinaldi said swiftly. We both laughed.

'The old superman,' I said.

'I am jealous maybe,' Rinaldi said.

'No, you're not.'

'I don't mean like that. I mean something else. Have you any married friends?'

'Yes,' I said.

'I haven't,' Rinaldi said. 'Not if they love each other.'

'Why not?'

'They don't like me.'

'Why not?'

'I am the snake. I am the snake of reason.'

'You're getting it mixed. The apple was reason.'

'No, it was the snake.' He was more cheerful.

'You are better when you don't think so deeply,' I said.

'I love you, baby,' he said. 'You puncture me when I become

a great Italian thinker. But I know many things I can't say. I know more than you.'

'Yes. You do.'

'But you will have a better time. Even with remorse you will have a better time.'

'I don't think so.'

'Oh, yes. That is true. Already I am only happy when I am working.' He looked at the floor again.

'You'll get over that.'

'No. I only like two other things; one is bad for my work and the other is over in half an hour or fifteen minutes. Sometimes less.'

'Sometimes a good deal less.'

'Perhaps I have improved, baby. You do not know. But there are only the two things and my work.'

'You'll get other things.'

'No. We never get anything. We are born with all we have and we never learn. We never get anything new. We all start complete. You should be glad not to be a Latin.'

'There's no such thing as a Latin. That is "Latin" thinking. You are so proud of your defects.' Rinaldi looked up and laughed.

'We'll stop, baby. I am tired from thinking so much.' He had looked tired when he came in. 'It's nearly time to eat. I'm glad you're back. You are my best friend and my war brother.'

'When do the war brothers eat?' I asked.

'Right away. We'll drink once more for your liver's sake.'

'Like Saint Paul.'

'You are inaccurate. That was wine and the stomach. Take a little wine for your stomach's sake.'

'Whatever you have in the bottle,' I said. 'For any sake you mention.'

'To your girl,' Rinaldi said. He held out his glass.

'All right.'

'I'll never say a dirty thing about her.'

'Don't strain yourself.'

He drank off the cognac. 'I am pure,' he said. 'I am like you, baby. I will get an English girl too. As a matter of fact I knew your girl first but she was a little tall for me. A tall girl for a sister,' he quoted.

'You have a lovely pure mind,' I said.

'Haven't I? That's why they call me Rinaldo Purissimo.'

'Rinaldo Sporchissimo.'

'Come on, baby, we'll go down to eat while my mind is still pure.'

I washed, combed my hair and we went down the stairs. Rinaldi was a little drunk. In the room where we ate, the meal was not quite ready.

'I'll go get the bottle,' Rinaldi said. He went off up the stairs. I sat at the table and he came back with the bottle and poured us each a half tumbler of cognac.

'Too much,' I said and held up the glass and sighted at the lamp on the table.

'Not for an empty stomach. It is a wonderful thing. It burns out the stomach completely. Nothing is worse for you.'

'All right.'

'Self-destruction day by day,' Rinaldi said. 'It ruins the stomach and makes the hand shake. Just the thing for a surgeon.'

'You recommend it?'

'Heartily. I use no other. Drink it down, baby, and look forward to being sick.'

I drank half the glass. In the hall I could hear the orderly calling, 'Soup! Soup is ready!'

The major came in, nodded to us and sat down. He seemed very small at table.

'Is this all we are?' he asked. The orderly put the soup bowl down and he ladled out a plateful.

'We are all,' Rinaldi said. 'Unless the priest comes. If he knew Federico was here he would be here.'

'Where is he?' I asked.

'He's at 307,' the major said. He was busy with his soup. He wiped his mouth, wiping his upturned grey moustache carefully. 'He will come I think. I called them and left word to tell him you were here.'

'I miss the noise of the mess,' I said.

'Yes, it's quiet,' the major said.

'I will be noisy,' said Rinaldi.

'Drink some wine, Enrico,' said the major. He filled my glass. The spaghetti came in and we were all busy. We were finishing the spaghetti when the priest came in. He was the same as ever, small and brown and compact-looking. I stood up and we shook hands. He put his hand on my shoulder.

'I came as soon as I heard,' he said.

'Sit down,' the major said. 'You're late.'

'Good evening, priest,' Rinaldi said, using the English word. They had taken that up from the priest-baiting captain who spoke a little English. 'Good evening, Rinaldi,' the priest said. The orderly brought him soup but he said he would start with the spaghetti.

'How are you?' he asked me.

'Fine,' I said. 'How have things been?'

'Drink some wine, priest,' Rinaldi said. 'Take a little wine for your stomach's sake. That's Saint Paul, you know.'

'Yes, I know,' said the priest politely. Rinaldi filled his glass.

'That Saint Paul,' said Rinaldi. 'He's the one who makes all the trouble.' The priest looked at me and smiled. I could see that the baiting did not touch him now.

'That Saint Paul,' Rinaldi said. 'He was a rounder and a chaser and then when he was no longer hot he said it was no good. When he was finished he made the rules for us who are still hot. Isn't it true, Federico?'

The major smiled. We were eating meat stew now.

'I never discuss a Saint after dark,' I said. The priest looked up from the stew and smiled at me.

'There he is, gone over with the priest,' Rinaldi said. 'Where are all the good old priest-baiters? Where is Cavalcanti? Where is Brundi? Where is Cesare? Do I have to bait this priest alone without support?'

'He is a good priest,' said the major.

'He is a good priest,' said Rinaldi. 'But still a priest. I try to make the mess like the old days. I want to make Federico happy. To hell with you, priest!'

I saw the major look at him and notice that he was drunk. His thin face was white. The line of his hair was very black against the white of his forehead.

'It's all right, Rinaldo,' said the priest. 'It's all right.'

'To hell with you,' said Rinaldi. 'To hell with the whole damn business.' He sat back in his chair.

'He's been under a strain and he's tired,' the major said to me. He finished his meat and wiped up the gravy with a piece of bread.

'I don't give a damn,' Rinaldi said to the table. 'To hell with the whole business.' He looked defiantly around the table, his eyes flat, his face pale.

'All right,' I said. 'To hell with the whole damn business.'

'No, no,' said Rinaldi. 'You can't do it. You can't do it. I say you can't do it. You're dry and you're empty and there's nothing else. There's nothing else I tell you. Not a damned thing. I know, when I stop working.'

The priest shook his head. The orderly took away the stew dish.

'What are you eating meat for?' Rinaldi turned to the priest. 'Don't you know it's Friday?'

'It's Thursday,' the priest said.

'It's a lie. It's Friday. You're eating the body of our Lord. It's God-meat. I know. It's dead Austrian. That's what you're eating.'

'The white meat is from officers,' I said, completing the old joke.

Rinaldi laughed. He filled his glass.

'Don't mind me,' he said. 'I'm just a little crazy.'

'You ought to have a leave,' the priest said.

The major shook his head at him. Rinaldi looked at the priest.

'You think I ought to have a leave?'

The major shook his head at the priest. Rinaldi was looking at the priest.

'Just as you like,' the priest said. 'Not if you don't want.'

'To hell with you,' Rinaldi said. 'They try to get rid of me. Every night they try to get rid of me. I fight them off. What if I have it. Everybody has it. The whole world's got it. First,' he went on, assuming the manner of a lecturer, 'it's a little pimple. Then we notice a rash between the shoulders. Then we notice nothing at all. We put our faith in mercury.'

'Or salvarsan,' the major interrupted quietly.

'A mercurial product,' Rinaldi said. He acted very elated now. 'I know something worth two of that. Good old priest,' he said. 'You'll never get it. Baby will get it. It's an industrial accident. It's a simple industrial accident.'

The orderly brought in the sweet and coffee. The sweet was a sort of black bread pudding with hard sauce. The lamp was smoking; the black smoke going close up inside the chimney.

'Bring two candles and take away the lamp,' the major said. The orderly brought two lighted candles each in a saucer, and took out the lamp blowing it out. Rinaldi was quiet now. He seemed all right. We talked and after the coffee we all went out into the hall.

'You want to talk to the priest. I have to go in the town,' Rinaldi said. 'Good night, priest.'

'Good night, Rinaldo,' the priest said.

'I'll see you, Fredi,' Rinaldi said.

'Yes,' I said. 'Come in early.' He made a face and went out the door. The major was standing with us. 'He's very tired and overworked,' he said. 'He thinks too he has syphilis. I don't believe it but he may have. He is treating himself for it. Good night. You will leave before daylight, Enrico?'

'Yes.'

'Goodbye then,' he said. 'Good luck. Peduzzi will wake you and go with you.'

'Goodbye, Signor Maggiore.'

'Goodbye. They talk about an Austrian offensive but I don't believe it. I hope not. But anyway it won't be here. Gino will tell you everything. The telephone works well now.'

'I'll call regularly.'

'Please do. Good night. Don't let Rinaldi drink so much brandy.'

'I'll try not to.'

'Good night, priest.'

'Good night, Signor Maggiore.'

He went off into his office.

CHAPTER 26

I WENT to the door and looked out. It had stopped raining but there was a mist.

'Should we go upstairs?' I asked the priest.

'I can only stay a little while.'

'Come on up.'

We climbed the stairs and went into my room. I lay down on Rinaldi's bed. The priest sat on my cot that the orderly had set up. It was dark in the room.

'Well,' he said, 'how are you really?'

'I'm all right. I'm tired tonight.'

'I'm tired too, but from no cause.'

'What about the war?'

'I think it will be over soon. I don't know why, but I feel it.'

'How do you feel it?'

'You know how your major is? Gentle? Many people are like that now.'

'I feel that way myself,' I said.

'It has been a terrible summer,' said the priest. He was surer of himself now than when I had gone away. 'You cannot believe how it has been. Except that you have been there and you know how it can be. Many people have realized the war this summer. Officers whom I thought could never realize it realize it now.'

'What will happen?' I stroked the blanket with my hand.

'I do not know but I do not think it can go on much longer.'

'What will happen?'

'They will stop fighting.'

'Who?'

'Both sides.'

'I hope so,' I said.

'You don't believe it?'

'I don't believe both sides will stop fighting at once.'

'I suppose not. It is too much to expect. But when I see the changes in men I do not think it can go on.'

'Who won the fighting this summer?'

'No one.'

'The Austrians won,' I said. 'They kept them from taking San Gabriele. They've won. They won't stop fighting.'

'If they feel as we feel they may stop. They have gone through the same thing.'

'No one ever stopped when they were winning.'

'You discourage me.'

'I can only say what I think.'

'Then you think it will go on and on? Nothing will ever happen?'

'I don't know. I only think the Austrians will not stop when they have won a victory. It is in defeat that we become Christian.'

'The Austrians are Christians — except for the Bosnians.'

'I don't mean technically Christian. I mean like Our Lord.'

He said nothing.

'We are all gentler now because we are beaten. How would Our Lord have been if Peter had rescued Him in the Garden?'

'He would have been just the same.'

'I don't think so,' I said.

'You discourage me,' he said. 'I believe and I pray that something will happen. I have felt it very close.'

'Something may happen,' I said. 'But it will happen only to us. If they felt the way we do, it would be all right. But they have beaten us. They feel another way.'

'Many of the soldiers have always felt this way. It is not because they were beaten.'

'They were beaten to start with. They were beaten when they took them from their farms and put them in the army. That is why the peasant has wisdom, because he is defeated from the start. Put him in power and see how wise he is.'

He did not say anything. He was thinking.

'Now I am depressed myself,' I said. 'That's why I never think about these things. I never think and yet when I begin to talk I say the things I have found out in my mind without thinking.'

'I had hoped for something.'

'Defeat?'

'No. Something more.'

'There isn't anything more. Except victory. It may be worse.'

'I hoped for a long time for victory.'

'Me too.'

'Now I don't know.'

'It has to be one or the other.'

'I don't believe in victory any more.'

'I don't. But I don't believe in defeat. Though it may be better.'

'What do you believe in?'

'In sleep,' I said. He stood up.

'I am very sorry to have stayed so long. But I like so to talk with you.'

'It is very nice to talk again. I said that about sleeping, meaning nothing.'

We stood up and shook hands in the dark.

'I sleep at 307 now,' he said.

'I go out on post early tomorrow.'

'I'll see you when you come back.'

'We'll have a walk and talk together.' I walked with him to the door.

'Don't go down,' he said. 'It is very nice that you are back. Though not so nice for you.' He put his hand on my shoulder.

'It's all right for me,' I said. 'Good night.'

'Good night. Ciaou!'

'Ciaou!' I said. I was deadly sleepy.

CHAPTER 27

I WOKE when Rinaldi came in but he did not talk and I went back to sleep again. In the morning I was dressed and gone before it was light. Rinaldi did not wake when I left.

I had not seen the Bainsizza before and it was strange to go up the slope where the Austrians had been, beyond the place on the river where I had been wounded. There was a steep new road and many trucks. Beyond the road flattened out and I saw woods and steep hills in the mist. There were woods that had been taken quickly and not smashed. Then beyond where the road was not protected by the hills it was screened by matting on the sides and over the top. The road ended in a wrecked village. The lines were up beyond. There was much artillery around. The houses were badly smashed but things were very well organized and there were signboards everywhere. We found Gino and he got us some coffee and later I went with him and met various people and saw the posts. Gino said the British cars were working further down the Bainsizza at Ravne. He had great admiration for the British. There was still a certain amount of shelling, he said, but not many wounded. There would be many sick now the rains had started. The Austrians were supposed to attack but he did not believe it. We were supposed to attack too, but they had not brought up any new troops so he thought that was off too. Food was scarce and he would be glad to get a full meal in Gorizia. What kind of supper had I had? I told him and he said that would be wonderful. He was especially impressed by the *dolce*. I did not describe it in detail, only said it was a *dolce*, and I think he believed it was something more elaborate than bread pudding.

Did I know where he was going to go? I said I didn't but that some of the other cars were at Caporetto. He hoped he would go up that way. It was a nice little place and he liked the high mountain hauling up beyond. He was a nice boy and everyone seemed to like him. He said where it really had been hell was at San Gabriele and the attack beyond Lom that had gone bad. He said the Austrians had a great amount of artillery in the woods along Ternova ridge beyond and above us, and shelled the roads badly at night. There was a battery of naval guns that had gotten on his nerves. I would recognize them because of their flat trajectory. You heard the report and then the shriek commenced almost instantly. They usually fired two guns at once, one right after the other, and the fragments from the burst were enormous. He showed me one, a smoothly jagged piece of metal over a foot long. It looked like babbiting metal.

'I don't suppose they are so effective,' Gino said. 'But they scare me. They all sound as though they came directly for you. There is the boom, then instantly the shriek and burst. What's the use of not being wounded if they scare you to death?'

He said there were Croats in the lines opposite us now and some Magyars. Our troops were still in the attacking positions. There was no wire to speak of and no place to fall back to if there should be an Austrian attack. There were fine positions for defence along the low mountains that came up out of the plateau but nothing had been done about organizing them for defence. What did I think about the Bainsizza anyway?

I had expected it to be flatter, more like a plateau. I had not realized it was so broken up.

'Alto piano,' Gino said, 'but no piano.'

We went back to the cellar of the house where he lived. I said I thought a ridge that flattened out on top and had a little depth would be easier and more practical to hold than a succession of small mountains. It was no harder to attack up a mountain than on the level, I argued. 'That depends on the mountains,' he said. 'Look at San Gabriele.'

'Yes,' I said, 'but where they had trouble was at the top where it was flat. They got up to the top easy enough.'

'Not so easy,' he said.

'Yes,' I said, 'but that was a special case because it was a fortress rather than a mountain anyway. The Austrians had been fortifying it for years.' I meant tactically speaking in a war where there was some movement. A succession of mountains were nothing to hold as a line because it was too easy to turn them. You should have possible mobility and a mountain is not very mobile. Also, people always over-shoot down hill. If the flank were turned, the best men would be left on the highest mountain. I did not believe in a war in mountains. I had thought about it a ot, I said. You pinched off one mountain and they pinched off another but when something really started everyone had to get down off the mountains.

'What were you going to do if you had a mountain frontier?' he asked.

'I had not worked that out yet,' I said, and we both laughed. 'But,' I said, 'in the old days the Austrians were always whipped in the quadrilateral around Verona. They let them come down on to the plain and whipped them there.'

'Yes,' said Gino. 'But those were Frenchmen and you can work out military problems clearly when you are fighting in somebody else's country.'

160

'Yes,' I agreed, 'when it is your own country you cannot use it so scientifically.'

'The Russians did, to trap Napoleon.'

'Yes, but they had plenty of country. If you tried to retreat to trap Napoleon in Italy you would find yourself in Brindisi.'

'A terrible place,' said Gino. 'Have you ever been there?'

'Not to stay.'

'I am a patriot,' Gino said. 'But I cannot love Brindisi or Taranto.'

'Do you love the Bainsizza?' I asked.

'The soil is sacred,' he said. 'But I wish it grew more potatoes. You know when we came here we found fields of potatoes the Austrians had planted.'

'Has the food really been short?'

'I myself have never had enough to eat but I am a big eater and I have not starved. The mess is average. The regiments in the line get pretty good food but those in support don't get so much. Something is wrong somewhere. There should be plenty of food.'

'The dogfish are selling it somewhere else.'

'Yes, they give the battalions in the front line as much as they can but the ones in back are very short. They have eaten all the Austrians' potatoes and chestnuts from the woods. They ought to feed them better. We are big eaters. I am sure there is plenty of food. It is very bad for the soldiers to be short of food. Have you ever noticed the difference it makes in the way you think?'

'Yes,' I said. 'It can't win a war but it can lose one.'

'We won't talk about losing. There is enough talk about losing. What has been done this summer cannot have been done in vain.'

I did not say anything. I was always embarrassed by the words sacred, glorious and sacrifice and the expression in vain. We had heard them, sometimes standing in the rain almost out of earshot, so that only the shouted words came through, and had read them, on proclamations that were slapped up by billposters over other proclamations, now for a long time, and I had seen nothing sacred, and the things that were glorious had no glory and the sacrifices were like the stock-yards at Chicago if nothing was done with the meat except to bury it. There were many words that you could not stand to hear and finally only the names of places had dignity. Certain numbers were the same way and certain dates and these with the names of the places were all you could say and have them mean anything. Abstract words such as glory, honour, courage, or hallow were obscene beside the concrete names of villages, the numbers of roads, the names of rivers, the numbers of regiments and the dates. Gino was a patriot, so he said things that separated us sometimes, but he was also a fine boy and I understood his being a patriot. He was born one. He left with Peduzzi in the car to go back to Gorizia.

It stormed all that day. The wind drove down the rain and everywhere there was standing water and mud. The plaster of the broken houses was grey and wet. Late in the afternoon the rain stopped and from our number two post I saw the bare wet autumn country with clouds over the tops of the hills and the straw screening over the roads wet and dripping. The sun came out once before it went down and shone on the bare woods beyond the ridge. There were many Austrian guns in the woods on that ridge but only a few fired. I watched the sudden round puffs of shrapnel smoke in the sky above a broken farmhouse near where the line was; soft puffs with a yellow-white flash in the centre. You saw the flash, then heard the crack, then saw the smoke ball distort and thin in the wind. There were many iron shrapnel balls in the rubble of the houses and on the road beside the broken house where the post was, but they did not shell near the post that afternoon. We loaded two cars and drove down the road that was screened with wet mats and the last of the sun came through in the breaks between the strips of matting. Before we were out on the clear road behind the hill the sun was down. We went on down the clear road and as it turned a corner into the open and went into the square arched tunnel of matting the rain started again.

The wind rose in the night and at three o'clock in the morning with the rain coming in sheets there was a bombardment and the Croatians came over across the mountain meadows and through patches of woods and into the front line. They fought in the dark in the rain and a counter-attack of scared men from the second line drove them back. There was much shelling and many rockets in the rain and machine-gun and rifle fire all along the line. They did not come again and it was quieter and between the gusts of wind and rain we could hear the sound of a great bombardment far to the north.

The wounded were coming into the post, some were carried on stretchers, some walking and some were brought on the backs of men that came across the field. They were wet to the skin and all were scared. We filled two cars with stretcher cases as they came up from the cellar of the post and as I shut the door of the second car and fastened it I felt the rain on my face turn to snow. The flakes were coming heavy and fast in the rain.

When daylight came the storm was still blowing but the snow had stopped. It had melted as it fell on the wet ground and now it was raining again. There was another attack just after daylight but it was unsuccessful. We expected an attack all day but it did not come until the sun was going down. The bombardment started to the south below the long wooded ridge where the Austrian guns were concentrated. We expected a bombardment but it did not come. It was getting dark. Guns were firing from the field behind the village and the shells, going away, had a comfortable sound.

We heard that the attack to the south had been unsuccessful. They did not attack that night but we heard that they had broken through to the north. In the night word came that we were to prepare to retreat. The captain at the post told me this. He had it from the Brigade. A little while later he came from the telephone and said it was a lie. The Brigade had received orders that the line of the Bainsizza should be held no matter what happened. I asked about the break through and he said that he had heard at the Brigade that the Austrians had broken through the twenty-seventh army corps up towards Caporetto. There had been a great battle in the north all day.

'If those bastards let them through we are cooked,' he said.

'It's Germans that are attacking,' one of the medical officers said. The word Germans was something to be frightened of. We did not want to have anything to do with the Germans.

'There are fifteen divisions of Germans,' the medical officer said. 'They have broken through and we will be cut off.'

'At the Brigade they say this line is to be held. They say they have not broken through badly and that we will hold a line across the mountains from Monte Maggiore.'

'Where do they hear this?'

'From the Division.'

'The word that we were to retreat came from the Division.'

'We work under the Army Corps,' I said. 'But here I work under you. Naturally when you tell me to go I will go. But get the orders straight.'

'The orders are that we stay here. You clear the wounded from here to the clearing station.'

'Sometimes we clear from the clearing station to the field hospitals, too,' I said. 'Tell me, I have never seen a retreat — if there is a retreat how are all the wounded evacuated?'

'They are not. They take as many as they can and leave the rest.'

'What will I take in the cars?'

'Hospital equipment.'

'All right,' I said.

The next night the retreat started. We heard that Germans and Austrians had broken through in the north and were coming down the mountain valleys towards Cividale and Udine. The retreat was orderly, wet and sullen. In the night, going slowly along the crowded roads we passed troops marching under the rain, guns, horses pulling wagons, mules, motor trucks, all moving away from the front. There was no more disorder than in an advance.

That night we helped empty the field hospitals that had been set up in the least ruined villages of the plateau, taking the wounded down to Plava on the river-bed: and the next day hauled all day in the rain to evacuate the hospitals and clearing station at Plava. It rained steadily and the army of the Bainsizza moved down off the plateau in the October rain and across the river where the great victories had commenced in the spring of that year. We came into Gorizia in the middle of the next day. The rain had stopped and the town was nearly empty. As we came up the street they were loading the girls from the soldiers' whorehouse into a truck. There were seven girls and they had on their hats and coats and carried small suitcases. Two of them were crying. Of the others one smiled at us and put out her tongue and fluttered it up and down. She had thick full lips and black eyes.

I stopped the car and went over and spoke to the matron. The girls from the officers' house had left early that morning, she said. Where were they going? To Conegliano, she said. The truck started. The girl with thick lips put out her tongue again at us. The matron waved. The two girls kept on crying. The others looked interestedly out at the town. I got back in the car.

'We ought to go with them,' Bonello said. 'That would be a good trip.'

'We'll have a good trip,' I said.

'We'll have a hell of a trip.'

'That's what I mean,' I said. We came up the drive to the villa.

'I'd like to be there when some of those tough babies climb in.'

'You think they will?'

'Sure. Everybody in the Second Army knows that matron.' We were outside the villa.

'They call her the Mother Superior,' Bonello said. 'The girls

165

are new but everybody knows her. They must have brought them up just before the retreat.'

'They'll have a time.'

'I'll say they'll have a time. I'd like to have a crack at them for nothing. They charge too much at that house anyway. The government gyps us.'

'Take the car out and have the mechanics go over it,' I said. 'Change the oil and check the differential. Fill it up and then get some sleep.'

'Yes, Signor Tenente.'

The villa was empty. Rinaldi was gone with the hospital. The major was gone taking hospital personnel in the staff car. There was a note on the window for me to fill the cars with the material piled in the hall and to proceed to Pordenone. The mechanics were gone already. I went out back to the garage. The other two cars came in while I was there and their drivers got down. It was starting to rain again.

'I'm so — sleepy I went to sleep three times coming here from Plava,' Piani said. 'What are we going to do, Tenente?'

'We'll change the oil, grease them, fill them up, then take them around in front and load up the junk they've left.'

'Then do we start?'

'No, we'll sleep for three hours.'

'Christ, I'm glad to sleep,' Bonello said. 'I couldn't keep awake driving.'

'How's your car, Aymo?' I asked.

'It's all right.'

'Get me a monkey suit and I'll help you with the oil.'

'Don't you do that, Tenente,' Aymo said. 'It's nothing to do. You go and pack your things.'

'My things are all packed,' I said. 'I'll go and carry out the stuff that they left for us. Bring the cars around as soon as they're ready.'

They brought the cars around to the front of the villa and we loaded them with the hospital equipment which was piled in the hallway. When it was all in, the three cars stood in line down the driveway under the trees in the rain. We went inside.

'Make a fire in the kitchen and dry your things,' I said.

'I don't care about dry clothes,' Paini said. 'I want to sleep.'

'I'm going to sleep on the major's bed,' Bonello said.

'I don't care where I sleep,' Piani said.

'There are two beds in here.' I opened the door.

'I never knew what was in that room,' Bonello said.

'That was old fish-face's room,' Piani said.

'You two sleep in there,' I said. 'I'll wake you.'

'The Austrians will wake us if you sleep too long, Tenente,' Bonello said.

'I won't oversleep,' I said. 'Where's Aymo?'

'He went out in the kitchen.'

'Get to sleep,' I said.

'I'll sleep,' Piani said. 'I've been asleep sitting up all day. The whole top of my head kept coming down over my eyes.'

'Take your boots off,' Bonello said. 'That's old fish-face's bed.'

'Fish-face is nothing to me.' Piani lay on the bed, his muddy boots straight out, his head on his arm. I went out to the kitchen. Aymo had a fire in the stove and a kettle of water on.

'I thought I'd start some *pasta asciutta*,' he said. 'We'll be hungry when we wake up.'

'Aren't you sleepy, Bartolomeo?'

'Not so sleepy. When the water boils I'll leave it. The fire will go down.'

'You'd better get some sleep,' I said. 'We can eat cheese and monkey meat.'

'This is better,' he said. 'Something hot will be good for those two anarchists. You go to sleep, Tenente.'

'There's a bed in the major's room.'

'You sleep there.'

'No, I'm going up to my old room. Do you want a drink, Bartolomeo?'

'When we go, Tenente. Now it wouldn't do me any good.'

'If you wake in three hours and I haven't called you, wake me, will you?'

'I haven't any watch, Tenente.'

'There's a clock on the wall in the major's room.'

'All right.'

I went out then through the dining-room and the hall and up the marble stairs to the room where I had lived with Rinaldi. It was raining outside. I went to the window and looked out. It was getting dark and I saw the three cars standing in line under the trees. The trees were dripping in the rain. It was cold and the drops hung to the branches. I went back to Rinaldi's bed and lay down and let sleep take me.

We ate in the kitchen before we started. Aymo had a basin of spaghetti with onions and tinned meat chopped up in it. We sat around the table and drank two bottles of the wine that had been left in the cellar of the villa. It was dark outside and still raining. Piani sat at the table very sleepy.

'I like a retreat better than an advance.' Bonello said. 'On a retreat we drink barbera.'

'We drink it now. Tomorrow maybe we drink rainwater,' Aymo said.

'Tomorrow we'll be in Udine. We'll drink champagne.'

'That's where the slackers live. Wake up, Piani! We'll drink champagne tomorrow in Udine!'

'I'm awake,' Piani said. He filled his plate with the spaghetti and meat. 'Couldn't you find tomato sauce, Barto?'

'There wasn't any,' Aymo said.

'We'll drink champagne in Udine,' Bonello said. He filled his glass with the clear red barbera.

'Have you eaten enough, Tenente?' Aymo asked.

'I've got plenty. Give me the bottle, Bartolomeo.'

'I have a bottle apiece to take in the cars,' Aymo said.

'Did you sleep at all?'

'I don't need much sleep. I slept a little.'

'Tomorrow we'll sleep in the king's bed,' Bonello said. He was feeling very good.

'I'll sleep with the queen,' Bonello said. He looked to see how I took the joke.

'Shut up,' I said. 'You get too funny with a little wine.' Outside it was raining hard. I looked at my watch. It was half-past nine.

'It's time to roll,' I said and stood up.

'Who are you going to ride with, Tenente?' Bonello asked.

'With Aymo. Then you come. Then Piani. We'll start out on the road for Cormons.'

'I'm afraid I'll go to sleep,' Piani said.

'All right. I'll ride with you. Then Bonello. Then Aymo.'

'That's the best way,' Piani said. 'Because I'm so sleepy.'

'I'll drive and you sleep awhile.'

'No. I can drive just so long as I know somebody will wake me up if I go to sleep.'

'I'll wake you up. Put out the lights, Barto.'

'You might as well leave them,' Bonello said. 'We've got no more use for this place.'

'I have a small locker trunk in my room,' I said. 'Will you help take it down, Piani?'

'We'll take it,' Piani said. 'Come on, Aldo.' He went off into the hall with Bonello. I heard them going upstairs.

'This was a fine place,' Bartolomeo Aymo said. He put two bottles of wine and half a cheese into his haversack. 'There won't be a place like this again. Where will they retreat to, Tenente?'

'Beyond the Tagliamento, they say. The hospital and the sector are to be at Pordenone.'

'This is a better town than Pordenone.'

'I don't know Pordenone,' I said. 'I've just been through there.'

'It's not much of a place,' Aymo said.

CHAPTER 28

As we moved out through the town it was empty in the rain and the dark except for columns of troops and guns that were going through the main street. There were many trucks too and some carts going through on other streets and converging on the main road. When we were out past the tanneries on to the main road the troops, the motor trucks, the horse-drawn carts and the guns were in one wide slow-moving column. We moved slowly but steadily in the rain, the radiator cap of our car almost against the tailboard of a truck that was loaded high, the load covered with wet canvas. Then the truck stopped. The whole column was stopped. It started again and we went a little farther, then stopped. I got out and walked ahead, going between the trucks and carts and under the wet necks of the horses. The block was farther ahead. I left the road, crossed the ditch on a footboard and walked along the field beyond the ditch. I could see the stalled column between the trees in the rain as I went forward across from it in the field. I went about a mile. The column did not move, although on the other side beyond the stalled vehicles I could see the troops moving. I went back to the cars. This block might extend as far as Udine. Piani was asleep over the wheel. I climbed up beside him and went to sleep too. Several hours later I heard the truck ahead of us grinding into gear. I woke Piani and we started, moving a few yards, then stopping, then going on again. It was still raining.

The column stalled again in the night and did not start. I got down and went back to see Aymo and Bonello. Bonello had two sergeants of engineers on the seat of his car with him. They stiffened when I came up.

'They were left to do something to a bridge,' Bonello said. 'They can't find their unit so I gave them a ride.'

'With the Sir Lieutenant's permission.'

'With permission,' I said.

'The lieutenant is an American,' Bonello said. 'He'll give anybody a ride.'

One of the sergeants smiled. The other asked Bonello if I was an Italian from North or South America.

'He's not an Italian. He's North American English.'

The sergeants were polite but did not believe it. I left them and went back to Aymo. He had two girls on the seat with him and was sitting back in the corner and smoking.

'Barto, Barto,' I said. He laughed.

'Talk to them, Tenente,' he said. 'I can't understand them. Hey!' he put his hand on the girl's thigh and squeezed it in a friendly way. The girl drew her shawl tight around her and pushed his hand away. 'Hey!' he said. 'Tell the Tenente your name and what you're doing here.'

The girl looked at me fiercely. The other girl kept her eyes down. The girl who looked at me said something in a dialect I could not understand a word of. She was plump and dark and looked about sixteen.

'Sorella?' I asked and pointed at the other girl.

She nodded her head and smiled.

'All right,' I said and patted her knee. I felt her stiffen away when I touched her. The sister never looked up. She looked perhaps a year younger. Aymo put his hand on the elder girl's thigh and she pushed it away. He laughed at her.

'Good man,' he pointed at himself. 'Good man,' he pointed at me. 'Don't you worry.' The girl looked at him fiercely. The pair of them were like two wild birds.

'What does she ride with me for if she doesn't like me?' Aymo asked. 'They got right up in the car the minute I motioned to them.' He turned to the girl. 'Don't worry,' he said. 'No danger of —,' using the vulgar word. 'No place for —.' I could see she understood the word and that was all. Her eyes looked at him very scared. She pulled the shawl tight. 'Car all full,' Aymo said. 'No danger of —. No place for —.' Every time he said the word the girl stiffened a little. Then sitting stiffly and looking at him she began to cry. I saw her lips working and then tears came down her plump cheeks. Her sister, not looking up, took her hand and they sat there together. The older one, who had been so fierce, began to sob.

'I guess I scared her,' Aymo said. 'I didn't mean to scare her.'

Bartolomeo brought out his knapsack and cut off two pieces of cheese. 'Here,' he said. 'Stop crying.'

The older girl shook her head and still cried, but the younger girl took the cheese and commenced to eat. After a while the younger girl gave her sister the second piece of cheese and they both ate. The older sister still sobbed a little.

'She'll be all right after a while,' Aymo said.

An idea came to him. 'Virgin?' he asked the girl next to him. She nodded her head vigorously. 'Virgin too?' he pointed to the sister. Both the girls nodded their heads and the elder said something in dialect.

'That's all right,' Bartolomeo said. 'That's all right.'

Both the girls seemed cheered.

I left them sitting together with Aymo sitting back in the corner and went back to Piani's car. The column of vehicles did not move but the troops kept passing alongside. It was still raining hard and I thought some of the stops in the movement of the column might be from cars with wet wiring. More likely they were from horses or men going to sleep. Still, traffic could tie up in cities when everyone was awake. It was the combination of horse and motor vehicles. They did not help each other any. The peasants' carts did not help much either. Those were a couple of fine girls with Barto. A retreat was no place for two virgins. Real virgins. Probably very religious. If there were no war we would probably all be in bed. In bed I lay me down my head. Bed and board. Stiff as a board in bed. Catherine was in bed now between two sheets, over her and under her. Which side did she sleep on? Maybe she wasn't asleep. Maybe she was lying thinking about me. Blow, blow, ye western wind. Well, it blew and it wasn't the small rain but the big rain down that rained. It rained all night. You knew it rained down that rain. Look at it. Christ, that my love were in my arms and I in my bed again. That my love Catherine. That my sweet love Catherine down might rain. Blow her again to me. Well, we were in it. Everyone was caught in it and the small rain would not quiet it. 'Good night, Catherine,' I said out loud. 'I hope you sleep well. If it's too uncomfortable, darling, lie on the other side,' I said. 'I'll get you some cold water. In a little while it will be morning and then it won't be so bad. I'm sorry he makes you so uncomfortable. Try and go to sleep, sweet.'

I was asleep all the time, she said. You've been talking in your sleep. Are you all right?

Are you really there?

Of course, I'm here. I wouldn't go away. This doesn't make any difference between us.

You're so lovely and sweet. You wouldn't go away in the night, would you?

Of course I wouldn't go away. I'm always here. I come whenever you want me.

'—,' Piani said. 'They've started again.'

'I was dopey,' I said. I looked at my watch. It was three o'clock in the morning. I reached back behind the seat for a bottle of the barbera.

'You talked out loud,' Piani said.

'I was having a dream in English,' I said.

The rain was slacking and we were moving along. Before daylight we were stalled again and when it was light we were at a little rise in the ground and I saw the road of the retreat stretched out far ahead, everything stationary except for the infantry filtering through. We started to move again but seeing the rate of progress in the daylight, I knew we were going to have to get off that main road some way and go across country if we ever hoped to reach Udine.

In the night many peasants had joined the column from the roads of the country and in the column there were carts loaded

with household goods; there were mirrors projecting up between mattresses, and chickens and ducks tied to carts. There was
a sewing machine on the cart ahead of us in the rain. They had
saved the most valuable things. On some carts the women sat
huddled from the rain and others walked beside the carts keeping
as close to them as they could. There were dogs now in the
column, keeping under the wagons as they moved along. The
road was muddy, the ditches at the side were high with water
and beyond the trees that lined the road the fields looked too
wet and too soggy to try to cross. I got down from the car and
worked up the road a way, looking for a place where I could see
ahead to find a side-road we could take across country. I knew
there were many side-roads but did not want one that would
lead to nothing. I could not remember them because we had
always passed them bowling along in the car on the main road
and they all looked much alike. Now I knew we must find one
if we hoped to get through. No one knew where the Austrians
were nor how things were going but I was certain that if the
rain should stop and planes come over and get to work on that
column that it would be all over. All that was needed was for a
few men to leave their trucks or a few horses to be killed to tie
up completely the movement on the road.

The rain was not falling so heavily now and I thought it might
clear. I went ahead along the edge of the road and when there
was a small road that led off to the north between two fields
with a hedge of trees on both sides, I thought that we had better
take it and hurried back to the cars. I told Piani to turn off and
went back to tell Bonello and Aymo.

'If it leads nowhere we can turn around and cut back in,' I
said.

'What about these?' Bonello asked. His two sergeants were
beside him on the seat. They were unshaven but still military
looking in the early morning.

'They'll be good to push,' I said. I went back to Aymo and
told him we were going to try it across country.

'What about my virgin family?' Aymo asked. The two girls were asleep.

'They won't be very useful,' I said. 'You ought to have some one that could push.'

'They could go back in the car,' Aymo said. 'There's room in the car.'

'All right if you want them,' I said. 'Pick up somebody with a wide back to push.'

'Bersaglieri,' Aymo smiled. 'They have the widest backs. They measure them. How do you feel, Tenente?'

'Fine. How are you?'

'Fine. But very hungry.'

'There ought to be something up that road and we will stop and eat.'

'How's your leg, Tenente?'

'Fine,' I said. Standing on the step and looking up ahead I could see Piani's car pulling out on to the little side-road and starting up it, his car showing through the hedge of bare branches. Bonello turned off and followed him and then Piani worked his way out and we followed the two ambulances ahead along the narrow road between hedges. It led to a farmhouse. We found Piani and Bonello stopped in the farmyard. The house was low and long with a trellis with a grape-vine over the door. There was a well in the yard and Piani was getting up water to fill his radiator. So much going in low gear had boiled it out. The farmhouse was deserted. I looked back down the road, the farmhouse was on a slight elevation above the plain, and we could see over the country, and saw the road, the hedges, the fields and the line of trees along the main road where the retreat was passing. The two sergeants were looking through the house. The girls were awake and looking at the courtyard, the well and the two big ambulances in front of the farmhouse, with three drivers at the well. One of the sergeants came out with a clock in his hand.

'Put it back,' I said. He looked at me, went in the house and came back without the clock.

'Where's your partner?' I asked.

'He's gone to the latrine.' He got up on the seat of the ambulance. He was afraid we would leave him.

'What about breakfast, Tenente?' Bonello asked. 'We could eat something. It wouldn't take very long.'

'Do you think this road going down on the other side will lead to anything?'

'Sure.'

'All right. Let's eat.' Piani and Bonello went in the house.

'Come on,' Aymo said to the girls. He held his hand to help them down. The older sister shook her head. They were not going into any deserted house. They looked after us.

'They are difficult,' Aymo said. We went into the farmhouse together. It was large and dark and abandoned feeling. Bonello and Piani were in the kitchen.

'There's not much to eat,' Piani said. 'They've cleaned it out.'

Bonello sliced a big white cheese on the heavy kitchen table.

'Where was the cheese?'

'In the cellar. Piani found wine too and apples.'

'That's a good breakfast.'

Piani was taking the wooden cork out of a big wicker-covered wine-jug. He tipped it and poured a copper pan full.

'It smells all right,' he said. 'Find some beakers, Barto.'

The two sergeants came in.

'Have some cheese, sergeants,' Bonello said.

'We should go,' one of the sergeants said, eating his cheese and drinking a cup of wine.

'We'll go. Don't worry,' Bonello said.

'An army travels on its stomach,' I said.

'What?' asked the sergeant.

'It's better to eat.'

'Yes. But time is precious.'

'I believe the bastards have eaten already,' Piani said. The sergeants looked at him. They hated the lot of us.

'You know the road?' one of them asked me.

176

'No,' I said. They looked at each other.

'We would do best to start,' the first one said.

'We are starting,' I said. I drank another cup of the red wine. It tasted very good after the cheese and apple.

'Bring the cheese,' I said and went out. Bonello came out carrying the great jug of wine.

'That's too big,' I said. He looked at it regretfully.

'I guess it is,' he said. 'Give me the canteens to fill.' He filled the canteens and some of the wine ran out on the stone paving of the courtyard. Then he picked up the wine jug and put it just inside the door.

'The Austrians can find it without breaking the door down,' he said.

'We'll roll,' I said. 'Piani and I will go ahead.' The two engineers were already on the seat beside Bonello. The girls were eating cheese and apples. Aymo was smoking. We started off down the narrow road. I looked back at the two cars coming and the farmhouse. It was a fine, low, solid stone house and the ironwork of the well was very good. Ahead of us the road was narrow and muddy and there was a high hedge on either side. Behind, the cars were following closely.

CHAPTER 29

At noon we were stuck in a muddy road about, as nearly as we could figure, ten kilometres from Udine. The rain had stopped during the forenoon and three times we had heard planes coming, seen them pass overhead, watched them go far to the left and heard them bombing on the main high road. We had worked through a network of secondary roads and had taken many roads that were blind, but had always, by backing up and finding another road, gotten closer to Udine. Now, Aymo's car, in backing so that we might get out of a blind road, had gotten into the soft earth at the side and the wheels, spinning, had dug deeper and deeper until the car rested on its differential. The thing to do now was to dig out in front of the wheels, put in brush so that the chains could grip, and then push until the car was on the road. We were all down on the road around the car. The two sergeants looked at the car and examined the wheels. Then they started off down the road without a word. I went after them.

'Come on,' I said. 'Cut some brush.'

'We have to go,' one said.

'Get busy,' I said, 'and cut brush.'

'We have to go,' one said. The other said nothing. They were in a hurry to start. They would not look at me.

'I order you to come back to the car and cut brush,' I said. The one sergeant turned. 'We have to go on. In a little while you will be cut off. You can't order us. You're not our officer.'

'I order you to cut brush,' I said. They turned and started down the road.

'Halt,' I said. They kept on down the muddy road, the hedge on either side. 'I order you to halt,' I called. They went a little faster. I opened up my holster, took the pistol, aimed at the one who had talked the most, and fired. I missed and they both started to run. I shot three times and dropped one. The other went through the hedge and was out of sight. I fired at him through the hedge as he ran across the field. The pistol clicked empty and I put in another clip. I saw it was too far to shoot at the second sergeant. He was far across the field, running, his head held low. I commenced to reload the empty clip. Bonello came up.

'Let me go finish him,' he said. I handed him the pistol and he walked down to where the sergeant of engineers lay face down across the road. Bonello leaned over, put the pistol against the man's head and pulled the trigger. The pistol did not fire.

'You have to cock it,' I said. He cocked it and fired twice. He

178

took hold of the sergeant's legs and pulled him to the side of the road so he lay beside the hedge. He came back and handed me the pistol.

'The son of a bitch,' he said. He looked towards the sergeant. 'You see me shoot him, Tenente?'

'We've got to get the brush quickly,' I said. 'Did I hit the other one at all?'

'I don't think so,' Aymo said. 'He was too far away to hit with a pistol.'

'The dirty scum,' Piani said. We were all cutting twigs and branches. Everything had been taken out of the car. Bonello was digging out in front of the wheels. When we were ready Aymo started the car and put it into gear. The wheels spun round throwing brush and mud. Bonello and I pushed until we could feel our joints crack. The car would not move.

'Rock her back and forth, Barto,' I said.

He drove the engine in reverse, then forward. The wheels only dug in deeper. Then the car was resting on the differential again, and the wheels spun freely in the holes they had dug. I straightened up.

'We'll try her with a rope,' I said.

'I don't think it's any use, Tenente. You can't get a straight pull.'

'We have to try it,' I said. 'She won't come out any other way.'

Piani's and Bonello's cars could only move straight ahead down the narrow road. We roped both cars together and pulled. The wheels only pulled sideways against the ruts.

'It's no good,' I shouted. 'Stop it.'

Piani and Bonello got down from their cars and came back. Aymo got down. The girls were up the road about forty yards sitting on a stone wall.

'What do you say, Tenente?' Bonello asked.

'We'll dig out and try once more with the brush,' I said. I looked down the road. It was my fault. I had led them up here.

The sun was almost out from behind the clouds and the body of the sergeant lay beside the hedge.

'We'll put his coat and cape under,' I said. Bonello went to get them. I cut brush and Aymo and Piani dug out in front and between the wheels. I cut the cape, then ripped it in two, and laid it under the wheel in the mud, then piled brush for the wheels to catch. We were ready to start and Aymo got up on the seat and started the car. The wheels spun and we pushed and pushed. But it wasn't any use.

'It's finished,' I said. 'Is there anything you want in the car, Barto?'

Aymo climbed up with Bonello, carrying the cheese and two bottles of wine and his cape. Bonello, sitting behind the wheel was looking through the pockets of the sergeant's coat.

'Better throw the coat away,' I said. 'What about Barto's virgins?'

'They can get in the back,' Piani said. 'I don't think we are going far.'

I opened the back door of the ambulance.

'Come on,' I said. 'Get in.' The two girls climbed in and sat in the corner. They seemed to have taken no notice of the shooting. I looked back up the road. The sergeant lay in his dirty long-sleeved underwear. I got up with Piani and we started. We were going to try to cross the field. When the road entered the field I got down and walked ahead. If we could get across, there was a road on the other side. We could not get across. It was too soft and muddy for the cars. When they were finally and completely stalled, the wheels dug in to the hubs, we left them in the field and started on foot for Udine.

When we came to the road which led back towards the main highway I pointed down it to the two girls.

'Go down there,' I said. 'You'll meet people.' They looked at me. I took out my pocket-book and gave them each a ten-lira note. 'Go down there,' I said, pointing. 'Friends! Family!'

They did not understand but they held the money tightly and

started down the road. They looked back as though they were afraid I might take the money back. I watched them go down the road, their shawls close around them, looking back apprehensively at us. The three drivers were laughing.

'How much will you give me to go in that direction, Tenente?' Bonello asked.

'They're better off in a bunch of people than alone if they catch them,' I said.

'Give me two hundred lire and I'll walk straight back towards Austria,' Bonello said.

'They'd take it away from you,' Piani said.

'Maybe the war will be over,' Aymo said. We were going up the road as fast as we could. The sun was trying to come through. Beside the road were mulberry trees. Through the trees I could see our two big moving-vans of cars stuck in the field. Piani looked back too.

'They'll have to build a road to get them out,' he said.

'I wish to Christ we had bicycles,' Bonello said.

'Do they ride bicycles in America?' Aymo asked.

'They used to.'

'Here it is a great thing,' Aymo said. 'A bicycle is a splendid thing.'

'I wish to Christ we had bicycles,' Bonello said. 'I'm no walker.'

'Is that firing?' I asked. I thought I could hear firing a long way away.

'I don't know,' Aymo said. He listened.

'I think so,' I said.

'The first thing we will see will be the cavalry,' Piani said.

'I don't think they've got any cavalry.'

'I hope to Christ not,' Bonello said. 'I don't want to be stuck on a lance by any cavalry.'

'You certainly shot that sergeant, Tenente,' Piani said. We were walking fast.

'I killed him,' Bonello said. 'I never killed anybody in this war, and all my life I've wanted to kill a sergeant.'

'You killed him on the sit all right,' Piani said. 'He wasn't flying very fast when you killed him.'

'Never mind. That's one thing I can always remember. I killed that — of a sergeant.'

'What will you say in confession?' Aymo asked.

'I'll say, Bless me, father, I killed a sergeant.' They all laughed.

'He's an anarchist,' Piani said. 'He doesn't go to church.'

'Piani's an anarchist too,' Bonello said.

'Are you really anarchists?' I asked.

'No, Tenente. We're socialists. We come from Imola.'

'Haven't you ever been there?'

'No.'

'By Christ it's a fine place, Tenente. You come there after the war and we'll show you something.'

'Are you all socialists?'

'Everybody.'

'Is it a fine town?'

'Wonderful. You never saw a town like that.'

'How did you get to be socialists?'

'We're all socialists. Everybody is a socialist. We've always been socialists.'

'You come, Tenente. We'll make you a socialist too.'

Ahead the road turned off to the left and there was a little hill and, beyond a stone wall, an apple orchard. As the road went uphill they ceased talking. We walked along together all going fast against time.

CHAPTER 30

LATER we were on a road that led to a river. There was a long line of abandoned trucks and carts on the road leading up to the bridge. No one was in sight. The river was high and the bridge had been blown up in the centre; the stone arch was fallen into the river and the brown water was going over it. We went on up the bank looking for a place to cross. Up above I knew there was a railway bridge and I thought we might be able to get across there. The path was wet and muddy. We did not see any troops; only abandoned trucks and stores. Along the river bank there was nothing and no one but the wet brush and muddy ground. We went up to the bank and finally we saw the railway bridge.

'What a beautiful bridge,' Aymo said. It was a long plain iron bridge across what was usually a dry river-bed.

'We better hurry and get across before they blow it up,' I said.

'There's nobody to blow it up,' Piani said. 'They're all gone.'

'It's probably mined,' Bonello said. 'You cross first, Tenente.'

'Listen to the anarchist,' Aymo said. 'Make him go first.'

'I'll go,' I said. 'It won't be mined to blow up with one man.'

'You see,' Piani said. 'That is brains. Why haven't you brains, anarchist?'

'If I had brains I wouldn't be here,' Bonello said.

'That's pretty good, Tenente,' Aymo said.

'That's pretty good,' I said. We were close to the bridge now. The sky had clouded over again and it was raining a little. The bridge looked long and solid. We climbed up the embankment.

'Come one at a time,' I said and started across the bridge. I watched the ties and the rails for any trip-wires or signs of explosive but I saw nothing. Down below the gaps in the ties the river ran muddy and fast. Ahead across the wet countryside I could see Udine in the rain. Across the bridge I looked back. Just up the river was another bridge. As I watched, a yellow mud-coloured motor-car crossed it. The sides of the bridge were high and the body of the car, once on, was out of sight. But I saw the heads of the driver, the man on the seat with him, and the two men on the rear seat. They all wore German helmets. Then the car was over the bridge and out of sight behind the trees and the abandoned vehicles on the road. I waved to Aymo who was crossing and to the others to come on. I climbed down and crouched beside the railway embankment. Aymo came down with me.

'Did you see the car?' I asked.

'No. We were watching you.'

'A German staff car crossed on the upper bridge.'

'A staff car?'

'Yes.'

'Holy Mary!'

The others came and we all crouched in the mud behind the embankment, looking across the rails at the bridge, the line of trees, the ditch and the road.

'Do you think we're cut off then, Tenete?'

'I don't know. All I know is a German staff car went along that road.'

'You don't feel funny, Tenete? You haven't got strange feelings in the head?'

'Don't be funny, Bonello.'

'What about a drink?' Piani asked. 'If we're cut off we might as well have a drink.' He unhooked his canteen and uncorked it.

'Look! Look!' Aymo said and pointed towards the road. Along the top of the stone bridge we could see German helmets moving. They were bent forward and moved smoothly, almost supernaturally, along. As they came off the bridge we saw them. They were bicycle troops. I saw the faces of the first two. They were ruddy and healthy-looking. Their helmets came low down over their foreheads and the side of their faces. Their carbines were clipped to the frame of the bicycles. Stick bombs hung handle down from their belts. Their helmets and their grey uniforms were wet and they rode easily, looking ahead and to both sides. There were two — then four in line, then two, then almost a dozen; then another dozen — then one alone. They did not talk but we could not have heard them because of the noise from the river. They were gone out of sight up the road.

'Holy Mary,' Aymo said.

'They were Germans,' Piani said. 'Those weren't Austrians.'

'Why isn't there somebody here to stop them?' I said. 'Why haven't they blown the bridge up? Why aren't there machine-guns along this embankment?'

'You tell us, Tenente,' Bonello said.

I was very angry.

'The whole bloody thing is crazy. Down below they blow up a little bridge. Here they leave a bridge on the main road. Where is everybody? Don't they try and stop them at all?'

'You tell us, Tenente,' Bonello said. I shut up. It was none of my business; all I had to do was to get to Pordenone with three ambulances. I had failed at that. All I had to do now was get to Pordenone. I probably could not even get to Udine. The hell I couldn't. The thing to do was to be calm and not get shot or captured.

'Didn't you have a canteen open?' I asked Piani. He handed it to me. I took a long drink. 'We might as well start,' I said. 'There's no hurry though. Do you want to eat something?'

'This is no place to stay,' Bonello said.

'All right. We'll start.'

'Should we keep on this side — out of sight?'

'We'll be better off on top. They may come along this bridge too. We don't want them on top of us before we see them.'

We walked along the railroad track. On both sides of us stretched the wet plain. Ahead across the plain was the hill of Udine. The roofs fell away from the castle on the hill. We could see the campanile and the clock-tower. There were many mulberry trees in the fields. Ahead I saw a place where the rails were torn up. The ties had been dug out too and thrown down the embankment.

'Down! down!' Aymo said. We dropped down beside the embankment. There was another group of bicyclists passing along the road. I looked over the edge and saw them go on.

'They saw us but they went on,' Aymo said.

'We'll get killed up there, Tenente,' Bonello said.

'They don't want us,' I said. 'They're after something else. We're in more danger if they should come on us suddenly.'

'I'd rather walk here out of sight,' Bonello said.

'All right. We'll walk along the tracks.'

'Do you think we can get through?' Aymo asked.

'Sure. There aren't very many of them yet. We'll go through in the dark.'

'What was that staff car doing?'

'Christ knows,' I said. We kept on up the tracks. Bonello tired of walking in the mud of the embankment and came up with the rest of us. The railway moved south away from the highway now and we could not see what passed along the road. A short bridge over a canal was blown but up we climbed across on what was left of the span. We heard firing ahead of us.

We came up on the railway beyond the canal. It went on straight towards the town across the low fields. We could see the line of the other railway ahead of us. To the north was the main road where we had seen the cyclists; to the south there was a small branch-road across the fields with thick trees on each side. I thought we had better cut to the south and work around the town that way and across country towards Campoformio and the main road to the Tagliamento. We could avoid the main line of the retreat by keeping to the secondary roads beyond Udine. I knew there were plenty of side-roads across the plain. I started down the embankment.

'Come on,' I said. We would make for the side-road and work to the south of the town. We all started down the embankment. A shot was fired at us from the side-road. The bullet went into the mud of the embankment.

'Go on back,' I shouted. I started up the embankment, slipping in the mud. The drivers were ahead of me. I went up the embankment as fast as I could go. Two more shots came from the thick brush and Aymo, as he was crossing the tracks, lurched, tripped and fell face down. We pulled him down on the other side and turned him over. 'His head ought to be uphill,' I said.

Piani moved him around. He lay in the mud on the side of the embankment, his feet pointing downhill, breathing blood irregularly. The three of us squatted over him in the rain. He was hit low in the back of the neck and the bullet had ranged upward and come out under the right eye. He died while I was stopping up the two holes. Piani laid his head down, wiped at his face with a piece of the emergency dressing, then let it alone.

'The bastards,' he said.

'They weren't Germans,' I said. 'There can't be any Germans over there.'

'Italians,' Piani said, using the word as an epithet, 'Italiani!' Bonello said nothing. He was sitting beside Aymo, not looking at him. Piani picked up Aymo's cap where it had rolled down the embankment and put it over his face. He took out his canteen.

'Do you want a drink?' Piani handed Bonello the canteen.

'No,' Bonello said. He turned to me. 'That might have happened to us any time on the railway tracks.'

'No,' I said. 'It was because we started across the field.'

Bonello shook his head. 'Aymo's dead,' he said. 'Who's dead next, Tenente? Where do we go now?'

'Those were Italians that shot,' I said. 'They weren't Germans.'

'I suppose if they were Germans they'd have killed all of us,' Bonello said.

'We are in more danger from Italians than Germans,' I said. 'The rear guard are afraid of everything. The Germans know what they're after.'

'You reason it out, Tenente,' Bonello said.

'Where do we go now?' Piani asked.

'We better lie up some place till it's dark. If we could get south we'd be all right.'

'They'd have to shoot us all to prove they were right the first time,' Bonello said. 'I'm not going to try them.'

'We'll find a place to lie up as near to Udine as we can get and then go through when it's dark.'

'Let's go then,' Bonello said. We went down the north side of the embankment. I looked back. Aymo lay in the mud within the angle of the embankment. He was quite small and his arms were by his side, his puttee-wrapped legs and muddy boots together, his cap over his face. He looked very dead. It was raining. I had liked him as well as anyone I ever knew. I had his papers in my pocket and would write to his family.

Ahead across the fields was a farmhouse. There were trees around it and the farm buildings were built against the house. There was a balcony along the second floor held up by columns.

'We better keep a little way apart,' I said. 'I'll go ahead.' I started towards the farmhouse. There was a path across the field.

Crossing the field, I did not know but that someone would fire on us from the trees near the farmhouse or from the farm-house itself. I walked towards it, seeing it very clearly. The balcony of the second floor merged into the barn and there was hay coming out between the columns. The courtyard was of stone blocks and all the trees were dripping with the rain. There was a big empty two-wheeled cart, the shafts tipped high up in the rain. I came to the courtyard, crossed it, and stood under the shelter of the balcony. The door of the house was open and I went in. Bonello and Piani came in after me. It was dark inside. I went back to the kitchen. There were ashes of a fire on the big open hearth. The pots hung over the ashes, but they were empty. I looked around but I could not find anything to eat.

'We ought to lie up in the barn,' I said. 'Do you think you could find anything to eat, Piani, and bring it up there?'

'I'll look,' Piani said.

'I'll look too,' Bonello said.

'All right,' I said. 'I'll go up and look at the barn.' I found a stone stairway that went up from the stable underneath. The stable smelt dry and pleasant in the rain. The cattle were all gone, probably driven off when they left. The barn was half full of hay. There were two windows in the roof, one was blocked with boards, the other was a narrow dormer window on the north side. There was a chute so that hay might be pitched down to the cattle. Beams crossed the opening down into the main floor where the hay carts drove in when the hay was hauled in to be pitched up. I heard the rain on the roof and smelled the hay, and, when I went down, the clean smell of dried dung in the stable. We could pry a board loose and see out of the south window down into the courtyard. The other window looked out on the field towards the north. We could get out of either window on to the roof and down, or go down the hay chute if the stairs were impracticable. It was a big barn and we could hide in the hay if we heard anyone. It seemed like a good place. I was sure we could have gotten through to the south if they had not fired on us. It was impossible that there were Germans there. They were coming from the north and down the road from Cividale. They could not have come through from the south. The Italians were even more dangerous. They were frightened and firing on anything they saw. Last night on the retreat we had heard that there had been many Germans in Italian uniforms mixing with the retreat in the north. I did not believe it. That was one of those things you always heard in the war. It was one of the things the enemy always did to you. You did not know anyone who went over in German uniform to confuse them. Maybe they did but it sounded difficult. I did not believe the Germans did it. I did not believe they had to. There was no need to confuse our retreat. The size of the army and the fewness of the roads did that. Nobody gave any orders, let alone Germans. Still, they would shoot us for Germans. They shot Aymo. The hay smelled good and lying in a barn in the hay took away all the years in between. We had lain in hay and talked and shot sparrows with an air-rifle when they perched in the triangle cut high up in the wall of the barn. The barn was gone now and one year they had cut the hemlock woods and there were only stumps, dried tree-tops, branches and fireweed where the woods had been. You could not go back. If you did not go forward what happened? You never got back to Milan. And if you got back to Milan what happened? I listened to the firing to the north toward Udine. I could hear machine-gun firing. There was no shelling. That was something. They must have gotten some troops along the road. I looked down in the half-light of the hay barn and saw Piani standing on the hauling floor. He had a long sausage, a jar of something and two bottles of wine under his arm.

'Come up,' I said. 'There is the ladder.' Then I realized that I should help him with the things and went down. I was vague in the head from lying in the hay. I had been nearly asleep.

'Where's Bonello?' I asked.

'I'll tell you,' Piani said. We went up the ladder. Up on the hay we set the things down. Piani took out his knife with the corkscrew and drew the cork of a wine-bottle.

'They have sealing-wax on it,' he said. 'It must be good.' He smiled.

'Where's Bonello?' I asked.

Piani looked at me.

'He went away, Tenente,' he said. 'He wanted to be a prisoner.'

I did not say anything.

'He was afraid we would get killed.'

I held the bottle of wine and did not say anything.

'You see we don't believe in the war anyway, Tenente.'

'Why didn't you go?' I asked.

'I did not want to leave you.'

'Where did he go?'

'I don't know, Tenente. He went away.'

'All right,' I said. 'Will you cut the sausage?'

Piani looked at me in the half-light.

'I cut it while we were talking,' he said. We sat in the hay and ate the sausage and drank the wine. It must have been wine they had saved for a wedding. It was so old that it was losing its colour.

'You look out of this window, Luigi,' I said. 'I'll go look out the other window.'

We had each been drinking out of one of the bottles and I took my bottle with me and went over too and lay flat on the hay and looked out the narrow window at the wet country. I do not know what I expected to see, but I did not see anything except the fields and the bare mulberry trees and the rain falling. I drank the wine and it did not make me feel good. They had kept it too long and it had gone to pieces and lost its quality and colour. I watched it get dark outside; the darkness came very quickly. It would be a black night with the rain. When it was dark there was no use watching any more, so I went over to Piani. He was lying asleep and I did not wake him but sat down beside him for a while. He was a big man and he slept heavily. After a while I woke him and we started.

That was a very strange night. I do not know what I had expected — death perhaps, and shooting in the dark, and running, but nothing happened. We waited, lying flat beyond the ditch along the main road while a German battalion passed, then when they were gone we crossed the road and went on to the north. We were very close to Germans twice in the rain but they did not see us. We got past the town to the north without seeing any Italians, then after a while came on the main channels of the retreat and walked all night toward the Tagliamento. I had not realized how gigantic the retreat was. The whole country was moving, as well as the army. We walked all night, making better time than the vehicles. My leg ached and I was tired but we made good time. It seemed so silly for Bonello to have decided to be taken prisoner. There was no danger. We had walked through two armies without incident. If Aymo had not been killed there would never have seemed to be any danger. No one had bothered us when we were in plain sight along the railway. The killing came suddenly and unreasonably. I wondered where Bonello was.

'How do you feel, Tenente?' Piani asked. We were going

along the side of a road crowded with vehicles and troops.

'Fine.'

'I'm tired of this walking.'

'Well, all we have to do is walk now. We don't have to worry.'

'Bonello was a fool.'

'He was a fool all right.'

'What will you do about him, Tenente?'

'I don't know.'

'Can't you just put him down as taken prisoner?'

'I don't know.'

'You see if the war went on they would make bad trouble for his family.'

'The war won't go on,' a soldier said. 'We're going home. The war is over.'

'Everybody's going home.'

'We're all going home.'

'Come on, Tenente,' Piani said. He wanted to get past them.

'Tenente? Who's a Tenente? *A basso gli ufficiali!* Down with the officers!'

Piani took me by the arm. 'I better call you by your name,' he said. 'They might try and make trouble. They've shot some officers.' We worked up past them.

'I won't make a report that will make trouble for his family.' I went on with our conversation.

'If the war is over it makes no difference,' Piani said. 'But I don't believe it's over. It's too good that it should be over.'

'We'll know pretty soon,' I said.

'I don't believe it's over. They all think it's over but I don't believe it.'

'*Evviva la Pace!*' a soldier shouted out. 'We're going home.'

'It would be fine if we all went home,' Piani said. 'Wouldn't you like to go home?'

'Yes.'

'We'll never go. I don't think it's over.'

192

'*Andiamo a casa!*' a soldier shouted.

'They throw away their rifles,' Piani said. 'They take them off and drop them down while they're marching. Then they shout.'

'They ought to keep their rifles.'

'They think if they throw away their rifles they can't make them fight.'

In the dark and the rain, making our way along the side of the road I could see that many of the troops still had their rifles. They stuck up above the capes.

'What brigade are you?' an officer called out.

'*Brigata di Pace,*' someone shouted. 'Peace Brigade!' The officer said nothing.

'What does he say? What does the officer say?'

'Down with the officer. *Evviva la Pace!*'

'Come on,' Piani said. We passed two British ambulances, abandoned in the block of vehicles.

'They're from Gorizia,' Piani said. 'I know the cars.'

'They got further than we did.'

'They started earlier.'

'I wonder where the drivers are?'

'Up ahead probably.'

'The Germans have stopped outside Udine,' I said. 'These people will all get across the river.'

'Yes,' Piani said. 'That's why I think the war will go on.'

'The Germans could come on,' I said. 'I wonder why they don't come on.'

'I don't know. I don't know anything about this kind of war.'

'They have to wait for their transport I suppose.'

'I don't know,' Piani said. Alone he was much gentler. When he was with the others he was a very rough talker.

'Are you married, Luigi?'

'You know I am married.'

'Is that why you did not want to be a prisoner?'

'That is one reason. Are you married, Tenente?'

'No.'

'Neither is Bonello.'

'You can't tell anything by a man's being married. But I should think a married man would want to get back to his wife,' I said. I would be glad to talk about wives.

'Yes.'

'How are your feet?'

'They're sore enough.'

Before daylight we reached the bank of the Tagliamento and followed down along the flooded river to the bridge where all the traffic was crossing.

'They ought to be able to hold at this river,' Piani said. In the dark the flood looked high. The water swirled and it was wide. The wooden bridge was nearly three-quarters of a mile across, and the river that usually ran in narrow channels in the wide stony bed far below the bridge, was close under the wooden planking. We went along the bank and then worked our way into the crowd that were crossing the bridge. Crossing slowly in the rain a few feet above the flood, pressed tight in the crowd, the box of an artillery caisson just ahead, I looked over the side and watched the river. Now that we could not go our own pace I felt very tired. There was no exhilaration in crossing the bridge. I wondered what it would be like if a plane bombed it in the daytime.

'Piani,' I said.

'Here I am, Tenente.' He was a little ahead in the jam. No one was talking. They were all trying to get across as soon as they could: thinking only of that. We were almost across. At the far end of the bridge there were officers and carabinieri standing on both sides flashing lights. I saw them silhouetted against the sky-line. As we came close to them I saw one of the officers point to a man in the column. A carabiniere went in after him and came out holding the man by the arm. He took him away from the road. We came almost opposite them. The officers were scrutinizing everyone in the column, sometimes speaking to each other, going forward to flash a light in someone's face. They took someone else out just before we came opposite. I saw the man. He was a lieutenant-colonel. I saw the stars in the box on his sleeve as they flashed a light on him. His hair was grey and he was short and fat. The carabiniere pulled him in behind the line of officers. As we came opposite I saw one or two of them look at me. Then one pointed at me and spoke to a carabiniere. I saw the carabiniere start for me, come through the edge of the column towards me, then felt him take me by the collar.

'What's the matter with you?' I said and hit him in the face. I saw his face under the hat, upturned moustaches, and blood coming down his cheek. Another one dived in towards us.

'What's the matter with you?' I said. He did not answer. He was watching a chance to grab me. I put my arm behind me to loosen my pistol.

'Don't you know you can't touch an officer?'

The other one grabbed me from behind and pulled my arm up so that it twisted in the socket. I turned with him and the other one grabbed me around the neck. I kicked his shins and got my left knee into his groin.

'Shoot him if he resists,' I heard someone say.

'What's the meaning of this?' I tried to shout but my voice was not very loud. They had me at the side of the road now.

'Shoot him if he resists,' an officer said. 'Take him over back.'

'Who are you?'

'You'll find out.'

'Who are you?'

'Battle police,' another officer said.

'Why don't you ask me to step over instead of having one of these airplanes grab me?'

They did not answer. They did not have to answer. They were battle police.

'Take him back there with the others,' the first officer said. 'You see. He speaks Italian with an accent.'

'So do you, you bastard,' I said.

'Take him back with the others,' the first officer said. They took me down behind the line of officers below the road towards a group of people in a field by the river bank. As we walked towards them shots were fired. I saw flashes of the rifles and heard the reports. We came up to the group. There were four officers standing together, with a man in front of them with a carabiniere on each side of him. A group of men were standing guarded by carabinieri. Four other carabinieri stood near the questioning officers, leaning on their carbines. They were wide-hatted carabinieri. The two who had me shoved me in with the group waiting to be questioned. I looked at the man the officers were questioning. He was the fat, grey-haired, little lieutenant-colonel they had taken out of the column. The questioners had all the efficiency, coldness and command of themselves of Italians who are firing and are not being fired on.

'Your Brigade?'

He told them.

'Regiment?'

He told them.

'Why are you not with your regiment?'

He told them.

'Do you not know that an officer should be with his troops?'

He did.

That was all. Another officer spoke.

'It is you and such as you that have let the barbarians on to the sacred soil of the fatherland.'

'I beg your pardon,' said the lieutenant-colonel.

'It is because of treachery such as yours that we have lost the fruits of victory.'

'Have you ever been in a retreat?' the lieutenant-colonel asked.

'Italy should never retreat.'

We stood there in the rain and listened to this. We were facing the officers and the prisoner stood in front and a little to one side of us.

'If you are going to shoot me,' the lieutenant-colonel said, 'please shoot me at once without further questioning. The questioning is stupid.' He made the sign of the cross. The officers spoke together. One wrote something on a pad of paper.

'Abandoned his troops, ordered to be shot,' he said.

Two carabinieri took the lieutenant-colonel to the river bank. He walked in the rain, an old man with his hat off, a carabiniere on either side. I did not watch them shoot him but I heard the shots. They were questioning someone else. This officer too was separated from his troops. He was not allowed to make an explanation. He cried when they read the sentence from the pad of paper and cried while they led him off, and they were questioning another when they shot him. They made a point of being intent on questioning the next man while the man who had been questioned before was being shot. In this way there was obviously nothing they could do about it. I did not know whether I should wait to be questioned or make a break now. I was obviously a German in Italian uniform. I saw how their minds worked; if they had minds and if they worked. They were all young men and they were saving their country. The second army was being reformed beyond the Tagliamento. They were executing officers of the rank of major and above who were separated from their troops. They were also dealing summarily with German agitators in Italian uniform. They wore steel helmets. Only two of us had steel helmets. Some of the carabinieri had them. The other carabinieri wore the wide hat. Airplanes we called them. We stood in the rain and were taken out one at a time to be questioned and shot. So far they had shot everyone they had questioned. The questioners had that beautiful detachment and devotion to stern justice of men dealing in death without being in any danger of it. They were questioning a full colonel of a line regiment. Three more officers had just been put in with us.

Where was his regiment?

I looked at the carabinieri. They were looking at the newcomers. The others were looking at the colonel. I ducked down, pushed between two men, and ran for the river, my head down. I tripped at the edge and went in with a splash. The water was very cold and I stayed under as long as I could. I could feel the current swirl me and I stayed under until I thought I could never come up. The minute I came up I took a breath and went down again. It was easy to stay under with so much clothing and my boots. When I came up the second time I saw a piece of timber ahead of me and reached it and held on with one hand. I kept my head behind it and did not even look over it. I did not want to see the bank. There were shots when I ran and shots when I came up the first time. I heard them when I was almost above water. There were no shots now. The piece of timber swung in the current and I held it with one hand. I looked at the bank. It seemed to be going by very fast. There was much wood in the stream. The water was very cold. We passed the brush of an island above the water. I held on to the timber with both hands and let it take me along. The shore was out of sight now.

CHAPTER 31

You do not know how long you are in a river when the current moves swiftly. It seems a long time and it may be very short. The water was cold and in flood and many things passed that had been floated off the banks when the river rose. I was lucky to have a heavy timber to hold on to, and I lay in the icy water with my chin on the wood, holding as easily as I could with both hands. I was afraid of cramps and I hoped we would move towards the shore. We went down the river in a long curve. It was beginning to be light enough so I could see the bushes along the shore-line. There was a brush island ahead and the current moved towards the shore. I wondered if I should take off my boots and clothes and try to swim ashore, but decided not to. I had never thought of anything but that I would reach the shore some way, and I would be in a bad position if I landed barefoot. I had to get to Mestre some way.

I watched the shore come close, then swing away, then come closer again. We were floating more slowly. The shore was very close now. I could see twigs on the willow bush. The timber swung slowly so that the bank was behind me and I knew we were in an eddy. We went slowly around. As I saw the bank again, very close now, I tried holding with one arm and kicking and swimming the timber towards the bank with the other, but I did not bring it any closer. I was afraid we would move out of the eddy and, holding with one hand, I drew up my feet so they were against the side of the timber and shoved hard towards the bank. I could see the brush but even with my momentum and swimming as hard as I could, the current was taking me away. I thought then I would drown because of my boots, but I thrashed and fought through the water, and when I looked up the bank was coming towards me, and I kept thrashing and swimming in a heavy-footed panic until I reached it. I hung to the willow branch and did not have strength to pull myself up but I knew I would not drown now. It had never occurred to me on the timber that I might drown. I felt hollow and sick in my stomach and chest from the effort, and I held to the branches and waited. When the sick feeling was gone I pulled in to the willow bushes and rested again, my arms around some brush, holding tight with my hands to the branches. Then I crawled out, pushed on through the willows and on to the bank. It was half-daylight and I saw no one. I lay flat on the bank and heard the river and the rain.

After a while I got up and started along the bank. I knew there was no bridge across the river until Latisana. I thought I might be opposite San Vito. I began to think out what I should do. Ahead there was a ditch running into the river. I went towards it. So far I had seen no one and I sat down by some bushes along the bank of the ditch and took off my shoes and emptied them of water. I took off my coat, took my wallet with my papers and my money all wet in it out of the inside pocket and then wrung the coat out. I took off my trousers and wrung them too, then my shirt and underclothing. I slapped and rubbed myself and then dressed again. I had lost my cap.

Before I put on my coat I cut the cloth stars off my sleeves and put them in the inside pocket with my money. My money was wet but was all right. I counted it. There were three thousand and some lire. My clothes felt wet and clammy and I slapped my arms to keep the circulation going. I had woollen underwear and I did not think I would catch cold if I kept moving. They had taken my pistol at the road and I put the holster under my coat. I had no cape and it was cold in the rain. I started up the bank of the canal. It was daylight and the country was wet, low and dismal looking. The fields were bare and wet; a long way away I could see a campanile rising out of the plain. I came up on to a road. Ahead I saw some troops coming down the road. I limped along the side of the road and they passed me and paid no attention to me. They were a machine-gun detachment going up towards the river. I went on down the road.

That day I crossed the Venetian plain. It is a low level country and under the rain it is even flatter. Towards the sea there are salt marshes and very few roads. The roads all go along the river mouths to the sea and to cross the country you must go along the paths beside the canals. I was working across the country from the north to the south and had crossed two railway lines and many roads and finally I came out at the end of a path on to a railway line where it ran beside a marsh. It was the main line from Venice to Trieste, with a high solid embankment, a solid roadbed and double track. Down the track a way was a flag-station and I could see soldiers on guard. Up the line there was a bridge over a stream that flowed into the marsh. I could see a guard too at the bridge. Crossing the fields to the north I had seen a train pass on this railroad, visible a long way across the flat plain, and I thought a train might come from Portogruaro. I watched the guards and lay down on the embankment so that I could see both ways along the track. The guard at the bridge walked a little way up the line towards where I lay, then turned and went back towards the bridge. I lay, and was hungry, and waited for the train. The one I had seen was so long that the engine moved it very slowly, and I was sure I could get aboard it. After I had almost given up hoping for one I saw a train coming. The engine, coming straight on, grew larger slowly. I looked at the guard at the bridge. He was walking on the near side of the bridge but on the other side of the track. That would put him out of sight when the train passed. I watched the engine come nearer. It was working hard. I could see there were many cars. I knew there would be guards on the train, and tried to see where they were, but, keeping out of sight, I could not. The engine was almost to where I was lying. When it came opposite, working and puffing even on the level, and I saw the engineer pass, I stood up and stepped up close to the passing cars. If the guards were watching I was a less suspicious object standing beside the track. Several closed freight-cars passed. Then I saw a low open car of the sort they call gondolas coming, covered with canvas. I stood until it had almost passed, then jumped and caught the rear hand-rods and pulled up. I crawled down between the gondola and the shelter of the high freight-car behind. I did not think anyone had seen me. I was holding to the hand-rods and crouching low, my feet on the coupling. We were almost opposite the bridge. I remembered the guard. As we passed him he looked at me. He was a boy and his helmet was too big for him. I stared at him contemptuously and he looked away. He thought I had something to do with the train.

We were past. I saw him still looking uncomfortable, watching the other cars pass and I stopped to see how the canvas was fastened. It had grummets and was laced down at the edge with cord. I took out my knife, cut the cord and put my arm under. There were hard bulges under the canvas that tightened in the rain. I looked up and ahead. There was a guard on the freight-car ahead but he was looking forward. I let go of the hand-rails and ducked under the canvas. My forehead hit something that gave me a violent bump and I felt blood on my face but I crawled on in and lay flat. Then I turned around and fastened down the canvas.

I was in under the canvas with guns. They smelled cleanly of oil and grease. I lay and listened to the rain on the canvas and the clicking of the car over the rails. There was a little light came through and I lay and looked at the guns. They had their canvas jackets on. I thought they must have been sent ahead from the third army. The bump on my forehead was swollen and I stopped the bleeding by lying still and letting it coagulate, then picked away the dried blood except over the cut. It was nothing. I had no handkerchief, but feeling with my fingers I washed away where the dried blood had been, with rain-water that dripped from the canvas, and wiped it clean with the sleeve of my coat. I did not want to look conspicuous. I knew I would have to get out before they got to Mestre because they would be taking care of these guns. They had no guns to lose or forget about. I was terrifically hungry.

CHAPTER 32

LYING on the floor of the flat-car with the guns beside me under the canvas I was wet, cold, and very hungry. Finally I rolled over and lay flat on my stomach with my head on my arms. My knee was stiff, but it had been very satisfactory. Valentini had done a fine job. I had done half the retreat on foot and swum part of the Tagliamento with his knee. It was his knee all right. The other knee was mine. Doctors did things to you and then it was not your body any more. The head was mine, and the inside of the belly. It was very hungry in there. I could feel it turn over on itself. The head was mine, but not to use, not to think with; only to remember and not too much remember.

I could remember Catherine but I knew I would get crazy if I thought about her when I was not sure yet I would see her, so I would not think about her, only about her a little, only about her with the car going slowly and clickingly, and some light through the canvas, and my lying with Catherine on the floor of the car. Hard as the floor of the car to lie not thinking only feeling, having been away too long, the clothes wet and the floor moving only a little each time and lonesome inside and alone with wet clothing and hard floor for a wife.

You did not love the floor of a flat-car nor guns with canvas jackets and the smell of vaselined metal or a canvas that rain leaked through, although it is very fine under a canvas and pleasant with guns; but you loved someone else whom now you knew was not even to be pretended there; you seeing now very clearly and coldly — not so coldly as clearly and emptily. You saw emptily, lying on your stomach, having been present when one army moved back and another came forward. You had lost your cars and your men as a floorwalker loses the stock of his department in a fire. There was, however, no insurance. You were out of it now. You had no more obligation. If they shot floorwalkers after a fire in the department store because they spoke with an accent they had always had, then certainly the floorwalkers would not be expected to return when the store opened again for business. They might seek other employment; if there was any other employment and the police did not get them.

Anger was washed away in the river along with any obligation. Although that ceased when the carabiniere put his hands on my collar. I would like to have had the uniform off although I did not care much about the outward forms. I had taken off the stars, but that was for convenience. It was no point of honour. I was not against them. I was through. I wished them all the luck. There were the good ones, and the brave ones, and the calm ones and the sensible ones, and they deserved it. But it was not my show any more and I wished this bloody train would get to Mestre and I would eat and stop thinking. I would have to stop.

Piani would tell them they had shot me. They went through the pockets and took the papers of the people they shot. They would not have my papers. They might call me drowned. I wondered what they would hear in the States. Dead from wounds and other causes. Good Christ, I was hungry. I wondered what had become of the priest at the mess. And Rinaldi. He was probably at Pordenone. If they had not gone further back. Well, I would never see him now. I would never see any of them now. That life was over. I did not think he had syphilis. It was not a serious disease anyway if you took it in time, they said. But he would worry. I would worry too if I had it. Anyone would worry.

I was not made to think. I was made to eat. My God, yes. Eat and drink and sleep with Catherine. Tonight maybe. No, that was impossible. But tomorrow night, and a good meal and sheets and never going away again except together. Probably have to go damned quickly. She would go. I knew she would go. When would we go? That was something to think about. It was getting dark. I lay and thought where we would go. There were many places.

BOOK IV

CHAPTER 33

I DROPPED off the train in Milan as it slowed to come into the station early in the morning before it was light. I crossed the track and came out between some buildings and down on to the street. A wine shop was open and I went in for some coffee. It smelled of early morning, of swept dust, spoons in coffee-glasses and the wet circles left by wine-glasses. The proprietor was behind the bar. Two soldiers sat at a table. I stood at the bar and drank a glass of coffee and ate a piece of bread. The coffee was grey with milk, and I skimmed the milk scum off the top with a piece of bread. The proprietor looked at me.

'You want a glass of grappa?'

'No thanks.'

'On me,' he said and poured a small glass and pushed it towards me. 'What's happening at the front?'

'I would not know.'

'They are drunk,' he said, moving his hand towards the two soldiers. I could believe him. They looked drunk.

'Tell me,' he said, 'what is happening at the front?'

'I would not know about the front.'

'I saw you come down the wall. You came off the train.'

'There is a big retreat.'

'I read the papers. What happens? Is it over?'

'I don't think so.'

He filled the glass with grappa from a short bottle.

'If you are in trouble,' he said, 'I can keep you.'

'I am not in trouble.'

'If you are in trouble stay here with me.'

'Where does one stay?'

'In the building. Many stay here. Any who are in trouble stay here.'

'Are many in trouble?'

'It depends on the trouble. You are a South American?'

'No.'

'Speak Spanish?'

'A little.'

He wiped off the bar.

'It is hard now to leave the country but in no way impossible.'

'I have no wish to leave.'

'You can stay here as long as you want. You will see what sort of man I am.'

'I have to go this morning but I will remember the address to return.'

He shook his head. 'You won't come back if you talk like that. I thought you were in real trouble.'

'I am in no trouble. But I value the address of a friend.'

I put a ten-lira note on the bar to pay for the coffee.

'Have a grappa with me,' I said.

'It is not necessary.'

'Have one.'

He poured the two glasses.

'Remember,' he said. 'Come here. Do not let other people take you in. Here you are all right.'

'I am sure.'

'You are sure?'

'Yes.'

He was serious. 'Then let me tell you one thing. Do not go about with that coat.'

'Why?'

'On the sleeves it shows very plainly where the stars have been cut away. The cloth is a different colour.'

I did not say anything.

'If you have no papers I can give you papers.'

'What papers?'

'Leave papers.'

'I have no need for papers. I have papers.'

'All right,' he said. 'But if you need papers I can get what you wish.'

'How much are such papers?'

'It depends on what they are. The price is reasonable.'

'I don't need any now.'

He shrugged his shoulders.

'I'm all right,' I said.

When I went out he said, 'Don't forget that I am your friend.'

'No.'

'I will see you again,' he said.

'Good,' I said.

Outside I kept away from the station, where there were military police, and picked up a cab at the edge of the little park. I gave the driver the address of the hospital. At the hospital I went to the porter's lodge. His wife embraced me. He shook my hand.

'You are back. You are safe.'

'Yes.'

'Have you had breakfast?'

'Yes.'

'How are you, Tenente? How are you?' the wife asked.

'Fine.'

'Won't you have breakfast with us?'

'No, thank you. Tell me is Miss Barkley here at the hospital now?'

'Miss Barkley?'

'The English lady nurse.'

'His girl,' the wife said. She patted my arm and smiled.

'No,' the porter said. 'She is away.'

My heart went down. 'You are sure? I mean the tall blonde English young lady.'

'I am sure. She is gone to Stresa.'

'When did she go?'

'She went two days ago with the other lady English.'

'Good,' I said. 'I wish you to do something for me. Do not tell anyone you have seen me. It is very important.'

'I won't tell anyone,' the porter said. I gave him a ten-lira note. He pushed it away.

'I promise you I will tell no one,' he said. 'I don't want any money.'

'What can we do for you, Signor Tenente?' his wife asked.

'Only that,' I said.

'We are dumb,' the porter said. 'You will let me know anything I can do?'

'Yes,' I said. 'Goodbye. I will see you again.'

They stood in the door, looking after me.

I got into the cab and gave the driver the address of Simmons, one of the men I knew who was studying singing.

Simmons lived a long way out in the town towards the Porta Magenta. He was still in bed and sleepy when I went to see him.

'You get up awfully early, Henry,' he said.

'I came in on the early train.'

'What's all this retreat? Were you at the front? Will you have a cigarette? They're in that box on the table.' It was a big room with a bed beside the wall, a piano over on the far side and a dresser and table. I sat on a chair by the bed. Simmons sat propped up by the pillows and smoked.

'I'm in a jam, Sim,' I said.

'So am I,' he said. 'I'm always in a jam. Won't you smoke?'

'No,' I said. 'What's the procedure in going to Switzerland?'

'For you? The Italians wouldn't let you out of the country.'

'Yes. I know that. But the Swiss. What will they do?'

'They intern you.'

'I know. But what's the mechanics of it?'

'Nothing. It's very simple. You can go anywhere. I think you just have to report or something. Why? Are you fleeing the police?'

'Nothing definite yet.'

'Don't tell me if you don't want. But it would be interesting to hear. Nothing happens here. I was a great flop at Piacenza.'

'I'm awfully sorry.'

'Oh, yes — I went very badly. I sang well too. I'm going to try it again at the Lyrico here.'

'I'd like to be there.'

'You're awfully polite. You aren't in a bad mess, are you?'

'I don't know.'

'Don't tell me if you don't want. How do you happen to be away from the bloody front?'

'I think I'm through with it.'

'Good boy. I always knew you had sense. Can I help you any way?'

'You're awfully busy.'

'Not a bit of it, my dear Henry. Not a bit of it. I'd be happy to do anything.'

'You're about my size. Would you go out and buy me an outfit of civilian clothes? I've clothes but they're all at Rome.'

'You did live there, didn't you? It's a filthy place. How did you ever live there?'

'I wanted to be an architect.'

'That's no place for that. Don't buy clothes. I'll give you all the clothes you want. I'll fit you out so you'll be a great success. Go in that dressing-room. There's a closet. Take anything you want. My dear fellow, you don't want to buy clothes.'

'I'd rather buy them, Sim.'

'My dear fellow, it's easier for me to let you have them than go out and buy them. Have you got a passport? You won't get far without a passport.'

'Yes. I've still got my passport.'

'Then get dressed, my dear fellow, and off to old Helvetia.'

'It's not that simple. I have to go up to Stresa first.'

'Ideal, my dear fellow. You just row a boat across. If I wasn't trying to sing, I'd go with you. I'll go yet.'

'You could take up yodelling.'

'My dear fellow, I'll take up yodelling yet. I really can sing though. That's the strange part.'

'I'll bet you can sing.'

He lay back in bed smoking a cigarette.

'Don't bet too much. But I can sing though. It's damned funny, but I can. I like to sing. Listen.' He roared into 'Africana', his neck swelling, the veins standing out. 'I can sing,' he said. 'Whether they like it or not.' I looked out of the window. 'I'll go down and let my cab go.'

'Come back up, my dear fellow, and we'll have breakfast.' He stepped out of bed, stood straight, took a deep breath and commenced doing bending exercises. I went downstairs and paid off the cab.

CHAPTER 34

In civilian clothes I felt a masquerader. I had been in uniform a long time and I missed the feeling of being held by your clothes. The trousers felt very floppy. I had bought a ticket at Milan for Stresa. I had also bought a new hat. I could not wear Sim's hat but his clothes were fine. They smelled of tobacco and as I sat in the compartment and looked out the window the new hat felt very new and the clothes very old. I myself felt as sad as the wet Lombard country that was outside through the window. There were some aviators in the compartment who did not think much of me. They avoided looking at me and were very scornful of a civilian my age. I did not feel insulted. In the old days I would have insulted them and picked a fight. They got off at Gallarate and I was glad to be alone. I had the paper but I did not read it because I did not want to read about the war. I was going to forget the war. I had made a separate peace. I felt damned lonely and was glad when the train got to Stresa.

At the station I had expected to see the porters from the hotels but there was no one. The season had been over a long time and no one met the train. I got down from the train with my bag, it was Sim's bag, and very light to carry, being empty except for two shirts, and stood under the roof of the station in the rain while the train went on. I found a man in the station and asked him if he knew what hotels were open. The Grand Hôtel des Iles Borromées was open and several small hotels that stayed open all the year. I started in the rain for the Iles Borromées carrying my bag. I saw a carriage coming down the street and signalled to the driver. It was better to arrive in a carriage. We drove up to the carriage entrance of the big hotel and the concierge came out with an umbrella and was very polite.

I took a good room. It was very big and light and looked out on the lake. The clouds were down over the lake but it would be beautiful with the sunlight. I was expecting my wife, I said. There was a big double-bed, a *letto matrimoniale*, with a satin coverlet. The hotel was very luxurious. I went down the long halls, down the wide stairs, through the rooms to the bar. I knew the barman and sat on a high stool and ate salted almonds and potato chips. The martini felt cool and clean.

'What are you doing here in *borghese*?' the barman asked after he had mixed a second martini.

'I am on leave. Convalescing-leave.'

'There is no one here. I don't know why they keep the hotel open.'

'Have you been fishing?'

'I've caught some beautiful pieces. Trolling this time of year you catch some beautiful pieces.'

'Did you ever get the tobacco I sent?'

'Yes. Didn't you get my card?'

I laughed. I had not been able to get the tobacco. It was American pipe-tobacco that he wanted, but my relatives had stopped sending it or it was being held up. Anyway it never came.

'I'll get some somewhere,' I said. 'Tell me have you seen two English girls in the town? They came here day before yesterday.'

'They are not at the hotel.'

'They are nurses.'

'I have seen two nurses. Wait a minute, I will find out where they are.'

'One of them is my wife,' I said. 'I have come here to meet her.'

'The other is my wife.'

'I am not joking.'

'Pardon my stupid joke,' he said. 'I did not understand.' He went away and was gone quite a little while. I ate olives, salted almonds and potato chips and looked at myself in civilian clothes in the mirror behind the bar. The bartender came back. 'They are at the little hotel near the station,' he said.

How about some sandwiches?'

'I'll ring for some. You understand there is nothing here, now there are no people.'

'Isn't there really anyone at all?'

'Yes. There are a few people.'

The sandwiches came and I ate three and drank a couple more martinis. I had never tasted anything so cool and clean. They made me feel civilized. I had had too much red wine, bread, cheese, bad coffee and grappa. I sat on the high stool before the pleasant mahogany, the brass and the mirrors and did not think at all. The barman asked me some question.

'Don't talk about the war,' I said. The war was a long way away. Maybe there wasn't any war. There was no war here. Then I realized it was over for me. But I did not have the feeling that it was really over. I had the feeling of a boy who thinks of what is happening at a certain hour at the schoolhouse from which he has played truant.

* * *

Catherine and Helen Ferguson were at supper when I came to their hotel. Standing in the hallway I saw them at table. Catherine's face was away from me and I saw the line of her hair and her cheek and her lovely neck and shoulders. Ferguson was talking. She stopped when I came in.

'My God,' she said.

'Hello,' I said.

'Why it's you!' Catherine said. Her face lighted up. She looked too happy to believe it. I kissed her. Catherine blushed and I sat down at the table.

'You're a fine mess,' Ferguson said. What are you doing here? Have you eaten?'

'No.' The girl who was serving the meal came in and I told her to bring a plate for me. Catherine looked at me all the time, her eyes happy.

'What are you doing in mufti?' Ferguson asked.

'I'm in the Cabinet.'

'You're in some mess.'

'Cheer up, Fergy. Cheer up just a little.'

'I'm not cheered by seeing you. I know the mess you've gotten this girl into. You're no cheerful sight to me.'

Catherine smiled at me and touched me with her foot under the table.

'No one got me in a mess, Fergy. I get in my own messes.'

'I can't stand him,' Ferguson said. 'He's done nothing but ruin you with his sneaking Italian tricks. Americans are worse than Italians.'

'The Scotch are such a moral people,' Catherine said.

'I don't mean that. I mean his Italian sneakiness.'

'Am I sneaky, Fergy?'

'You are. You're worse than sneaky. You're like a snake. A snake with an Italian uniform: with a cape around your neck.'

'I haven't got an Italian uniform now.'

'That's just another example of your sneakiness. You had a

love affair all summer and got this girl with child and now I suppose you'll sneak off.'

I smiled at Catherine and she smiled at me.

'We'll both sneak off,' she said.

'You're two of the same thing,' Ferguson said. 'I'm ashamed of you, Catherine Barkley. You have no shame and no honour and you're as sneaky as he is.'

'Don't, Fergy,' Catherine said and patted her hand. 'Don't denounce me. You know we like each other.'

'Take your hand away,' Ferguson said. Her face was red. 'If you had any shame it would be different. But you're God knows how many months gone with child and you think it's a joke and are all smiles because your seducer's come back. You've no shame and no feelings.' She began to cry. Catherine went over and put her arm around her. As she stood comforting Ferguson, I could see no change in her figure.

'I don't care,' Ferguson sobbed. 'I think it's dreadful.'

'There, there, Fergy,' Catherine comforted her. 'I'll be ashamed. Don't cry, Fergy. Don't cry, old Fergy.'

'I'm not crying,' Ferguson sobbed. 'I'm not crying. Except for the awful thing you've gotten into.' She looked at me. 'I hate you,' she said. 'She can't make me not hate you. You dirty sneaking American Italian.' Her eyes and nose were red with crying.

Catherine smiled at me.

'Don't you smile at him with your arm around me.'

'You're unreasonable, Fergy. '

'I know it,' Ferguson sobbed. 'You mustn't mind me, either of you. I'm so upset. I'm not reasonable. I know it. I want you both to be happy.'

'We're happy,' Catherine said. 'You're a sweet Fergy.'

Ferguson cried again. 'I don't want you happy the way you are. Why don't you get married? You haven't got another wife have you?'

'No,' I said. Catherine laughed.

'It's nothing to laugh about,' Ferguson said. 'Plenty of them have other wives.'

'We'll be married, Fergy,' Catherine said, 'if it will please you.'

'Not to please me. You should want to be married.'

'We've been very busy.'

'Yes. I know. Busy making babies.' I thought she was going to cry again but she went into bitterness instead. 'I suppose you'll go off with him now tonight?'

'Yes,' said Catherine. 'If he wants me.'

'What about me?'

'Are you afraid to stay here alone?'

'Yes, I am.'

'Then I'll stay with you.'

'No, go on with him. Go with him right away. I'm sick of seeing both of you.'

'We'd better finish dinner.'

'No. Go right away.'

'Fergy, be reasonable.'

'I say get out right away. Go away both of you.'

'Let's go then,' I said. I was sick of Fergy.

'You do want to go. You see you want to leave me even to eat dinner alone. I've always wanted to go to the Italian lakes and this is how it is. Oh, Oh,' she sobbed, then looked at Catherine and choked.

'We'll stay till after dinner,' Catherine said. 'And I'll not leave you alone if you want me to stay. I won't leave you alone, Fergy.'

'No. No. I want you to go. I want you to go.' She wiped her eyes. 'I'm so unreasonable. Please don't mind me.'

The girl who served the meal had been upset by all the crying. Now as she brought in the next course she seemed relieved that things were better.

That night at the hotel, in our room with the long empty hall outside and our shoes outside the door, a thick carpet on the floor of the room, outside the windows the rain falling and in the room light and pleasant and cheerful, then the light out and it exciting with smooth sheets and the bed comfortable, feeling that we had come home, feeling no longer alone, waking in the night to find the other one there, and not gone away; all other things were unreal. We slept when we were tired and if we woke the other one woke too so one was not alone. Often a man wishes to be alone and a girl wishes to be alone too and if they love each other they are jealous of that in each other, but I can truly say we never felt that. We could feel alone when we were together, alone against the others. It has only happened to me like that once. I have been alone while I was with many girls and that is the way that you can be most lonely. But we were never lonely and never afraid when we were together. I know that the night is not the same as the day: that all things are different, that the things of the night cannot be explained in the day, because they do not then exist, and the night can be a dreadful time for lonely people once their loneliness has started. But with Catherine there was almost no difference in the night except that it was an even better time. If people bring so much courage to this world the world has to kill them to break them, so of course it kills them. The world breaks everyone and afterward many are strong at the broken places. But those that will not break it kills. It kills the very good and the very gentle and the very brave impartially. If you are none of these you can be sure it will kill you too but there will be no special hurry.

I remember waking in the morning. Catherine was asleep and the sunlight was coming in through the window. The rain had stopped and I stepped out of bed and across the floor to the window. Down below were the gardens, bare now but beautifully regular, the gravel paths, the trees, the stone wall by the lake and the lake in the sunlight with the mountains beyond. I stood at the window looking out and when I turned away I saw Catherine was awake and watching me.

'How are you, darling?' she said. 'Isn't it a lovely day?'

'How do you feel?'

'I feel very well. We had a lovely night.'

'Do you want breakfast?'

She wanted breakfast. So did I and we had it in bed, the November sunlight coming in the window, and the breakfast tray across my lap.

'Don't you want the paper? You always wanted the paper in the hospital.'

'No,' I said. 'I don't want the paper now.'

'Was it so bad you don't want even to read about it?'

'I don't want to read about it.'

'I wish I had been with you so I would know about it too.'

'I'll tell you about it if I ever get it straight in my head.'

'But won't they arrest you if they catch you out of uniform?'

'They'll probably shoot me.'

'Then we'll not stay here. We'll get out of the country.'

'I'd thought something of that.'

'We'll get out. Darling, you shouldn't take silly chances. Tell me how did you come from Mestre to Milan?'

'I came on the train. I was in uniform then.'

'Weren't you in danger then?'

'Not much. I had an old order of movement. I fixed the dates on it in Mestre.'

'Darling, you're liable to be arrested here any time. I won't have it. It's silly to do something like that. Where would we be if they took you off?'

'Let's not think about it. I'm tired of thinking about it.'

'What would you do if they came to arrest you?'

'Shoot them.'

'You see how silly you are, I won't let you go out of the hotel until we leave here.'

'Where are we going to go?'

'Please don't be that way, darling. We'll go wherever you say. But please find some place to go right away.'

'Switzerland is down the lake, we can go there.'

'That will be lovely.'

It was clouding over outside and the lake was darkening.

'I wish we did not always have to live like criminals,' I said.

'Darling, don't be that way. You haven't lived like a criminal very long. And we'll never live like criminals. We're going to have a fine time.'

'I feel like a criminal. I've deserted from the army.'

'Darling, *please* be sensible. It's not deserting from the army. It's only the Italian army.'

I laughed. 'You're a fine girl. Let's get back into bed. I feel fine in bed.'

A little while later Catherine said, 'You don't feel like a criminal do you?'

'No,' I said. 'Not when I'm with you.'

'You're such a silly boy,' she said. 'But I'll look after you. Isn't it splendid, darling, that I don't have any morning-sickness?'

'It's grand.'

'You don't appreciate what a fine wife you have. But I don't care. I'll get you some place where they can't arrest you and then we'll have a lovely time.'

'Let's go there right away.'

'We will, darling. I'll go any place any time you wish.'

'Let's not think about anything.'

'All right.'

CHAPTER 35

CATHERINE went along the lake to the little hotel to see Ferguson and I sat in the bar and read the papers. There were comfortable leather chairs in the bar and I sat in one of them and read until the barman came in. The army had not stood at the Tagliamento. They were falling back to the Piave. I remembered the Piave. The railroad crossed it near San Dona going up to the front. It was deep and slow there and quite narrow. Down below there were mosquito marshes and canals. There were some lovely villas. Once, before the war, going up to Cortina D'Ampezzo I had gone along it for several hours in the hills. Up there it looked like a trout stream, flowing swiftly with shallow stretches and pools under the shadow of the rocks. The road turned off from it at Cadore. I wondered how the army that was up there would come down. The barman came in.

'Count Greffi was asking for you,' he said.

'Who?'

'Count Greffi. You remember the old man who was here when you were here before.'

'Is he here?'

'Yes, he's here with his niece. I told him you were here. He wants you to play billiards.'

'Where is he?'

'He's taking a walk.'

'How is he?'

'He's younger than ever. He drank three champagne cocktails last night before dinner.'

'How's his billiard game?'

'Good. He beat me. When I told him you were here he was very pleased. There's nobody here for him to play with.'

Count Greffi was ninety-four years old. He had been a contemporary of Metternich, and was an old man with white hair and moustache and beautiful manners. He had been in the diplomatic service of both Austria and Italy and his birthday parties were the great social event of Milan. He was living to be one hundred years old and played a smoothly fluent game of billiards that contrasted with his own ninety-four-year-old brittleness. I had met him when I had been at Stresa once before out of season and while we played billiards we drank champagne.

I thought it was a splendid custom and he gave me fifteen points in a hundred and beat me.

'Why didn't you tell me he was here?'

'I forgot it.'

'Who else is here?'

'No one you know. There are only six people altogether.'

'What are you doing now?'

'Nothing.'

'Come on out fishing.'

'I could come for an hour.'

'Come on. Bring the trolling line.'

The barman put on a coat and we went out. We went down and got a boat and I rowed while the barman sat in the stern and let out the line with a spinner and a heavy sinker on the end to troll for lake trout. We rowed along the shore, the barman holding the line in his hand and giving it occasional jerks forward. Stresa looked very deserted from the lake. There were the long rows of bare trees, the big hotels and the closed villas. I rowed across to Isola Bella and went close to the walls, where the water deepened sharply, and you saw the rock wall slanting down in the water, and then up and along to the fisherman's island. The sun was under a cloud and the water was dark and smooth and very cold. We did not have a strike though we saw some circles on the water from rising fish.

I rowed up opposite the fisherman's island where there were boats drawn up and men were mending nets.

'Should we get a drink?'

'All right.'

I brought the boat up to the stone pier and the barman pulled in the line, coiling it on the bottom of the boat and hooking the spinner on the edge of the gunwale. I stepped out and tied the boat. We went into a little café, sat at a bare wooden table and ordered vermouth.

'Are you tired from rowing?'

'No.'

'I'll row back,' he said.

'I like to row.'

'Maybe if you hold the line it will change the luck.'

'All right.'

'Tell me how goes the war.'

'Rotten.'

'I don't have to go. I'm too old, like Count Greffi.'

'Maybe you'll have to go yet.'

'Next year they'll call my class. But I won't go.'

'What will you do?'

'Get out of the country. I wouldn't go to war. I was at the war once in Abyssinia. Nix. Why do you go?'

'I don't know. I was a fool.'

'Have another vermouth?'

'All right.'

The barman rowed back. We trolled up the lake beyond Stresa and then down not far from shore. I held the taut line and felt the faint pulsing of the spinner revolving while I looked at the dark November water of the lake and the deserted shore. The barman rowed with long strokes and on the forward thrust of the boat the line throbbed. Once I had a strike: the line hardened suddenly and jerked back, I pulled and felt the live weight of the trout and then the line throbbed again. I had missed him.

'Did he feel big?'

'Pretty big.'

'Once when I was out trolling alone I had the line in my teeth and one struck and nearly took my mouth out.'

'The best way is to have it over your leg,' I said. 'Then you feel it and don't lose your teeth.'

I put my hand in the water. It was very cold. We were almost opposite the hotel now.

'I have to go in,' the barman said, 'to be there for eleven o'clock. *L'heure du cocktail.*'

'All right.'

221

I pulled in the line and wrapped it on a stick notched at each end. The barman put the boat in a little slip in the stone wall and locked it with a chain and padlock.

'Any time you want it,' he said, 'I'll give you the key.'

'Thanks.'

We went up to the hotel and into the bar. I did not want another drink so early in the morning so I went up to our room. The maid had just finished doing the room and Catherine was not back yet. I lay down on the bed and tried to keep from thinking.

When Catherine came back it was all right again. Ferguson was downstairs, she said. She was coming to lunch.

'I knew you wouldn't mind,' Catherine said.

'No,' I said.

'What's the matter, darling?'

'I don't know.'

'I know. You haven't anything to do. All you have is me and I go away.'

'That's true.'

'I'm sorry, darling. I know it must be a dreadful feeling to having nothing at all suddenly.'

'My life used to be full of everything,' I said. 'Now if you aren't with me I haven't a thing in the world.'

'But I'll be with you. I was only gone for two hours. Isn't there anything you can do?'

'I went fishing with the barman.'

'Wasn't it fun?'

'Yes.'

'Don't think about me when I'm not here.'

'That's the way I worked it at the front. But there was something to do then.'

'Othello with his occupation gone,' she teased.

'Othello was a nigger,' I said. 'Besides, I'm not jealous. I'm just so in love with you that there isn't anything else.'

'Will you be a good boy and be nice to Ferguson?'

'I'm always nice to Ferguson unless she curses me.'

'Be nice to her. Think how much we have and she hasn't anything.'

'I don't think she wants what we have.'

'You don't know much, darling, for such a wise boy.'

'I'll be nice to her.'

'I know you will. You're so sweet.'

'She won't stay afterward, will she?'

'No. I'll get rid of her.'

'And then we'll come up here.'

'Of course. What do you think I want to do?'

We went downstairs to have lunch with Ferguson. She was very impressed by the hotel and the splendour of the dining-room. We had a good lunch with a couple of bottles of white capri. Count Greffi came into the dining-room and bowed to us. His niece, who looked a little like my grandmother, was with him. I told Catherine and Ferguson about him and Ferguson was very impressed. The hotel was very big and grand and empty but the food was good, the wine was very pleasant and finally the wine made us all feel very well. Catherine had no need to feel any better. She was very happy. Ferguson became quite cheerful. I felt very well myself. After lunch Ferguson went back to her hotel. She was going to lie down for a while after lunch she said.

Along late in the afternoon someone knocked on our door.

'Who is it?'

'The Count Greffi wishes to know if you will play billiards with him.'

I looked at my watch; I had taken it off and it was under the pillow.

'Do you have to go, darling?' Catherine whispered.

'I think I'd better.' The watch said a quarter past four o'clock. Out loud I said, 'Tell the Count Greffi I will be in the billiard-room at five o'clock.'

At a quarter to five I kissed Catherine goodbye and went into the bathroom to dress. Knotting my tie and looking in the glass I looked strange to myself in the civilian clothes. I must remember to buy some more shirts and socks.

'Will you be away a long time?' Catherine asked. She looked lovely in the bed. 'Would you hand me the brush?'

I watched her brushing her hair, holding her head so the weight of her hair all came on one side. It was dark outside and the light over the head of the bed shone on her hair and on her neck and shoulders. I went over and kissed her and held her hand with the brush and her head sank back on the pillow. I kissed her neck and shoulders. I felt faint with loving her so much.

'I don't want to go away.'

'I don't want you to go away.'

'I won't go then.'

'Yes. Go. It's only for a little while and then you'll come back.'

'We'll have dinner up here.'

'Hurry and come back.'

I found the Count Greffi in the billiard-room. He was practising strokes, looking very fragile under the light that came down above the billiard table. On a card table a little way beyond the light was a silver icing-bucket with the necks and corks of two champagne bottles showing above the ice. The Count Greffi straightened up when I came towards the table and walked towards me. He put out his hand, 'It is such a great pleasure that you are here. You were very kind to come to play with me.'

'It was very nice of you to ask me.'

'Are you quite well? They told me you were wounded on the Isonzo. I hope you are well again.'

'I'm very well. Have you been well?'

'Oh, I am always well. But I am getting old. I detect signs of age now.'

'I can't believe it.'

'Yes. Do you want to know one? It is easier for me to talk Italian. I discipline myself but I find when I am tired that it is so much easier to talk Italian. So I know I must be getting old.'

'We could talk Italian. I am a little tired too.'

'Oh, but when you are tired it will be easier for you to talk English.'

'American.'

'Yes. American. You will please talk American. It is a delightful language.'

'I hardly ever see Americans.'

'You must miss them. One misses one's countrymen and especially one's countrywomen. I know that experience. Should we play or are you too tired?'

'I'm not really tired. I said that for a joke. What handicap will you give me?'

'Have you been playing very much?'

'None at all.'

'You play very well. Ten points in a hundred?'

'You flatter me.'

'Fifteen?'

'That would be fine but you will beat me.'

'Should we play for a stake? You always wished to play for a stake.'

'I think we'd better.'

'All right. I will give you eighteen points and we will play for a franc a point.'

He played a lovely game of billiards and with the handicap I was only four ahead at fifty. Count Greffi pushed a button on the wall to ring for the barman.

'Open one bottle, please,' he said. Then to me, 'We will take a little stimulant.' The wine was icy cold and very dry and good.

'Should we talk Italian? Would you mind very much? It is my great weakness now.'

We went on playing, sipping the wine between shots, speaking in Italian, but talking little, concentrated on the game. Count Greffi made his one-hundredth point and with the handicap I was only at ninety-four. He smiled and patted me on the shoulder.

'Now we will drink the other bottle and you will tell me about the war.' He waited for me to sit down.

'About anything else,' I said.

'You don't want to talk about it? Good. What have you been reading?'

'Nothing,' I said. 'I'm afraid I am very dull.'

'No. But you should read.'

'What is there written in war-time?'

'There is *Le Feu* by a Frenchman, Barbusse. There is *Mr. Britling Sees Through It*.'

'No, he doesn't.'

'What?'

'He doesn't see through it. Those books were at the hospital.'

'Then you have been reading?'

'Yes, but nothing any good.'

'I thought *Mr. Britling* a very good study of the English middle-class soul.'

'I don't know about the soul.'

'Poor boy. We none of us know about the soul. Are you *Croyant?*'

'At night.' Count Greffi smiled and turned the glass with his fingers.

'I had expected to become more devout as I grow older but somehow I haven't,' he said. 'It is a great pity.'

'Would you like to live after death?' I asked and instantly felt a fool to mention death. But he did not mind the word.

'It would depend on the life. This life is very pleasant. I would like to live for ever,' he smiled. 'I very nearly have.'

We were sitting in the deep leather chairs, the champagne in the ice-bucket and our glasses on the table between us.

'If you ever live to be as old as I am you will find many things strange.'

'You never seem old.'

'It is the body that is old. Sometimes I am afraid I will break off a finger as one breaks a stick of chalk. And the spirit is no older and not much wiser.'

'You are wise.'

'No, that is the great fallacy, the wisdom of old men. They do not grow wise. They grow careful.'

'Perhaps that is wisdom.'

'It is a very unattractive wisdom. What do you value most?'

'Someone I love.'

'With me it is the same. That is not wisdom. Do you value life?'

'Yes.'

'So do I. Because it is all I have. And to give birthday parties,' he laughed. 'You are probably wiser than I am. You do not give birthday parties.'

We both drank the wine.

'What do you think of the war really?' I asked.

'I think it is stupid.'

'Who will win it.?'

'Italy.'

'Why?'

'They are a younger nation.'

'Do younger nations always win wars?'

'They are apt to for a time.'

'Then what happens?'

'They become older nations.'

'You said you were not wise.'

'Dear boy, that is not wisdom. That is cynicism.'

'It sounds very wise to me.'

'It's not particularly. I could quote you the examples on the other side. But it is not bad. Have we finished the champagne?'

'Almost.'

'Should we drink some more? Then I must dress.'

'Perhaps we'd better not now.'

'You are sure you don't want more?'

'Yes.' He stood up.

'I hope you will be very fortunate and very happy and very, very healthy.'

'Thank you. And I hope you will live forever.'

'Thank you. I have. And if you ever become devout pray for me if I am dead. I am asking several of my friends to do that. I had expected to become devout myself but it has not come.' I thought he smiled sadly but I could not tell. He was so old and his face was very wrinkled, so that a smile used so many lines that all gradations were lost.

'I might become very devout,' I said. 'Anyway, I will pray for you.'

'I had always expected to become devout. All my family died very devout. But somehow it does not come.'

'It's too early.'

'Maybe it is too late. Perhaps I have outlived my religious feeling.'

'My own comes only at night.'

'Then too you are in love. Do not forget that is a religious feeling.'

'You believe so?'

'Of course.' He took a step towards the table. 'You were very kind to play.'

'It was a great pleasure.'

'We will walk upstairs together.'

CHAPTER 36

THAT night there was a storm and I woke to hear the rain lashing the window-panes. It was coming in the open window. Someone had knocked on the door. I went to the door very softly, not to disturb Catherine, and opened it. The barman stood there. He wore his overcoat and carried his wet hat.

'Can I speak to you, Tenente?'

'What's the matter?'

'It's a very serious matter.'

I looked around. The room was dark. I saw the water on the floor from the window. 'Come in,' I said. I took him by the arm into the bathroom; locked the door and put on the light. I sat down on the edge of the bathtub.

'What's the matter, Emilio? Are you in trouble?'

'No. You are, Tenente.'

'Yes?'

'They are going to arrest you in the morning.'

'Yes?'

'I came to tell you. I was out in the town and I heard them talking in a café.'

'I see.'

He stood there, his coat wet, holding his wet hat and said nothing.

'Why are they going to arrest me?'

'For something about the war.'

'Do you know what?'

'No. But I know that they know you were here before as an officer and now you are here out of uniform. After this retreat they arrest everybody.'

I thought a minute.

'What time do they come to arrest me?'

'In the morning. I don't know the time.'

'What do you say to do?'

He put his hat in the washbowl. It was very wet and had been dripping on the floor.

'If you have nothing to fear an arrest is nothing. But it is always bad to be arrested, especially now.'

'I don't want to be arrested.'

'Then go to Switzerland.'

'How?'

'In my boat.'

'There is a storm,' I said.

'The storm is over. It is rough but you will be all right.'

'When should we go?'

'Right away. They might come to arrest you early in the morning.'

'What about our bags?'

'Get them packed. Get your lady dressed. I will take care of them.'

'Where will you be?'

'I will wait here. I don't want anyone to see me outside in the hall.'

I opened the door, closed it, and went into the bedroom. Catherine was awake.

'What is it, darling?'

'It's all right, Cat,' I said. 'Would you like to get dressed right away and go in a boat to Switzerland?'

'Would you?'

'No,' I said. 'I'd like to go back to bed.'

'What is it about?'

'The barman says they are going to arrest me in the morning.'

'Is the barman crazy?'

'No.'

'Then please hurry, darling, and get dressed so we can start.' She sat up on the side of the bed. She was still sleepy. 'Is that the barman in the bathroom?'

'Yes.'

'Then I won't wash. Please look the other way, darling, and I'll be dressed in just a minute.'

I saw her white back as she took off her nightgown and then I looked away because she wanted me to. She was beginning to be a little big with the child and she did not want me to see her. I dressed hearing the rain on the windows. I did not have much to put in my bag.

'There's plenty of room in my bag, Cat, if you need any.'

'I'm almost packed,' she said. 'Darling, I'm awfully stupid, but why is the barman in the bathroom?'

'Sh — he's waiting to take our bags down.'

'He's awfully nice.'

'He's an old friend,' I said. 'I nearly sent him some pipe-tobacco once.'

I looked out the open window at the dark night. I could not see the lake, only the dark and the rain but the wind was quieter.

'I'm ready, darling,' Catherine said.

'All right.' I went to the bathroom door. 'Here are the bags, Emilio,' I said. The barman took the two bags.

'You're very good to help us,' Catherine said.

'That's nothing, lady,' the barman said. 'I'm glad to help you just so I don't get in trouble myself. Listen,' he said to me, 'I'll take these out the servants' stairs and to the boat. You just go out as though you were going for a walk.'

'It's a lovely night for a walk,' Catherine said.

'It's a bad night all right.'

'I'm glad I've an umbrella,' Catherine said.

We walked down the hall and down the wide thickly carpeted stairs. At the foot of the stairs by the door the porter sat behind his desk.

He looked surprised at seeing us.

'You're not going out, sir?' he said.

'Yes,' I said. 'We're going to see the storm along the lake.'

'Haven't you got an umbrella, sir?'

'No,' I said. 'This coat sheds water.'

He looked at it doubtfully. 'I'll get you an umbrella, sir,' he said. He went away and came back with a big umbrella. 'It is a little big, sir,' he said. I gave him a ten-lira note. 'Oh, you are too good, sir. Thank you very much,' he said. He held the door open and we went out into the rain. He smiled at Catherine and she smiled at him. 'Don't stay out in the storm,' he said. 'You will get wet, sir and lady.' He was only the second porter, and his English was still literally translated.

'We'll be back,' I said. We walked down the path under the giant umbrella and out through the dark wet gardens to the road and across the road to the trellised pathway along the lake. The wind was blowing off-shore now. It was a cold, wet November wind and I knew it was snowing in the mountains. We came along past the chained boats in the slips along the quay to where the barman's boat should be. The water was dark against the stone. The barman stepped out from beside the row of trees.

'The bags are in the boat,' he said.

'I want to pay you for the boat,' I said.

'How much money have you?'

'Not so much.'

'You send me the money later. That will be all right.'

'How much?'

'What you want.'

'Tell me how much.'

'If you get through send me five hundred francs. You won't mind that if you get through.'

'All right.'

'Here are sandwiches.' He handed me a package. 'Everything there was in the bar. It's all here. This is a bottle of brandy and a bottle of wine.' I put them in my bag. 'Let me pay for those.'

'All right, give me fifty lire.'

I gave it to him. 'The brandy is good,' he said. 'You don't need to be afraid to give it to your lady. She better get in the boat.' He held the boat, it rising and falling against the stone wall and I helped Catherine in. She sat in the stern and pulled her cape around her.

'You know where to go?'

'Up the lake.'

'You know how far?'

'Past Luino.'

'Past Luino, Cannero, Cannobio, Tranzano. You aren't in Switzerland until you come to Brissago. You have to pass Monte Tamara.'

'What time is it?' Catherine asked.

'It's only eleven o'clock,' I said.

'If you row all the time you ought to be there by seven o'clock in the morning.'

'Is it that far?'

'It's thirty-five kilometres.'

'How should we go? In this rain we need a compass.'

'No. Row to Isola Bella. Then on the other side of Isola Madre go with the wind. The wind will take you to Pallanza. You will see the lights. Then go up the shore.'

'Maybe the wind will change.'

'No,' he said. 'This wind will blow like this for three days. It comes straight down from the Motterone. There is a can to bail with.'

'Let me pay you something for the boat now.'

'No, I'd rather take a chance. If you get through you pay me all you can.'

'All right.'

'I don't think you'll get drowned.'

'That's good.'

'Go with the wind up the lake.'

'All right,' I stepped in the boat.

'Did you leave the money for the hotel?'

'Yes. In an envelope in the room.'

'All right. Good luck, Tenente.'

'Good luck. We thank you many times.'

'You won't thank me if you get drowned.'

'What does he say?' Catherine asked.

'He says good luck.'

'Good luck,' Catherine said. 'Thank you very much.

'Are you ready?'

'Yes.'

He bent down and shoved us off. I dug at the water with the oars, then waved one hand. The barman waved back deprecatingly. I saw the lights of the hotel and rowed out, rowing straight out until they were out of sight. There was quite a sea running but we were going with the wind.

CHAPTER 37

I ROWED in the dark keeping the wind in my face. The rain had stopped and only came occasionally in gusts. It was very dark, and the wind was cold. I could see Catherine in the stern but I could not see the water where the blades of the oars dipped. The oars were long and there were no leathers to keep them from slipping out. I pulled, raised, leaned forward, found the water, dipped and pulled, rowing as easily as I could. I did not feather the oars because the wind was with us. I knew my hands would blister and I wanted to delay it as long as I could. The boat was light and rowed easily. I pulled it along in the dark water. I could not see, and hoped we would soon come opposite Pallanza.

We never saw Pallanza. The wind was blowing up the lake and we passed the point that hides Pallanza in the dark and never saw the lights. When we finally saw some lights much further up the lake and close to the shore it was Intra. But for a long time we did not see any lights, nor did we see the shore but rowed steadily in the dark riding with the waves. Sometimes I missed the water with the oars in the dark as a wave lifted the boat. It was quite rough; but I kept on rowing, until suddenly we were close ashore against a point of rock that rose beside us; the waves striking against it, rushing high up, then falling back. I pulled hard on the right oar and backed water with the other and we went out into the lake again; the point was out of sight and we were going on up the lake.

'We're across the lake,' I said to Catherine.

'Weren't we going to see Pallanza?'

'We've missed it.'

'How are you, darling?'

'I'm fine.'

'I could take the oars awhile.'

'No, I'm fine.'

'Poor Ferguson,' Catherine said. 'In the morning she'll come to the hotel and find we're gone.'

'I'm not worrying so much about that,' I said, 'as about getting into the Swiss part of the lake before it's daylight and the custom guards see us.'

'Is it a long way?'

'It's thirty some kilometres from here.'

I rowed all night. Finally my hands were so sore I could hardly close them over the oars. We were nearly smashed up on the shore several times. I kept fairly close to the shore because I was afraid of getting lost on the lake and losing time. Sometimes we were so close we could see a row of trees and the road along the shore with the mountains behind. The rain stopped and the wind drove the clouds so that the moon shone through and looking back I could see the long dark point of Castagnola and the lake with white-caps and beyond, the moon on the high snow mountains. Then the clouds came over the moon again and the mountains and the lake were gone, but it was much lighter than it had been before and we could see the shore. I could see it too clearly and pulled out where they would not see the boat if there were custom guards along the Pallanza road. When the moon came out again we could see white villas on the shore on the slopes of the mountain and the white road where it showed through the trees. All the time I was rowing.

The lake widened and across it on the shore at the foot of the mountains on the other side we saw a few lights that should be Luino. I saw a wedgelike gap between the mountains on the other shore and I thought that must be Luino. If it was we were making good time. I pulled in the oars and lay back on the seat. I was very, very tired of rowing. My arms and shoulders and back ached and my hands were sore.

'I could hold the umbrella,' Catherine said 'We could sail with that with the wind.'

'Can you steer?'

'I think so.'

'You take this oar and hold it under your arm close to the side of the boat and steer and I'll hold the umbrella.' I went back to the stern and showed her how to hold the oar. I took the big umbrella the porter had given me and sat facing the bow and opened it. It opened with a clap. I held it on both sides, sitting astride the handle hooked over the seat. The wind was full in it and I felt the boat suck forward while I held as hard as I could to the two edges. It pulled hard. The boat was moving fast.

'We're going beautifully,' Catherine said, All I could see was umbrella ribs. The umbrella strained and pulled and I felt us driving along with it. I braced my feet and held back on it, then suddenly, it buckled; I felt a rib snap on my forehead, I tried to grab the top that was bending with the wind and the whole thing buckled and went inside out and I was astride the handle of an inside-out, ripped umbrella, where I had been holding a wind-filled pulling sail. I unhooked the handle from the seat, laid the umbrella in the bow and went back to Catherine for the oar. She was laughing. She took my hand and kept on laughing.

'What's the matter?' I took the oar.

'You looked so funny holding that thing.'

'I suppose so.'

'Don't be cross, darling. It was awfully funny. You looked about twenty feet broad and very affectionate holding the umbrella by the edges —' she choked.

'I'll row.'

'Take a rest and a drink. It's a grand night and we've come a long way.'

'I have to keep the boat out of the trough of the waves.'

'I'll get you a drink. Then rest a little while, darling.'

I held the oars up and we sailed with them. Catherine was opening the bag. She handed me the brandy bottle. I pulled the cork with my pocket-knife and took a long drink. It was smooth and hot and the heat went all through me and I felt warmed and cheerful. 'It's lovely brandy,' I said. The moon was under again but I could see the shore. There seemed to be another point going out a long way ahead into the lake.

'Are you warm enough, Cat?'

'I'm splendid. I'm a little stiff.'

'Bail out that water and you can put your feet down.'

Then I rowed and listened to the rowlocks and the dip and scrape of the bailing tin under the stern seat.

'Would you give me the bailer?' I said. 'I want a drink.'

'It's awfully dirty.'

'That's all right. I'll rinse it.'

I heard Catherine rinsing it over the side. Then she handed it to me dipped full of water. I was thirsty after the brandy and the water was icy cold, so cold it made my teeth ache. I looked towards the shore. We were closer to the long point. There were lights in the bay ahead.

'Thanks,' I said and handed back the tin pail.

'You're ever so welcome,' Catherine said. 'There's much more if you want it.'

'Don't you want to eat something?'

'No. I'll be hungry in a little while. We'll save it till then.'

'All right.'

What looked like a point ahead was a long high headland. I went further out in the lake to pass it. The lake was much narrower now. The moon was out again and the *guardie di finanza* could have seen our boat black on the water if they had been watching.

'How are you, Cat?' I asked.

'I'm all right. Where are we?'

'I don't think we have more than about eight miles more.'

'That's a long way to row, you poor sweet. Aren't you dead?'

'No. I'm all right. My hands are sore, that's all.'

We went on up the lake. There was a break in the mountains on the right bank, a flattening-out with a low shore line that I thought must be Cannobio. I stayed a long way out because it was from now on that we ran the most danger of meeting a *guardia*. There was a high dome-capped mountain on the other shore away ahead. I was tired. It was no great distance to row but when you were out of condition it had been a long way. I knew I had to pass that mountain and go up the lake at least five miles further before we would be in Swiss water. The moon was almost down now but before it went down the sky clouded over again and it was very dark. I stayed well out in the lake, rowing awhile, then resting and holding the oars so that the wind struck the blades.

'Let me row awhile,' Catherine said.

'I don't think you ought to.'

'Nonsense. It would be good for me. It would keep me from being too stiff.'

'I don't think you should, Cat.'

'Nonsense. Rowing in moderation is very good for the pregnant lady.'

'All right, you row a little moderately. I'll go back, then you come up. Hold on to both gunwales when you come up.'

I sat in the stern with my coat on and the collar turned up and watched Catherine row. She rowed very well but the oars were too long and bothered her. I opened the bag and ate a couple of sandwiches and took a drink of the brandy. It made everything much better, and I took another drink.

'Tell me when you're tired,' I said. Then a little later, 'Watch out the oar doesn't pop you in the tummy.'

'If it did' — Catherine said between strokes — 'life might be much simpler.'

I took another drink of the brandy.

'How are you going?'

'All right.'

'Tell me when you want to stop.'

'All right.'

I took another drink of the brandy, then took hold of the two gunwales of the boat and moved forward.

'No. I'm going beautifully.'

'Go on back to the stern. I've had a grand rest.'

For a while, with the brandy, I rowed easily and steadily. Then

I began to catch crabs and soon I was just chopping along again with a thin brown taste of bile from having rowed too hard after the brandy.

'Give me a drink of water, will you?' I said.

'That's easy,' Catherine said.

Before daylight it started to drizzle. The wind was down or we were protected by mountains that bounded the curve the lake had made. When I knew daylight was coming I settled down and rowed hard. I did not know where we were and I wanted to get into the Swiss part of the lake. When it was beginning to be daylight we were quite close to the shore. I could see the rocky shore and the trees.

'What's that?' Catherine said. I rested on the oars and listened. It was a motor-boat chugging out on the lake. I pulled close up to the shore and lay quiet. The chugging came closer; then we saw the motor-boat in the rain a little astern of us. There were four *guardia di fianza* in the stern, their *alpini* hats pulled down, their cape collars turned up and their carbines slung across their backs. They all looked sleepy so early in the morning. I could see the yellow on their hats and the yellow marks on their cape collars. The motor-boat chugged on and out of sight in the rain.

I pulled out into the lake. If we were that close to the border I did not want to be hailed by a sentry along the road. I stayed out where I could just see the shore and rowed on for three-quarters of an hour in the rain. We heard a motor-boat once more but I kept quiet until the noise of the engine went away across the lake.

'I think we're in Switzerland, Cat,' I said.

'Really?'

'There's no way to know until we see Swiss troops.'

'Or the Swiss navy.'

'The Swiss navy's no joke for us. That last motor-boat we heard was probably the Swiss navy.'

'If we're in Switzerland let's have a big breakfast. They have wonderful rolls and butter and jam in Switzerland.'

It was clear daylight now and a fine rain was falling. The wind was still blowing outside up the lake and we could see the tops of the white-caps going away from us and up the lake. I was sure we were in Switzerland now. There were many houses back in the trees from the shore and up the shore a way was a village with stone houses, some villas on the hills and a church. I had been looking at the road that skirted the shore for guards but did not see any. The road came quite close to the lake now and I saw a soldier coming out of a café on the road. He wore a grey-green uniform and a helmet like the Germans. He had a healthy-looking face and a little toothbrush moustache. He looked at us.

'Wave to him,' I said to Catherine. She waved and the soldier smiled embarrassedly and gave a wave of his hand. I eased up rowing. We were passing the water-front of the village.

'We must be well inside the border,' I said.

'We want to be sure, darling. We don't want them to turn us back at the frontier.'

'The frontier is a long way back. I think this is the customs town. I'm pretty sure it's Brissago.'

'Won't there be Italians there? There are always both sides at a customs town.'

'Not in war-time. I don't think they let the Italians cross the frontier.'

It was a nice-looking little town. There were many fishing-boats along the quay and nets were spread on racks. There was a fine November rain falling but it looked cheerful and clean even with the rain.

'Should we land then and have breakfast?'

'All right.'

I pulled hard on the left oar and came in close, then straightened out when we were close to the quay and brought the boat alongside. I pulled in the oars, took hold of an iron ring, stepped up on the wet stone and was in Switzerland. I tied the boat and held my hand down to Catherine.

'Come on up, Cat. It's a grand feeling.'

'What about the bags?'

'Leave them in the boat.'

Catherine stepped up and we were in Switzerland together.

'What a lovely country,' she said.

'Isn't it grand?'

'Let's go and have breakfast!'

'Isn't it a grand country? I love the way it feels under my shoes.'

'I'm so stiff I can't feel it very well. But it feels like a splendid country. Darling, do you realize we're here and out of that bloody place?'

'I do. I really do. I've never realized anything before.'

'Look at the houses. Isn't this a fine square? There's a place we can get breakfast.'

'Isn't the rain fine? They never had rain like this in Italy. Its cheerful rain.'

'And we're here, darling! Do you realize we're here?'

We went inside the café and sat down at a clean wooden table. We were cockeyed excited. A splendid clean-looking woman with an apron came and asked us what we wanted.

'Rolls and jam and coffee,' Catherine said.

'I'm sorry, we haven't any rolls in war-time.'

'Bread then.'

'I can make you some toast.'

'All right.'

'I want some eggs fried too.'

'How many eggs for the gentleman?'

'Three.'

'Take four, darling.'

'Four eggs.'

The woman went away. I kissed Catherine and held her hand very tight. We looked at each other and at the café.

'Darling, darling, isn't it lovely?'

'It's grand,' I said.

'I don't mind there not being rolls,' Catherine said. 'I thought about them all night. But I don't mind it. I don't mind it a all.'

'I suppose pretty soon they will arrest us.'

'Never mind, darling. We'll have breakfast first. You won't mind being arrested after breakfast. And then there's nothing they can do to us. We're British and American citizens in good standing.'

'You have a passport, haven't you?'

'Of course. Oh let's not talk about it. Let's be happy.'

'I couldn't be any happier,' I said. A fat grey cat with a tail that lifted like a plume crossed the floor to our table and curved against my leg to purr each time she rubbed. I reached down and stroked her. Catherine smiled at me very happily. 'Here comes the coffee,' she said.

They arrested us after breakfast. We took a little walk through the village then went down to the quay to get our bags. A soldier was standing guard over the boat.

'Is this your boat?'

'Yes.'

'Where do you come from?'

'Up the lake.'

'Then I have to ask you to come with me.'

'How about the bags?'

'You can carry the bags.'

I carried the bags and Catherine walked beside me and the soldier walked along behind us to the old custom-house. In the custom-house a lieutenant, very thin and military, questioned us.

'What nationality are you?'

'American and British.'

'Let me see your passports.'

I gave him mine and Catherine got hers out of her handbag. He examined them for a long time.

'Why do you enter Switzerland this way in a boat?'

'I am a sportsman,' I said. 'Rowing is my great sport. I always row when I get a chance.'

'Why do you come here?'

'For the winter sport. We are tourists and we want to do the winter sport.'

'This is no place for winter sport.'

'We know it. We want to go where they have the winter sport.'

'What have you been doing in Italy?'

'I have been studying architecture. My cousin has been studying art.'

'Why do you leave there?'

'We want to do the winter sport. With the war going on you cannot study architecture.'

'You will please stay where you are,' the lieutenant said. He went back into the building with our passports.

'You're splendid, darling,' Catherine said. 'Keep on the same track. You want to do the winter sport.'

'Do you know anything about art?'

'Rubens,' said Catherine.

'Large and fat,' I said.

'Titian,' Catherine said.

'Titian-haired,' I said. 'How about Mantegna?'

'Don't ask hard ones,' Catherine said. 'I know him though — very bitter.'

'Very bitter,' I said. 'Lots of nail holes.'

'You see I'll make you a fine wife,' Catherine said. 'I'll be able to talk art with your customers.'

'Here he comes,' I said. The thin lieutenant came down the length of the custom-house, holding our passports.

'I will have to send you into Locarno,' he said. 'You can get a carriage and a soldier will go in with you.'

'All right,' I said. 'What about the boat?'

'The boat is confiscated. What have you in those bags?'

He went all through the two bags and held up the quarter

bottle of brandy. 'Would you join me in a drink?' I asked.

'No thank you.' He straightened up. 'How much money have you?'

'Twenty-five hundred lire.'

He was favourably impressed. 'How much has your cousin?'

Catherine had a little over twelve hundred lire. The lieutenant was pleased. His attitude towards us became less haughty.

'If you are going for winter sports,' he said. 'Wengen is the place. My father has a very fine hotel at Wengen. It is open all the time.'

'That's splendid,' I said. 'Could you give me the name?'

'I will write it on a card.' He handed me the card very politely.

'The soldier will take you into Locarno. He will keep your passports. I regret this but it is necessary. I have good hopes they will give you a visa or a police permit at Locarno.'

He handed the two passports to the soldier and carrying the bags we started into the village to order a carriage. 'Hi,' the lieutenant called to the soldier. He said something in a German dialect to him. The soldier slung his rifle on his back and picked up the bags.

'It's a great country,' I said to Catherine.

'It's so practical.'

'Thank you very much,' I said to the lieutenant. He waved his hand.

'*Service!*' he said. We followed our guard into the village.

We drove to Locarno in a carriage with the soldier sitting on the front seat with the driver. At Locarno we did not have a bad time. They questioned us but they were polite because we had passports and money. I do not think they believed a word of the story and I thought it was silly but it was like a law court. You did not want something reasonable, you wanted something technical and then stick to it without explanations. But we had passports and we would spend the money. So they gave us provisional visas. At any time these visas might be withdrawn. We were to report to the police wherever we went.

Could we go wherever we wanted? Yes. Where did we want to go?'

'Where do you want to go, Cat?'

'Montreux.'

'It is a very nice place,' the official said. 'I think you will like that place.'

'Here at Locarno is a very nice place,' another official said. 'I am sure you would like it here very much at Locarno. Locarno is a very attractive place.'

'We would like some place where there is winter sport.'

'There is no winter sport at Montreux.

'I beg your pardon,' the other official said. 'I come from Montreux. There is very certainly winter sport on the Montreux Oberland Bernois railway. It would be false for you to deny that.'

'I do not deny it. I simply said there is no winter sport at Montreux.'

'I question that,' the other official said. 'I question that statement.'

'I hold to that statement.'

'I question that statement. I myself have luge-ed into the streets of Montreux. I have done it not once but several times. Luge-ing is certainly winter sport.'

The other official turned to me.

'Is luge-ing your idea of winter sport, sir? I tell you you would be very comfortable here in Locarno. You would find the climate healthy, you would find the environs attractive. You would like it very much.'

'The gentleman has expressed a wish to go to Montreux.'

'What is luge-ing?' I asked.

'You see he has never even heard of luge-ing!'

That meant a great deal to the second official. He was pleased by that.

'Luge-ing,' said the first official, 'is tobogganing.'

'I beg to differ,' the other official shook his head. 'I must differ again. The toboggan is very different from the luge. The toboggan is constructed in Canada of flat laths. The luge is a common sled with runners. Accuracy means something.'

'Couldn't we toboggan?' I asked.

'Of course you could toboggan,' the first official said. 'You could toboggan very well. Excellent Canadian toboggans are sold in Montreux. Ochs Brothers sell toboggans. They import their own toboggans.'

The second official turned away. 'Tobogganing,' he said, 'requires a special *piste*. You could not toboggan into the streets of Montreux. Where are you stopping here?'

'We don't know,' I said. 'We just drove in from Brissago. The carriage is outside.'

'You make no mistake in going to Montreux,' the first official said. 'You will find the climate delightful and beautiful. You will have no distance to go for winter sport.'

'If you really want winter sport,' the second official said, 'you will go to the Engadine or to Mürren. I must protest against your being advised to go to Montreux for the winter sport.'

'At Les Avants above Montreux there is excellent winter sport of every sort.' The champion of Montreux glared at his colleague.

'Gentlemen,' I said, 'I am afraid we must go. My cousin is very tired. We will go tentatively to Montreux.'

'I congratulate you,' the first official shook my hand.

'I believe that you will regret leaving Locarno,' the second official said. 'At any rate you will report to the police at Montreux.'

'There will be no unpleasantness with the police,' the first official assured me. 'You will find all the inhabitants extremely courteous and friendly.'

'Thank you both very much,' I said. 'We appreciate your advice very much.'

'Goodbye,' Catherine said. 'Thank you both very much.'

They bowed us to the door, the champion of Locarno a little coldly. We went down the steps and into the carriage

'My God, darling,' Catherine said. 'Couldn't we have gotten away any sooner?' I gave the name of a hotel one of the officials had recommended to the driver. He picked up the reins.

'You've forgotten the army,' Catherine said. The soldier was standing by the carriage. I gave him a ten-lira note. 'I have no Swiss money yet,' I said. He thanked me, saluted and went off. The carriage started and we drove to the hotel.

'How did you happen to pick out Montreux?' I asked Catherine. 'Do you really want to go there?'

'It was the first place I could think of,' she said. 'It's not a bad place. We can find some place up in the mountains.'

'Are you sleepy?'

'I'm asleep right now.'

'We'll get a good sleep. Poor Cat, you had a long bad night.'

'I had a lovely time,' Catherine said. 'Especially when you sailed with the umbrella.'

'Can you realize we're in Switzerland?'

'No, I'm afraid I'll wake up and it won't be true.'

'I am too.'

'It is true, isn't it, darling? I'm not just driving down to the *stazione* in Milan to see you off.'

'I hope not.'

'Don't say that. It frightens me. Maybe that's where we're going.'

'I'm so groggy I don't know,' I said.

'Let me see your hands.'

I put them out. They were both blistered raw.

'There's no hole in my side,' I said.

'Don't be sacrilegious.'

I felt very tired and vague in the head. The exhilaration was all gone. The carriage was going along the street.

'Poor hands,' Catherine said.

'Don't touch them,' I said. 'By God I don't know where we

are. Where are we going, driver?' The driver stopped his horse.

'To the Hotel Metropole. Don't you want to go there?'

'Yes,' I said. 'It's all right, Cat.'

'It's all right, darling. Don't be upset. We'll get a good sleep and you won't feel groggy tomorrow.'

'I get pretty groggy,' I said. 'It's like a comic opera today. Maybe I'm hungry.'

'You're just tired, darling. You'll be fine.' The carriage pulled up before the hotel. Someone came out to take our bags.

'I feel all right,' I said. We were down on the pavement going into the hotel.

'I know you'll be all right. You're just tired. You've been up a long time.'

'Anyhow we're here.'

'Yes, we're really here.'

We followed the boy with the bags into the hotel.

BOOK V

CHAPTER 38

THAT fall the snow came very late. We lived in a brown wooden house in the pine trees on the side of the mountain and at night there was frost so that there was thin ice over the water in the two pitchers on the dresser in the morning. Mrs. Guttingen came into the room early in the morning to shut the windows and started a fire in the tall porcelain stove. The pine wood crackled and sparkled and then the fire roared in the stove and the second time Mrs. Guttingen came into the room she brought big chunks of wood for the fire and a pitcher of hot water. When the room was warm she brought in breakfast. Sitting up in bed eating breakfast we could see the lake and the mountains across the lake on the French side. There was snow on the tops of the mountains and the lake was a grey steel-blue.

Outside, in front of the chalet a road went up the mountain. The wheel-ruts and ridges were iron hard with the frost, and the road climbed steadily through the forest and up and around the mountain to where there were meadows, and barns and cabins in the meadows at the edge of the woods looking across the valley. The valley was deep and there was a stream at the bottom that flowed down into the lake and when the wind blew across the valley you could hear the stream in the rocks.

Sometimes we went off the road and on a path through the pine forest. The floor of the forest was soft to walk on; the frost did not harden it as it did the road. But we did not mind the hardness of the road because we had nails in the soles and heels of our boots and the heel nails bit on the frozen ruts and with nailed boots it was good walking on the road and invigorating. But it was lovely walking in the woods.

In front of the house where we lived the mountain went down

steeply to the little plain along the lake and we sat on the porch of the house in the sun and saw the winding of the road down the mountain-side and the terraced vineyards on the side of the lower mountain, the vines all dead now for the winter and the fields divided by stone walls, and below the vineyards the houses of the town on the narrow plain along the lake shore. There was an island with two trees on the lake and the trees looked like the double sails of a fishing-boat. The mountains were sharp and steep on the other side of the lake and down at the end of the lake was the plain of the Rhone Valley flat between the two ranges of mountains; and up the valley where the mountains cut it off was the Dent du Midi. It was a high snowy mountain and it dominated the valley but it was so far away that it did not make a shadow.

When the sun was bright we ate lunch on the porch but the rest of the time we ate upstairs in a small room with plain wooden walls and a big stove in the corner. We bought books and magazines in the town and a copy of *Hoyle* and learned many two-handed card games. The small room with the stove was our living-room. There were two comfortable chairs and a table for books and magazines and we played cards on the dining-table when it was cleared away. Mr. and Mrs. Guttingen lived downstairs and we would hear them talking sometimes in the evening and they were very happy together too. He had been a head waiter and she had worked as maid in the same hotel and they had saved their money to buy this place. They had a son who was studying to be a head waiter. He was at a hotel in Zurich. Downstairs there was a parlour where they sold wine and beer, and sometimes in the evening we would hear carts stop outside on the road and men come up the steps to go in the parlour to drink wine.

There was a box of wood in the hall outside the living-room and I kept up the fire from it. But we did not stay up very late. We went to bed in the dark in the big bedroom and when I was undressed I opened the windows and saw the night and the cold stars and the pine trees below the window and then got into bed as fast as I could. It was lovely in bed with the air so cold and clear and the night outside the window. We slept well and if I woke in the night I knew it was from only one cause and I would shift the feather bed over, very softly so that Catherine would not be wakened, and then go back to sleep again, warm and with the new lightness of thin covers. The war seemed far away. But I knew from the papers that they were still fighting in the mountains because the snow would not come.

Sometimes we walked down the mountain into Montreux. There was a path went down the mountain but it was steep and so usually we took the road and walked down on the wide hard road between fields and then below between the stone walls of the vineyards and on down between the houses of the villages along the way. There were three villages Chernex, Fontanivant, and the other I forget. Then along the road we passed an old square-built stone château on a ledge on the side of the mountain-side with the terraced fields of vines, each vine tied to a stick to hold it up, the vines dry and brown and the earth ready for the snow and the lake down below flat and grey as steel. The road went down a long grade below the château and then turned to the right and went down very steeply and paved with cobbles, into Montreux.

We did not know anyone in Montreux. We walked along beside the lake and saw the swans and the many gulls and terns that flew up when you came close and screamed while they looked down at the water. Out on the lake there were flocks of grebes, small and dark, and leaving trails in the water when they swam. In the town we walked along the main street and looked in the windows of the shops. There were many big hotels that were closed but most of the shops were open and the people were very glad to see us. There was a fine coiffeur's place where Catherine went to have her hair done. The woman who ran it was very cheerful and the only person we knew in Montreux. While Catherine was there I went up to a beer place and drank dark Munich beer and read the papers. I read the *Corriere della Sera* and the English and American papers from Paris. All the advertisements were blacked out, supposedly to prevent communication in that way with the enemy. The papers were bad reading. Everything was going very badly everywhere. I sat back in the corner with a heavy mug of dark beer and an opened glazed-paper package of pretzels and ate the pretzels for the salty flavour and the good way they made the beer taste and read about disaster. I thought Catherine would come by but she did not come so I hung the papers back on the rack, paid for my beer and went up the street to look for her. The day was cold and dark and wintry and the stone of the houses looked cold. Catherine was still in the hairdresser's shop. The woman was waving her hair. I sat in the little booth and watched. It was exciting to watch and Catherine smiled and talked to me and my voice was a little thick from being excited. The tongs made a pleasant clicking sound and I could see Catherine in three mirrors and it was pleasant and warm in the booth. Then the woman put up Catherine's hair, and Catherine looked in the mirror and changed it a little, taking out and putting in pins; then stood up. 'I'm sorry to have taken such a long time.'

'Monsieur was very interested. Were you not, monsieur?' the woman smiled.

'Yes,' I said.

We went out and up the street. It was cold and wintry and the wind was blowing. 'Oh, darling, I love you so,' I said.

'Don't we have a fine time?' Catherine said. 'Look. Let's go some place and have beer instead of tea. It's very good for young Catherine. It keeps her small.'

'Young Catherine,' I said. 'That loafer.'

'She's been very good,' Catherine said. 'She makes very little trouble. The doctor says beer will be good for me and keep her small.'

'If you keep her small enough and she's a boy, maybe he will be a jockey.'

'I suppose if we really have this child we ought to get married,' Catherine said. We were in the beer place at the corner table. It was getting dark outside. It was still early but the day was dark and the dusk was coming early.

'Let's get married now,' I said.

'No,' Catherine said. 'It's too embarrassing now. I show too plainly. I won't go before anyone and be married in this state.'

'I wish we'd gotten married.'

'I suppose it would have been better. But when could we, darling?'

'I don't know.'

'I know one thing. I'm not going to be married in this splendid matronly state.'

'You're not matronly.'

'Oh, yes, I am, darling. The hairdresser asked me if this was our first. I lied and said no, we had two boys and two girls.'

'When will we be married?'

'Any time after I'm thin again. We want to have a splendid wedding with everyone thinking what a handsome young couple.'

'And you're not worried?'

'Darling, why should I be worried? The only time I ever felt badly was when I felt like a whore in Milan, and that only lasted seven minutes and besides it was the room furnishings. Don't I make you a good wife?'

'You're a lovely wife.'

'Then don't be too technical, darling. I'll marry you as soon as I'm thin again.'

'All right.'

'Do you think I ought to drink another beer? The doctor said I was rather narrow in the hips and it's all for the best if we keep young Catherine small.'

'What else did he say?' I was worried.

'Nothing. I have a wonderful blood-pressure, darling. He admired my blood-pressure greatly.'

'What did he say about you being too narrow in the hips?'

'Nothing. Nothing at all. He said I shouldn't ski.'

'Quite right.'

'He said it was too late to start if I'd never done it before. He said I could ski if I wouldn't fall down.'

'He's just a big-hearted joker.'

'Really he was very nice. We'll have him when the baby comes.'

'Did you ask him if you ought to get married?'

'No. I told him we'd been married four years. You see, darling, if I marry you I'll be an American and any time we're married under American law the child is legitimate.'

'Where did you find that out?'

'In the New York *World Almanac* in the library.'

'You're a grand girl.'

'I'll be very glad to be an American and we'll go to America, won't we, darling? I want to see Niagara Falls.'

'You're a fine girl.'

'There's something else I want to see but I can't remember it.'

'The stockyards?'

'No. I can't remember it.'

'The Woolworth building?'

'No.'

'The Grand Canyon?'

'No. But I'd like to see that.'

'What was it?'

'The Golden Gate! That's what I want to see. Where is the Golden Gate?'

'San Francisco.'

'Then let's go there. I want to see San Francisco anyway.'

'All right. We'll go there.'

'Now let's go up the mountain. Should we? Can we get the M.O.B.?' ♦

'There's a train a little after five.'

'Let's get that.'

'All right. I'll drink one more beer first.'

When we went out to go up the street and climb the stairs to the station it was very cold. A cold wind was coming down the Rhone valley. There were lights in the shop windows and we climbed the steep stone stairway to the upper street, then up another stair to the station. The electric train was there waiting, all the lights on. There was a dial that showed when it left. The clock hands pointed to ten minutes after five. I looked at the station clock. It was five minutes after. As we got on board I saw the motorman and conductor coming out of the station wine-shop. We sat down and opened the window. The train was electrically heated and stuffy but fresh cold air came in through the window.

'Are you tired, Cat?' I asked.

'No. I feel splendid.'

'It isn't a long ride.'

'I like the ride,' she said. 'Don't worry about me, darling. I feel fine.'

Snow did not come until three days before Christmas. We woke one morning and it was snowing. We stayed in bed with the fire roaring in the stove and watched the snow fall. Mrs. Guttingen took away the breakfast trays and put more wood in the stove. It was a big snowstorm. She said it had started about midnight. I went to the window and looked out but could not see across the road. It was blowing and snowing wildly. I went back to bed and we lay and talked.

'I wish I could ski,' Catherine said. 'It's rotten not to be able to ski.'

'We'll get a bobsled and come down the road. That's no worse for you than riding in a car.'

'Won't it be rough?'

'We can see.'

'I hope it won't be too rough.'

'After a while we'll take a walk in the snow'

'Before lunch,' Catherine said, so we'll have a good appetite.'

'I'm always hungry.'

'So am I.'

We went out in the snow but it was drifted so that we could not walk far. I went ahead and made a trail down to the station but when we reached there we had gone far enough. The snow was blowing so we could hardly see and we went into the little inn by the station, and swept each other off with a broom and sat on a bench and had vermouths.

'It is a big storm,' the barmaid said.

'Yes.'

'The snow is very late this year.'

'Yes.'

'Could I eat a chocolate bar?' Catherine asked. 'Or is it too close to lunch? I'm always hungry.'

'Go on and eat one,' I said.

'I'll take one with filberts,' Catherine said.

'They are very good,' the girl said, 'I like them the best.'

'I'll have another vermouth,' I said.

When we came out to start back up the road our track was filled in by the snow. There were only faint indentations where the holes had been. The snow blew in our faces so we could hardly see. We brushed off and went in to have lunch. Mr. Guttingen served the lunch.

'Tomorrow there will be ski-ing,' he said. 'Do you ski, Mr Henry?'

'No. But I want to learn.'

'You will learn very easily. My boy will be here for Christmas and he will teach you.'

'That's fine. When does he come?'

'Tomorrow night.'

When we were sitting by the stove in the little room after lunch looking out the window at the snow coming down Catherine said, 'Wouldn't you like to go on a trip somewhere by yourself, darling, and be with men and ski?'

'No. Why should I?'

'I should think sometimes you would want to see other people besides me.'

'Do you want to see other people?'

'No.'

'Neither do I.'

'I know. But you're different. I'm having a child and that makes me contented not to do anything. I know I'm awfully stupid now and I talk too much, and I think you ought to get away so you won't be tired of me.'

'Do you want me to go away?'

'No. I want you to stay.'

'That's what I'm going to do.'

'Come over here,' she said. 'I want to feel the bump on your head. It's a big bump.' She ran her finger over it. 'Darling, would you like to grow a beard?'

'Would you like me to?'

'It might be fun. I'd like to see you with a beard.'

'All right. I'll grow one. I'll start now, this minute. It's a good idea. It will give me something to do.'

'Are you worried because you haven't anything to do?'

'No. I like it. I have a fine life. Don't you?'

'I have a lovely life. But I was afraid because I'm big now that maybe I was a bore to you.'

'Oh, Cat. You don't know how crazy I am about you.'

'This way?'

'Just the way you are. I have a fine time. Don't we have a good life?'

'I do, but I thought maybe you were restless.'

'No. Sometimes I wonder about the front and about people I know but I don't worry. I don't think about anything much.'

'Who do you wonder about?'

'About Rinaldi and the priest and lots of people I know. But I don't think about them much. I don't want to think about the war. I'm through with it.'

'What are you thinking about now?'

'Nothing.'

'Yes you were. Tell me.'

'I was wondering whether Rinaldi had the syphilis.'

'Was that all?'

'Yes.'

'Has he the syphilis?'

'I don't know.'

'I'm glad you haven't. Did you ever have anything like that?'

'I had gonorrhoea.'

'I don't want to hear about it. Was it very painful, darling?'

'Very.'

'I wish I'd had it.'

'No you don't.'

'I do. I wish I'd had it to be like you. I wish I'd stayed with all your girls so I could make fun of them to you.'

'That's a pretty picture.'

'It's not a pretty picture you having gonorrhoea.'

'I know it. Look at it snowing now.'

'I'd rather look at you. Darling, why don't you let your **hair** grow?'

'How grow?'

'Just grow a little longer.'

'It's long enough now.'

'No, let it grow a little longer and I could cut mine and we'd be just alike only one of us blonde and one of us dark.'

'I wouldn't let you cut yours.'

'It would be fun. I'm tired of it. It's an awful nuisance in the bed at night.'

'I like it.'

'Wouldn't you like it short?'

'I might. I like it the way it is.'

'It might be nice short. Then we'd both be alike. Oh, darling. I want you so much I want to be you too.'

'You are. We're the same one.'

'I know it. At night we are.'

'The nights are grand.'

'I want us to be all mixed up. I don't want you to go away. I just said that. You go if you want to. But hurry right back. Why, darling, I don't live at all when I'm not with you.'

'I won't ever go away,' I said. 'I'm no good when you're not there. I haven't any life at all any more.'

'I want you to have a life. I want you to have a fine life. But we'll have it together, won't we?'

'And now do you want me to stop growing my beard or let it go on?'

'Go on. Grow it. It will be exciting. Maybe it will be done for New Year's.'

'Now do you want to play chess?'

'I'd rather play with you.'

'No. Let's play chess.'

'And afterward we'll play?'

'Yes.'

'All right.'

I got out the chess-board and arranged the pieces. It was still snowing hard outside.

One time in the night I woke up and knew that Catherine was awake too. The moon was shining in the window and made shadows on the bed from the bars on the window-panes.

'Are you awake, sweetheart?'

'Yes. Can't you sleep?'

'I just woke up thinking about how I was nearly crazy when I first met you. Do you remember?'

'You were just a little crazy.'

'I'm never that way any more. I'm grand now. You say grand so sweetly. Say grand.'

'Grand.'

'Oh, you're sweet. And I'm not crazy now. I'm just very, very, very happy.'

259

'Go on to sleep,' I said.

'All right. Let's go to sleep at exactly the same moment.

'All right.'

But we did not. I was awake for quite a long time thinking about things and watching Catherine sleeping, the moonlight on her face. Then I went to sleep, too.

CHAPTER 39

By the middle of January I had a beard and the winter had settled into bright cold days and hard cold nights. We could walk on the roads again. The snow was packed hard and smooth by the hay-sleds and wood-sleds and the logs that were hauled down the mountain. The snow lay over all the country, down almost to Montreux. The mountains on the other side of the lake were all white and the plain of the Rhone valley was covered. We took long walks on the other side of the mountain to the Bains d'Alliez. Catherine wore hob-nailed boots and a cape and carried a stick with a sharp steel point. She did not look big with the cape and we would not walk too fast but stopped and sat on logs by the roadside to rest when she was tired.

There was an inn in the trees at the Bains d'Alliez where the woodcutters stopped to drink, and we sat inside warmed by the stove and drank hot red wine with spices and lemon in it. They called it *glühwein* and it was a good thing to warm you and to celebrate with. The inn was dark and smoky inside and afterward when you went out the cold air came sharply into your lungs and numbed the edge of your nose as you inhaled. We looked back at the inn with light coming from the windows and the woodcutters' horses stamping and jerking their heads outside to keep warm. There was frost on the hairs of their muzzles and their breathing made plumes of frost in the air. Going up the road towards home the road was smooth and slippery for a while and the ice orange from the horses until the wood-hauling track turned off. Then the road was clean-packed snow and led through the woods, and twice coming home in the evening we saw foxes.

It was fine country and every time that we went out it was fun.

'You have a splendid beard now,' Catherine said. 'It looks just like the woodcutters'. Did you see the man with the tiny gold earrings?'

'He's a chamois hunter,' I said. 'They wear them because they say it makes them hear better.'

'Really? I don't believe it. I think they wear them to show they are chamois hunters. Are there chamois near here?'

'Yes, beyond the Dent du Jaman.'

'It was fun seeing the fox.'

'When he sleeps he wraps that tail around him to keep warm.'

'It must be a lovely feeling.'

'I always wanted to have a tail like that. Wouldn't it be fun if we had brushes like a fox?'

'It might be very difficult dressing.'

'We'd have clothes made, or live in a country where it wouldn't make any difference.'

'We live in a country where nothing makes any difference. Isn't it grand how we never see anyone? You don't want to see people, do you, darling?'

'No.'

'Should we sit here just a minute? I'm a little bit tired.'

We sat close together on the logs. Ahead the road went down through the forest.

'She won't come between us, will she? The little brat.'

'No. We won't let her.'

'How are we for money?'

'We have plenty. They honoured the last sight draft.'

'Won't your family try and get hold of you now they know you're in Switzerland?'

'Probably. I'll write them something.'

'Haven't you written them?'

'No. Only the sight draft.'

'Thank God I'm not your family.'

'I'll send them a cable.'

'Don't you care anything about them?'

'I did, but we quarrelled so much it wore itself out.'

'I think I'd like them. I'd probably like them very much.'

'Let's not talk about them or I'll start to worry about them.' After a while I said, 'Let's go on if you're rested.'

'I'm rested.'

We went on down the road. It was dark now and the snow squeaked under our boots. The night was dry and cold and very clear.

'I love your beard,' Catherine said. 'It's a great success. It looks so stiff and fierce and it's very soft and a great pleasure.'

'Do you like it better than without?'

'I think so. You know, darling, I'm not going to cut my hair now until after young Catherine's born. I look too big and matronly now. But after she's born and I'm thin again I'm going to cut it and then I'll be a fine new and different girl for you. We'll go together and get it cut, or I'll go alone and come and surprise you.'

I did not say anything.

'You won't say I can't, will you?'

'No. I think it would be exciting.'

'Oh, you're so sweet. And maybe I'd look lovely, darling, and be so thin and exciting to you and you'll fall in love with me all over again.'

'Hell,' I said, 'I love you enough now. What do you want to do? Ruin me?'

'Yes. I want to ruin you.'

'Good,' I said, 'that's what I want too.'

CHAPTER 40

WE had a fine life. We lived through the months of January and February and the winter was very fine and we were happy. There had been short thaws when the wind blew warm and the snow softened and the air felt like Spring, but always the clear hard cold had come again and the winter had returned. In March came the first break in the winter. In the night it started raining. It rained on all morning and turned the snow to slush and made the mountain-side dismal. There were clouds over the lake and over the valley. It was raining high up the mountain. Catherine wore heavy overshoes and I wore Mr. Guttingen's rubber-boots and we walked to the station under an umbrella, through the slush and the running water that was washing the ice of the roads bare, to stop at the pub before lunch for a vermouth. Outside we could hear the rain.

'Do you think we ought to move into town?'

'What do you think?' Catherine asked.

'If the winter is over and the rain keeps up it won't be fun up here. How long is it before young Catherine?'

'About a month. Perhaps a little more.'

'We might go down and stay in Montreux.'

'Why don't we go to Lausanne? That's where the hospital is.'

'All right. But I thought maybe that was too big a town.'

'We can be as much alone in a bigger town and Lausanne might be nice.'

'When should we go?'

'I don't care. Whenever you want, darling. I don't want to leave here if you don't want.'

'Let's see how the weather turns out.'

It rained for three days. The snow was all gone now on the mountain-side below the station. The road was a torrent of muddy snow-water. It was too wet and slushy to go out. On the morning of the third day of rain we decided to go down into town.

'That is all right, Mr. Henry,' Guttingen said. 'You do not have to give me any notice. I did not think you would want to stay now the bad weather is come.'

'We have to be near the hospital anyway on account of Madame,' I said.

'I understand,' he said. 'Will you come back some time and stay, with the little one?'

'Yes, if you would have room.'

'In the Spring when it is nice you could come and enjoy it. We could put the little one and the nurse in the big room that is closed now and you and Madame could have your same room looking out over the lake.'

'I'll write about coming,' I said. We packed and left on the train that went down after lunch. Mr. and Mrs. Guttingen came down to the station with us and he hauled our baggage down on a sled through the slush. They stood beside the station in the rain waving goodbye.

'They were very sweet,' Catherine said.

'They were fine to us.'

We took the train to Lausanne from Montreux. Looking out the window towards where we had lived you could not see the mountains for the clouds. The train stopped in Vevey, then went on, passing the lake on one side and on the other the wet brown fields and the bare woods and the wet houses. We came into Lausanne and went into a medium-sized hotel to stay. It was still raining as we drove through the streets and into the carriage entrance of the hotel. The concierge with brass keys on his lapels, the elevator, the carpets on the floors and the white wash-bowls with shining fixtures, the brass bed and the big comfortable bedroom all seemed very great luxury after the Guttingens'. The windows of the room looked out on a wet garden with a wall topped by an iron fence. Across the street, which sloped steeply, was another hotel with a similar wall and garden. I looked out at the rain falling in the fountain of the garden.

Catherine turned on all the lights and commenced unpacking.

I ordered a whisky and soda and lay on the bed and read the papers I had bought at the station. It was March 1918, and the German offensive had started in France. I drank the whisky and soda and read while Catherine unpacked and moved around the room.

'You know what I have to get, darling,' she said.

'What?'

'Baby clothes. There aren't many people reach my time without baby things.'

'You can buy them.'

'I know. That's what I'll do tomorrow. I'll find out what is necessary.'

'You ought to know. You were a nurse.'

'But so few of the soldiers had babies in the hospitals.'

'I did.'

She hit me with the pillow and spilled the whisky and soda.

'I'll order you another,' she said. 'I'm sorry I spilled it.'

'There wasn't much left. Come on over to the bed.'

'No. I have to try and make this room look like something.'

'Like what?'

'Like our home.'

'Hang out the Allied flags.'

'Oh shut up.'

'Say it again.'

'Shut up.'

'You say it so cautiously,' I said. 'As though you didn't want to offend anyone.'

'I don't.'

'Then come over to the bed.'

'All right.' She came and sat on the bed. 'I know I'm no fun for you, darling. I'm like a big flour-barrel.'

'No you're not. You're beautiful and you're sweet.'

'I'm just something very ungainly that you've married.'

'No you're not. You're more beautiful all the time.'

'But I will be thin again, darling.'

'You're thin now.'

'You've been drinking.'

'Just whisky and soda.'

'There's another one coming,' she said. 'And then should we order dinner up here?'

'That will be good.'

'Then we won't go out, will we? We'll just stay in tonight.'

'And play,' I said.

'I'll drink some wine.' Catherine said. 'It won't hurt me. Maybe we can get some of our old white capri.'

'I know we can,' I said. 'They'll have Italian wines at a hotel this size.'

The waiter knocked at the door. He brought the whisky in a glass with ice and beside the glass on a tray a small bottle of soda.

'Thank you,' I said. 'Put it down there. Will you please have dinner for two brought up here and two bottles of dry white capri in ice.'

'Do you wish to commence your dinner with soup?'

'Do you want soup, Cat?'

'Please.'

'Bring soup for one.'

'Thank you, sir.' He went out and shut the door. I went back to the papers and the war in the papers, and poured the soda slowly over the ice into the whisky. I would have to tell them not to put ice in the whisky. Let them bring the ice separately. That way you could tell how much whisky there was and it would not suddenly be too thin from the soda. I would get a bottle of whisky and have them bring ice and soda. That was the sensible way. Good whisky was very pleasant. It was one of the pleasant parts of life.

'What are you thinking, darling?'

'About whisky.'

'What about whisky?'

'About how nice it is.'

Catherine made a face. 'All right,' she said.

We stayed at that hotel three weeks. It was not bad; the dining-room was usually empty and very often we ate in our room at night. We walked in the town and took the cogwheel railway down to Ouchy and walked beside the lake. The weather became quite warm and it was like Spring. We wished we were back in the mountains but the Spring weather lasted only a few days and then the cold rawness of the breaking up of winter came again.

Catherine bought the things she needed for the baby, up in the town. I went to a gymnasium in the arcade to box for exercise. I usually went up there in the morning while Catherine stayed late in bed. On the days of false Spring it was very nice, after boxing and taking a shower, to walk along the streets smelling the Spring in the air and stop at a café to sit and watch the people and read the paper and drink a vermouth; then go down to the hotel and have lunch with Catherine. The professor at the boxing gymnasium wore moustaches and was very precise and jerky and went all to pieces if you started after him. But it was pleasant in the gym. There was good air and light and I worked quite hard, skipping rope, shadow-boxing, doing abdominal exercises lying on the floor in a patch of sunlight that came through the open window, and occasionally scaring the professor when we boxed. I could not shadow-box in front of the narrow long mirror at first because it looked so strange to see a man with a beard boxing. But finally I just thought it was funny. I wanted to take off the beard as soon as I started boxing but Catherine did not want me to.

Sometimes Catherine and I went for rides out in the country in a carriage. It was nice to ride when the days were pleasant and we found two good places where we could ride out to eat. Catherine could not walk very far now and I loved to ride out along the country roads with her. When there was a good day we had a splendid time and we never had a bad time. We knew the baby was very close now and it gave us both a feeling as though something were hurrying us and we could not lose any time together.

CHAPTER 41

ONE morning I awoke about three o'clock hearing Catherine stirring in the bed.

'Are you all right, Cat?'

'I've been having some pains, darling.'

'Regularly?'

'No, not very.'

'If you have them at all regularly we'll go to the hospital.'

I was very sleepy and went back to sleep. A little while later I woke again.

'Maybe you'd better call up the doctor,' Catherine said. 'I think maybe this is it.'

I went to the phone and called the doctor. 'How often are the pains coming?' he asked.

'How often are they coming, Cat?'

'I should think every quarter of an hour.'

'You should go to the hospital then,' the doctor said. 'I will dress and go there right away myself.'

I hung up and called the garage near the station to send up a taxi. No one answered the phone for a long time. Then I finally got a man who promised to send up a taxi at once. Catherine was dressing. Her bag was all packed with the things she would need at the hospital and the baby things. Outside in the hall I rang for the elevator. There was no answer. I went downstairs. There was no one downstairs except the night-watchman. I brought the elevator up myself, put Catherine's bag in it, she stepped in and we went down. The night-watchman opened the door for us and we sat outside on the stone slabs beside the stairs down to the driveway and waited for the taxi. The night was clear and the stars were out. Catherine was very excited.

'I'm so glad it's started,' she said. 'Now in a little while it will be all over.'

'You're a good brave girl.'

'I'm not afraid. I wish the taxi would come, though.'

We heard it coming up the street and saw its headlights. It turned into the driveway and I helped Catherine in and the driver put the bag up in front.

'Drive to the hospital,' I said.

We went out of the driveway and started up the hill.

At the hospital we went in and I carried the bag. There was a woman at the desk who wrote down Catherine's name, age, address, relatives and religion, in a book. She said she had no religion and the woman drew a line in the space after that word. She gave her name as Catherine Henry.

'I will take you up to your room,' she said. We went up in an elevator. The woman stopped it and we stepped out and followed her down a hall. Catherine held tight to my arm.

'This is the room,' the woman said. 'Will you please undress and get into bed? Here is a nightgown for you to wear.'

'I have a nightgown,' Catherine said.

'It is better for you to wear this nightgown,' the woman said.

I went outside and sat on a chair in the hallway.

'You can come in now,' the woman said from the doorway. Catherine was lying in the narrow bed wearing a plain, square-cut nightgown that looked as though it were made of rough sheeting. She smiled at me.

'I'm having fine pains now,' she said. The woman was holding her wrist and timing the pains with a watch.

'That was a big one,' Catherine said. I saw it on her face.

'Where's the doctor?' I asked the woman.

'He's lying down sleeping. He will be here when he is needed.'

'I must do something for Madame, now,' the nurse said. 'Would you please step out again?'

I went out into the hall. It was a bare hall with two windows and closed doors all down the corridor. It smelled of hospital. I sat on the chair and looked at the floor and prayed for Catherine.

'You can come in,' the nurse said. I went in.

'Hello, darling,' Catherine said.

'How is it?'

'They are coming quite often now.' Her face drew up. Then she smiled.

'That was a real one. Do you want to put your hand on my back again, nurse?'

'If it helps you,' the nurse said.

'You go away, darling,' Catherine said. 'Go out and get something to eat. I may do this for a long time the nurse says.'

'The first labour is usually protracted,' the nurse said.

'Please go out and get something to eat,' Catherine said. 'I'm fine, really.'

'I'll stay awhile,' I said.

The pains came quite regularly, then slackened off. Catherine was very excited. When the pains were bad she called them good ones. When they started to fall off she was disappointed and ashamed.

'You go out, darling,' she said. 'I think you are just making me self-conscious.' Her face tied up. 'There. That was better. I so want to be a good wife and have this child without any foolishness. Please go and get some breakfast, darling, and then come back. I won't miss you. Nurse is splendid to me.'

'You have plenty of time for breakfast,' the nurse said.

'I'll go then. Goodbye, sweet.'

'Goodbye,' Catherine said, 'and have a fine breakfast for me too.'

'Where can I get breakfast?' I asked the nurse.

'There's a café down the street at the square,' she said. 'It should be open now.'

Outside it was getting light. I walked down the empty street to the café. There was a light in the window. I went in and stood at the zinc bar and an old man served me a glass of white wine and a brioche. The brioche was yesterday's. I dipped it in the wine and then drank a glass of coffee.

'What do you do at this hour?' the old man asked.

'My wife is in labour at the hospital.'

'So. I wish you good luck.'

'Give me another glass of wine.'

He poured it from the bottle slopping it over a little so some ran down on the zinc. I drank this glass, paid and went out. Outside along the street were the refuse cans from the houses waiting for the collector. A dog was nosing at one of the cans.

'What do you want?' I asked and looked in the can to see if there was anything I could pull out for him; there was nothing on top but coffee-grounds, dust and some dead flowers.

'There isn't anything, dog,' I said. The dog crossed the street. I went up the stairs in the hospital to the floor Catherine was on and down the hall to her room. I knocked on the door. There was no answer. I opened the door; the room was empty, except for Catherine's bag on a chair and her dressing-gown hanging on a hook on the wall. I went out and down the hall, looking for somebody. I found a nurse.

'Where is Madame Henry?'

'A lady has just gone to the delivery room.'

'Where is it?'

'I will show you.'

She took me down to the end of the hall. The door of the room was partly open. I could see Catherine lying on a table, covered by a sheet. The nurse was on one side and the doctor stood on the other side of the table beside some cylinders. The doctor held a rubber mask attached to a tube in one hand.

'I will give you a gown and you can go in,' the nurse said. 'Come in here, please.'

She put a white gown on me and pinned it at the neck in back with a safety-pin.

'Now you can go in,' she said. I went into the room.

'Hello, darling,' Catherine said in a strained voice. 'I'm not doing much.'

'You are Mr. Henry?' the doctor asked.

'Yes. How is everything going, doctor?'

'Things are going very well,' the doctor said. 'We came in here where it is easy to give gas for the pains.'

'I want it now,' Catherine said. The doctor placed the rubber mask over her face and turned a dial and I watched Catherine breathing deeply and rapidly. Then she pushed the mask away. The doctor shut off the petcock.

'That wasn't a very big one. I had a very big one a while ago. The doctor made me go clear out, didn't you, doctor?' Her voice was strange. It rose on the word doctor.

The doctor smiled.

'I want it again,' Catherine said. She held the rubber tight to her face and breathed fast. I heard her moaning a little. Then she pulled the mask away and smiled.

'That was a big one,' she said. 'That was a very big one. Don't you worry, darling. You go away. Go have another breakfast.'

'I'll stay,' I said.

We had gone to the hospital about four o'clock in the morning. At noon Catherine was still in the delivery room. The pains had slackened again. She looked very tired and worn now but she was still cheerful.

'I'm not any good, darling,' she said. 'I'm so sorry. I thought I would do it very easily. Now — there's one —' she reached out her hand for the mask and held it over her face. The doctor moved the dial and watched her. In a little while it was over.

'It wasn't much,' Catherine said. She smiled. 'I'm a fool about the gas. It's wonderful.'

'We'll get some for the home,' I said.

'*There one comes*,' Catherine said quickly. The doctor turned the dial and looked at his watch.

'What is the interval now?' I asked.

'About a minute.'

'Don't you want lunch?'

'I will have something pretty soon,' he said.

'You must have something to eat, doctor,' Catherine said.

'I'm so sorry I go on so long. Couldn't my husband give me the gas?'

'If you wish,' the doctor said. 'You turn it to the numeral two.

'I see,' I said. There was a marker on a dial that turned with a handle.

'*I want it now,*' Catherine said. She held the mask tight to her face. I turned the dial to number two and when Catherine put down the mask I turned it off. It was very good of the doctor to let me do something

'Did you do it, darling?' Catherine asked. She stroked my wrist.

'Sure.'

'You're so lovely.' She was a little drunk from the gas.

'I will eat from a tray in the next room,' the doctor said. 'You can call me any moment.' While the time passed I watched him eat, then, after a while, I saw that he was lying down and smoking a cigarette. Catherine was getting very tired.

'Do you think I'll ever have this baby?' she asked.

'Yes, of course you will.'

'I try as hard as I can. I push down but it goes away. *There it comes. Give it to me.*'

At two o'clock I went out and had lunch. There were a few men in the café sitting with coffee and glasses of kirsch or marc on the tables. I sat down at a table. 'Can I eat?' I asked the waiter.

'It is past time for lunch.'

'Isn't there anything for all hours?'

'You can have *choucroute.*'

'Give me *choucroute* and beer.'

'A demi or a bock?'

'A light demi.'

The waiter brought a dish of sauerkraut with a slice of ham over the top and a sausage buried in the hot wine-soaked cabbage. I ate it and drank the beer. I was very hungry. I watched the

273

people at the tables in the café. At one table they were playing cards. Two men at the table next me were talking and smoking. The café was full of smoke. The zinc bar, where I had breakfasted, had three people behind it now; the old man. a plump woman in a black dress who sat behind a counter and kept track of everything served to the tables, and a boy in an apron. I wondered how many children the woman had and what it had been like.

When I was through with the *choucroute* I went back to the hospital. The street was all clean now. There were no refuse cans out. The day was cloudy but the sun was trying to come through. I rode upstairs in the elevator, stepped out and went down the hall to Catherine's room, where I had left my white gown. I put it on and pinned it in back at the neck. I looked in the glass and saw myself looking like a fake doctor with a beard. I went down the hall to the delivery room. The door was closed and I knocked. No one answered so I turned the handle and went in. The doctor sat by Catherine. The nurse was doing something at the other end of the room.

'Here is your husband,' the doctor said.

'Oh, darling, I have the most wonderful doctor,' Catherine said in a very strange voice. 'He's been telling me the most wonderful story and when the pain came too badly he put me all the way out. He's wonderful. You're wonderful, doctor.'

'You're drunk,' I said.

'I know it,' Catherine said. 'But you shouldn't say it.' Then 'Give it to me. Give it to me.' She clutched hold of the mask and breathed short and deep, pantingly, making the respirator click. Then she gave a long sigh and the doctor reached with his left hand and lifted away the mask.

'That was a very big one, Catherine said. Her voice was very strange. 'I'm not going to die now, darling. I'm past where I was going to die. Aren't you glad?'

'Don't you get in that place again.'

'I won't. I'm not afraid of it though. I won't die, darling.'

'You will not do any such foolishness,' the doctor said. 'You would not die and leave your husband.'

'Oh, no. I won't die. I wouldn't die. It's silly to die. There it comes. *Give it to me.*'

After a while the doctor said, 'You will go out, Mr. Henry, for a few moments and I will make an examination.'

'He wants to see how I am doing,' Catherine said. 'You can come back afterward, darling, can't he, doctor?'

'Yes,' said the doctor. 'I will send word when he can come back.'

I went out the door and down the hall to the room where Catherine was to be after the baby came. I sat in a chair there and looked at the room. I had the paper in my coat that I had bought when I went out for lunch and I read it. It was beginning to be dark outside and I turned the light on to read. After a while I stopped reading and turned off the light and watched it get dark outside. I wondered why the doctor did not send for me. Maybe it was better I was away. He probably wanted me away for a while. I looked at my watch. If he did not send for me in ten minutes I would go down anyway.

Poor, poor dear Cat. And this was the price you paid for sleeping together. This was the end of the trap. This was what people got for loving each other. Thank God for gas, anyway. What must it have been like before there were anaesthetics? Once it started they were in the mill-race. Catherine had a good time in the time of pregnancy. It wasn't bad. She was hardly ever sick. She was not awfully uncomfortable until towards the last. So now they got her in the end. You never got away with anything. Get away hell! It would have been the same if we had been married fifty times. And what if she should die? She won't die. People don't die in childbirth nowadays. That was what all husbands thought. Yes, but what if she should die? She won't die. She's just having a bad time. The initial labour is usually protracted. She's only having a bad time. Afterward we'd say what a bad time, and Catherine would say it wasn't really so bad. But what if she should die? She can't die. Yes, but what if she should die? She can't, I tell you. Don't be a fool. It's just a bad time. It's just nature giving her hell. It's only the first labour, which is almost always protracted. Yes, but what if she should die? She can't die. Why would she die? What reason is there for her to die? There's just a child that has to be born, the by-product of good nights in Milan. It makes trouble and is born and then you look after it and get fond of it maybe. But what if she should die? She won't die. But what if she should die? She won't. She's all right. But what if she should die? She can't die. But what if she should die? Hey, what about that? What if she should die?'

The doctor came into the room.

'How does it go, doctor?'

'It doesn't go,' he said.

'What do you mean?'

'Just that. I made an examination — ' He detailed the result of the examination. 'Since then I've waited to see. But it doesn't go.'

'What do you advise?'

'There are two things. Either a high forceps delivery which can tear and be quite dangerous besides being possibly bad for the child, and a Caesarean.'

'What is the danger of a Caesarean?' What if she should die!'

'It should be no greater than the danger of an ordinary delivery.'

'Would you do it yourself?'

'Yes. I would need possibly an hour to get things ready and to get the people I would need. Perhaps a little less.'

'What do you think?'

'I would advise a Caesarean operation. If it were my wife I would do a Caesarean.'

'What are the after effects?'

'There are none. There is only the scar.'

'What about infection?'

'The danger is not so great as in a high forceps delivery.'

'What if you just went on and did nothing?'

'You would have to do something eventually. Mrs. Henry is already losing much of her strength. The sooner we operate now the safer.'

'Operate as soon as you can,' I said.

'I will go and give the instructions.'

I went into the delivery room. The nurse was with Catherine who lay on the table, big under the sheet, looking very pale and tired.

'Did you tell him he could do it?' she asked.

'Yes.'

'Isn't that grand. Now it will be all over in an hour. I'm almost done, darling. I'm going all to pieces. *Please give me that.* It doesn't work. *Oh, it doesn't work!'*

'Breathe deeply.'

'I am. Oh, it doesn't work any more. It doesn't work!'

'Get another cylinder,' I said to the nurse.

'That is a new cylinder.'

'I'm just a fool, darling,' Catherine said. 'But it doesn't work any more.' She began to cry. 'Oh, I wanted so to have this baby and not make trouble, and now I'm all done and all gone to pieces and it doesn't work. Oh, darling, it doesn't work at all. I don't care if I die if it will only stop. Oh, please, darling, please make it stop. *There it comes. Oh Oh Oh!'* She breathed sobbingly in the mask. 'It doesn't work. It doesn't work. It doesn't work. Don't mind me, darling. Please don't cry. Don't mind me. I'm just gone all to pieces. You poor sweet. I love you so and I'll be good again I'll be good this time. *Can't they give me something?* If they could only give me something.'

'I'll make it work. I'll turn it all the way.'

'Give it to me now.'

I turned the dial all the way and as she breathed hard and deep her hand relaxed on the mask. I shut off the gas and lifted the mask. She came back from a long way away.

'That was lovely, darling. Oh, you're so good to me.'

'You be brave, because I can't do that all the time. It might kill you.'

'I'm not brave any more, darling. I'm all broken. They've broken me. I know it now.'

'Everybody is that way.'

'But it's awful. They just keep it up till they break you.'

'In an hour it will be over.'

'Isn't that lovely? Darling, I won't die, will I?'

'No. I promise you won't.'

'Because I don't want to die and leave you, but I get so tired of it and I feel I'm going to die.'

'Nonsense. Everybody feels that.'

'Sometimes I know I'm going to die.'

'You won't. You can't.'

'But what if I should?'

'I won't let you.'

'Give it to me quick. *Give it to me!*'

Then afterward, 'I won't die. I won't let myself die.'

'Of course you won't.'

'You'll stay with me?'

'Not to watch it.'

'No, just to be there.'

'Sure. I'll be there all the time.'

'You're so good to me. There, give it to me. Give me some more. *It's not working!*'

I turned the dial to three and then four. I wished the doctor would come back. I was afraid of the numbers above two.

Finally a new doctor came in with two nurses and they lifted Catherine on to a wheeled stretcher and we started down the hall. The stretcher went rapidly down the hall and into the elevator where everyone had to crowd against the wall to make room; then up, then an open door and out of the elevator and down the hall on rubber wheels to the operating room. I did not recognize the doctor with his cap and mask on. There was another doctor and more nurses.

'*They've got to give me something*,' Catherine said. '*They've got to give me something*. Oh please, doctor, give me enough to do some good!'

One of the doctors put a mask over her face and I looked through the door and saw the bright small amphitheatre of the operating room.

'You can go in the other door and sit up there,' a nurse said to me. There were benches behind a rail that looked down on the white table and the lights. I looked at Catherine. The mask was over her face and she was quiet now. They wheeled the stretcher forward. I turned away and walked down the hall. Two nurses were hurrying towards the entrance to the gallery.

'It's a Caesarean,' one said. 'They're going to do a Caesarean.'

The other one laughed, 'We're just in time. Aren't we lucky?' They went in the door that led to the gallery.

Another nurse came along. She was hurrying too.

'You go right in there. Go right in,' she said.

'I'm staying outside.'

She hurried in. I walked up and down the hall. I was afraid to go in. I looked out the window. It was dark but in the light from the window I could see it was raining. I went into a room at the far end of the hall and looked at the labels on bottles in a glass case. Then I came out and stood in the empty hall and watched the door of the operating room.

A doctor came out followed by a nurse. He held something in his two hands that looked like a freshly skinned rabbit and hurried across the corridor with it and in through another door. I went down to the door he had gone into and found them in the room doing things to a new-born child. The doctor held him up for me to see. He held him by the heels and slapped him.

'Is he all right?'

'He's magnificent. He'll weigh five kilos.'

I had no feeling for him. He did not seem to have anything to do with me. I felt no feeling of fatherhood.

'Aren't you proud of your son?' the nurse asked. They were washing him and wrapping him in something. I saw the little dark face and dark hand, but I did not see him move or hear him cry. The doctor was doing something to him again. He looked upset.

'No,' I said. 'He nearly killed his mother.'

'It isn't the little darling's fault. Didn't you want a boy?'

'No,' I said. The doctor was busy with him. He held him up by the feet and slapped him. I did not wait to see it. I went out in the hall. I could go in now and see. I went in the door and a little way down the gallery. The nurses who were sitting at the rail motioned for me to come where they were. I shook my head. I could see enough where I was.

I thought Catherine was dead. She looked dead. Her face was grey, the part of it that I could see. Down below, under the light, the doctor was sewing up the great long, forcep-spread, thick-edged wound. Another doctor in a mask gave the anaesthetic. Two nurses in masks handed things. It looked like a drawing of the Inquisition. I knew as I watched I could have watched it all, but I was glad I hadn't. I do not think I could have watched them cut, but I watched the wound closed into a high welted ridge with quick skilful-looking stitches like a cobbler's and was glad. When the wound was closed I went out into the hall and walked up and down again. After a while the doctor came out.

'How is she?'

'She is all right. Did you watch?'

He looked tired.

'I saw you sew up. The incision looked very long.'

'You thought so?'

'Yes. Will that scar flatten out?'

'Oh, yes.'

After a while they brought out the wheeled stretcher and took it very rapidly down the hallway to the elevator. I went along beside it. Catherine was moaning. Downstairs they put her in the bed in her room. I sat in a chair at the foot of the bed. There was a nurse in the room. I got up and stood by the bed. It was dark in the room. Catherine put out her hand, 'Hello, darling,' she said. Her voice was very weak and tired.

'Hello, you sweet.'

'What sort of baby was it?'

'Sh—don't talk,' the nurse said.

'A boy. He's long and wide and dark.'

'Is he all right?'

'Yes,' I said. 'He's fine.'

I saw the nurse look at me strangely.

'I'm awfully tired,' Catherine said. 'And I hurt like hell. Are you all right, darling?'

'I'm fine. Don't talk.'

'You were lovely to me. Oh darling, I hurt dreadfully. What does he look like?'

'He looks like a skinned rabbit with a puckered-up old-man's face.'

'You must go out,' the nurse said. 'Madame Henry must not talk.'

'I'll be outside,' I said.

'Go and get something to eat.'

'No. I'll be outside.' I kissed Catherine. She was very grey and weak and tired.

'May I speak to you?' I said to the nurse. She came out in the hall with me. I walked a little way down the hall.

'What's the matter with the baby?' I asked.

'Didn't you know?'

'No.'

'He wasn't alive.'

'He was dead?'

'They couldn't start him breathing. The cord was caught around his neck or something.'

'So he's dead.'

'Yes. It's such a shame. He was such a fine big boy. I thought you knew.'

'No,' I said. 'You better go back in with Madame.'

I sat down on the chair in front of a table where there were nurses' reports hung on clips at the side and looked out of the window. I could see nothing but the dark and the rain falling across the light from the window. So that was it. The baby was dead. That was why the doctor looked so tired. But why had they acted the way they did in the room with him? They supposed he would come around and start breathing probably. I had no religion but I knew he ought to have been baptized. But what if he never breathed at all. He hadn't. He had never been alive. Except in Catherine. I'd felt him kick there often enough. But I hadn't for a week. Maybe he was choked all the time. Poor little kid. I wished the hell I'd been choked like that. No I didn't. Still there would not be all this dying to go through. Now Catherine would die. That was what you did. You died. You did not know what it was about. You never had time to learn. They threw you in and told you the rules and the first time they caught you off base they killed you. Or they killed you gratuitously like Aymo. Or gave you the syphilis like Rinaldi. But they killed you in the end. You could count on that. Stay around and they would kill you.

Once in camp I put a log on top of the fire and it was full of ants. As it commenced to burn, the ants swarmed out and went first towards the centre where the fire was; then turned back and ran towards the end. When there were enough on the end they fell off into the fire. Some got out, their bodies burnt and flattened, and went off not knowing where they were going. But most of them went towards the fire and then back towards the end and swarmed on the cool end and finally fell off into the fire. I remember thinking at the time that it was the end of the world and a splendid chance to be a messiah and lift the log off the fire and throw it out where the ants could get off on to the ground.

But I did not do anything but throw a tin cup of water on the log, so that I would have the cup empty to put whisky in before I added water to it. I think the cup of water on the burning log only steamed the ants.

So now I sat out in the hall and waited to hear how Catherine was. The nurse did not come out, so after a while I went to the door and opened it very softly and looked in. I could not see at first because there was a bright light in the hall and it was dark in the room. Then I saw the nurse sitting by the bed and Catherine's head on a pillow, and she all flat under the sheet. The nurse put her finger to her lips, then stood up and came to the door.

'How is she?' I asked.

'She's all right,' the nurse said. 'You should go and have your supper and then come back if you wish.'

I went down the hall and then down the stairs and out the door of the hospital and down the dark street in the rain to the café. It was brightly lighted inside and there were many people at the tables. I did not see a place to sit, and a waiter came up to me and took my wet coat and hat and showed me a place at a table across from an elderly man who was drinking beer and reading the evening paper. I sat down and asked the waiter what the *plat du jour* was.

'Veal stew — but it is finished.'

'What can I have to eat?'

'Ham and eggs, eggs with cheese, or *choucroute*.'

'I had *choucroute* this noon,' I said.

'That's true,' he said. 'That's true. You ate *choucroute* this noon.' He was a middle-aged man with a bald top to his head and his hair slicked over it. He had a kind face.

'What do you want? Ham and eggs or eggs with cheese?'

'Ham and eggs,' I said, 'and beer.'

'A demi-blonde?'

'Yes,' I said.

'I remembered,' he said. 'You took a demi-blonde this noon.'

I ate the ham and eggs and drank the beer. The ham and eggs

were in a round dish — the ham underneath and the eggs on top. It was very hot and at the first mouthful I had to take a drink of beer to cool my mouth. I was hungry and I asked the waiter for another order. I drank several glasses of beer. I was not thinking at all but read the paper of the man opposite me. It was about the break through on the British front. When he realized I was reading the back of his paper he folded it over. I thought of asking the waiter for a paper, but I could not concentrate. It was hot in the café and the air was bad. Many of the people at the tables knew one another. There were several card games going on. The waiters were busy bringing drinks from the bar to the tables. Two men came in and could find no place to sit. They stood opposite the table where I was. I ordered another beer. I was not ready to leave yet. It was too soon to go back to the hospital. I tried not to think and to be perfectly calm. The men stood around but no one was leaving, so they went out. I drank another beer. There was quite a pile of saucers now on the table in front of me. The man opposite me had taken off his spectacles, put them away in a case, folded his paper and put it in his pocket and now sat holding his liqueur glass and looking out at the room. Suddenly I knew I had to get back. I called the waiter, paid the reckoning, got into my coat, put on my hat and started out the door. I walked through the rain up to the hospital.

Upstairs I met the nurse coming down the hall.

'I just called you at the hotel,' she said. Something dropped inside me.

'What is wrong?'

'Mrs. Henry has had a haemorrhage.'

'Can I go in?'

'No, not yet. The doctor is with her.'

'Is it dangerous?'

'It is very dangerous.' The nurse went into the room and shut the door. I sat outside in the hall. Everything was gone inside of me. I did not think. I could not think. I knew she was going to die and I prayed that she would not. Don't let her die. Oh,

God, please don't let her die. I'll do anything for you if you won't let her die. Please, please, please, dear God, don't let her die. Dear God, don't let her die. Please, please, please don't let her die. God, please make her not die. I'll do anything you say if you don't let her die. You took the baby but don't let her die —that was all right but don't let her die. Please, please, dear God, don't let her die.

The nurse opened the door and motioned with her finger for me to come. I followed her into the room. Catherine did not look up when I came in. I went over to the side of the bed. The doctor was standing by the bed on the opposite side. Catherine looked at me and smiled. I bent down over the bed and started to cry.

'Poor darling,' Catherine said very softly. She looked grey.

'You're all right, Cat,' I said. 'You're going to be all right.'

'I'm going to die,' she said; then waited and said, 'I hate it.'

I took her hand.

'Don't touch me,' she said. I let go of her hand. She smiled. 'Poor darling. You touch me all you want.'

'You'll be all right, Cat. I know you'll be all right.'

'I meant to write you a letter to have if anything happened, but I didn't do it.'

'Do you want me to get a priest or anyone to come and see you?'

'Just you,' she said. Then a little later, 'I'm not afraid. I just hate it.'

'You must not talk so much,' the doctor said.

'All right,' Catherine said.

'Do you want me to do anything, Cat? Can I get you anything?'

Catherine smiled, 'No.' Then a little later, 'You won't do our things with another girl, or say the same things, will you?'

'Never.'

'I want you to have girls though.'

'I don't want them.'

You are talking too much,' the doctor said. 'You cannot talk. Mr. Henry must go out. He can come back again later. You are not going to die. You must not be silly.'

'All right,' Catherine said. 'I'll come and stay with you nights,' she said. It was very hard for her to talk.

'Please go out of the room,' the doctor said. Catherine winked at me, her face grey. 'I'll be right outside,' I said.

'Don't worry, darling,' Catherine said. 'I'm not a bit afraid. It's just a dirty trick.'

'You dear, brave sweet.'

I waited outside in the hall. I waited a long time. The nurse came to the door and came over to me. 'I'm afraid Mrs. Henry is very ill,' she said. 'I'm afraid for her.'

'Is she dead?'

'No, but she is unconscious.'

It seems she had one haemorrhage after another. They couldn't stop it. I went into the room and stayed with Catherine until she died. She was unconscious all the time, and it did not take her very long to die.

Outside the room in the hall I spoke to the doctor. 'Is there anything I can do tonight?'

'No. There is nothing to do. Can I take you to your hotel?'

'No, thank you. I am going to stay here a while.'

'I know there is nothing to say. I cannot tell you —'

'No,' I said. 'There's nothing to say.'

'Good night,' he said. 'I cannot take you to your hotel?'

'No, thank you.'

'It was the only thing to do,' he said. 'The operation proved—'

'I do not want to talk about it,' I said.

'I would like to take you to your hotel.'

'No, thank you.'

He went down the hall. I went to the door of the room.

'You can't come in now,' one of the nurses said.

'Yes, I can,' I said.

'You can't come in yet.'

'You get out,' I said. 'The other one too.'

But after I had got them out and shut the door and turned off the light it wasn't any good. It was like saying goodbye to a statue. After a while I went out and left the hospital and walked back to the hotel in the rain.

COMMENTARY

Biographical Background

ERNEST HEMINGWAY was born in 1899 in Oak Park, Illinois, and as a child he made many trips into Michigan where he learned to enjoy intimate contact with unspoiled nature—an experience which in one way or another would influence all his subsequent writing. In 1917 he went to Kansas City to work as a newspaper reporter and extend his experience of the world. He was also very keen to get into the First World War somehow, although his defective vision prevented him from enlisting as a soldier. However, in 1918 he joined the Red Cross and in May he sailed to France. From there he was moved to Italy and was posted to Schio in the foothills of the Dolomites where he drove an ambulance for a few weeks. At this age Hemingway still regarded war rather as a game. ('I was an awful dope when I went to the last war,' he said in 1941. 'I can remember just thinking that we were the home team and the Austrians were the visiting team.') The Austrians were attacking in the Piave River valley north of Venice, and when volunteers were asked for to man emergency canteens near the Italian front lines, Hemingway, keen to see some real action, immediately applied. He was posted to Fossalta, and it was there, during the night of July 8th, that he was severely wounded while he was delivering chocolate and cigarettes to the men in the trenches. He managed to carry another wounded man to the command post before collapsing himself. He was taken to a field hospital near Treviso before being transferred to hospital in Milan. Later he was awarded the Silver Medal of Valour. He was still eighteen, and the experience of being badly wounded had such a profound effect on the form his fiction would subsequently take, that a few words should be said about it.

When Hemingway came to the war he was still an innocent

who could hardly differentiate war from sport, and who was looking forward to adult experience as he might have done a fishing trip. His initiation into what war really meant, what adults could do to each other in their 'games', was shattering. Hit by an Austrian trench-mortar shell and shortly afterwards machine-gunned in the knee, he was very near death. Indeed he once said 'I died then', and the three Italian soldiers with him were killed. Hemingway himself in due course had over two hundred fragments of steel taken from his right knee. This was only the first of many wounds he received in a life that proved to be incredibly injury-prone, but it was the one he never forgot. From a state of innocence he had passed in a moment of unforgettable pain into a state which, for a while, he actually thought was death; life which had seemed to be such an open field of exciting possibilities suddenly turned into nightmare as the healthy young American boy woke up to find himself desperately wounded and lying among corpses. (Apparently for some time after this Hemingway could not sleep with the light out.) All of the heroes in Hemingway's fiction have the ability to absorb punishment and to maintain that 'grace under pressure' which became the basis of the Hemingway code, and many of them — Nick Adams (*In Our Time*), Jake Barnes (*The Sun Also Rises*), Robert Jordan (*For Whom the Bell Tolls*), Richard Cantwell (*Across the River and Into the Trees*) as well as Frederic Henry in *A Farewell to Arms* — are wounded in wars. As the critic Philip Young has shown in his book *Ernest Hemingway: A Reconsideration*, both the topographical and physical details of the woundings in the last two named books are unmistakably autobiographical. Using the vocabulary of the psychoanalyst Otto Fenichel, Young has suggested that this first wounding was 'traumatic' for Hemingway, who thereafter kept compulsively returning to the scene and moment of the injury. I will quote Young:

> It is the first characteristic of this neurosis that the trauma is constantly being repeated: 'The patient cannot free himself from thinking about the occurrence over and over again.' Both Hemingway and his hero

testify to this, of course—whether asleep, in the nightmares which repeat the wounding in Italy, for example, or awake, in writing of the incidents which hurt. The hero keeps saying he can 'get rid of' the experiences which have damaged him by writing about them later. This is precisely the view of Fenichel, who argues that the function of these repetitions is that they 'represent attempts to achieve a belated mastery, fractionally, of the unmastered amounts of excitation.'

In other words Hemingway was constantly having to master, in his writing style and in his life style, the terror and horror of that moment on the Italian front which in retrospect he could control but could never forget.

While Hemingway was recovering in the hospital in Milan, one of the nurses who helped to look after him was Agnes Hannah von Kurowsky, an American girl of Polish ancestry. She served as the original for Catherine Barkley, the heroine of *A Farewell to Arms*. Like his hero Frederic Henry, Hemingway was successfully operated on in Milan, like Henry he had drink smuggled into the hospital, and like Henry he fell in love with his nurse. There are other figures from this period of Hemingway's life who contributed to the fictional characters in the novel—a priest called Don Giuseppe Bianchi whom Hemingway liked and respected; Captain Enrico Serena who called Hemingway 'Baby'; Conte Emanuele Greppi, an elderly Italian who talked politics, played billiards, and drank champagne with the young convalescent Hemingway—but Agnes is by far the most important. For the first time in his life Hemingway thought that he was deeply in love with a woman, and like Catherine, Agnes often volunteered for night work so that she could spend time with him. When they were separated, she to Florence, he back to the front (where, like Henry, he went down with jaundice), they kept up an intense correspondence, perhaps more intense on his side than hers, for it seems that she could see that this was a youthful infatuation bound to end. Nevertheless when Hemingway returned to America after the Armistice he still intended to bring Agnes over and marry her, and it was clearly a real shock when she wrote to break off the relationship, explaining that she had fallen in love with a Neapolitan, Domenico Caracciolo. A few months later she wrote again saying that the marriage with Caracciolo was off, but for Hemingway it was now a closed episode. Thus ended what Carlos Baker calls 'the most romantic chapter in the first twenty years of his life'. He had been to the war and earned what Stephen Crane had called a 'red badge of courage'; and he had experienced the intensity of first love and the anguish of loss. Out of these two contemporaneous experiences he would make *A Farewell to Arms*, one of his most successful fictions.*

The Title and the Structure

For over a decade Hemingway wanted to make use of his experiences of 1918 and write a story about love and war. Apparently he had wanted to use as an epigraph Marlowe's lines 'but that was

---

* A very contracted, and bitter, version of this episode in Hemingway's life may be found in 'A Very Short Story' in *In Our Time* (1923). Like every story in that book it is preceded by a short prose sketch concerning a moment of violence apparently unrelated to the story that follows. This sketch is particularly important because it is the only one which refers to Nick Adams (who features in the stories), and because it anticipates a crucial theme in *A Farewell to Arms*. I shall therefore quote most of it:

> Nick sat against the wall of the church where they had dragged him to be clear of machine-gun fire in the street. Both legs stuck out awkwardly. He had been hit in the spine. His face was sweaty and dirty. The sun shone on his face. The day was very hot. Rinaldi, big backed, his equipment sprawling, lay face downward against the wall ... Stretcher bearers would be along any time now. Nick turned his head carefully and looked at Rinaldi. 'Senta Rinaldi. Senta. You and me we've made a separate peace.' Rinaldi lay still in the sun breathing with difficulty. 'Not patriots.' Nick turned his head carefully away smiling sweatily. Rinaldi was a disappointing audience.

Thus in the prose passage and the following story Hemingway had juxtaposed his wounding and his subsequent love affair and loss. *A Farewell to Arms* is, however, a much richer merging of the two incidents.

in another country, and besides the wench is dead'. But he used 'In Another Country' as the title of a story in *Men Without Women*, and he decided on the more felicitous *A Farewell to Arms*, a title taken, as he said, from a poem by the Elizabethan poet George Peele to be found in *The Oxford Book of English Verse*. The poem itself is not particularly relevant to the novel, except inasmuch as it touches on the passing of Time and the transitoriness of youth and beauty, but the title is peculiarly apposite because of the pun which can legitimately be found in the word 'arms'. In Hemingway's novel, Frederic Henry deserts from the war and goes away with Catherine, only to see her die in childbirth. He says farewell, in turn, to the harsh arms of battle and the soft arms of his lover; the first farewell is liberating, the second is a devastating loss. The ambiguity inherent in the word 'arms' points to the basic struggle in Existence between the forces of destruction and the creative, or procreative drives—as Freud would say, between *Thanatos* and *Eros*. It is the registered tension between these two that sustains Hemingway's novel and gives it a timeless relevance.

The novel is divided into five 'Books', the first three roughly of equal length, the last two somewhat shorter but again about the same length as each other. The structure does suggest a five-act drama, and it is worth noting that Hemingway himself apparently once referred to the novel as his *Romeo and Juliet*. As Carlos Baker has commented, this could mean that he regarded Frederic Henry and Catherine Barkley as star-crossed lovers, or it could more specifically suggest that his two lovers caught up in the war on the Austrian-Italian front are comparable to the victims of the Montague-Capulet feud.

The Style

The best way to start to appreciate the theory or creed behind Hemingway's style is to consider the famous passage in Chapter Twenty-Seven.

I was always embarrassed by the words sacred, glorious, and sacrifice and the expression in vain. We had heard them sometimes standing in the rain almost out of earshot, so that only the shouted words came through, and had read them, on proclamations that were slapped up by billposters over other proclamations, now for a long time, and I had seen nothing sacred, and the things that were glorious had no glory and the sacrifices were like the stockyards at Chicago if nothing was done with the meat except to bury it. There were many words that you could not stand to hear and finally only the names of places had dignity. Certain numbers were the same way and certain dates and these with the names of places were all you could say and have them mean anything. Abstract words such as glory, honour, courage, or hallow were obscene beside the concrete names of villages, the numbers of roads, the names of rivers, the numbers of regiments and the dates.

One of the first victims in any war is language as the distortions and exhortations and lies of propaganda take over the available media. Like millions of others, Hemingway had seen what horrors could be perpetrated in the name of patriotism or glory, and one of the reasons his writing made such an impact on the generations following the First World War was the way in which it seemed to be restoring the integrity to language, ruthlessly cutting out any vague rhetoric, any false appeal to the emotions, any abstract speculations. After a very dirty war, and in the confused decade that followed, Hemingway's prose offered something clean and refreshingly lucid and direct and honest. It has been called a 'tough guy' style, full of laconic understatement and unemotional, anti-intellectual brusqueness. But although the style is related to Hemingway's creation of a stance which could confront all that life might have to offer with a cool clear-eyed stoicism, the apparent simplifications in his writing are not the result of a pose. A statement from his book *Death in the Afternoon* might be helpful here.

If a writer of prose knows enough about what he is writing about he may omit things that he knows and the reader, if the writer is writing truly enough, will have a feeling of those things as strongly as though the writer had stated them. The dignity of movement of an iceberg is due to only one-eighth of it being above water. A writer who omits things because he does not know them only makes hollow places in his writing.

It is as important for a writer to know what to omit as to decide what to include, and part of Hemingway's genius was his ability to omit a very great deal, leaving only those bare essentials which carry an impact out of all proportion to their apparent simplicity. He does not tell us what he is feeling or what we, the readers, ought to feel. He very seldom moves inside his characters' heads and hearts to give us long internal surveys of their thoughts and feelings, or their stream of consciousness. What he does give us is what the senses register—sights, sounds, tastes, conversations, movements—for at a time when all faiths are in doubt and all abstractions suspect, these at least could be trusted. He will go into minute detail about meals—as for instance in describing what Henry is eating when he is wounded, or while he is waiting for Catherine to be delivered of her child; he is careful to be complete and exact about topography and geography ('We live by accidents of terrain, you know. And terrain is what remains in the dreaming part of the mind,' says Cantwell in *Across the River and Into the Trees*), and in recounting his adventures Henry is meticulous in describing the disposition of roads, the situations of villages, the way a river bends or widens or the mountains loom; and he always makes a point of recording the season, the climate, the atmosphere—the book starts with the falling leaves of 'late summer' and ends in the rain of a 'false spring'. Like Robert Jordan in *For Whom the Bell Tolls*, Hemingway wants to 'Keep it accurate. . . . Quite accurate'. The characters in the book differentiate themselves and imprint themselves on our memories by their gestures, conversations, changing appearances. Conrad (whom Hemingway admired) once wrote that his task was 'by the written word to make you hear, to make you feel—it is, before all, to make you *see*'. Hemingway makes us see, and hear and feel, and he does it, not by directing our responses or summarizing those of his characters, but by putting the terrain, the objects, the equipment, the weather, the places, the people, before us in a series of cleanly defined, carefully separated, perceptions and notations. But of course in addition to choosing what to omit and what to include, Hemingway is responsible for the arrangement of all the concrete particulars which make up his novel; and it is the sequence and juxtaposition, as well as the selection, of the details which gives his prose not only the dignity of movement of the iceberg but conveys to us something of the enormous emotional power hidden below the surface.

There is another aspect of Hemingway's prose worth mentioning here, and it can be suggested by two more quotations. In *The Sun Also Rises* (1926) Hemingway's first important novel which most successfully evoked the expatriate existence of what Gertrude Stein called 'the lost generation', the wounded hero Jake Barnes says to himself 'Perhaps as you went along you did learn something. I did not care what it was all about. All I wanted to know was how to live in it. Maybe if you found out how to live in it you learned from that what it was all about.' And in the story 'A Clean, Well-Lighted Place' a waiter meditates on the nature of his fear of the darkness. 'What did he fear; it was not fear or dread. It was a nothing that he knew only too well. It was all a nothing and a man was nothing too. It was only that and light was all it needed and a certain cleanness and order.' The first quotation points attention towards man's relationship to his concrete environment and away from philosophical and metaphysical theories; the second one invites us to see Hemingway's own prose as a constant ritual of maintaining 'cleanness and order', creating a 'well-lighted place' to keep the darkness out and the dread of nothingness at bay. Taken together they help us to appreciate an additional reason for the famous Hemingway objectivity which proved at once both irresistible and inimitable for so many contemporary readers and writers.

The Book

A Farewell to Arms was written in 1928 in Paris and America. In 1948 Hemingway said

> During the time I was writing the first draft my second son Patrick was delivered in Kansas City by Caesarean section, and while I was rewriting my father killed himself in Oak Park, Illinois. . . . I remember all these things happening and all the places we lived in and the fine times and the bad times we had in that year. But much more vividly I remember living in the book making up what happened in it every day. Making the country and the people and the things that happened I was happier than I had ever been. . . . The fact that the book was a tragic one did not make me unhappy since I believed that life was a tragedy and knew it could have only one end.*

The book was published in 1929 and was a great success. It not only evoked the basic futility of the First World War as seen by an American outsider. It also obviously, in its account of a doomed idyll, caught something of the disillusion and the doomed exhausted feeling in the air in Europe and America as the rather desperately gay Twenties approached the great Depression of the Thirties.

In outline it is a simple story about an American in an Italian ambulance brigade, Frederic Henry, and a British nurse serving in Italy, Catherine Barkley. In Book One Frederic Henry, who is the narrator, describes his life with the army in Italy and his first meeting with Catherine. He is badly wounded and at the end of Book One he is on a train to Milan, going for treatment to a hospital to which it turns out Catherine has been posted. Book Two describes their happy love affair in the hospital and on his convalescent leave. It ends, again with Henry on a train, this time going back to the front. Book Three describes the failure of the Italian campaign and the big retreat in which Henry is also

* Quoted by Carlos Baker in *Hemingway: The Writer as Artist.*

involved. About to be shot as a traitor by carabinieri he escapes by diving into a river and swimming away. The third Book ends with Henry again on a train, this time in hiding on it as he makes his way back to Milan. In Book Four he follows Catherine to Stresa where she is now working. There they renew their love affair and enjoy happy days, oblivious of the war, until Henry is warned that he is to be arrested as a deserter. He and Catherine make their escape at night by rowing down the lake into Switzerland. At the end of the Book they are entering a hotel in Montreux together. Book Five records their idyllic period alone together in the mountains. But Catherine is now pregnant and after the winter they have to go down to Lausanne for the child to be properly delivered. Despite medical attention both the child and Catherine die in the hospital after the birth. The final Book ends with Henry again approaching an hotel, but this time alone.

Book One

Chapter One. The opening chapter gives no information about the identity of 'we', nor does it locate the scene at a specific date or in a particular country. Instead the emphasis is on climate and terrain — the turning of the seasons, the running of the river, and the movements of men towards an unidentified war. The first paragraph is one of Hemingway's most dazzling pieces of writing, and while seeming only to describe a setting it carries much of the book in embryo. The first sentence mentions three key features of the geography which subtly recur throughout the book. The plain, on which the war is largely fought and thus becomes associated with death; the river, which is ambiguous since armies fight across it but Henry also escapes down it; and the mountains, their cool clear eminences suggesting an area far above the battles of men and associated in the book with a good clean life and a refuge where the lovers are out of the reach of war. The next two sentences juxtapose the running water which runs forever clear; and the marching troops who raise dust as they make their way towards war. The repetition of the word 'dust' twice in the next sentence makes us aware of an echo of the phrase in the funeral service — 'ashes to ashes, dust to dust' — and we realize that, unlike the river, the men are walking along the dusty road to death. In addition the season has now changed from late summer to autumn and the leaves are falling, thus establishing the more ubiquitous autumnal feeling which hangs over the book. By repeating, in slightly different ways, references to the leaves falling and the soldiers marching, Hemingway very unobtrusively makes us aware of the movement of all things to death, leaving afterwards a vacancy — 'the road bare and white'. But the seasons are cyclical and the trees will put forth new leaves in their season, whereas man walks down the road of his life only once and does not return. Thus in the opening paragraph by forgoing dates and names and restricting himself to a few very carefully placed generalizations about concrete details of scenery, seasons, and troops, Hemingway has in fact managed to portray for us the human condition — the relation of man to terrain and the difference between human and nature's time (notice the apt use of past tenses and participles suggesting that mixture of events, which happen once, and processes, which are ongoing and recurrent, which is what the paragraph, like the book, is about) — without any of those abstractions or portentous statements which he distrusted. In addition he has created a mood both ominous and melancholy which will finally pervade the book.

In the following paragraphs other subtle suggestive details are given. The plain is rich in crops but men are bringing guns and battle equipment — a depressing grey — into it. The contrast between nature's fruitful products and man's instruments of death is brought home when the guns are covered with green branches. Again there is a reference to the 'fall' coming, and with it the 'rains' —rain which will fall with increasing persistence and menace until the end of the book. The country is now wet and stripped bare and 'dead', the atmosphere a mixture of mud and mists and clouds through which the silent anonymous men in uniform carrying arms continue to move to an unnamed war. It is Hemingway's version of the modern wasteland. Notice that the soldiers carrying cartridge-boxes under their capes look 'as though they were six months gone with child'. This simile brings in the idea of pregnancy incongruously related to desolation and death. It is an incongruity which will conclude the book. The chapter ends with the start of winter and the coming of the 'permanent rain' bringing a disease which kills 'only seven thousand' men. The frailty, futility, and ephemerality of human life is quietly brought home to us. It is the rains which are 'permanent'; man is transitory.

Obviously it will be impossible to go through each chapter in this sort of detail. But these few observations should serve to show how carefully Hemingway's deceptively simple prose deserves to be studied. He once described prose as 'architecture' and we can see that every verbal brick is placed with infinite care.

Chapters Two and Three. For the first time 'I' appears, and we are brought into much closer proximity with the specific situation of the narrator, the mess where he eats, the situation of the war, the soldiers around him and so on. We have moved into a definite time and place. The conversation in the mess reveals a priest being teased by his unbelieving companions who treat religion and sex as matters mainly for ridicule and raillery. Then the discussion turns to where the narrator should spend his leave. The priest suggests his home town of Abruzzi, but the others mock at this idea of going to see 'peasants' and instead advise the narrator to go to the 'centres of culture and civilization' — meaning places where he can enjoy night-life with whores and drink. Here again Hemingway is subtly setting up an opposition between sacred and profane attitudes to life which will develop in the course of the book. The priest has not only his faith, but a reverence for nature and for love, which he does not like to hear reduced to a dirty joke. Also he speaks up for the value of 'home' a very important concept in Hemingway: ('Where a man feels at home, outside of where he's born, is where he's meant to be' — *The Green Hills of Africa*). Since the narrator is a deracinated American (the tone of almost complete anonymity which he maintains for most of the book adds to the feeling of his being a person without roots, almost without identity), he should have listened to the priest who invited him to visit his home. But instead he goes to the big cities indulging in the transient excitements of too much drinking and whoring. When he comes back he suddenly regrets that he did not go to Abruzzi which is a mountain place where life is healthy and it is cold and 'clear and dry'. Again the contrast between life in the mountains and in the cities of the plains is made, and just as the narrator has an instinctive liking and respect for the priest, though he does not believe in God, so he will come to share his attitude towards love, and his preference for the pure life in the mountains.

Chapters Four to Six. The narrator finds that things have run perfectly well in his absence, an early sign of his increasing feeling of dissociation from the war. At the same time he now meets Miss Barkley, and although their first conversation is about the horrors of war, their meeting is in a garden, suggesting that almost paradisal refuge which for a brief time will be theirs. In one of their meetings Catherine Barkley calls the narrator by his name for the first time — 'Mr. Henry' — as if it is in contact with her that he has started to take on a distinct identity. They talk of 'dropping' the war, and for the first time 'I put my arm around under her arm'. Dropping the war in order to take up her 'arms' is exactly what he is going to do in the rest of the book. But at this moment he is still regarding her as a sexual object and thinks he can see all the steps in the affair 'like the moves in a chess game'. He lies by saying he loves her, and again thinks of making progress with her as like a game, this time a card game. Thus when Catherine, who seems a little mentally upset, suddenly announces 'This is a rotten game we play, isn't it?', it is as if she has seen through his initially superficial attitude to their relationship. We are prepared for more serious feelings to emerge.

Chapters Seven and Eight. Chapter Seven starts by the narrator describing how he tried to assist a man who wanted to be hospitalized out of the war with a self-inflicted wound. The attempt fails, but it anticipates the narrator's own coming defection from the war which, he decides, 'did not have anything to do with me'. Notice also that he finds he has nothing to write home to America about. He is detached both from his home and his present situation and thus his voice sounds alienated, as though he has no connections with anything or anyone. He likes to drink and joins in the mess banter occasionally, but he comes across to us as an outsider. It is at this time that he realizes that when he cannot see Catherine he feels 'lonely and hollow'. It is the beginning of his falling properly in love with her. However, he has to leave for the front where an attack is to be made (notice again the references to the dust, the river, the mountains, etc.), and she gives him a Saint Anthony medallion to wear for protection.

Chapter Nine. It is in this chapter that the narrator describes the terrible moment when he is hit and badly wounded in the knee while eating some of the food he has brought to the men. (The mechanic Passini, who has recently offered the opinion that 'There is nothing worse than war', is hideously wounded and dies while Henry is trying to help him.) Henry gives the details of his wounding, the treatment he received, and the scene in the dressing-station, in a dispassionate tone which only serves to make the horrible experience more clear and real to us.

Chapters Ten and Eleven. These describe visits to Henry in the field hospital from two very different men. With his friend Rinaldi—a fine surgeon who is a good comrade but who cannot believe in anything more than drink and whores—the conversation, hearty and jocular, is about war and women, but it almost ends in a quarrel when Henry thinks Rinaldi is making sexually cynical remarks about Catherine Barkley. By contrast, the priest seems tired, for the hopelessness and hatefulness of the war is getting him down. He speaks to Henry of his belief in God. Henry tells him that he is not a man capable of much love, but the priest tells him he has confused lust with love, and that in time he will learn what real love—the desire to sacrifice for another person—is. The visit of the priest reminds Henry of the priest's picture of his home town, Abruzzi, and conjuring up an image of the clean, beautiful life up there, he falls asleep—a more peaceful conclusion to the visit than the previous one had afforded him.

Chapter Twelve. There is conversation about the war situation, but Henry learns that he is to be sent to Milan for operations and therapy. Rinaldi brings the good news that Catherine is also being sent to Milan. On the train Henry gets drunk and is sick. It is 'a bad trip', the first of several he will make, and it concludes the Book.

Book Two

Chapters Thirteen to Eighteen. Although this part of the book deals with Henry's time in hospital, his operations and recuperation, it is almost the most idyllic section of the book. He is legitimately out of the war and in this new private time he falls properly in love with Catherine. From the start the auguries are good. The building he is taken to has only just been converted for use as a hospital, and he is the first patient in a clean and well-lighted place. From his window he looks out into a blue sky, and the sunlight streams in. It is true he has nightmares—his night panics help to make him more of a real character to us—but when Catherine Barkley arrives he is suddenly truly in love with her: 'The wildness was gone and I felt finer than I had ever felt.' With drinks being smuggled in and secret night meetings with Catherine, Henry is entirely happy. A bat flies into the room one night, but if it is an omen it does not disturb them. It is at this stage that Catherine says 'There isn't any me any more. Just what you want,' as she will later say to Henry, 'There isn't any me. I'm you. . . . You're my religion. You're all I've got,' and makes other such protestations of simple and entire devotion. Some critics think that Catherine is more like a fantasy woman, a wish-fulfilment on Hemingway's part, rather than a plausible character. It is true that she is not shown as having a very complex nature and we do not think of her as highly individuated. But then nor is Henry. They are more like generic lovers, simplified down to certain essentials, and we should not look for the same sort of detailed individuality such as other novelists give their characters. As a pair of doomed representative figures, passing through various phases and across varying landscapes, they are unforgettable.

Just before his operation Henry looks out of the window and sees the sun shining on the cathedral. He feels 'clean inside and outside', and it is as though he has mentally and spiritually disengaged himself from the mire and filth of war in order to concentrate wholly on loving Catherine. They spend a lovely summer together, and when you remember that it is after her death that Henry is recalling all the tiny details of the good times they had together they take on a real poignancy; they are at once so vivid and so past.

Chapters Nineteen to Twenty-One. The summer is passing away, and the war is still going pointlessly on — Henry wonders if wars now go on for ever, and in a sense he is right. The lovers start to meet other people, including Ettore, 'a legitimate hero who bored everyone he met'. Because bravery is such an important idea in the book, it is worth noting that it is not enough to be brave; ideally one must be brave quietly and without any vanity or ostentation. This is the basis of Hemingway's particular kind of modern stoicism. The meeting with Ettore is followed by a return of the rain and it turns out that Catherine is afraid of the rain — 'because sometimes I see me dead in it'. This increases the ominousness of the rain which seems to come down more regularly and heavily now that the summer is over, and of course Catherine's irrational foreboding is finally justified.

They pay a visit to the horse-races where some mildly crooked betting goes on, but Catherine prefers to disengage herself from the rigged gambling. That way she feels 'cleaner', and once more the distant mountains are mentioned. Similarly she prefers it when the two of them are alone; it is all part of an instinct to isolate themselves from contaminating company. With the summer gone the mood begins to change. Catherine tells Henry that she is pregnant and he makes the unconsidered statement, 'You always feel trapped biologically.' This is of course unfair to Catherine who puts no pressures on him and does not even ask for the social contract of marriage. But in the larger sense it is of course true, and it is a biological process which will prove the fatal trap for Catherine. Once again the subject of bravery comes up and, contradicting a famous line of Shakespeare's, Catherine says 'The brave dies perhaps two thousand deaths if he is intelligent. He simply doesn't mention them.' Once again, it is not the absence of fear but the control of it that is important for Hemingway. As it turns out she will indeed be brave.

Chapters Twenty-Two to Twenty-Four. The mood continues to darken. It is raining 'very hard', and Henry goes down with jaundice. The head nurse finds the empty bottles illicitly concealed in his cupboard (as happened to Hemingway), and his leave is cancelled, thus bringing separation from Catherine suddenly very close. On the night he is due to return to the front he spends all the time before the train leaves with Catherine. The evening is cold and misty and wet as they walk through the city. At one point they pause in front of the cathedral. It looks 'fine' but they do not go in. Noticing a couple huddling together by one of the buttresses Henry comments that 'Everybody ought to have somewhere to go'. In the proximity of the cathedral the remark has added connotations. Although it is a splendid building, it can no longer serve as a home to an age that has lost its faith. The general problem then is what exactly will serve as a home for modern man, just as it is Catherine's and Henry's more specific problem to find a place where they can be alone together and make love. Before they do so Henry goes to a shop to buy a pistol which he needs now that he is about to return to the front. Again we can sense how his having to take up military arms again will involve him in separation from Catherine's human arms. They finally hire a room in an hotel by the station—the fog has now turned to rain—and at first Catherine feels like a 'whore' as they book a room for the evening. However, their feelings for each other and delight in being together transform the room: 'we felt very happy and in a little time the room felt like our own home. My room at the hospital had been our own home and this room was our home too in the same way.' I have commented on how important the idea of 'home' is for Hemingway, as it is for his deracinated characters. More generally, in an age without secure beliefs and full of uprooted people, many have to improvise and create 'homes' out of neutral and alien places. It is a comment on the world of the book that two of the places Henry makes into temporary homes are a hospital and a station hotel.

Although theirs is theoretically an illicit liaison, Catherine speaks for the quality of their relationship when she says 'Everything we do seems so innocent and simple. I can't believe we do anything wrong.' By comparison with what they have together, whatever the world might say or think seems utterly irrelevant. But the rain continues to pour down, and with a quotation from Marvell's poem 'To His Coy Mistress' Henry brings in a sense of the inexorable passing of time, and he soon has to leave for his train. Whereas this Book had started in the freshness of a new hospital and sunlight, it ends with them passing out over the worn stair carpet of an old hotel into the now incessant rain. The train is crowded and Henry finally has to travel lying in the corridor in an ungainly uncomfortable position. It is another bad trip, and it is going back towards the war.

Book Three

Chapters Twenty-Five to Twenty-Seven. On his return to the front Henry finds that the war has gone badly. It is now fall, and once again references to mud, dead leaves, rain, and the mountains enforce a pervasive sense of desolation. As he says, this does *not* feel like a 'home-coming'. Almost the first thing Henry does is lie down to rest, and throughout this whole book there are frequent references to his going to sleep, or trying to, adding to the sense of general fatigue as well as suggesting his increasing desire to be quit of the war. On his return he has two long conversations, again with Rinaldi and then the priest. Rinaldi is overworked and tense and admits that he has no 'sacred subjects', as Catherine now is to Henry. The priest is also tired but believes that peace will come soon, although Henry's pessimism on that score discourages him. When the priest asks Henry what he believes in, Henry answers, only half jocularly, 'in sleep'. Away from Catherine his waking hours bring him no joy. Henry starts out on a mission to take some cars where they are needed, and the combination of such things as a wrecked village, the rain, the noise of guns, the wounded being brought in, serve to make this seem about the darkest point in the war. In the night there is a storm and a bombardment, and rumours follow that the dreaded Germans are now attacking them. A retreat is ordered and begins. Henry sets out with his other drivers in the cars—in the rain.

Chapters Twenty-eight to Thirty. These chapters describe the retreat, slow, sullen, miserable. During the retreat they pick up two frightened young virgins, to whom they are kind, and two unscrupulous sergeants, one of whom Henry shoots when he refuses to help them to free a car from the mud and tries to run away—such different temporary companions in close proximity show up yet another of the incongruities precipitated by the mess of a war. While resting Henry starts to think of Catherine, and going to sleep, and the rain, and the images become mixed together so that he recalls fragments of a famous sixteenth-century anonymous poem which in its entirety runs:

> Western wind, when will thou blow
>   The small rain down can rain?
> Christ, if my love were in my arms
>   And I in my bed again!
>
> *(Oxford Book of English Verse)*

Catherine's are indeed the only arms he wants now.

In an attempt to go faster than the main column, which is almost at a complete standstill, Henry decides to take the cars as far as possible across country. Finally the cars get stuck in a muddy field and they take to walking. They come to a river and then follow a railroad track. 'On both sides of us stretched the wet plain.' This is ominous terrain in the geography of this book. Soon they see some Germans, and then one of them is shot—probably by Italians who suspect them of being enemies. It is part of the insane confusion of war. This insanity comes to a head when they finally cross a bridge with other retreating Italians. Carabinieri are picking out all those they think are officers and shooting them for treachery and 'abandoning' their troops. To anyone who, unlike the carabinieri, has seen what the conditions were at the front, the charge is utterly mad. But the executions continue. Although he is in an ambulance brigade, Henry has the rank of officer, and he too is pulled out to await his turn to be shot. But he takes advantage of a momentary lapse of attention on the part of the carabinieri and makes a desperate jump into the river, staying under the fast-moving water until he is out of range of their guns.

Chapters Thirty-One and Thirty-Two. On his own now, when he gets out of the river Henry finds he has lost his cap — which is often regarded as a symbol of one's official role. He strips off the markings from the rest of his uniform, not only as a precaution one feels, but because he is now dissociating himself entirely from the army. He crosses the Venetian plain and jumps on to a slow-moving train. He hides under the canvas covering one of the freight cars and finds that he is on a great load of guns, while the rain beats down on the canvas above him. Lying on guns he thinks of Catherine — again the two kinds of arms are juxtaposed, quite unobtrusively and yet with distinct impact. Among his thoughts at this time is his clear and unemotional recognition that he is 'out of it now'. 'Anger was washed away in the river along with any obligation.' You often find in literature that a writer will use some sort of watery immersion to suggest a second baptism into a new way of life, and clearly Henry's jump was a self-preserving leap right out of the world of war altogether. 'I was through.' All he thinks of now is Catherine, and food — these two very basic appetites have been starved for too long. Like other Hemingway heroes he even tries to suppress the very act of thinking, since it can bring such torments. 'I was not made to think. I was made to eat. . . . Eat and drink and sleep with Catherine.' After seeing the chaos and cruelty and desolation of war, one can appreciate the elemental simplicity of the kind of life he now wishes to turn to, as he makes his third significant train journey — away from the war for ever.

Book Four

Chapters Thirty-Three to Thirty-Seven. Dropping off the train in Milan, Henry now has to take on the identity of a civilian. He visits a friend who fits him out with some clothes, and it is interesting that he feels something of a masquerader and misses the feeling of wearing a uniform, of 'being held by your clothes'. He is indeed held by nothing now – he has disengaged himself from all commitments, except the one to Catherine. But it is a psychologically relevant point that he still feels as if he is somehow playing 'truant' in his new civilian role. As he travels in the train to Stresa, where he learns Catherine has gone, he knows that people look at him suspiciously since at his age he should be in uniform. But, although he feels as 'sad as the wet Lombard country', he is quite bent on putting the war out of his mind altogether. He won't even read the newspapers. 'I had made a separate peace.'

At Stresa he enjoys a happy reunion with Catherine, and they go to the large light room he has booked at an hotel. His memory of the sixteenth-century poem has come true. His love is in his arms while the rain comes down. With her the nights are not frightening and lonely, as we know they can be for Henry, but even more private and satisfying because of the intimacy they enjoy. At this point – i.e. when their idyll has been resumed – there is an important statement about courage.

> If people bring so much courage to this world the world has to kill them to break them, so of course it kills them. The world breaks every one and afterward many are strong at the broken places. But those that will not break it kills. It kills the very good and the very gentle and the very brave impartially. If you are none of these you can be sure it will kill you too but there will be no special hurry.

This is one of the most famous passages in Hemingway and it certainly clarifies the pessimistic mood generated by the book.

But it is not just a gratuitous piece of philosophizing. From now on they will both need their courage; and Catherine who is very brave is killed.

The next morning the sun is up, the rain has stopped, and the garden (remember that it was in a garden Henry first saw Catherine) is 'bare but beautifully regular' in front of the window. All these are good auguries, but later in the day the clouds come over and the day darkens, as if in anticipation of the brevity of the good time together that remains for them. You will notice that Henry often says, 'Let's not think about anything' or, 'I tried to keep from thinking.' This not only indicates his desire not to spoil the moment by worrying about the war or what will happen if he is arrested; it is almost as though he knows there is no future ahead of them, that 'there is nothing else than now' as another Hemingway hero, Robert Jordan, comes to realize.

One problem for Henry is that his occupation is gone; when Catherine is at work he has nothing to do. He goes fishing and catches nothing. He plays billiards and talks with the aged Count Greffi about ultimate matters – the soul, life, death. Count Greffi and Henry agree that what they value most is a loved person, and life itself ('Because it is all I have'). The Count assures Henry that though he has no orthodox religious faith, love 'is a religious feeling'. What the priest had predicted is now true for Henry. All this does not add up to a way of life for Henry. Once his life seemed so full; now, without Catherine 'I haven't a thing in the world'. But the situation is suddenly changed when Henry is woken up in the night – during a storm – by the barman who warns him that he is about to be arrested in the morning and advises him to escape by boat to Switzerland. To effect this Henry has to row all night, but the rain stops and the clear moonlight gives him a glimpse of a mountainside, which offers an anticipatory hint of the refuge they are to find in Switzerland. When they land in a little town in Switzerland – which of course was neutral and thus unmarked by evidence of war – 'it looked cheerful and clean even with the rain'. This is not the rain of the war-swept plains of Italy. After going through the necessary business of obtaining visas from the officials in the town, they set out for Montreux. This is Catherine's choice, because 'We can find some place up in the mountains.' The end of the book sees them arriving at an hotel there, exhausted but at last out of the war altogether. 'Yes, we're really here.'

Book Five

Chapters Thirty-Eight and Thirty-Nine. These describe the idyllic time they have together up in the mountains. They don't know anyone and even though bad news of the war gets through to them, it does not violate the special atmosphere they have created with each other. There are one or two interesting echoes worth noting. You will remember that at the beginning of the book when Henry returned from his leave he regretted that he had not gone to a clean mountain place 'where the roads were frozen and hard as iron' (Chapter Three). Now, outside their mountain chalet, in the road 'the wheel-ruts and ridges were iron hard with the frost'. He has come to the good place the priest outlined for him. Again, they play card games and chess together – the two games Henry had in mind when he thought he was simply planning a tactical seduction of Catherine. Now they share the 'games'. But even as Henry sets up the pieces on the chess board, a more deadly move in the larger game of existence is being prepared for them. Henry lets his beard grow – a further step away from his military identity – and the emphasis is on the good life they have, their coming child, the total exclusiveness of their love, and their plans to go to the Golden Gate when they return to America. 'It was a fine country and every time that we went out it was fun.' Because of his gift for detail Hemingway is able to convey the vivid happiness of this lovers' interlude without lapsing into sentimental clichés.

Chapters Forty and Forty-One. Their 'fine life' comes to an end. Once again the rains start and it even rains 'high up the mountain'. Their retreat has been penetrated and is now sullied with slush and mud. On account of this change in the weather (it rains for three days), and Catherine's advanced state of pregnancy, they decide to go down the mountain and take the train to Lausanne. All the signs are increasingly ominous. They cannot see the mountains for the clouds; it continues to rain; the windows of their hotel look out over a wet garden and a wall with an iron fence on top. It is worth noting that it is at this moment that Henry gives us the one and only date in the book — March 1918. As it is the first time a date has been given it has a slightly sinister effect, as though he is recording the moment in history when something ended. They try to make their hotel room 'like a home' and there is a brief burst of good weather which, however, turns out to be a false spring. They continue to have good times, but they have a new feeling 'as though something were hurrying us and we could not lose any time together'. That date does indeed mark the imminent end of their time together.

The last chapter in the book describes how Catherine is taken to hospital and how she dies after a difficult Caesarean delivery and after her baby son has already died. It is a chapter of great poignancy as all the gathering menace and sense of desolation of the book comes together in the moment of Catherine's death and Henry's loss. For in losing her he loses everything. While he is waiting for the delivery he walks out of the hospital into 'the empty street', which may remind us of the bare road that is mentioned in the first paragraph of the book, and certainly prefigures the emptiness of his life to come without Catherine. He also notices a dog scavenging in some refuse cans. Henry's noticing of this refuse — 'coffee-grounds, dust, and some dead leaves' — again suggests, if not ashes to ashes and dust to dust, at least the sense of the mere trash that is left behind after life has departed, and it hints perhaps at the more general decline of all things to the universal rubbish dump.

Watching the severe pains Catherine is experiencing, inter-mittently alleviated by gas, Henry realizes that 'This was the end of the trap'—the biological trap he had mentioned earlier. 'It's just Nature giving her hell.' At one point Catherine cries out 'They've broken me', again reminding us of an earlier passage on courage; and during the operation, with the masked figures working on her, Henry says 'It looked like a drawing of the Inquisition.' It all serves to make Catherine seem like a victim. Anticipating her death and trying to formulate his feelings about it, Henry makes use of two examples which convey a very grim, pessimistic and fatalistic attitude to an indifferent, if not actively malign, universe. First he once again makes use of an image from a game, this time baseball. 'You died. You did not know what it was about. You never had time to learn. They threw you in and told you the rules and the first time they caught you off base they killed you. . . .' and so on. Whoever the 'they' are, they are certainly not any human agencies. Then Henry remembers putting a log that was swarming with ants on a fire. Their sub-sequent behaviour, running this way and that but always finally into the fire, obviously suggests to Henry an analogy for the posi-tion and plight of human beings, since whichever way we run it is always finally towards death. As he says, he thought at the time he could have played a messiah by lifting the log from the fire, thus rescuing the ants. But he did not, and by the same token he does not expect any help in this life from some unseen God. This need not be taken as a definitive statement of Hemingway's philosophy. It is a manifestation of the feelings of a man about to lose the only person in the world he cares for—apparently quite gratuitously. After protracted suffering Catherine dies, her last words being 'I'm not a bit afraid. It's just a dirty trick.' She is broken, but she still has her courage. Henry goes into the room to say farewell to the only arms he loved, but he finds that it is no use. 'It was like saying good-bye to a statue.' He concludes only by stating that he walked back to the hotel in the rain. But the submerged part of the iceberg of Hemingway's prose is hitting us with its total force by now, and we can appreciate that the misery and sense of loss and emptiness which Henry feels as he steps into the void of a future without Catherine are feelings, or absences of feeling, which could not be adequately expressed by language. His silence — and the rain — tell us all we need to know.

Suggested Further Reading

The most comprehensive biographical study of Hemingway is Carlos Baker's *Ernest Hemingway: A Life Story* (Collins, London 1969); there is also a lot of interesting material in *My Brother, Ernest Hemingway* by Leicester Hemingway (Weidenfeld and Nicolson, London 1962). See also *The Apprenticeship of Ernest Hemingway* by Charles Fenton (New York 1954). There is of course a vast amount of criticism of Hemingway's work available. One of the most important early appraisals of his work was an essay by Edmund Wilson called 'Hemingway: Gauge of Morale'. It originally appeared in 1939 and can be found in his book *The Wound and the Bow* (New York 1951). Two of the most important studies of Hemingway's work are *Ernest Hemingway: A Reconsideration* by Philip Young (Pennsylvania State University Press, 1966), and *Hemingway: The Writer as Artist* by Carlos Baker (Princeton University Press, 1963). A selection of essays on his work may be found in the *Twentieth Century Views* volume devoted to him, edited by Robert P. Weeks. For some detailed consideration of Hemingway's style see the chapters on Hemingway in *The Colloquial Style in America* by Richard Bridgman (Oxford University Press, New York 1966) and in *The Reign of Wonder* by Tony Tanner (Cambridge University Press, Cambridge 1965).